Praise for Kare[...]

"A nice backstory and excit[...] is a must-read."
—*RT Book Reviews* on *The Wolf Siren* (4.5 stars)

"*The Lost Wolf's Destiny* is action-packed with a lot of twists and turns that lead the reader on an amazing ride."
—*Fresh Fiction*

Praise for Sharon Ashwood

"Ms. Ashwood's characters leap from the pages."
—*Romance Junkies*

"Sharon Ashwood is all that is good and right in the paranormal romance genre."
—*Bitten by Books*

"Ms. Ashwood knows how to write paranormal novels, leaving the reader with one heck of an impression of her talent."
—*Coffee Time Romance & More*

Karen Whiddon started weaving fanciful tales for her younger brothers at the age of eleven. Amid the gorgeous Catskill Mountains, then the majestic Rocky Mountains, she fueled her imagination with the natural beauty surrounding her. Karen now lives in north Texas, writes full-time and volunteers for a boxer dog rescue. She shares her life with her hero of a husband and four to five dogs, depending on if she is fostering. You can email Karen at kwhiddon1@aol.com. Fans can also check out her website, karenwhiddon.com.

Books by Karen Whiddon

Harlequin Nocturne

The Pack Series

Wolf Whisperer
The Wolf Princess
The Wolf Prince
Lone Wolf
The Lost Wolf's Destiny
The Wolf Siren
Shades of the Wolf
Billionaire Wolf
A Hunter Under the Mistletoe (with Addison Fox)
Her Guardian Shifter

Visit the Author Profile page
at Harlequin.com for more titles.

HER GUARDIAN SHIFTER

KAREN WHIDDON

ROYAL ENCHANTMENT

SHARON ASHWOOD

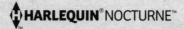
HARLEQUIN® NOCTURNE™

Recycling programs
for this product may
not exist in your area.

ISBN-13: 978-0-373-20859-3

Her Guardian Shifter & Royal Enchantment

Copyright © 2017 by Harlequin Books S.A.

The publisher acknowledges the copyright holders
of the individual works as follows:

Her Guardian Shifter
Copyright © 2017 by Karen Whiddon

Royal Enchantment
Copyright © 2017 by Naomi Lester

Printed in U.S.A.

www.Harlequin.com

CONTENTS

HER GUARDIAN SHIFTER 7
Karen Whiddon

ROYAL ENCHANTMENT 295
Sharon Ashwood

HER GUARDIAN SHIFTER

Karen Whiddon

To my dog-rescue family.
Your love and support and kindheartedness
help make this world brighter.

Chapter 1

Damned if he did and damned if he didn't. Truer words had never been uttered. Hightailing it out of California with his infant son made Eric Mikkelson feel like some sort of criminal, even though he'd never broken a single law in his entire thirty-six years. Basically, he considered himself one of the good guys. Though his kind, the Vedjorn—bear shape-shifters—were by and large ostracized by the wolves, aka The Pack, since no one went around revealing what kind of shifter they were, his life hadn't been impacted as much as it could have been otherwise.

No, this journey had nothing to do with him, and everything to do with protecting his son. He wasn't sure why he felt as if he'd gone on the lam. After all, he'd been granted full legal custody of three-month-old Garth in a court of law. Without restrictions. So if he wanted to drive across the country to New York in the middle of winter, infant son in tow, there was absolutely no reason why he shouldn't or couldn't.

He had his reasons, of course. Even before Garth had

been born, he'd asked for and received permission to take a sabbatical from his job as a college professor. As soon as his then-wife, Yolanda, had begun showing, so had her disdain for the *thing* she carried inside her.

The more she'd ranted and raved, the more worried he'd grown. She, too, was bear, and their kind were dwindling. A pregnancy would normally be a time for celebration. Not with her. Instead, she appeared to be coming unhinged.

In her third trimester, she'd finally come to him and asked for her freedom. She hadn't meant she only wanted out of the marriage. She wanted out of motherhood, as well. He'd negotiated with her carefully. Since he'd offered her a hefty settlement, she'd carried their son full term. Once Garth had been born, she'd refused even to look at the tiny, red-faced infant. She'd handed over the baby to Eric, checked herself out of the hospital and took off to have fun without being tied to anyone or anything.

The divorce had gone through without a hitch. Eric settled into his new life as a single father with bemused dedication and love. He'd been shocked to learn how much he loved his newborn son, and vowed to be the best parent he could.

He'd researched everything about babies. Heavily. Some things, such as the ingrained habits borne of years spent educating others, wouldn't be changed. He'd felt competent and prepared, until the first time Garth came down with a high fever that wouldn't break.

But he'd managed, and now, three months in, he would lay down his life for his son. Which was why, when his unstable ex-wife started showing up on his doorstep unannounced, insisting something was wrong with the baby and she needed to take him somewhere to have him fixed, he'd realized he needed to leave California for a while.

While he made his preparations, he'd received phone

calls from colleagues and friends, informing him that Yolanda had been declaring to anyone who would listen that Eric had stolen her son from her and cheated her out of motherhood.

After he'd placated numerous people, the news got worse. Now it seemed that Yolanda not only wanted her son back, but she also wanted Eric dead. She'd gone twice to the Wolf Pack authorities, the Pack Protectors, and tried to convince them that Eric was a Berserker, a form of insanity unique to the Vedjorn. When a Berserker shifted from human to bear, he or she became a crazed killing machine. If Eric had truly been one, he'd be a danger to not only her son, but others. She also had hinted a few times that Garth might be a Berserker, as well. It was this last claim that worried Eric. He could defend himself against her attacks. His son could not.

The infrequent gene mutation among the bear shifters was the reason the others—especially wolves—avoided them. Since they were the largest group, the Wolf Pack had an entire division, called the Pack Protectors, devoted to ensuring humankind didn't learn about their existence. True Berserkers with their indiscriminate killing would endanger not only the bears, but all the others, as well. This could not be allowed. Anyone even seriously suspected of being a Berserker was brought in and contained, until the accusations could either be verified or denied. True Berserkers, though few and far between, were exterminated.

And Yolanda had named Eric a Berserker. Since this accusation was serious, one might have expected her to have some proof. Something to back her up, incidents of killing and maiming. Since she didn't, no one took her seriously. Including Eric.

Then, without warning, Yolanda had shown up on Eric's doorstep demanding to see *her* baby. She hadn't been even close to sober. He'd turned her away. She'd finally left, shouting about how their son needed healing. And how she was the only one who could provide it.

After that, she'd had an attorney friend contact him. Even though she'd willingly signed away all parenting rights, she'd now decided she'd changed her mind. Except she hadn't really. He knew all this was somehow related to her intense need to *heal* her son. From what, he wasn't sure. Maybe she truly did believe little Garth would grow up to be Berserker. But everyone understood those signs wouldn't start to exhibit themselves until Garth was able to shape-shift, which would be in his early teens. And if he truly ended up being Berserker, there was no cure.

With a bone-deep certainty, Eric knew his son wasn't Berserker. Unfortunately, Yolanda appeared equally convinced he was, despite having no evidence to support her.

She'd shown up twice more at his front door, cursing, screaming and crying. And threatening. He began to understand his son was in real danger from the woman who'd birthed him. When he caught her breaking the window on the back door in order to gain entry to his home so she could grab the baby, he'd realized it would be better to disappear. In fact, his Pack Protector friend Jason had strongly suggested it.

So early one morning Eric had quietly packed his SUV, locked his house and taken off cross-country with Garth securely strapped in his infant car seat in back. The rest of his belongings had already been picked up by a moving company and would be delivered a week later, including his painstakingly restored 1969 classic Camaro SS.

His destination was the tiny town of Forestwood, New York, where he'd rented the bottom floor of a house from a website he'd found on the internet, hoping it would look the same as the pictures that had been posted. He no longer would be teaching college. Instead he would open his own business doing something that until now he'd considered only a hobby. He planned to start an entirely new life, focusing on his son and keeping his head down.

Though her new tenant was supposed to pick up his keys today, Julia Jacobs eyed the blizzard raging outside and figured he'd call her to reschedule. According to the stern yet clearly excited weatherman on TV, officials were advising people to stay off the roads. Whiteout conditions and extreme cold didn't make for safe travel.

JJ didn't mind. She'd been anticipating the snow with the eagerness of a child. She'd dreamed it, after all. And snowfall brought her joy. In all kinds of ways. At the first sight of big, fat snowflakes drifting down from the leaden gray sky, she was filled with the excited anticipation of a kid on Christmas Eve.

Though she knew she was out of sync with the rest of the world, winter was her favorite season. The crisp bite of the cold air, her breath pluming as she exhaled. She loved the bundling up, the sweater and scarf and coat and hat and gloves and boots. Stepping out into the white wonderland and making the first set of footprints to mar the unblemished perfection. The way the world went absolutely still and quiet the morning after a snowfall, and how wonderful it felt to sit inside her warm house by the fire drinking cocoa and watching the snow fall. Snow always felt like a new beginning, a chance to start over.

She sighed, glad once again that she was alone, that she'd left Shawn and the hustle and bustle of New York City behind. Even before his true abusive nature came out, her ex-boyfriend had ridiculed her love of all things winter, one of her many character traits that he'd found distasteful and disgusting. Of course, he'd been a summer person, while heat and blazing sunshine had only depressed her. That had just been the beginning and she'd finally broken free. This blizzard, already being ominously forecasted as the storm of the century, brought her nothing but joy.

She felt sorry for her new tenant, though. When he'd rented out the bottom floor of her house, his Norwegian accent had intrigued her. Of course, she'd Googled him after getting his name, noting he'd immigrated to California. She'd been impressed by his academic credentials. A college professor on sabbatical, he'd said. With an infant son.

The last might have given other landlords pause. After all, babies cried, and even though he'd be on another floor entirely, sound drifted in older houses like hers.

But JJ had never been a landlord before—heck, she was a brand-new homeowner—and she adored babies, so she'd immediately granted Mr. Eric Mikkelson the lease. He'd paid for two months up front, along with a perfectly reasonable security deposit. He didn't smoke or have pets, so she privately thought she might have actually managed to find the perfect tenant.

Even the few fuzzy photos of him she'd seen online jibed with his career. He looked the part, a stereotypical professor, round wire glasses and hair in a ponytail. She hadn't been able to tell if his hair was blond or gray, but supposed it didn't matter. He had a baby, which made up for a whole lot of other things, including any lingering intellectual snobbishness. Lord knew she'd had enough of that with Shawn and his Wall Street friends.

Again, she quickly put the thought from her mind. Enough time had passed that she ought to be able to relax, but she still jumped every time someone moved too fast or she heard a loud, unexpected noise. At least she'd retaught herself not to keep her gaze trained on the ground anymore lest she be accused of flirting.

And the nightmares featuring Shawn had finally stopped. The horrible, awful dreams had her questioning her own sanity.

Heaving a sigh, she walked to the window to watch the beautiful snow fall, knowing this would instantly put her in a better frame of mind.

Meanwhile, meeting her new tenant would have to wait until after the storm. Which meant she was free to putter around the house, put a pot of butternut squash soup to simmer on the stove and go out and play in the snow.

Until she'd moved in with Shawn, she'd lived all her life in an apartment in New York City with her parents. If she and her friends had wanted to make a snowman, they'd gone to the park. Now, thanks to a distant great-aunt she'd barely known leaving her this house upstate in Forestwood, New York, she could make a snowman in her own front yard. The prospect excited her, probably more than it should considering she'd just turned thirty-four. She'd have to wait to build it until after the snowfall stopped, but still wanted to go outside and check out the snow.

After bundling up—two pairs of socks inside her snow boots, scarf, and wearing a soft knit cap under her hood—she took a deep breath and stepped out into the swirling storm.

Wow. Stopping just outside the front door on her stoop, she stared. This was coming down fast and furious. She guesstimated already six to seven inches had fallen.

And so beautiful. Slowly she turned, squinting as she tried to see down the street to the other houses. Other houses! She'd lived her entire life surrounded by tall buildings, in the crowded city. She thought she could get used to this new life. Everything moved slower here. The pace suited her just fine.

One month and she'd unpacked nearly everything. Of

course, she hadn't had much to unpack. Luckily, all her great-aunt's furniture had come with the house, since JJ had none of her own. When she'd moved in with Shawn, he'd convinced her to get rid of her own few eclectic pieces. After all, they'd clashed with his sleek, modern furniture. Bohemian, he'd called it, with the same disparaging intonation one would use with a curse word.

Shawn. She hated how her thoughts kept returning to him when they shouldn't. That part of her life was over. He no longer had any hold on her. He would never find her here. Even her mother had been sworn to secrecy, though she hadn't been told why. Pushing him and her former life out of her head, JJ returned her focus to the perfect snowstorm.

Unable to resist, she dropped to the ground and made a snow angel, even though fresh flakes would fill it in quickly. With her face lifted to the sky, she felt like a kid. The icy flakes stuck to her eyelashes and her lips, even her teeth, since she was grinning. The cold air hurt her skin, which meant she wouldn't be able to stay outside much longer, but she planned to enjoy what time she had.

The sound of a car door slamming made her sit up and blink away the snowflakes stuck to her lashes. What the… Someone had pulled up to the curb in front of her house. Driving some sort of compact SUV that she'd never in a million years have believed could make it more than a mile in this snow without snow tires and chains.

A tall, bare-headed man came around from the driver's side. As she stared, her first thought was of the mythological Norse god Thor. She forgot about the icy wind, the snowflakes swirling like dervishes. Because as he strode toward her, his long, wavy blond hair swirling around his shoulders, her entire body came alive. He moved with a confident, easy stride, as if the snow and ice didn't exist for him.

Damn. Realizing she was still on the ground, she clambered to her feet, dusting as much snow off her as she could before she looked up at him. And she meant up. This guy had to be way over six feet tall. Shawn had been six-two, and she'd bet this man would tower over him. Norse god, she thought again. Odd that she hadn't had a single dream of him. She'd bet she would from now on.

"Um, hi?" she squeaked.

"Ms. Jacobs?" he rumbled, his bright blue eyes sharp. Oh heck, his voice definitely suited him. Made her go weak in the knees. And that accent…

Belatedly she knew who this must be. "Eric Mikkelson?" She couldn't keep the disbelief from showing.

"Yes." He tilted his massive, unbelievably gorgeous head. "You weren't expecting me? I believe I confirmed I'd be here this afternoon to pick up the keys."

"I know, but…" She gestured helplessly at the storm raging around them. "You drove up here in this?"

"This?" Frowning, he didn't appear to understand what she meant. Before she could elaborate, he turned back toward his car. "I need to get my son. Do you mind if we continue this discussion inside?"

His son. Struck dumb by both his recklessness and his masculine beauty, she nodded. Then, because she loved babies as much as she loved snow, she followed him over to the car and tried to peer around him as he unbuckled his son's infant carrier.

She caught a glimpse of bright blue eyes peering out from a tiny, bundled up face. As she leaned in closer, her tenant, clearly not realizing she'd moved in so close, caught her with his elbow under the chin and sent her flying backward.

"Oof." Down she went, right on her behind. Luckily, all her layers plus the several inches of fluffy snow provided lots of padding. Nothing got hurt except her pride.

Her tenant glanced back over his shoulder at her, clearly unaware what had happened. "Are you all right?" he asked, his cautious tone telling her he'd begun to consider the possibility that she might be nuts.

For a split second she debated telling him what had happened. Pushing to her feet, she once again dusted off snow, the cold dampness beginning to seep through her layers to her skin. And then she caught sight of Eric's son, and completely forgot what she'd been about to say.

The instant the baby locked eyes with her, he grinned and wrinkled his cute little nose. All bundled up in his snowsuit, cap and mittens, he looked like a precious baby seal with bright blue eyes. As his daddy lifted him up, he cooed.

Like his father, his cuteness factor was off the charts.

"Come on," she said, conscious of the freezing temperature and icy wind. "I don't want him to get frostbite."

Eric Mikkelson stared and shook his head. "He has Norwegian blood," he said, as if that explained everything. "This snowstorm is nothing compared to the ones I grew up with in Norway. I dressed him warmly. He'll be fine."

Fine? She managed to refrain from shaking her head while she tromped her way through the deepening snow to her front door. When she turned back to look for him, for a second she couldn't see him, the baby or his car due to the blowing, swirling snow.

Chapter 2

An instant of panic disappeared the moment JJ caught sight of her new tenant striding up her walk, his son clutched securely to his massive chest.

Again with the striding? As if the snow wasn't even there. Maybe it had something to do with his height.

Then, before she had time to pretend she wasn't gaping, he reached her. Fumbling, her hands cold even in her lined ski gloves, she opened the door. "Come on inside."

As she began the laborious process of removing her many layers of warm clothes, she watched him shrug out of his coat and then get busy undressing the baby. In disbelief, she processed not only the fact that Eric wore just a black sweater under his parka, but that his infant son did, too.

Unable to tear her gaze away, even though she knew her stare might be rude, she exhaled.

Eric Mikkelson was a big man. Not just tall, not just broad, but an appealing combination of the two. Throw in some killer muscles, a narrow waist and lean hips, and he was the stuff of which feminine fantasies were made.

She frowned. Since when did she need to even start thinking about another man, never mind fantasizing about one? If her relationship with Shawn had taught her anything, it had shown her she clearly needed to live alone and figure out how she'd let herself become so…

Since leaving Shawn, she'd tried out several different adjectives and discarded them, because no one single word could adequately describe how much of herself she'd let Shawn destroy. Thankfully, she'd finally gotten the courage to flee.

No, she thought, eyeing the gorgeous masculine specimen in front of her, a man was the last thing she needed.

Still, she'd have to be dead not to appreciate this man's appeal. And of course, there was his baby.

The infant made a curious snuffling sound. She wondered exactly what species of shape-shifter Eric might be. His aura, like hers, revealed him to be a shifter, though not what kind. And while she hadn't met too many others, she knew there were many different types of animals besides her wolf. In fact, this little town had recently gained notoriety among shifters for revealing another rare species of shifter, the Drakkor, or dragon shifter. They'd welcomed several into life in their town, even though most of the residents of Forestwood were Pack, or wolf, like JJ.

She'd bet Eric Mikkelson wasn't wolf. Still eyeing him, she figured he might be a big cat, like a lion or panther. Though his movements and size reminded her more of a grizzly. She swallowed hard. The Vedjorn bear shifters were as rare as Drakkor, and for good reason. They were unstable and frequently dangerous. They kept to themselves and, unlike the other species of shifters, rarely if ever intermarried outside of their own kind. Not that anyone else wanted anything to do with them.

"Are you all right?"

Crud. She'd been standing staring at him, most likely with her mouth wide-open or a big, dopey smile on her face. Flustered, she nodded. "Yes, sorry. I'm fine. It's just that…" she began. Horrified, she realized she'd been about to breach the most sacred etiquette between shifters. Yikes. There was no way she could ask him what kind of animal he changed into.

"Yes?" he asked, his tone patient, a smile playing along the edge of his sensual mouth. Once again she'd gotten lost in thought. Obviously, her social skills had also vanished with her previous life.

"I'm sorry," she finally repeated, wincing as the second apology crept out. "It's just, I wasn't expecting you today and now that you're here, you aren't at all what I expected." As she wound to the end of her rambling, her entire face flamed.

"But I confirmed that I would pick up the keys today," he said, his expression puzzled.

"Yes, but…" She waved her fingers at her large picture window. "With the storm, I thought you'd reschedule."

Tilting his big, shaggy head, he considered her. Then he grinned, his blue eyes sparking with amusement. And just like that, he went from great looking to absolutely drop-dead sexy.

So help her, her knees went weak again and her breath caught in her chest. Damn.

"You're joking, right?" His good-natured question prompted her to agree.

"Of course I am," she managed to reply, attempting a wobbly smile. Thank goodness she at least didn't sound breathless. "What's a little blizzard to someone from Norway, right?" Even if that someone had been living in California for years, according to his application.

"Exactly." The warm glance he sent her invited her to

share in his amusement. He swung his large head around to check out the central foyer, while expertly rocking his son's carrier. The stairs to her place were to the left. His front door was underneath the staircase.

"Would you mind showing me the way to my place? It's been a long day and I'd like to get settled in as quickly as possible."

"Of course." She matched his brisk tone. "Follow me."

When she'd arrived to claim the house she'd inherited, she'd been surprised to see it had been built as two separate living areas. Both the top floor and the bottom were self-contained dwellings, each with their own kitchen and bathrooms. She'd claimed the top floor. Years of living in the city had taught her she'd be safer there. And the bottom floor she'd rented out to him, her very first tenant ever.

Luckily, the top floor had its own separate entrance, so they'd both have plenty of privacy. And she would have some income to tide her over until she figured out exactly what she wanted to do.

"You'll have the entire bottom floor," she said, opening his front door and stepping aside. "Here it is. All yours."

Still bouncing the baby, he pushed past her and stopped, turning in a half circle to take it all in.

"Wow." His deep laugh reminded her of hot cocoa spiced with Kahlúa. "When you said it came furnished, I was relieved. I confess, I actually pictured Ikea or maybe an eclectic mix of garage sale and discount store. What I didn't envision was this. It's very…" Words seemed to fail him.

"Old lady-ish?" she suggested helpfully, unable to keep from smiling. "All of this stuff belonged to my great-aunt Olivia." She didn't tell him the reason she'd kept the fussy, outdated furniture was because she not only didn't have any of her own, but currently didn't have the funds to re-place it.

"I see," he said, eyeing a particularly delicate looking chair. "To be honest, I'm afraid I'll break that if I sit in it."

She had to admit he was probably right. "I'll switch it out with something else," she said, trying to sound busi-nesslike. "Here are your keys."

When she went to hand them off, her fingers brushed his. Damn. A curious swooping pull swept through her, momentarily making her head spin.

"Are you all right?" he asked yet again, watching her closely, as if he expected her to fall over in a dead faint at any second.

"Yes." Biting back her second almost automatic apol-ogy, she forced a smile. Life with Shawn had compelled her to apologize for everything, even stuff that wasn't her fault. She'd been consciously trying to break the habit ever since she'd gotten free.

"I guess I'd better leave you to it," she continued brightly. "I'm just upstairs if you need anything."

He nodded. "I've got your number, as well. Thank you for everything." As she moved back out into their shared foyer, he firmly and quietly closed his door. A second later, she heard the sound of the dead bolt clicking into place. She couldn't help but wish she'd dream of him once she went to sleep.

Exhaustion had Eric wishing he could undress and crawl into bed, but little Garth would need a diaper change and some formula first. Shame about the landlord woman. Though she really was stunning with her fiery red hair, large green eyes and curvy body, she seemed a little daft in the head. The way she'd eyed his baby—as if she'd like to eat him up—had worried Eric. Had he escaped one crazy woman only to relocate with another?

Surely not. Most likely, he was overreacting out of fear. Still, just in case, until he knew her better, he'd make sure to keep his distance.

After he got Garth cleaned up, fed and burped, and put down for a nap, he finally rummaged in his backpack for the sandwich he'd bought at the last gas station. It had gotten crushed and didn't look the least bit appetizing, but was still cold. He wolfed it down in four bites, wishing he'd had the foresight to buy two. Tomorrow, he'd stock up on food, but for now he had enough of the two things that really mattered—formula and diapers. He had a portable crib in the back of his SUV and the rest of his things would be arriving as soon as the transport company got there.

The one thing he worried most about was his other car. The one he didn't want to take a chance on damaging by driving cross-country. And he sure as hell wouldn't be taking it out on icy roads recently coated with salt. He'd park it until the winter season had long passed. Late spring, at the earliest.

One of the reasons he'd chosen to rent this place over the others was that it came with a garage. According to the lease, his landlord got one side of the two-car, detached garage and he got the other. He didn't plan to use it for the SUV he'd driven across the country. No. He planned to store the 1969 Camaro SS he'd lovingly restored inside his slot in the garage. That car would be his advertisement for the business he planned to start.

Even in California, where customized hot rods were a dime a dozen, his car turned heads. He'd been asked several times where he'd had the work done. Plenty of people had wanted to hire him when he'd told them he'd done it himself. They'd been shocked to learn he worked as a college professor and that he'd restored the car as a hobby. He'd come to realize he might be able to do something he loved and actually earn a living at it. He'd started saving every penny he could, in the hope that one day he could actually start his own business. He'd just about had enough to get serious when Yolanda had gotten pregnant.

And then his life had gone to hell in a handbasket.

No sense in dwelling on the past. Tonight was the first night in his new home and tomorrow would be literally the first day of the rest of his new life. A life where he could keep Garth safe. A life where, hopefully, he could settle in, make friends, get his business established, and find peace and joy again.

The snow continued to fall all through the night. Eric knew because, restless, he got up several times to peer out the window to where the streetlight illuminated the now impassable street. The little house was snug—he'd give it that. No leaky windows, and the radiators put out plenty of heat. He felt cozy and oddly at peace, something he hadn't quite expected when he'd chucked his entire life and took off to start a new one on the opposite side of the country.

Now he suspected he knew what people who went into the Witness Protection Program felt like. Adrift, needing an anchor, but afraid to put down deep roots in case they needed to move on again. Hopefully, that wouldn't be the case here. No way would anyone—especially his ex—think to look for him this far from sunny California.

Finally, sometime around six, he got up, blinking at the brightness from the snow outside, and began puttering around his new living space. The old furniture reminded him of his maternal grandmother's house—fussy fabrics, lots of dark wood and elaborate ornamentation. He suspected there would have been a plethora of knickknacks covering every conceivable service, which Julia Jacobs had most likely cleared out once she'd arrived. The dark wood gleamed, evidently having recently been dusted and polished, and the space he'd rented looked clean.

Garth woke and Eric got busy changing his boy's diaper and warming formula so the little guy could have breakfast. Early on Eric had felt a sense of pride at the fact that he'd gotten quite adept at these basic parenting tasks, an accomplishment that had once both amazed and amused him. Now, taking care of his three-month-old was routine, second nature.

After Garth had been fed and burped, Eric sat on the couch and let his son play with a set of colorful plastic rattles. He'd brought only a few of the baby's toys with him; the others would arrive in the moving truck.

Eventually, Garth fell asleep again and Eric gently placed him back in his temporary crib. He stood for a moment watching his son sleep, his heart full. Finally, he felt like a weight had been lifted off his shoulders.

The knock on his door was decisive, yet quiet enough that it didn't wake the baby. When Eric opened it, he wasn't surprised to see his petite landlady standing there. If anything, she looked even more intriguing than she had the night before. He'd never been partial to redheads, but he'd never seen one as beautiful as her. Her emerald-green eyes and lush mouth contrasted with her spattering of freckles, giving her a sexy, girl-next-door vibe. Eyeing her, he felt a jolt of lust, which of course he instantly tamped down.

"Yes?" he asked politely, keeping his body between her and the inside of his place.

A shadow darkened her eyes, almost as if his intense need for privacy wounded her. "I just wanted to apologize," she said softly. "I know I acted a little strange yesterday and I'm sorry." Her slight laugh sounded a bit forced, though she kept her chin up and her shoulders back. "Anyway, welcome to Forestwood." She held out her hand. He noticed her fingernails were short and looked uneven, as if she maybe chewed on them.

The two of them shook. She had a nice, firm grip, which he appreciated.

"I made you a map of town, showing you where all the shops are. If you need anything else, please don't hesitate to let me know."

Once he'd accepted the folded map, she turned to go.

"Wait."

Stopping, she turned, one eyebrow lifted.

"Thank you," he told her. "As soon as the roads are cleared, I need to hit the grocery store. Any idea what time the plows will come through?"

"I watched the news and this storm was pretty bad. They may not. If the plows don't make it out this way today, they'll get our road done tomorrow."

His heart sank. "Tomorrow?" As he spoke, his stomach rumbled, reminding him he hadn't had breakfast or even coffee. "I have absolutely no food. I don't suppose you'd care to sell me a few things to tide me over until then."

"No food?" Tilting her head, she considered him. "Please tell me you have formula for the baby."

"Of course I do. And diapers. You can't travel cross-country with an infant without those. Little Garth is taken care of. I'm the one who needs provisions."

Amusement sparked in her green eyes. "I'm not going to sell you food," she said, disappointing him. "But you won't starve, not in my house. Come with me. I can feed you. I'm an excellent cook."

Even though his stomach still rumbled with hunger, he wasn't sure he wanted her to feed him. The idea of her cooking for him seemed way too intimate. Yet what alternative did he have? He could starve or he could eat.

Both embarrassed and wary and, damn it, hungry, he shook his head. "I don't know," he said. "I mean, I barely know you. You shouldn't have to…"

"It's food." Her smile tugged at him, invited him to smile back. "Not gold or diamonds or even splitting a bottle of red wine. A couple of simple, hearty meals. Let me make you something, starting with breakfast. You can pay me back after you've made it to the store. Now what'll it be? I've got eggs and bread, or oatmeal if you prefer."

His stomach growled at the thought. Still, he felt obligated to at least make an effort to decline. "I don't want to impose," he began.

"You're not." She turned to go. "Come on. And bring that adorable baby with you."

Heaven help him, he went. The small sandwich from the night before had long ago faded from memory and he needed to eat something. Anything. Even cold cereal. He figured he'd go with oatmeal, since she probably had instant, and it would be less trouble and less intimate than asking her to fry him up a couple eggs.

Since Garth was still asleep, it was a simple matter of picking up the portable crib and carrying it with him. Good thing the kid was a sound sleeper. Eric tromped all the way up the steep flight of stairs and his son never woke. Garth had always been like that.

His lovely landlord had left her door open for him. He didn't know why he was making such a big deal out of a simple kindness on her part, but he chalked it up to being gun-shy after what had happened with Yolanda. Still, he couldn't stand outside on the landing forever. At least, not if he wanted to eat. .

Chapter 3

Taking a deep breath, Eric stepped inside and looked around. He didn't know what he'd expected, maybe a carbon copy of his, but her space looked completely different. Minimal furnishings, for one. Clearly, she'd chosen only what she wanted from the furniture her great-aunt had left behind. And then she'd added some other pieces, bright colors mostly. Lots of patterns, stripes and swirls and polka dots. Feminine stuff, but surprisingly comfortable looking.

Turning slowly, he wasn't sure what to make of it all. Instead of looking garish or confusing, the effect was cheerful and homey. In a bohemian sort of way. In fact, it reminded him of photos he'd seen of some of the dorms at the college where he used to work.

"In here," Julia called. He followed the sound of her voice and found her standing in front of the stove.

Her kitchen, too, appeared bright and clean. She'd made an attempt to modernize it, though the aging appliances and chipped counters showed its age. He set the travel crib near the table and against the wall, hopefully out of the way.

"Welcome. So what'll it be?" she asked, her friendly tone and relaxed posture inviting him to loosen his guard.

"Oatmeal is fine," he told her. "I don't want you to go to any trouble. You have instant, right?"

She eyed him, her expression thoughtful. "I do. Are you sure that's what you want?"

It wasn't, but he nodded. "Oatmeal is great on a snowy morning."

"Coffee?" Handing him a cup, she pointed toward a half-full coffeepot. "Help yourself."

In California, he'd come to appreciate good coffee. He'd even purchased a specialty brewer, which was on its way here with his other personal belongings. But right now, he would have settled for instant. With no expectations other than it being hot, he filled his cup and took a sip.

It was good. More than good. Right up there with the gourmet coffee served at the corner java shop he used to stop at every morning on his way to campus. A second sip and he made a small sound of pleasure, causing her to swing around and grin at him.

He felt the power of that grin like a punch in his stomach. Slightly disoriented, he finally smiled back. He definitely hadn't expected this. Expected her.

"I take it you like my coffee?"

"I do." His third sip made him widen his smile into a grin. "It's delicious. I can't tell you how badly I needed this."

"I can imagine." She gestured at the table, a round wooden one that she'd painted turquoise. Around it were four wooden chairs, all painted different colors. "Sit. I'll have your breakfast ready in a minute."

Slightly less uncomfortable, he pulled out a chair. After bustling around for a second, she put a bowl in the microwave. When it chimed, she used pot holders to remove it, dropped in a handful of raisins and carried it over to him, along with a spoon and a paper napkin. "Here you go."

After one bite, he had to fight not to inhale the entire bowl. "This doesn't taste like instant oatmeal," he commented, before shoveling another spoonful into his mouth.

"Oh yeah?" She took a seat across from him, cradling her own mug of coffee. "It is, but I mashed a banana in with it before I micro-zapped it. It's one of my favorite breakfasts in the world. Then I added raisins and cinnamon. Do you like it?"

Since he'd nearly finished his bowl, he nodded. Two more bites and he was done. "Thank you," he said, meaning it. "I was really hungry." So hungry that everything tasted better around her.

"I could tell. I made two packets, since one is never enough."

He could have eaten two more, but he'd already imposed enough. Sipping his coffee, he nodded before glancing out her kitchen window at the snow still piled up outside. "Judging from your porch railings, I'd say we must have gotten at least ten inches."

"Yep. They said on the news it was more like a foot."

"I believe it." One more swallow and he'd emptied his cup. He wondered if she'd mind if he had another. "Do you really think it will be tomorrow until the plows come through? I need to get to a grocery store at least."

She seemed remarkably unconcerned. "It'll probably be today. That all depends where they decide to go first. But if you don't make it to the store, I'll make sure you don't starve. Oh, and if you do get out, I'll be happy to watch the baby while you shop. No need to have to deal with taking him out into weather like this."

Watch the baby? He glanced at Garth, still sleeping peacefully. After his initial frisson of alarm, he considered her. He really needed to stop being so suspicious. No way could every woman he met turn out to be as psychotic and unbalanced as Yolanda. He had to admit, if only to himself, maybe he'd gotten paranoid. But then, who would blame him?

The truth was eventually he would have to find someone who could babysit Garth from time to time. More, once he started scouting for locations to open up his custom car shop. He'd definitely need to get day care during regular business hours so he could work. The thought tied his stomach in knots. He didn't like being away from his son, not for more than a few minutes at a time. He didn't know how people did it, returning to work out of necessity when their child was only a few months old. Like them, he'd have no choice but to do the same. Not yet, though. Not yet.

One thing at a time, he reminded himself.

"I might take you up on that," he replied. Surely he could let her watch Garth for an hour while he stocked his fridge and pantry.

"Just let me know when."

Again he glanced out her window at the pristine white snow. "As soon as the plows clear the streets."

"Do you have personal items arriving?" she asked. "Baby furniture, your television, that sort of thing?"

"My moving truck is supposed to arrive in a few days," he said, eyeing his empty mug longingly. "Assuming the roads are good enough for them to get through."

"Good." She grabbed the coffeepot and brought it over. "More coffee? Don't worry, I can always make more."

Relieved, he nodded. After she'd refilled his cup, he took another deep drink and sighed. Just as good the second time. "I promise I'll repay you as soon as I can."

The snorting sound she made surprised him. Humor danced in her eyes, inviting him to share it with her. "Don't worry about it. It's coffee, not Patrón Silver."

And then she laughed, the low sound pleasing and harmonious. "Occasionally there's nothing better than a shot of really good tequila, you know?"

He actually did. After a second of hesitation, he nodded in agreement. "Thanks again for everything. I'm just not used to mooching off anyone."

When she pulled out the chair across from him, he saw she'd refilled her mug, too. Like him, she drank her coffee black. "Tell me about yourself, Eric Mikkelson. Why are you moving to the Catskills from sunny and hip California? Is it for a new job or do you have family here?"

Personal questions. Though instead of immediately putting him on the defensive once again, the friendly, casual way she phrased her questions actually relaxed him. She sounded *interested* rather than inquisitive. "No family. I moved here to go into a new line of work. I'm planning on opening my own business in town, once I find the perfect space."

"Awesome." To his surprise, she didn't ask him what kind of business. "But still. Why Forestwood? We're not exactly a metropolis. We're barely even on the map."

Since he knew from her aura that she, too, was a shifter, he felt comfortable enough to tell her the truth. "Because I read the article about the Drakkor. Any town that will lovingly shelter an individual without knowing or understanding what kind of being she might be is the kind of place where I feel I'll fit in."

At first, she didn't move. Didn't comment or respond, just watched him, her big green eyes contemplative. "The Drakkor. After that article was published, we got a lot of tourists. Mostly, they just wanted to see a real, live dragon. But no one actually wanted to move here."

"For me, it isn't about seeing a Drakkor." The earnestness in his voice surprised him. "It's about finding friendly people. Neighbors who don't judge you because you're different. The sort of kindhearted community where I can raise my son." He stopped, slightly embarrassed to have revealed so much to a stranger.

Tilting her head, she considered him. Then a slow smile bloomed, transforming her from really attractive to stunningly beautiful. His heart actually skipped a beat.

"That's really pretty damn amazing," she said finally, her warm voice imbibing the compliment with more.

What was it about this woman? Though they'd just met the day before, he felt as if he'd known her for a long time. He wasn't sure what to think about that.

Instead of allowing himself to bask in the glow of her praise, he turned the discussion to her. "How about you?" he asked. "Were you born and raised here or did you make your way from somewhere else, too?"

Her smile faded. "I'd never been here before until a month ago. A great-aunt whom I didn't even know existed died. She left me this house and all the furniture, so I moved here."

"What about your job? Did you leave that, too, or are you able to work from home?"

Ducking her head, she shrugged. "I worked at a few different things. Dog walking, which is really in demand in the city, some waitressing and even some temporary secretarial work. None of it was difficult to leave."

"In the city?" He couldn't help but notice she didn't say where precisely she'd lived before. Since he'd been open with her, he figured he'd ask. "What city?"

"New York. Manhattan to be exact." Again a shadow crossed her face. "Only a couple of hours' drive from here, but it might as well be across the country."

He knew what she meant. The difference between some areas of California was also like that.

When he finished his second cup of coffee, she poured

him more without asking. Then she emptied the last of the pot into her own cup before she sat back down. "So far, I like it here a lot," she said. "Though I haven't been here very long. I guess we can learn the town together."

Together. What the... No, he was overreacting. No doubt she didn't mean anything by that. Again, he couldn't let what had happened with his ex-wife destroy his future. He would be vigilant and careful. And cautious. Yes, cautious. But his new landlord appeared kind and genuine. He would believe her to be so unless she proved otherwise.

"About watching Garth," he began. "What's your experience with infants?"

"Experience?" Shaking her head, she chuckled. "I just love babies. Always have. I'm not a professional nanny or anything, though I did once have a job working in a day care. Not in the baby room, though. But I'm reasonably sure I can manage taking care of him for an hour while you get groceries."

She was right. It wasn't as if he was asking her to be a full-time nanny. "Sorry." Glancing at his son, still peacefully sleeping, he sighed. "I've never left him with anyone before. I don't—"

"Really know me all that well," she finished for him. "I get it. Believe me, I was only trying to help. If you'd rather take him with you, I completely understand."

Her statement brought him a measure of relief. "I'll think about it," he said. "Out of curiosity, have you found work here yet or are you still looking?"

She glanced down, which made his stomach twist, though he wasn't sure why.

"Oh." She flushed. "Right now, I'm still unemployed. My aunt left me a small inheritance as well as this house. I've only been here a month and haven't looked for anything yet."

Wishing he hadn't asked, he tried to lighten the mood. "Well then, we're two of a kind, since I don't have a job yet, either."

Her smile came back, a quick flash of self-deprecating humor. "I guess we are."

Startled, he realized he actually *liked* Julia Jacobs. At least what he knew about her so far. And he would need someone to watch Garth, at least part-time. For now, he'd keep his eyes open and not make any rash decisions.

"What kind of work do you do?" she asked.

Briefly, he considered and decided he didn't see any harm in telling her the truth. "I was a college professor, but I took a sabbatical when Garth was born. Now, I'm planning to open up a customized car shop. It used to be a hobby, but I'm thinking I can make a living doing it full-time."

"Customize cars? Like painting them?"

"That's part of it. Restoring older cars to their original condition, only better. Turning them into hot rods." Oversimplified, but adequate.

"Interesting." The little shrug that accompanied her comment told him she either knew zero about cars or didn't care to. "That's kind of the polar opposite from higher education, isn't it?"

"Maybe." He smiled. "I figure since I came to the complete other side of the country, I might as well make a major change to my life. It's something I've always wanted to do."

"Then good for you." She smiled back. "Not to be nosy, but what about Garth's mother? Where is she in all of this?"

He froze, aware his expression had completely shut down. But she couldn't know and her question had actually been perfectly reasonable, if a bit intrusive. "She and

I are divorced. Turns out she didn't actually want a child. She signed over all parental rights to me."

If they'd been discussing any other subject, her disbelief and shock might have been comical. He could almost read her thoughts. Right now, she was dying to ask what kind of woman could abandon an innocent, tiny baby like Garth. From the grim set of her mouth and the way she'd narrowed her eyes, she must be wondering if Eric's ex was a monster. He didn't have the heart to tell her Yolanda actually was.

When he didn't comment further, she sighed. "I'm sorry. I didn't mean to pry."

Now he felt like an ass. After all, she'd opened her home to him and fed him. She'd been nothing but kind and friendly. "It's okay," he finally said. "It's just a sore subject."

"I can imagine." The grimness in her tone told him she agreed. "Anyway, if you need anything, please let me know."

He could take a hint. She'd fed him, chatted with him and now was ready for him to go. He stood, collected his son and let himself out the door.

Once back in his new, empty living quarters, Eric found he missed her. Or maybe he just missed having company. Someone to talk to. With the streets still impassable, he couldn't leave, couldn't drive around and check out the rest of the town the way he'd initially planned on his second day. Being stuck inside an unfamiliar house felt confining, to say the least. Plus he was impatient to begin scouting out a possible location to open his shop.

All in good time, he reminded himself. He needed to exercise a little patience.

He considered himself lucky that he had electricity and water. Since she'd never had them turned off, all he'd needed to do was change them into his name. And even though his television was on the moving truck, she'd left a smallish one in the living room, for which he was grateful.

Garth finally woke. Eric passed some time bathing and changing his son, giving him another bottle, and then just talking to him. Though at three months, little Garth couldn't do much other than wave his hands around and coo, being around him filled Eric with love.

Time passed slowly. He'd grown hungry again, but stubbornly remained in his part of the house, not wanting his landlord to feel compelled to feed him again. He didn't want to turn into a giant moocher, so decided to make do until he could get out and go to the store.

To his relief, he heard the unmistakable sound of the plow shortly after three. Rushing to the front window, he watched the big machine lumber down the street, plumes of snow shooting up to the side. Too late, he realized his vehicle would be buried, but since there was nothing he could do to avert this, he simply continued to watch. It wasn't like he hadn't dug out a car before, back when he'd lived in Norway.

Once the plow had passed, he shrugged into his parka and eyed Garth, now wide-awake and happily batting at the bright plastic toys Eric had strung across the front of his portable crib. He didn't want to leave his son alone, but couldn't just bring him outside while he cleared the snow from his car. Which meant he'd have to impose on his new landlord once again. Good thing she claimed to love babies.

Fifteen minutes, he told himself, picking up the carrier and trudging upstairs to Julia's place. He would ask her to keep an eye on the baby while he cleared his car. Then he'd retrieve Garth, bundle him up and put him in his car seat for a quick trip to the store.

Chapter 4

She answered the door on his second knock. To Eric's amusement, her gaze slid past him, right to the baby watching her with wide-eyed interest. "Well, hello there," she said, crouching down so she and Garth were at eye level. "I see you're finally awake, little sleepyhead."

Garth made a gurgling sound, jingling his plastic keys as he gazed up at her.

"You're so precious," Julia cooed. She glanced up at Eric. "Is everything all right?"

He cleared his throat. "I was wondering if you'd mind keeping an eye on him for a few minutes. The plow covered my SUV and I need to dig it out so I can head into town. I'll come back for him as soon as I'm done."

"No problem." She took the infant carrier and brought it inside. "Like I told you earlier, if you want, I can watch him while you go to the store."

Tempting, but again, he barely knew her and she'd already done more than enough for him. Leaving her in charge of Garth while he was a few feet away, outside, was entirely different than driving away without his son. "I appreciate that, but I'd rather bring him with me." He cast her a sideways look, trying to judge how she would take this news.

To his surprise, she smiled. "I understand. You don't know me yet and he's your entire world. Believe me, I wouldn't leave my baby for very long with someone I just met, either."

Relieved, he nodded. "I'm glad you understand. Fifteen minutes, okay? He's already been fed and has a clean diaper. I'm thinking this won't take much more than that."

"No rush." Her gaze had already strayed back to his son. "We'll be right here whenever you finish."

After the door closed behind her new tenant, JJ let out a sigh of relief. She liked looking at him, plain and simple. Even though another man in her life was the absolute last thing she needed right now. She hadn't worked through her recent past yet. Hell, she didn't even recognize the woman who'd fled New York City as if the hounds of hell were after her, with giant teeth. And of course, her dreams still haunted her.

This appalled her. She'd always been fierce, a fighter, but not a killer. She'd often questioned how she could have let herself become the woman Shawn had made her into, a woman afraid of her own shadow, too terrified to speak or even look at something the wrong way. She'd walked on eggshells, never knowing what might set him off.

Initially, she'd gone into the relationship a strong, female shifter. A she-wolf, proud of her heritage, confident in her humanness. Shawn might have been only human, but in the beginning he'd seemed kind and thoughtful and handsome. She'd also liked his size, instinctively feeling a large man like him would always protect her.

In fact, it had been the opposite. He'd used his size to intimidate and threaten and hurt. What she'd become after three years with Shawn...

Now, she knew personally how some abused animals felt. She understood the impulse that had them cringing at sudden movements or a raised hand. Objectively, she could see how several years of conditioning by a man she'd thought had loved her had made her this way. What confused and astounded her was how she'd let it happen. How she'd managed to come to believe it was all her fault. If she'd been prettier, smarter, quicker... A better girlfriend, a harder worker, more... As if he was the rational person and she was the one spiraling out of control.

She deserved everything she got. He'd actually said that to her, numerous times. Until finally, something had broken inside her and she'd known she'd had enough. That had been when she'd gotten the news of her great-aunt's death and learned she'd inherited a house in a town she'd never known existed. That had been when she'd realized she'd be all right, that she could leave.

She'd grabbed on with both hands and secretly planned her escape. When she'd fled, she'd taken care to make sure he was at work and had no idea. Even so, she'd been terrified he'd find out and catch her, and make her pay.

And she'd done it! Freed herself, and most likely saved Shawn's life. Because she'd always known, deep down inside herself, if he pushed her too far, she'd snap and shift to wolf. A cornered wolf would kill in self-defense. Even Pack law allowed this, but she didn't want to be a killer.

This had been her first major victory in nearly three years. Now she was here, a few hours north of the city, and Shawn had no idea how to find her. After taking a few deep breaths, she let the tension drain off of her.

Her throat tight, she rolled her shoulders. Focus on

the positive. A house of her own in upstate New York. Enough money to tide her over until she figured out what she wanted to do, and now a paying tenant, which meant a nice revenue stream. Her way out, her ticket to another life.

When she'd first arrived, relieved to find the house completely furnished, she'd met with the attorney and signed the necessary paperwork. After, she'd slept for two days, not stirring from her bed except to guzzle water and use the bathroom. When she'd finally surfaced, she felt like a butterfly emerging from a cocoon. Full of possibilities and hope.

This was all still too new, only one short month along. She had the rest of winter to burrow in, claim her space and find her way. She needed to rebuild her life, piece by piece, not let herself get distracted by a man.

Or his too-adorable-for-words baby.

As if he knew her thoughts, the baby gurgled and flashed JJ a sweet smile. Her heart constricted.

"Hello there, Garth," she cooed, loving the way his bright blue eyes sparkled as he smiled up at her. Carefully, gently, she lifted him out of his portable crib, breathing in the sweet baby scent of him. Moving him to her shoulder, she murmured baby words and nonsense while swaying slightly. His tiny body nestled into her, relaxing in a way that let her know he trusted her to take care of him. She, who'd never even been able to keep a potted plant alive.

This would be her ideal job, taking care of this sweet baby while his daddy worked. Maybe once Eric got settled in and knew her better, he'd entrust her with his precious son for more than a few minutes.

Carrying the infant, she walked to the front window to check on Eric. He was still shoveling her sidewalk. Heart in her throat, she continued to watch him, holding the baby and pointing out his daddy. Even in his bulky parka, Eric's movements were both strong and graceful, an intriguing combination. He left his parka unzipped and wore no hat, his long blond hair tied back in a sexy ponytail.

Baby Garth squirmed, making her realize he'd just dirtied his diaper. Since Eric had brought a diaper bag, she located the spares—disposables, thank goodness—without difficulty, along with baby wipes, and clumsily managed her first diaper change since she'd done babysitting as a teenager years ago.

Feeling pretty accomplished, she picked up the now clean and dry infant and went back to the window. Still holding his shovel, Eric had stopped shoveling snow. Instead, he stood on the freshly cleared sidewalk talking to her next-door neighbor. Rhonda and JJ had hit it off immediately and, according to Rhonda, were destined to become best friends. Like JJ, she was in her thirties and single, though unlike JJ, she was divorced and now actively searching for The One. The Right One, she often quipped, winking.

Judging from the way she was eyeing JJ's new tenant, Rhonda considered him a viable possibility. She'd even ventured outside in a ski jacket and snow boots, shovel in hand, as if about to start shoveling her own driveway and sidewalk. Since it had snowed a couple times in the last few weeks, and JJ had yet to see her actually use her snow shovel, she knew exactly what Rhonda was up to.

Of course, a guy as nice as Eric would in no way stand around and watch a woman shovel snow, so when Eric began clearing Rhonda's sidewalk, the satisfied look on Rhonda's face told JJ she'd expected no less.

To her surprise, JJ felt a tiny twinge of jealously. With her long blond hair and perky upturned nose, Rhonda had the kind of looks and personality that attracted men like bees to a flower. From head to toe, she stood exactly five feet tall. Next to her, JJ felt like an ungainly giant. She and JJ were polar opposites, which was one of the reasons they got along so well, again according to Rhonda. JJ didn't mind; she actually found it a relief to let someone else do all the talking.

While she'd known Rhonda only a couple weeks, the two of them had been to dinner twice and had coffee together a few times. JJ genuinely liked the other woman.

Eric finished quickly and handed the shovel to Rhonda. With a quick smile, he went back to clearing the snow away from his car. His projected fifteen minutes had turned into thirty and he wasn't nearly done yet. JJ didn't mind. She not only enjoyed watching him, but spending time with tiny Garth brought her joy.

Her phone rang. Rhonda's number flashed up on the screen. Still holding the baby, JJ answered.

"Why didn't you call and tell me you had such a gorgeous male specimen living in your house?" Rhonda shrieked.

Since JJ had no real answer for that, she didn't say anything. As usual, her silence didn't bother Rhonda in the slightest. "So what's the story on him?" she asked. "I want details. All of them."

"I don't know very much," JJ finally admitted. "He's from California. Says he's going to open his own business. And his baby is adorable."

For once, she'd stunned her neighbor into silence. "Baby?" Rhonda finally said. She'd never made any secret of the fact that she didn't like children. "He has a baby?"

"Yes. A son named Garth. I think he's three or four months old. I'm watching him while Eric digs his vehicle out from under the snow."

"Wow." Again the silence. But Rhonda being Rhonda, she didn't miss a beat. "Eric, huh? I didn't catch his name.

He was kind enough to clear my driveway and sidewalk for me."

"So I saw," JJ drawled, continuing to bounce the baby. "Um, are you and he…?"

JJ pretended not to understand. "Listen, I've got to go." As if on cue, little Garth let out a loud cry. "I'll talk to you later, okay?" She ended the call without waiting for a response.

Garth squealed again, his bright blue eyes fixed on the doorway. She heard the clump of boots on the stairs, and eyed the baby thoughtfully. He seemed way too young to understand that the sound signaled his father's return, but judging from the way he waved his tiny hands, he clearly was excited about something.

When Eric came through the door, JJ smiled. Little Garth made a chortling sound when he saw his father, continuing to wave his chubby fists. Eric grinned, his bright blue eyes sparkling the same as his son's. "Hey there, little man," he said. Cheeks reddened by exertion and cold, he seemed to have been energized by the exercise. After he peeled off his gloves and shrugged out of his coat, he reached for his son. "Come to Daddy, baby boy."

Then and only then did she think to rush to the stove and put a kettle of water on. If she'd been paying more attention, she would have already done this and had a mug of hot cocoa waiting for him. As it was, he'd have to wait a minute or two for the kettle to whistle.

"Are you cold?" she asked, wincing at the unnecessary question. Of course he was cold. The wind-chill factor was in the teens.

Looking up from playing with his son, he shrugged. "It's a little chilly out there, but I find it exhilarating."

Stunned, she stared. He might be the only other person she'd ever met who'd described feeling that way in blowing snow.

The teakettle finally whistled, startling her out of her thoughts. She hurried to get it. "Hot cocoa?" she asked. Even though it was only instant, nothing beat hot chocolate after shoveling snow in the cold.

"Sounds great."

She made them each a cup, adding a little whipped cream on top. When she turned back, he'd placed his son in his portable crib, where Garth happily played with the bright plastic keys.

With her heart hammering for no good reason, JJ brought Eric his hot drink. Her mouth went dry as he wrapped his long fingers around the mug, and she let her gaze follow the line of his throat as he took a sip and swallowed.

She couldn't blame Rhonda for being excited. Eric looked like a movie star, or a comic book superhero come to life. Even better, the size of his aura indicated when he shape-shifted, it was into something large and magnificent. No doubt Rhonda had noticed that as well, since she, too, was a shifter.

On that, JJ agreed with her neighbor. Shifter to shifter, she couldn't help but appreciate everything about her new tenant.

Artwork, she told herself. She'd decided to try and simply appreciate his amazingly rugged good looks the way she would enjoy a great painting. Like art.

And if she got a tingly feeling every once in a while, so be it. Some things couldn't be helped. She was healing, learning to make her own way in the world, but she wasn't dead.

He caught her watching him and cocked his head. "I think I like it here," he said, taking another long drink of his cocoa. "California is nice, but they don't have real winters. Something about the cold makes me feel alive."

"Me, too." Another flash of delight made her insides quiver. She looked down to hide her excitement. "Most everyone thinks I'm crazy because I love cold and snow." Glancing at him through her lashes, she confessed, "No one likes winter as much as I do."

"Except maybe me." The easy smile he flashed made her catch her breath. "Thanks for the cocoa." Draining the last of it, he set the cup down on her counter. "Garth and I need to drive into town. You're welcome to come with us if you'd like. I could use someone familiar with the place to point me in the right direction."

Her heart gave an entirely unnecessary leap. "I'd love to go," she said, working to quash her enthusiasm so it didn't show. "But I've only lived here one month. I do know where the stores are and some of the restaurants, but I'm in no way a native." About to tell him asking Rhonda would be his best bet, she managed to bite back the comment.

"I forgot." Tilting his head, he eyed her. "You said you were from Manhattan."

"Right."

He continued to watch her, clearly waiting for her to elaborate.

"I needed a fresh start," she finally said, keeping her chin up. "Like you, I had some emotional stuff going on I needed to get away from."

To her relief, he nodded. "I know the feeling."

"It's not easy, that's for sure."

"What about your parents?" he asked. "Do they live close by?"

Normal conversation, she told herself. Asking casual questions, like regular people do. Not everything was suspect. Shawn wasn't his friend.

"My father died a year ago," she said, her words bringing back the pain of his crossing as if it had happened yesterday. "And right after his funeral, my mom closed up their apartment and hopped a plane to Australia. Turns out she'd always wanted to live there."

And her abandonment had felt like a second death, though JJ didn't begrudge her mom her happiness. The two of them talked on the phone about once a month.

"Wow. Adventurous," he said. "You have to admire that."

Out of habit, she caught herself looking around, as if someone else might be listening. Shawn had been human, and she'd grown used to hiding her true nature. Ironic that. In her wolf form, she could have taken Shawn down permanently. He might never have hit her if he'd known that.

Then again, he probably would have just swung harder. Some people never changed, no matter what the circumstances. And Pack law forbade her to reveal her true nature to anyone unless they were going to be mates. Since Shawn and she hadn't been engaged, she'd kept her mouth shut. Truth be told, she'd come to like having a part of herself untouched by him.

"It's okay," Eric said, correctly interpreting her movement. "It's just the two of us. No one else can hear."

"Sorry. I feel foolish, but you know how it is."

"I do." He reached for his son's portable bed, hefting it in one hand.

"What about Garth?" she asked, blurting out the question before she had time to think it through. "Is he full or a halfling?"

"Full." The shortness of his answer told her how dangerously close to the line her question skirted. "Thanks for the cocoa. Are you ready to go now? I'd like to get out there and back before it starts snowing again, just in case."

"Sure." After grabbing her winter coat, she shrugged it on. "I'll probably pick up a few things, too." Like wine. She couldn't believe she'd forgotten to get at least one bottle. Nothing better than a fire crackling in the fireplace, a glass of wine and an old movie in the DVR.

With Garth securely buckled into his infant car carrier, they started to town. Initially tense, JJ relaxed her death grip on the door handle when she realized Eric, despite having lived in California, truly appeared to know how to navigate his SUV on snowy roads.

The small local grocery store appeared to be empty.

"Is it even open?" Eric asked, pulling into a parking spot right near the front door.

She laughed. "The day before the storm hit, you couldn't even park in the lot. And yes, I'm going to say they're open, judging by that neon sign above the doorway."

"Great." Hurrying around to the back, he unbuckled Garth. "Hopefully, it won't take me long to get enough provisions to tide me over for a while."

She nodded. "I just need a few things, so I'll walk with you. Would you like me to hold Garth?"

"Sure." Without a second of hesitation, he handed over the baby. Garth cooed, apparently already recognizing her. In response, her heart squeezed. Ever since she'd realized how Shawn had been using her desire to have a baby as a trick to keep her on a leash, she'd pushed that ache deep down inside her. Being around this little one brought her longing right back to the surface. Maybe someday she'd be lucky enough to have a child of her own.

Chapter 5

By the time they'd reached the other side of the grocery store, Eric had a full basket. JJ had grabbed a bottle of red wine and some cheese and put both in the cart, feeling ridiculously domestic. When they reached the checkout, Eric grabbed those and put them on the belt first, followed by his own groceries.

"Let me pay for my things," JJ said, fumbling in her purse for her wallet while holding Garth.

"I got it." The easy smile Eric flashed had her insides going all tingly again. "A bottle of wine and a block of cheese are the least I can do for you after all the help you've been to me."

"Okay."

When they walked outside, it had started snowing again. Eric gave a good-natured groan, making her laugh.

"I like it," she said, twirling around in the parking lot.

"Which would explain why I found you making a snow angel when I first arrived." After placing little Garth into his infant seat, he began loading groceries into the back of his SUV. At her laugh, he glanced over his shoulder at her, then returned his attention to the task at hand.

Too happy to care, she stuck her tongue out at his back. "This is why I couldn't live anywhere else but New York," she told him. "Well, this and autumn. I'm definitely a fan of the fall."

He closed the back door of his vehicle and walked the shopping cart to the front of the store. "No sense leaving it out here in the snow," he said. "Let's go home before the roads get too bad."

Home. How many times had she said that word back in the city, not really meaning it? Now, hearing him refer to her house that way made hope blossom in her chest. Not for him, not for them, but for her. She really could make this place her home. She really could start her life over.

Once at the house, she took baby Garth inside while Eric carried in his provisions. "Here you go." He handed her the bag with her wine and cheese. "Thanks for your help."

Though plainly, she needed to go, she lingered, searching for a valid reason to stay. Busy unpacking his groceries, he didn't issue an invitation. Finally, though, she thanked him again for the wine and made her way upstairs.

When the snowfall finally stopped an hour before midnight, her measuring stick on the back porch showed they'd gotten eighteen inches. She was giddy with happiness, deciding then and there that she'd go into the woods and become wolf as soon as darkness had fallen. Since moving here, she tried to shape-shift at least once a week. It was much easier to do so here than it had been in the city. Just walking alone into Central Park had been nerve-racking, though once she disappeared into the trees and changed into wolf, it had been fun. Though there had been wooded areas remote enough that a wolf could hunt unnoticed, always, always, always, she and all the others of her kind couldn't help but be aware of the perimeter. As wolf, of necessity they'd remained on alert, just in case they encountered a human, or worse, a gang of humans.

In Forestwood, all that had changed. Judging from the abundance of auras she'd seen, more than two-thirds of the town inhabitants were some kind of shape-shifter. The rest were human and seemed oblivious to the others living in their midst.

She'd never been so glad to see the first snowfall here. One of the things she loved best about snow was changing into her wolf self and going for a run in it. Her entire life, she'd never felt free. Especially, she thought ruefully, since she'd had to lie to Shawn about where she'd been when she disappeared for a few hours every couple weeks. But she couldn't tell him the truth, so she'd done what she must, because she'd had no choice.

Now she could finally experience a space without boundaries. The idea both fascinated and terrified her. Ever since arriving in the Catskills, she'd been itching to get out and do exactly that. Her inner wolf, the curious beast, had been pushing at the edge of her consciousness every other day now. She didn't mind, as this was the purest kind of freedom. Limitless and joyful.

Each day, she felt better and better. Her burden of insecurity had gradually lessened, day by day, the entire time she'd been here in her new home. With such tremendous possibilities open to her, how could she remain afraid to take the first, vital step?

Downstairs, her new tenant and his adorable baby were hopefully asleep. The full moon lit up the freshly fallen snow, silver and white ice crystals beckoning. She'd dressed warmly, aware she'd need to walk deep into the woods behind her house as a human, before shedding her layers and beginning the process that would result in setting her wolf form free.

Anticipation had her moving fast. Her inner wolf felt she'd waited too long to change, which wasn't a good thing for her mental health, though in actuality she hadn't. Still, each time she let her wolf self out to play, when she'd returned to her human form she'd felt better, more balanced and better able to face any unexpected challenges that might lie ahead.

Tonight, she'd think of none of that. Tonight, as wolf, she'd hunt.

After crossing the large field between her house and the forest, she stopped and turned to look back. Pride of ownership filled her, making her heart swell. Her home sat on a small rise, surrounded by a grove of trees that appeared to shelter the two-story, wooden building. Rather than stand out, the house seemed to blend with the landscape, as though it had always been there, standing the test of time.

Hers. Something permanent, a place she could hold on to. Where she could put down roots and change the path of her life. As she often did, she offered up a silent thank-you to the great-aunt she'd never known.

Turning back toward the dark forest, she began moving once again, lifting her feet higher as she trudged through the deepening snow. Here, near the edge of the trees, snowdrifts were deeper, making progress more difficult.

But she powered through, her heart rate quickening as the wolf inside her paced and pushed, ready to be set free.

Finally, she judged she'd gone far enough into the woods. She found a fallen tree and hung her empty backpack from one of the branches. Slowly, she began peeling back layers, already shivering from the cold, though she knew in a few minutes her thick wolf pelt would keep her more than warm.

Stuffing each article of clothing into her backpack, she eventually stood naked, the chill seeping up from her bare feet. She knew she had to act quickly before her poor toes got frostbite. Inhaling, she dropped to the ground and initiated the change.

The familiar sensation never got old. The changes that occurred to her human body—especially her skeleton—could occasionally be painful. More so when a long time had gone by since her last change.

Since she was rushing herself as she shifted, she expected this one to really hurt. Surprisingly, it didn't. Maybe the combination of adrenaline, anticipation and cold combined to deaden the pain somewhat.

Either way, as her bones lengthened, her hands and feet turning into paws, a savage sort of joy filled her.

Wolf-JJ was almost free. In a moment, she'd give herself over to the primitive nature of the beast.

Done. Immediately, myriad tantalizing scents beckoned. Her wolf nose, a thousand times more sensitive than her human one, picked up on the fact that a rabbit had recently crossed nearby, as had a skunk and a small herd of white-tailed deer.

Eager to explore, she bounded off through the snow.

Eric had heard Julia tromp down the stairs right around twelve, just as he was about to turn off the TV and head to bed. Curious, he waited for the sound of a car engine starting, but then caught sight of her moving slowly across a large, open field. Her bulky parka and layered clothing made movement a bit difficult as she headed toward the forest, no doubt to change into her beast, whatever kind that might be.

An instant of longing rocked him, his inner beast protesting with a roar that reverberated in his soul. He felt it had been forever since he'd shape-shifted, and his bear self was not at all happy about that. But what could he do? Taking care of an infant made it damn near impossible to go off by himself and change. While he'd gotten Jason, his Pack Protector friend, to watch Garth a time or two, he'd been able to shape-shift only twice in three months. Not good. At all. To go too long without letting his inner bear free was dangerous. He knew, as did all shifters, that doing so could lead to insanity or even death. Right now, Eric felt as if he could be pushing the limit. Maybe he'd see if his landlord would be willing to watch Garth for an hour or two tomorrow night so Eric could take his own solitary trip into the forest.

He resolved to ask her later. Right now, all he could do was watch until she disappeared from view, and push down his envy.

The hunt went well, JJ thought, as she hurriedly dressed after changing back to human. As usual, when in her wolf form, she had no sense of time passing, so she had no idea how long she'd explored the forest. She'd tracked and taken down a midsize rabbit, feasting until her belly was full. This would be her place, and though she knew there surely were other shifters in Forestwood, these few acres of woods were part of her property and would be where she went to let her wolf self run free.

Once again fully clothed, though everything retained a touch of a chill, she gave herself a few moments for the intense sexual arousal to recede. For whatever reason, this crazed need for bodily contact happened to everyone once they shifted back to human, no matter what kind of beast they became. Many people took advantage of this—she'd heard stories of wild and crazy orgies among groups who liked to shape-shift with others.

As for herself, she'd gotten used to tamping down the need. Even when she'd been with Shawn, she hadn't wanted to return home after having spent the night away and beg him to make love to her. Sex was another one of the things he used to control her.

So once the low thrum of desire had settled to a steady hum, she inhaled deeply and exhaled slowly, watching the plume her breath made in the frigid air. Centered, she felt normal again, so she wouldn't find herself at Eric's front door offering herself to him.

The thought sent a fresh wave of longing through her. Again she took deep breaths, focusing on the snow and the velvet ink of the sky, until she'd once again regained her equilibrium.

Then and only then did she turn to make her way back home. She followed her old footprints, glad they made the going much easier. The moon still provided illumination, though it no longer hung fat and sassy in the sky directly overhead.

A few hours then, she thought. Time well spent. Her entire body ached, a pleasant feeling. She let herself back into her silent house and went up the stairs, wincing as a few of them creaked.

She'd just about reached her landing when the downstairs door opened.

"Welcome back." The sound of Eric's deep voice sent an immediate thrum of need blazing through her bloodstream. Damn. So much for returning to normal.

Reluctant to face him, but glad of the several steps in between them, she turned, thankful for her bulky clothing. "Thank you. You're up kind of late, aren't you?" Then, as a worrisome thought occurred to her, she raised her gloved hand to her throat. "Is Garth all right?"

"He's fine." Eric dragged his own hand across his chin. "You went out to change, didn't you?"

Slowly, she nodded, aware once again they were skirting dangerously close to the edge of what was considered acceptable conversation.

Shifting his weight from foot to foot, he nodded. It dawned on her he was clearly uncomfortable. "It's been a while for me and…"

"You can't just leave Garth."

"Right. So I was wondering if you'd mind watching him for a few hours so I can change, too."

What she'd give to see him change, or to be more specific, to be there when he exchanged his animal form for that of a man. At the thought, a bolt of lust shot through her, so strong she nearly staggered. "Tonight?" she managed to ask. "Because I don't know if I—"

"No, not tonight." One corner of his mouth tugged up in a tired smile. "I was thinking maybe tomorrow night, if that would be okay with you. If not, I'm open to whenever you can spare the time."

"Tomorrow should be fine." *Casual*, she thought. She hoped she sounded casual. Not at all like a woman who wanted to pounce on him because she couldn't help imagining being the one to greet him when he became human again, fully and gloriously aroused.

In fact, she'd better get back to her own personal, private space before she did something foolish, like reach for him.

"I really appreciate it, Julia." He frowned. "Is it okay if I use your first name?"

"My friends call me JJ," she told him. "I'd rather you use that."

"I will." Again the blinding smile. "I really appreciate all your help. Someday I hope I can repay you."

Oh, she knew exactly how he could repay her. Dang it. Swallowing hard, she managed to smile back.

"Good night," she said firmly, unlocking her door and stepping inside. Once she had it closed firmly behind her, she sagged against it, her entire body throbbing. Residue from the change, she told herself. Nothing to do with her tenant. Nothing to do with him at all. After the disastrous relationship with Shawn, she didn't need to be wanting another man, not now. Maybe not ever.

In the morning, a phone call woke Eric. It was the moving company notifying him they'd be arriving the next afternoon, weather permitting. Finally, he'd be getting the few personal items he'd kept, along with Garth's actual baby furniture. And his car. Most important, his beautiful car. Of course, the baby furniture was important, too, but if it had gotten damaged or lost, he could replace it. His car was irreplaceable.

Things were starting to look up. Eric found himself waiting with barely concealed anticipation for the sun to go down so he could go into the woods alone and change.

He'd have to be careful, though he'd actually chosen this town because they'd reportedly been tolerant, even kind, to the Drakkor woman they'd sheltered for years. She'd become a celebrity of sorts among paranormal creatures, dispensing wisdom and baked goods from her cottage on the shores of the lake. Another Drakkor and his shifter mate had also settled here. He planned to visit all three of them once he got settled, as long as they were open to visitors. Being bear, he felt a sense of kinship with other outcasts, other species of shifter who were rare and few and often reviled.

When his family had left their small village in Norway, they'd chosen a town in California where other Vedjorn lived. Since most bear shifters mated with their own kind, they'd wanted their son to have the chance to find a mate.

While he missed his parents tremendously, he was glad they hadn't survived to see what kind of a mate he'd chosen. If he had his druthers, he'd never hook up with another bear shifter. And since most of the other shifters were afraid of the bears, he doubted he'd ever find another woman to mate with again.

Which suited him just fine. Once had been enough. He had his son. As long as he could find a female who was open to recreational sex, he'd consider his life a happy one.

For now, though, the only thing he needed to worry about was letting his inner beast free to run and hunt.

Anticipation built in him as he waited for dusk. Somehow, his nervous pacing communicated to his son, rendering Garth unusually fussy. Even though he'd been changed and fed and burped, he started crying and wouldn't be soothed. This had never happened before. Jiggling him, rocking him, speaking in a soothing tone over and over—none of it worked. In desperation, Eric searched the internet for a solution, but found only variations of what he already knew to do.

Finally, little Garth cried himself to sleep.

Exhausted, Eric quietly transferred his son to his temporary crib. Then he sat down with his head in his hands and tried to think.

Teething? Again he hit the search engines and learned teething usually starts at six months, but can start as early as three.

A soft tap at his door startled him. After a quick glance to make sure the sound hadn't made Garth wake, he hurried to answer.

"Is everything all right?" JJ murmured, as if she somehow knew the baby slept. She wore a flowing shirt and some sort of soft leggings that made her legs appear impossibly long.

"It is now," he said grimly, holding the door open and motioning her inside. "I couldn't get him to stop crying. He actually cried himself to sleep."

"Is he sick?" she asked, sounding worried. "From here, he looks feverish. Have you taken his temperature?"

That thought had never occurred to him. But then, Garth had only been sick once in his three months of life. Eric took comfort in the fact that his son was a full-blooded shape-shifter, and as such, only fire or silver could kill him. That could be both a curse and a blessing. He'd personally known a few people forced to live on in damaged bodies, enduring hell because they could not die. He wouldn't wish that on his worst enemy.

Chapter 6

Garth made a snuffling sound, drawing Eric's attention. His son might be all bear, but that didn't mean he couldn't suffer from illness. A fever could easily be rectified, however. Eric fumbled in the baby bag he'd packed, finally locating the thermometer. It was brand-new, still in the wrapping. He'd purchased the forehead kind, not wanting to deal with a rectal one.

Once he'd unwrapped it, he did a quick read of the instructions before swiping it over Garth's tiny brow.

"Ninety-nine point zero," he said. "Just a little over normal."

"Nothing to worry about, I don't think." JJ spoke with authority, despite claiming to know next to nothing about caring for babies.

"Maybe he's teething," she continued. "Is he drooling a lot?"

"Yeah." Eric hesitated, eyeing his sleeping son. "I don't think I can leave him if he's sick." Inside, his beast roared in protest. "I'm thinking I probably should reschedule."

When he looked back up, Julia studied him, her head

tilted. She appeared a bit shell-shocked, almost as if she'd heard his beast's roar. "It's up to you," she said. "I personally think he'll be fine. It's only for a few hours, anyway. But you're his father, so if you want to wait until another night, that's fine with me."

Again his beast made his presence known, rattling the proverbial bars of his invisible cage. Inside, Eric fought a minor battle. It had been too long since he'd let his bear out and the animal didn't take well to being confined for lengthy periods of time.

"I can see your problem," Julia said softly. "Your beast really needs to be free. Go change. Let your other self out to run and hunt. Make it short if you really feel you have to, but I'll be perfectly fine here with Garth."

Part of him wanted to leap for joy. The other, more rational part kept his feet planted firmly in place. "What would you do if he became sicker?"

"Take care of him," she said, turning away. "I seriously don't think there's anything wrong with him that a teething ring wouldn't fix. Do you have one of those?"

"A what?"

"A baby teething ring. You know, you put it in the fridge and once it's good and cold, you let the baby gum it." She frowned. "Though maybe those are for older babies. I doubt little Garth could hold it yet."

"I don't have one of those."

"That's okay. I've seen people use a cool, wet washcloth."

"You seem to have more experience with babies than you let on."

She smiled. "Just because I didn't work in the baby room at the day care doesn't mean I didn't spend a lot of time in there. As I said, I love babies."

Again, his inner beast roared, fighting to break free.

And once more, JJ cocked her head as though listening. He almost asked her what she heard, but restrained himself. "I'm going to go." He made a snap decision, knowing he'd have to shape-shift sooner or later, so he might as well do it and be done with it. A happy inner bear made life better all the way around.

"Good. I sense some discord between you and your beast."

Either she was unusually perceptive or he was giving far too much away.

"I'm fine," he lied. "Though I'll be better once I change and hunt." He studied his son. Garth made a snuffling sound and moved. Relief flooded Eric. Maybe she was right. Maybe his boy was just teething.

"I'm trusting you with my son." Even as he spoke, he couldn't believe what he was saying. He meant it, too, he realized. JJ, his landlord, was one of what his father used to call "good people."

"I promise I'll take good care of him," she said, smiling. "We'll be upstairs. I've got the perfect chair."

"Then let me carry up his diaper bag and portable crib."

Once everything had been set up, she smiled. "Now go. Run and hunt. I promise you'll feel much better once you've changed. Especially if it's been a while."

He nodded and then impulsively kissed her cheek. The instant he did it, he knew he'd made a huge mistake. Wide-eyed, she stared at him, while a rose color suffused her entire face.

Her scent—lavender—lingered on his lips after he moved away. "I'll see you in a little bit," he said, and hurried out the door before he did anything even more foolish.

Cheek still tingling, JJ watched from her window as Eric headed across the clearing toward the woods. With the full moon reflecting on the snow, she could see him outlined clearly, his parka dark against the glowing, magically pure whiteness.

Though she knew he hadn't meant anything with that casual kiss—on the cheek, no less—every fiber of her body had strained toward him, as if he were a lure she was unable to resist.

Luckily, she'd frozen in place instead of swaying toward him. Her blush had been the only sign of how his simple gesture affected her. Hopefully, he had no idea. Her secret attraction must remain just that—a secret.

Glancing at the still sleeping baby, she sighed. She'd need to be careful with these two. Both of them had the power to come dangerously close to stealing her heart.

Again her gaze drifted back to Eric, who was nearing the edge of the trees. Aching to be with him, she stood there until he vanished into the woods.

Her kind did best with others. They were called The Pack for a reason. But she'd always shape-shifted alone. Maybe it had been her natural reticence, but she hadn't been up for being around a group of people when she turned human again, battling a fierce arousal. She'd often wondered what it would be like, for curiosity's sake. She'd heard there were some groups for whom privacy was an option, who were not into random sex with strangers, but she'd always been afraid to take a chance. Though she'd often considered the idea, in the end she knew she did better alone.

Or so she'd told herself. Now, watching a gorgeous hunk of man on his way to shape-shift, she wanted nothing more than to do the same at his side.

Of course, assuming he was Pack. Why wouldn't he be, when 90 percent of the shifters she knew were wolves? There was no way to find out for sure, unless she accidentally came across him changing. Which was extremely unlikely to occur.

She sighed, unable to keep from imagining him as he transitioned from his animal form back to human. As always happened with their kind, he'd be fully aroused. Her body heated, the desire she'd experienced the night before back in full force.

And then she remembered he'd kissed her on the cheek. The cheek, not the lips. The kind of kiss a man gave to his mother or aunt or sister. Or friend.

That was what they were. Friends. She needed to constantly remind herself of that and she'd be fine.

She must have dozed, sitting in her armchair with a still slumbering Garth next to her. Eric's tread on her old wooden stairs woke her; no matter how quiet anyone tried to be, the third and seventh steps squeaked.

After pushing herself up and out of her chair, she pulled the door open before he reached it.

"Hey," he whispered. Even in the shadowy hallway, his blue eyes blazed. As he stepped into her living room, she could feel the satisfaction and coiled up energy rolling off him.

His inner beast had gone quiet. No longer restless, most likely sated by a run and a hunt. "How'd it go?" she asked, even though the question seemed unnecessary.

"It went well," he said. "Very well. I feel much better. How's Garth?"

"He slept the entire time you were gone. His color looks good. I checked his temperature one more time and it was the same. I'm sure he's fine."

Relief shone in her tenant's face. "I really appreciate this."

Mercilessly, she kept her gaze trained on his face, not daring to let it dip below his waist, though she badly wanted to see if his body revealed his certain arousal.

"I'd better go." He shifted his weight from one foot to the other. "See you tomorrow."

When he bent to retrieve the portable crib, she got a great view of his nicely shaped backside.

Giving herself a mental slap, she dragged her eyes toward the baby, where they needed to be.

"He's not moving," Eric said, panic edging his voice. "JJ, Garth isn't moving. I don't think he's breathing."

"What?" She reacted without conscious thought, reaching for the infant and lifting him up to pat him soundly on the back. He gasped, his eyes flying open.

And then he let out a cry, a screeching sort of wail, so wonderful she sagged in relief.

"Garth." Eric snatched him from her. "Baby boy?" Which only made him cry harder.

Trembling with relief, JJ reached into the crib and located the pacifier. She handed this to Eric, who held it to Garth's mouth. Latching on and suckling wildly, he instantly ceased crying.

"What the heck was that?" Eric asked, bewilderment and panic lacing his voice. "I swear, I put my finger under his nose and he wasn't breathing."

"I don't know." Privately, she wondered if Eric had imagined it. "He must have been deeply asleep." Tears stung the back of her eyes. "I'm so glad he's okay."

"Me, too." The fierce tone told her how much the man meant it.

Aware she needed to be careful, she took a deep breath. "Earlier, you said he was full-blooded. If so, you know illness wouldn't kill him."

"I'm aware." The shortness of Eric's answer told her he was angry at himself for overreacting. "And while it's true such a thing might not kill him, death isn't always the worst thing that could happen to our kind. Think of a soul trapped in a nonfunctioning body. I've seen that before. A fever can cause brain damage."

Slowly, she nodded. "I haven't ever thought of it like that."

"It's because you're not a parent." He had no way of knowing how much those words stung.

All she could do was nod.

"What a night," he continued. "I'm going take him downstairs now and get the both of us ready for bed."

Good. Because maybe then she could sit down before her legs gave out from under her.

Apparently, he felt the same way. After jerking his head in a brusque nod, he grabbed the diaper bag and portable crib, then turned and left.

As soon as the door clicked shut behind him, JJ dropped into her chair, her entire body shaking. Had Eric imagined everything in a moment of overprotective panic, or had Garth really stopped breathing?

Truth be told, she didn't know. Personally, she tended to lean more toward imagination, because every time she'd checked on him, the baby had been fine.

But after this, she had a feeling Eric wouldn't trust her to watch his son ever again. Full-blooded or not.

Once he'd gotten Garth back home, Eric shook his head. What the hell was wrong with him? He'd never been the overprotective type of parent, stressing about his baby's every sniffle. But for one split second there he'd been filled with a visceral dread, convinced something terrible and unimaginably awful had happened to his son.

Then Garth had drawn a breath and cried. Clearly, he was fine. Relief mixed with chagrin. His son was okay. Teething a little maybe, but all right. And Eric's first reaction, that awful gut-churning response, had been to turn on the woman who'd been trying to help him.

He felt awful, though his one consolation was that maybe she hadn't noticed.

Of course she had. He would find her tomorrow and offer an apology. Once he'd made sure his son had a clean diaper, he put him down for the night and climbed into bed.

When his cell phone rang at 1:00 a.m., waking him from a deep sleep, Eric fumbled for the phone and finally answered.

"Yolanda has gone off the deep end," a familiar voice said. "That woman is stark raving crazy."

Blinking, Eric didn't speak at first while he tried to figure out why his friend Jason was calling. This was old news, restating the obvious.

"I thought I'd pass along a warning." Jason worked for the Pack Protectors and acted as a liaison between the wolves and bears. He'd been helping Eric with his case ever since Yolanda had started her crazy accusations.

It helped that the Wolf Pack had lately been trying to end the divide between the bears and everyone else. It was slow going, as the distrust was mutual, but Eric gave them kudos for even trying. He certainly could always hope.

Eric had been brought up by two people who refused to accept the status quo. In Norway, they'd settled away from the small enclaves of their own kind, living among humans and other shifters before immigrating to the United States when Eric had been ten and settling in California, choosing a town with numerous other shifters, including Vedjorn.

Growing up, Eric hadn't known there was any prejudice against bears. He and Jason—who had to be Pack, though of course they'd never discussed it—had been best friends since kindergarten. When Jason had gone into the military and from there the Pack Protectors, he'd never once lost contact with Eric. Even when his top-secret clearance revealed that his best friend was a Vedjorn bear shifter, Jason hadn't turned away. Instead, he'd asked to work on the task force dedicated to keeping the few remaining Vedjorn safe.

Yawning, Eric rubbed his eyes. Luckily, the ringing phone hadn't disturbed Garth, who still slept. Eric couldn't stop himself from once again checking to make sure his son was breathing. He was, of course.

"Thanks, man, but couldn't this have waited until morning? Is it really the kind of thing that warrants a phone call at 1:00 a.m.?"

Jason cursed. "I'm so sorry. I forgot you were on the East Coast. It's only ten here. I just got home from work. It's been a long day. Most of my afternoon and evening were spent dealing with your ex."

"She doesn't know where I am." Eric felt quite confident in that knowledge. "You're still the only one who knows, right? Everyone else—faculty, friends—all still think I went up to Seattle."

"Yeah, still true. But you know what? I really didn't get it before. Why you felt the need to put as much distance as possible between you and her." Jason's wry tone told Eric he did now. "Sure, she seemed a bit emotional. Dramatic, even. But not unstable."

"Is she still trying to brand me a Berserker?" Though he hated to even speak the word, Eric didn't have a choice. A true Berserker, though rare among their kind, was extremely dangerous. When Berserkers shifted into their bear selves, they could become uncontrollable killing machines. The Wolf Pack Protectors had been working in conjunction with the Vedjorn Bear Council in making sure any true Berserkers were destroyed before they killed any humans and brought unwelcome notice to the entire shape-shifter population. In Eric's lifetime, he'd heard of only two, both back in Norway.

"Yes." Jason sounded tired. "I've shifted with you, remember. I know you're not. And I really don't understand her plan. What is she hoping to achieve?"

"If I knew, I'd tell you. Despite her claims otherwise, it's not like she truly wants our son—she handed him over without a backward glance and signed papers waiving all parental rights." Again, rehashing old news. The two men had speculated endlessly over Yolanda's motives. Since she wanted nothing to do with Garth, her reasons for stalking Eric remained a mystery.

"She flew into a rage at the office today when no one would tell her where she could find you. Something about having a score to settle. And needing to protect Garth."

"Again, that makes no sense." Before Eric could finish his statement, he heard an alarm that began shrieking in the background at Jason's place. "Are you all right?"

"Yeah. That's my burglar alarm. Perimeter alert. I need to check this out, so I'm going to let you go." He ended the call.

Setting down his phone, Eric shook his head. With her rants and raves about Berserkers and the possibility that a sweet, innocent baby could be one, Yolanda presented a very real danger. He understood she wanted to harm their child and destroy Eric himself, which was why he'd high-tailed it out of Cali. Eventually, she would turn back to her partying friends and forget about them. Until then—and maybe forever—he'd keep a low profile. All that mattered was making sure Garth stayed safe.

The phone call had startled Eric, making him wonder if he'd be able to go back to sleep. But apparently shape-shifting and hunting earlier had exhausted him, because he drifted off as soon as he laid his head on his pillow. When he opened his eyes again, bright sunlight reflecting on the snow outside lit up his room.

Instinctively, he checked on Garth. His son still slumbered, the rise and fall of his chest steady. The sight filled Eric with so much joy his throat felt tight.

The possibilities of this new life, with this child…he could ask for nothing more.

Once his son woke up, cheerful as always, Eric changed him and fed him. Then he ate his own breakfast.

The chime of his cell phone broke into his thoughts. He grabbed it. Caller ID showed Jason's number.

"Jason," he said, bracing himself for more tales of craziness. "What's Yolanda done now?"

Silence on the other end. Then an unfamiliar male voice spoke. "This is Officer Frank DeLeon with the Pack Protectors. I regret to inform you that Jason is dead."

"Dead?" Eric swallowed hard, pain knifing through him. "I just talked to him around one this morning. His alarm went off in the middle of our call. What happened? Intruders?"

A pause. "We're reviewing the surveillance tapes now. It was pretty violent."

Then, while Eric was still trying to wrap his mind around that, the voice continued. "And there's more, unfortunately. We've also got a severely injured woman here. Judging from what we can tell from the crime scene, she and Jason were battling."

"A woman?" At first he didn't understand.

"Yes. She knew the drill, since she came armed with a pistol and silver bullets. After she shot Jason, she turned the gun on herself."

"Who?" Eric cleared his throat, feeling as if he already knew the answer, but hoping he was wrong. "Who is the woman?"

"Mr. Mikkelson, we've tentatively identified her as your ex-wife, Yolanda. Your ex-wife and the person who was trying to make a case against you for allegedly being a true Berserker."

Chapter 7

Another pause. Had there been accusation in the Pack Protector's tone? When Officer DeLeon continued, Eric already knew exactly what he was going to say. "What I'll need from you, Mr. Mikkelson, is proof of your whereabouts since 1:00 a.m."

Stunned, shocked, Eric took a full twenty seconds to respond. "I'm in New York, sir. And yes, I can provide whatever proof you need."

It was only after he'd hung up that he allowed himself to give in to his grief. Jason was gone. Not only his best friend, but his contact inside the Pack Protectors. The guy who always had his back. And Yolanda had taken herself out along with him.

Unfortunately, the phone call had been all too real. Jason was dead. Yolanda was seriously injured and in intensive care. The doctor had told Eric he wasn't sure if she would pull through.

The taint of unspoken accusation had colored every sentence between Eric and Officer DeLeon. Even though it hadn't taken long for the Pack Protectors to verify that Eric was indeed in New York, on the opposite side of the country.

From what DeLeon had reluctantly revealed, it appeared Yolanda had gone to Jason's home to confront him. She'd purchased a pistol and some silver bullets, apparently with the intention of threatening him. Things had gone down-hill from there. Everyone in Jason's division had been fa-miliar with the woman and her crazy accusations. No one had seen her as a viable threat, least of all Jason.

Privately, Eric thought she'd purchased the one weapon that could kill a shifter in order to eliminate him, once she got Jason to reveal her ex-husband and son's location. He wondered if Jason had, before he died. Knowing his friend, Eric doubted it.

Poor Jason had been caught in the middle. A Pack Pro-tector, he clearly hadn't taken Yolanda seriously enough. This broke Eric's heart.

Meanwhile, Yolanda continued to recover at the hospi-tal. While a silver bullet could kill, she'd missed her heart and brain and any other vital organs. Now she had a fifty-fifty chance of survival.

One of their own had been killed and the Pack Protec-tors were in a frenzy to blame someone. At first it had seemed as if they were trying to figure out a way to accuse Eric, but in the end they'd had to acknowledge Yolanda had done this, and she'd acted alone.

However, Detective DeLeon's casual use of the word *Berserker* concerned Eric. He sounded as if he had no idea what a Berserker was. Yolanda definitely wasn't one, but the other man referred to her as a Berserker more than once. Luckily, as far as Eric and Garth were concerned, whatever caused bears to go wild was rarely passed down. Instead, it mostly appeared to be a random gene mutation.

Eric could not allow anything to happen to Garth, even

if his birth mother was determined to be Berserker by people who knew no better. Eric had shifted with Yolanda and he knew beyond a shadow of a doubt that she wasn't.

DeLeon had said Yolanda would be charged with murder if she lived. Right now, no one seemed certain she would. If she did, Eric could only hope she remained in police custody. He couldn't help but pray that Jason, in his final moments, had not revealed Eric and Garth's location.

Though most of the snow had melted, except for odd little pockets of dirty whiteness in the shadows of buildings or a particularly large tree, the slate-gray sky and icy, gusting wind promised another storm would be on the way sooner or later. After all, it was January.

JJ, like most of Forestwood, bustled around trying to run errands and stock up on supplies before she was snowed in again.

Her mother called from Australia just as JJ finished putting up the groceries. It was summer there, and her mom always loved to tell her how much fun she had at the beach in the blazing hot sun. She didn't seem to ever grasp the fact that her daughter really preferred fall and winter.

"I heard you got a big snowstorm," Anita Jacobs said by way of greeting.

"We did." JJ waited for her mom to gloat.

Instead, Anita sighed. "I miss the snow."

This statement so boggled her mind that JJ couldn't think of a response. Her mother had always complained bitterly when the first snowflake fluttered to the ground.

"Listen," her mom continued. "I was wondering. Have you and Shawn kissed and made up yet?"

JJ couldn't suppress a shudder. Her mother had loved Shawn. Of course, JJ hadn't given her a reason not to. She'd been too embarrassed to admit the truth. "No, Mom. That's not going to happen."

"Because he wants to live in Manhattan and you're now living upstate?"

"If only it were that simple," JJ said.

"He called me, you know."

JJ felt a stab of fear, like a steel blade plunging into the middle of her chest. She cursed herself for not telling her mother the truth. "Please tell me you didn't let him know where I am."

"Of course not." Anita sounded offended. "You asked me not to and I promised. I am a woman of my word. But I need to tell you how worried that man is. He seemed frantic. Said he's been searching for you in all five boroughs."

Frantic? More like pissed.

"Mom, there's something you should know about Shawn," JJ began.

"No." Her mother snorted. "If he had an affair, I don't want to know the details."

As far as JJ knew, Shawn could have had twenty affairs. Cheating would have been infinitely preferable to the facts. "It wasn't that, Mom." Pushing away the wave of shame, JJ forced herself to continue. "Shawn was abusive." There. Finally, she'd given her mom the truth. Though *abusive* seemed too tame a word, it nicely summed up things.

"Abusive?" Anita sounded confused. "What do you mean? That man positively doted on you."

"In public." Hearing the defeat in her own voice, JJ winced. "Listen, it's a long story. I'll tell it to you sometime, maybe next time you visit. But for now, believe me when I say it's not safe for me if Shawn finds out where I am."

"Wow. I had no idea. I'm shocked. Truly stunned. I also don't understand why you didn't tell me."

A hundred reasons. Chief among them, JJ had been ashamed. Also, she figured the less people knew, the better. She couldn't live with herself if she put anyone else's life in danger because of her.

Instead of answering, JJ sighed. "I'm sorry, Mom. It's just been kind of crazy."

"I imagine it has been. I'm so sorry you had to endure that. I honestly would have tried to help you if I'd known. You know you're always welcome to come live with me in Australia."

Closing her eyes against the wave of pain her mother's words brought, JJ tried to formulate a response. "Thanks, Mom. But I'm fine here. I like this house and this town. And I have a new tenant renting the space downstairs. For the first time in a long time, I think everything is going to be all right." Maybe if she said it enough, she'd believe it.

"Really?" JJ could hear the surprise in Anita's voice. "That's wonderful. Just remember, though. You always have a choice."

"We all have free will, Mom." This last came out sharper than JJ had intended. "Sorry." She took a deep breath and tried to take her tone down a notch. "I'm still adjusting to getting away and starting a new life."

Silence. Then her mother sighed. "I'm happy for you, sweetheart. Truly happy. Again, I find it painful that you never said anything to me. I could have helped you. Just because I moved away doesn't mean I abandoned you."

Hadn't she? JJ no longer had any idea what to think. To be fair, she'd told her mom as little as possible about that aspect of her life. It wasn't exactly something she wanted anyone else to know about. They hadn't really discussed it since her mother left.

This time, JJ didn't answer. After a few seconds of silence, Anita spoke. "Do you need me to come see you?

Maybe visit for a couple of weeks, just until you get settled? I still know a few people in that town."

Did she really mean that? Ever since the day her mom had packed up and moved to Australia, leaving alone a daughter still grieving over the loss of her father, JJ had struggled with the question of whether or not her mother really loved her.

She still didn't understand how a mom could move to the other side of the world from her young daughter who might need her. JJ got that they had both been in pain, shell-shocked and reeling over their mutual loss, but who simply took off without a backward glance, leaving behind the only family member you had left?

She still felt resentment, even after all these months. Another unwelcome emotion.

"Honey? Did you hear me? I can book a flight and be there in a few days if you want."

"That's okay," JJ finally said. "I'm still trying to find my footing. I told you I got a tenant to live in the downstairs unit. So I have his rent for income until I find a job. And I've made friends with the woman next door. So it's not like I'm all alone."

"Well, all right." Did her mom actually sound disappointed? "But promise me you'll let me know if you need me, okay?"

This was a new one. Her mother had never really appeared to care if JJ was in trouble. "Okay."

With that assurance, her mother hung up.

Odd. It was almost as if she was hoping JJ would actually need her. Shaking her head, JJ couldn't help but wonder if Anita had gotten bored with her life down under and was hoping for a little excitement to stir things up.

The next morning, JJ woke early. She showered and dried her hair, dressing warmly before heading into her kitchen to make a pot of coffee.

Even though it was below freezing, JJ bundled up and carried her coffee outside to the front porch to drink it. She needed to get out of the house. It felt like the walls were closing in around her.

Since snow had piled up on the outdoor chairs, JJ stood. Next door, the front door opened and Rhonda came outside and waved. "Come over here," she ordered, cupping her mouth with her hands to make sure the sound carried. "I just made a coffee cake. And I have plenty of java. We're overdue for a chat."

Thankful for the welcome distraction, JJ said she'd be right over. After draining the last of her coffee, she headed next door, glad of the still-shoveled sidewalk. Once inside Rhonda's cheery yellow kitchen, she shrugged out of her parka, hanging it on the wooden coatrack near the back door. Accepting a cup of steaming coffee, she chose one of the bar stools and sat at the bar instead of the kitchen table.

Smiling, Rhonda cut two large slices of coffee cake and brought them over, along with her own mug of coffee.

"It's so good to see you. But you don't look like you've been sleeping well," Rhonda drawled, her blue eyes sparkling with humor. "Is there a reason? Such as a certain handsome hunk of tenant keeping you up at night?"

Heaven help her, but JJ blushed. "I wish," she said, meaning it. "But no. I just had a bad night last night."

Taking a large bite prevented her from acting on the urge to over-confide. As if aware of this, her neighbor watched, sipping her coffee, while JJ chewed.

"Why?" Rhonda finally asked. Her coffee cake still sat untouched.

"I have no idea." JJ pointed toward her own half-demolished slice. "This is really good. Aren't you going to eat yours?"

"Maybe." Using her fork, Rhonda cut a teeny, tiny bite. "Mmm. It is good."

JJ shook her head, eyeing her neighbor in disbelief. "Unless you scarfed down three pieces before I got here, please tell me that's not all you're going to eat."

"Hey!" Rhonda's heavily penciled-in eyebrows rose. "Maybe I'm just trying to look good. Bikini season is right around the corner, you know."

This made JJ laugh. "It's January," she snorted. "I'd say you've got several months before you need to even think about bikini season. Unless you're going to Australia to visit my mom."

"Nope." Rhonda shook her head. Her expression got serious. "Listen, can I ask you something?"

"Sure."

"Are you and Thor involved?"

It took JJ a few seconds. "Thor? Oh, you mean Eric. My tenant. No, we're not. Why?" She asked the question even though she already knew what the answer would be.

"Because he's superhot." Rhonda sighed. "And also seems nice, which is rare in a guy who looks like him. But I didn't want to poach on your territory, so if you want dibs, let me know. Before I go making a fool of myself."

Dibs. Dismayed and alarmed at the rush of jealousy that flooded through her at the other woman's comment, JJ looked down at her half-eaten cake. To give herself time to decide how to respond, she took a long drink of her rapidly cooling coffee.

Finally, she decided to just go with the truth. "I don't know, Rhonda. He hasn't been here all that long." She met her friend's bright blue eyes. "But as far as who he might want to date in the future, I'm thinking it should be up to him, not us."

"True." Rhonda grabbed JJ's cup and refilled it. "But you're drop-dead gorgeous and you get to live with him.

You have the home field advantage. I'd have to put in some pretty intense effort to even get him to notice me."

JJ laughed. "Have you looked in the mirror lately, my friend? He might just be partial to petite, well-endowed blondes. He came here from California, after all."

"Did he?" Rhonda purred. "Then maybe I might have a chance."

Though it took an effort, JJ managed a casual shrug. "You might. As long as you can stand being around his baby."

Rhonda flashed her a horrified look. "I completely forgot about his kid. I know you mentioned it, but I must have blocked that from my mind." While she sulked, she shoveled a larger bite of her coffee cake into her mouth and washed it down with a gulp of coffee.

"Well, that's not going to work," Rhonda finally said. "Unless you'd be willing to watch the baby when he and I go out."

"Not a chance," JJ replied cheerfully. "You have to take one if you want the other. They're kind of a package deal."

"I'm not going to marry him," Rhonda protested. "Just have a little fun."

For whatever reason, JJ couldn't see Eric and Rhonda together. At all. Did that mean she wanted him for herself? She wasn't sure. "Good luck," she said.

Tilting her head, Rhonda searched her face. "You sound like you really mean it."

Again the twinge, which she disregarded more forcibly this time. "I just got out of a long-term relationship," she said. "And it wasn't a good one. I promise you, right now I'm not in the market for another."

She wondered why saying the words felt like a lie.

Staring out his front window at the slate-gray sky, Eric wondered if he'd made a mistake coming to Forestwood.

Did the sun ever shine here? Coming from sunny California, he'd read up and thought he was prepared for a New York winter. Apparently not. He had to admit, once or twice the idea of returning to Cali had crossed his mind, but he'd made a plan and committed himself to it. He had to give this town and this new life a chance. Plus, of course, his son was a lot safer this far from Yolanda.

At least there hadn't been any more snowstorms. Yet. The entire town appeared to be collectively holding its breath. He hadn't seen JJ since the incident when he'd thought Garth had stopped breathing. Two days. He found he missed talking with her. While he wasn't sure if that was because he knew absolutely no one else here, he didn't feel the urge to go next door and hang out with Rhonda.

No, it was JJ he wanted.

As if they were friends. Though they barely knew each other, he considered her a friend. As long as he pushed back his attraction—which he had to, since he had to focus on new beginnings and raising Garth—he believed he and JJ could become friends. Nothing more. Which he surprisingly regretted.

Right now, he couldn't help but wonder if she missed his company as much as he missed hers. He decided he'd go up to her place later that day and see if she wanted to talk.

Later that afternoon, when a sharp knock sounded on his front door, his heart stuttered as he jumped to his feet. Maybe JJ had come to visit. But when he yanked open the door, instead of a petite redhead, a dour-faced middle-aged man stood on his doorstep. The long overcoat he wore, along with his short, military-style haircut, proclaimed him law enforcement.

"Frank DeLeon," the man said, holding out his hand. "Pack Protector."

Chapter 8

Stunned, Eric shook the other man's hand.

"I hope you don't mind me dropping in on you like this."

Actually, Eric minded. He minded a lot. If this guy could find him, then so could Yolanda. Not just that, but he couldn't help but worry about his son's safety. As long as the Protectors were floating around the slightest possibility that Yolanda might be Berserker, Garth would be in danger.

"What do you want?" He didn't bother to keep the hostility from his tone. "Surely you're not here because of Yolanda."

"May I come in?"

Reluctantly, Eric stepped aside. In the long run, it would be better to make this man his friend. "Sure. Take a seat. Can I get you something to drink?"

"No, thanks. I'm good." Rather than sitting, DeLeon stood, awkwardly twisting a sheet of paper in his hand. "Listen, Yolanda took off from the hospital. We think she got into a car that exploded, though it's been extremely difficult to ID the body."

Eric stared. "What? A car explosion? I don't understand. How was she even well enough to leave the hospital? I thought she was in critical condition from her self-inflicted gunshot wound."

"She had help. Security footage showed another woman came and helped her. The hospital garage showed the two of them getting into a red Fiat. After that, we don't know where she went. Two hours later, the Fiat exploded on a construction lot three blocks west of the hospital. Only one body was recovered, so we aren't sure if it was Yolanda or the woman who helped her. Forensics is working on this as we speak."

Something in his tone didn't ring true. Or, Eric thought to himself, it was possible he was just being paranoid.

"Thanks for letting me know." Eric wasn't sure what else to say. "You came all the way out here just to tell me this?"

"No," DeLeon admitted, watching him closely. "There's more. A lot more. But I must say, you don't seem very grief stricken."

"I'm not. Shocked, yes. Sad, because she wasted her life and she was the mother of my son. But beyond that, there's nothing. Whatever we had between us died a long time ago."

"I see." But DeLeon's tone said he didn't.

Crossing his arms, Eric nodded. "Go ahead. You said there's more."

"In the course of this investigation, we've learned your ex was hanging around with a group of—and this is putting it mildly—deranged individuals."

"I'm not surprised," Eric said. "She always did like to party."

Now DeLeon dropped into the chair. Dragging his hand through his close-cropped hair, he sighed. "It's more than that, I'm afraid. These individuals have founded some sort of cult. The Bear Council as well as the Pack Protectors are extremely concerned with their activities. It seems they want to breed Berserkers. We're not sure why—their own little army, maybe? For whatever reason, this is why Yolanda was so focused on getting your son. She has convinced herself that the baby carries the necessary gene mutation to become Berserker."

As he tried to process DeLeon's words, Eric waited for the other man to laugh and admit he was joking. When he didn't, Eric swallowed hard. "That's crazy. Surely you're not serious."

"Unfortunately, I am." DeLeon grimaced. "Even worse, your ex-wife was one of the founders. There are reports—unsubstantiated as of yet—of her changing into a bear in front of some humans. Why, we aren't certain."

Immediately, Eric understood the rest of what the other man hadn't said. This was not only an extremely serious violation of shifter law, but dangerous. Doing something like this could bring everything crashing down, exposing millions of shape-shifters' lives, and sending humanity into chaos and war once they learned of the existence of others who previously had been only the stuff of legend and folktales.

"I see you understand the seriousness of this situation," DeLeon continued.

"I do. I don't see how it could get any worse."

DeLeon eyed him for a second. "It can and does. Even if the body we found was Yolanda's, there are many unknown people who belonged to her group. Your son's life is still in danger."

Dread shuddered up Eric's spine. "That's why I chose

to move so far away. In fact, Jason was the only Protector who knew where to find me. I'm assuming since you came all the way here, there are others who know my location, as well."

"Yes. I'm sorry. And we still don't know what Jason revealed to Yolanda before she killed him. Even if he kept your secret, his cell phone disappeared after he was murdered. We used the GPS to track it, and it was found in a Dumpster near where the car exploded. We aren't sure what may or may not have been on it. End result? We're afraid some members of the group might be coming after your baby."

Over his dead body. As the words sunk in, Eric's bear roared to life inside him, furious in defense of his cub. For a split second or two, he allowed his beast to rage unchecked, while he tried to throttle the anger boiling up inside him.

Watching, DeLeon recoiled, as if Eric's inner struggle had become visible. "Are you all right, man?"

It took another couple seconds before Eric could push a single word past the hard lump of fury in his throat. "Actually, I'm not. No way in hell any of them are getting near my son."

"I concur, I concur." DeLeon hurriedly raised his hand. "I just wanted to make you aware of the situation. The Pack Protectors have graciously offered to extend to you our Witness Protection Program, even though you're not exactly a witness."

The words didn't register at first. "What do you mean?"

His expression earnest, DeLeon leaned forward. "You and your son can have our protection. We'll set you up a new identity somewhere far away. Those crazies won't have any way to find you."

"This *is* my new location." Eric shook his head firmly.

"I just traveled all the way across the country, from one coast to another. I don't plan on going anywhere else. What kind of life would that be for Garth if I'm constantly on the run?"

"I understand." DeLeon's steady gaze was probably meant to be reassuring. "But we can't protect you here. If you come with us, we can. If you stay in Forestwood, you'll be on your own."

"Why?" Eric crossed his arms. "Why can't your people assign someone to watch over me here, just like they would if I went somewhere else? That doesn't even make sense."

Now DeLeon looked away. "I agree," he said quietly. "And I'm working very hard to convince my superiors. Right now, you have a fifty-fifty chance of them finding you. Please consider allowing us to use our vast network to help you and your son disappear."

Still stunned, upset and worried, Eric nodded. "I'll think about it," he said. The new life he'd so been looking forward to might not work out the way he'd hoped.

After her conversation with Rhonda, JJ kept expecting her neighbor to show up at Eric's. But Rhonda stayed home, at least for now. As for Eric, JJ hadn't seen him since he'd thought Garth had stopped breathing. She'd noticed a strange car parked in front of the house and assumed he'd had company, though she'd never seen the car leave or even who it belonged to. She wished she could ask him, but since it seemed he might be purposely avoiding her, she couldn't.

The strange thing was, she missed him far more than she should have missed a man she barely knew.

To be fair, she and Eric hadn't sought each other out. Not since the incident with little Garth. Though it had been only a couple days, it seemed longer. The few times she'd gone into town, she'd felt uncomfortable in her own stairway, rehearsing what she'd say if she ran into him.

Meanwhile, she set about enjoying the outdoors—and the winter weather—as much as she could.

Though the forecasters kept insisting they'd see another snowstorm soon, nothing happened. The already existing snow stuck around in the below-freezing temperatures, declining to melt. Of course, since it was January, it seemed the sun had taken a leave of absence, hiding behind a thick veil of gray clouds.

She, like probably everyone else in the area, had gotten to the point of completely disregarding the weather report, which seemed constantly to be all doom and gloom and unwarranted agitation. She was simply adopting a "wait and see" attitude. So when the next blizzard finally hit, she didn't see it coming.

Caught by surprise, she found her first warning was the howl of the wind. It woke her from a sound sleep and had her sitting up in her bed, disoriented. The wind whipped around the corners in a rage, testing the windows, seeking admission. She shivered, snuggling under the covers in search of sleep, even as the house stood stalwart, denying entrance.

In the morning she woke to the same sound. Exhilarated and thrilled, she hurried to the window and peered outside, seeing only wild swirls of wind-driven snow. Visibility was next to nothing, which meant whiteout conditions. When she turned on the TV, the weather forecaster was talking excitedly, calling this winter one for the record books. A travel advisory had been issued, and everyone was urged to hunker down until the storm passed.

Glad she'd stocked up at the grocery store the other day, JJ wondered if Eric had enough provisions. Because he was new to the East Coast, she couldn't help but worry, though she told herself it was none of her business.

Some might have felt trapped, housebound by the weather. Not JJ. She spent the day puttering around her little house, cleaning and baking, which filled her space with mouthwatering scents. She figured she'd take a few baked goods downstairs to Eric, as a sort of peace offering. Even in the city, none of Shawn's friends had been able to pass up her brownies.

The warm, cozy feeling she always got when snowed in relaxed her. After she'd cleaned the place and put some homemade stew in the Crock-Pot for dinner, she caught herself again wondering what Eric was up to. The brownies were wrapped up and ready to go. Briefly, JJ considered making a quick jog downstairs to deliver them, and inviting him to dinner while she was at it, but she wasn't sure how it would make her feel if he declined, so she didn't. She'd take him the baked goods when she could think of facing him without her heart thundering in her chest. Right now, humming as she puttered around, she just wanted to enjoy her space on this glorious snowy day.

She'd built a fire in her fireplace, opened her bottle of wine and gotten settled on the couch with a blanket, and a bowl of fresh-popped popcorn to tide her over until later. Now she was trying to decide on which of her favorite DVDs to watch, since cable TV had gone out. As she sorted through them, someone knocked on her door.

Someone. Right. Her heart kicked into a rapid beat. Because who else could it be but Eric? Even Rhonda wouldn't have attempted to slog through that mess outside to come over. Everyone else had been trapped in their homes by the storm.

And now her heart was racing again. Wishing she'd worn something other than the faded, yet oh-so-comfy sweatpants and old red sweatshirt—she could almost hear her mother lecturing her on how redheads didn't look good in red—she answered the door.

"Hey," Eric said, smiling. "The cable is out. There's no TV."

"Yeah." She managed to smile back, though she directed it at baby Garth, even though he appeared to be deeply asleep in his portable crib. "My neighbor told me that basically happens every time there's a really bad storm. Rain or snow."

"Really?" Peering past her, he eyed her setup on the couch. "What are you watching?"

"I don't know yet." She opened the door wider. "I'm going through my DVD collection now. You're welcome to join me if you'd like."

Part of her hoped he would. The other, more rational part figured he wouldn't.

Relief shone in his bright blue eyes. "I'd like that. I was feeling a bit trapped. I guess I've lived in sunny Cali for so long I'd forgotten what a beating it is when you're snowed in."

A beating? She'd never looked at it that way, but then she'd been told her entire life that she was unusual in her love of winter. Opening the door even wider, she gestured. "Come on in. I just made some popcorn. And we have wine."

Placing little Garth on the floor near but not too close to the fireplace, Eric grinned and held up a paper sack. Inside, she saw a six-pack. "I brought beer."

At her stunned look, he shrugged. "Just in case you were as bored as I am."

Which, she thought ruefully, put everything back into perspective.

"It smells amazing in here," he said. "Though I can't place that combination of scents."

Trying for nonchalance, she grinned anyway. "I made brownies and French bread and beef stew." She grabbed the plate of brownies she'd fixed for him. "I was going to take these down to you later."

Grinning back, he accepted. "Thank you. Chocolate is one of my weaknesses."

Funny how the room seemed to shrink with him in it.

"Did you have a lot of college coeds throwing themselves at you when you were a professor?" she asked, wincing as she realized she'd spoken her thoughts out loud.

One brow arched, he tilted his head. "That's kind of a strange question. Is it because of the Thor thing?"

Her shock must have shown on her face, because he laughed. "Your neighbor Rhonda called me that the other day. And I had a couple of friends who teased me relentlessly about looking like Thor. I honestly didn't see the resemblance. Until one of them took a photo of me when we were surfing and compared it to a movie poster of that guy that plays Thor."

Surfing? Her mouth watered at the image of him tanned and shirtless, riding a surfboard up into a giant wave.

"You mean Chris Hemsworth?" she asked, collecting her thoughts enough, hopefully, to sound coherent.

His grin widened. "Yeah, that's the guy. Don't tell me you think so, too."

"Of course not," she scoffed. "You're much shorter than him."

He laughed. "Touché."

Flustered but hoping she didn't show it, she gestured to the stack of DVDs she'd placed on her coffee table. "Take a look through those and see if there's anything you'd like to see."

"I don't care. You pick." He pulled a beer out of his sack. "Is it okay if I put the rest of these in your fridge?"

"Sure."

Once he'd done that, he returned and took a seat on the couch. After a second's hesitation, she dropped down next to him, wineglass in hand. Careful to keep as much space between them as possible, she grabbed the DVDs. "Romantic comedy or action adventure?"

He took a drink of beer and laughed again. "What do you think? Of course, I'll watch whatever you want."

"Bruce Willis it is then."

Once she'd popped the DVD in, she put the popcorn in between them. "Help yourself."

"Thanks." He sniffed. "Did you already eat the stew? It smells amazing."

"Not yet. That's what's in the Crock-Pot. It's still cooking." About to ask him if he wanted to stay for dinner, she held off. She was curious to see if he'd mention what had happened the last time she'd seen him, and if he actually had been avoiding her.

"I love beef stew," he said. A hint if there ever was one.

She only ducked her head, pretending to be focused on the popcorn. "Maybe I can dish up a bowl to take home with you later."

"That would be great." If he minded or even noticed she hadn't invited him to eat dinner with her, he didn't comment. "Sorry I haven't been around much," he continued. "I've been trying to get situated. In addition, I've been dealing with the moving company, trying to find out why my stuff isn't here yet." He sighed. "The weather has been bad all through the middle of the country, too. The trip that they originally estimated would take a week is taking much longer."

Inserting the DVD in the player, she waited until it cued

up and then hit the pause button. "Wow. That stinks. What all are you having brought here? If you need me to move some furniture out to make room for yours, let me know."

"I will." Taking another swig of his beer, he grinned at her. "Mainly, I'm worried about Garth's crib and my Camaro."

Perplexed, she eyed him over the rim of her wineglass. "You shipped a car?"

"Not just any car." His grin widened, captivating her. "A fully restored 1969 Camaro SS. My other baby."

"Oh." She wasn't sure what to say. She knew next to nothing about cars, though of course she was familiar with a Camaro. A new one, that is. She'd never understood what the big deal was with old cars.

At her expression, he laughed. "It's okay, I get it. I'll show you the car when she arrives, though. She's gorgeous. I plan to use her as an advertisement for my new business."

Relieved and slightly amused that he referred to the vehicle as a female, she nodded. "So you're opening up some kind of body shop, right?"

"A car customization shop." The happiness in his voice made her smile. "I've always wanted to do that. I've been saving for a few years. Now that I've sold everything I owned, I have enough cash for the startup."

"Isn't that kind of…specialized?"

He nodded. "It is."

"Forestwood is a really small town," she said cautiously. "Do you think there will be enough work here to keep you busy?"

He laughed before taking another drink of his beer. "Definitely. What you don't understand is that people will travel all over the country to find a good shop. All I need are the first few jobs. Once those are done, word will get out. People will flock to me."

Smiling back, she nodded. She liked his confidence. In fact, she liked a lot about him. "So you haven't been avoiding me?" Might as well clear things up.

"Avoiding you?" He couldn't be faking that level of astonishment. "Why would I do that?"

"Because of what you thought happened last time I watched your son." There. Best to have that finally out in the open. There was nothing she disliked more than playing games. Especially after living with the master game player, Shawn.

"Oh." Eric went quiet for a moment, as if considering her question. When he turned to fully face her, the serious expression he wore had her stomach tying up in a quick knot. "I panicked, JJ. Garth is everything to me. I wasn't blaming you or accusing you of doing anything."

"I didn't notice his lack of breathing," she stated. "If he really had stopped and I didn't see that, how could you not blame me?"

He frowned. "JJ, I'm not sure *I* would have noticed. Heck, I don't even know if he really stopped breathing or if it was just my overactive imagination kicking in. It's not like I expected you to do nothing but sit and stare at him."

She had to smile at that.

"Like right now," he continued. Gesturing toward his still-sleeping infant, he shook his head. "I'm here with him and you. I have no way to know if he is breathing unless I stick my finger under his nose, which would probably wake him up."

The humor in his tone coaxed a chuckle from her.

"Truce?" he asked, raising his beer can toward her wineglass.

"Okay." The clink of the glass and the metal made her smile again. "Are you ready to watch the movie?"

When he nodded, she hit the pause button again to un-freeze the DVD.

Überconscious of him next to her, she drank her wine faster than she usually did. When her glass was empty, she glanced sideways at him. He seemed to be totally engrossed in the film, one she'd watched a bazillion times. She could even recite the lines.

Getting up, she poured herself a second glass of wine and returned to the couch. He didn't even look away from the TV.

Reaching for popcorn at the exact same moment he did, JJ felt their fingers brush. She froze, resisting the urge to yank her hand away. What she really wanted to do was to hand-feed him, one kernel at a time.

Blinking, she looked down and took a deep breath. Where had that come from? She needed to get control of her crazy libido. Sleeping with her tenant would not be the smartest business move.

But oh, it would be fun. Possibly amazing, even. But a complication she definitely did not need.

As a distraction, she took another deep sip of wine.

"I'm sorry," he said, his voice a sensual rumble.

Forcing herself to look at him, she tilted her head. "For what?"

"Hogging the popcorn. Here." He pushed the bowl toward her. "There's still plenty left."

Eyes wide, she stared at him, unable to move. And then, just when she thought she'd be okay, she leaned in to get the popcorn and somehow winded up with her mouth pressed against his. Who moved first—did he kiss her or she him? Dizzy, she wondered if it even mattered.

She tasted the salty butter of the popcorn on his lips and then, when their tongues met, the yeasty flavor of his beer.

Kissing him was everything she'd ever imagined. And she had thought about it plenty.

When he deepened the kiss, she opened her mouth in welcome.

And then he broke away, pushing himself up off the sofa. "I'm so sorry," he muttered, dragging his hand through his unruly mane of hair. He wouldn't meet her gaze. She tried to speak and failed.

"That should never have happened," he said. "I can promise you, it won't happen again."

Chapter 9

Though JJ nodded in agreement, disappointment flooded her. She hadn't kissed anyone except Shawn in over three years. According to Shawn, no other man would ever find her desirable or want her, besides him. While she knew this was one of the numerous mental games he played on her, years of constant reaffirmation had made her wonder if it was the truth.

Which was no doubt why she took Eric's rejection way harder than she should. "It's okay," she managed to reply, her throat tight. He still kept his gaze averted, which hurt.

Pushing herself up, she walked to her kitchen and re-filled her wineglass. Then, staring at the half-empty bottle, she tried like hell not to cry.

"JJ." He'd followed her.

Fiercely wiping at her stinging eyes, she took a swig of her drink before turning to face him.

"Are you all right?" Gaze gentle, he crossed the space between them and cupped her chin with his big hand. She suppressed a shiver at his touch.

"I'm fine." Lifting her chin, she tried for carefree, but ended up only sounding sad. Aware she had to come up with something to say that would fix that, she took a deep breath. "We need to stay friends, okay? Nothing more. No more kissing."

Surprise flashed across his handsome face. "I agree. I went through a horrible divorce."

"And I an awful breakup." Crud. She hadn't meant to reveal so much.

"You did?" He met her gaze, his own warm. "So that was the emotional 'stuff' you had to get away from. At least, I assume he wasn't here, in Forestwood?"

"No." She felt like she shouldn't talk about it, as if by doing so she could somehow draw the darkness of Shawn's energy into her home, her safe haven.

When she didn't elaborate, Eric sighed. "Friends, okay? I'm sorry for what happened. I like you and I really don't want to lose your friendship."

"Same here," she told him, telling herself that she spoke the truth. If some small part of her wanted more, then she'd have to deal with that, until it went away for good. And she had no doubt it would. Right now, she was bruised and wounded.

They watched the rest of the movie in a silence she hoped was companionable—at least to him—but as far as she was concerned felt really awkward. She'd get over this. She had to. Because Eric had made an excellent point. She liked him and wanted to be his friend. That, in her humble opinion, was much more rare and valuable than a fleeting romance.

After the movie finished, he stood and stretched. Though she tried, she couldn't manage to keep her gaze on his face. Instead, she watched him with a kind of mindless hunger. The kind that made her feel hot and bothered and completely out of sorts. She served him a big bowl of stew—enough for two meals—and broke off some French bread for him to enjoy with it.

Juggling everything, he carried the food downstairs and then came back for Garth. They said their good-nights and he picked up his still-slumbering infant and left.

After he'd gone, she caught herself staring at the door, imagining him going downstairs and enjoying the meal she'd prepared. She felt an instant of regret, wishing she'd invited him to eat with her, but knew she'd probably done the right thing. Especially since she couldn't help but imagine him later, climbing between the sheets of her aunt's antique queen-size bed, probably naked. Her blood heated at the thought.

More foolish daydreaming. She figured this was her way of trying to distract herself from worrying that her ex would somehow find her and cause trouble. Shaking her head at herself, she rinsed the empty popcorn bowl, turned out the lights and went to bed. Hopefully, the plows would come through early so Eric wouldn't feel trapped in his home.

The strident sound of her fire alarm jolted her out of a sound sleep and extremely pleasurable dream. Sitting up, she breathed in, immediately swallowing a lungful of smoke.

Not. A. Malfunction. Coughing, heart pounding, she picked up her phone and dialed 911, even as she moved toward the doorway. She wondered if they'd even be able to get to her house with all the snow. On the way out, she snagged her parka off the coatrack near the door.

Clattering down the stairs, she pounded on Eric's doorway. "Fire," she yelled, and pounded again.

He yanked the door open, clearly half-asleep. "What's going on?"

"Fire. Grab the baby and come on. There's a fire in my unit. We've got to get out."

He didn't waste time questioning her. Turning, he ran for his son. She stepped inside, found the baby's coat, as well as Eric's. When he reappeared, holding his sound-asleep infant, she urged him outside.

Eric saw her eyeing his son. "This kid can sleep through anything," he said wryly.

Once they were outside, she could see flames shooting from her upstairs windows. The sight chilled her even more than the brisk wind, making her want to weep.

They struggled to move through the deep snow, trying to get some distance from the house. On the front lawn, she helped Eric make sure Garth's coat was zipped and they put a knit cap on his little head before pulling up the hood and turning him to keep his face out of the wind. This startled him awake. Of course, he immediately wanted his bottle, which Eric didn't have, though he'd had the foresight to grab a pacifier, which seemed to satisfy him.

"This is awful," she said. "I called 911 but I don't know if they'll be able to make it, since the road isn't plowed." Amazing how things could change in the matter of a few hours. Before she'd gone to sleep, she'd wondered if she'd feel shy around Eric after the hot kisses they'd shared, but this crisis shoved all that out the window. Talk about perspective.

He eyed her and then squinted out toward the street. "It looks like the plow might have come through earlier. Maybe when we were watching the movie. There are really high snowdrifts on the other side."

Trying to hide her agitation, she tromped through the snow to see. "Thank goodness," she told him when she returned. "I hope they hurry." She pointed to the flames. "It appears to be getting more intense. I don't want the entire house to burn down."

As she finished speaking, she heard the sirens. "I hope they can put the fire out in time." She felt like chewing her nails, a habit she'd cured herself of shortly after moving here. Her thick gloves helped with that, too.

"They will. It'll be fine. Let's move a little farther away, just to be safe. Even though the fire is upstairs, you never know if it'll burn through the floor or something. Let's go. Just to be safe," he repeated.

He had a point. Huddled together, they all moved closer to Rhonda's house, hoping the structure would provide some shelter from the bitterly cold wind. From there, JJ could see flames were now shooting from the attic area above her unit. It looked like her entire floor and above might be a total loss.

The fire engine pulled up, lights flashing. The siren gave one final whoop before the driver cut it off. A police car came around the corner, fishtailing as it took the slippery turn too fast. The officer at the wheel parked right behind the fire truck.

"I'm surprised they didn't send an ambulance," Eric remarked. "At home when the fire department comes, they always send a paramedic, too."

"We only have one," JJ told him. "They aren't going to tie it up unless they know for sure it's needed." Though she stood perfectly still, her insides jumped and jangled. How could this have happened, just when she'd begun to feel settled and happy? "They have to put this fire out," she whispered. "I can't lose my home."

Instead of answering, Eric squeezed her shoulder.

Over the next hour, everything seemed to happen in slow motion, while she watched as if from a distance. It felt like someone else's nightmare. Using a huge hose, they doused her pretty little house with water, firemen in yellow suits heading inside. She winced when she heard the sound of an ax hitting wood. And she prayed silently, head bowed, as hard as she'd prayed the last time Shawn had come home drunk and mean. There had been no divine interference then and she didn't really expect it now.

As she swayed from exhaustion, barely containing her panic, Eric put his arm around her. He'd shifted little Garth to against his chest and under his coat. "It's all going to be all right," he said. "I promise."

"Is it?" Turning on him, unable to control her shivering, which wasn't from the cold, she gave in and let herself collapse against his strong chest right next to his son.

"I'm wondering if you should wake Rhonda," he said. "Get inside and warm up."

She started to shake her head, but he continued. "I'll go with you. I'm worried about little Garth. Even though he's bundled up, he's shivering."

Stunned, JJ raised her head to check on the baby. Wide-awake, he watched her from Eric's chest. His bright blue eyes, so similar to Eric's, were wide-open. He should have been snug as a bug in his little hooded parka, but his cheeks were rosy from the cold.

Instantly contrite, she nodded. "Oh, my gosh. I'm so sorry, I didn't even think. You and Garth need to go inside. I can't. I've got to see what happens with my house. I'll go with you and then come back. Follow me."

The sidewalks weren't shoveled, either. Crossing the remaining distance between her house and Rhonda's was slow going and surprisingly treacherous. Several times she paused, looking back over her shoulder to make sure Eric and Garth were behind her. She was glad he allowed her to go first, though normally he would have been the one to forge the path, since he was taller and larger. But she figured he was glad to use this to distract her. As if anything could. Once she'd delivered him to Rhonda, she planned to go right back to her own house.

Finally, they reached the wooden steps leading up to Rhonda's porch. The house remained silent and dark. It seemed really odd that Rhonda hadn't come outside to check out the commotion.

JJ climbed onto the first step and nearly wiped out. Only a quick grab for the railing kept her from landing on her behind. "Careful," she told Eric. "It's black ice."

When they all were finally up on the porch, JJ pressed Rhonda's doorbell and waited. She heard the chimes echo inside. Nothing. After a few seconds, she rang it again. Still nothing.

"This isn't like her," she told Eric. "It's weird."

"Try knocking."

So she knocked, though with gloves on the sound was muted. Again, no response.

"Maybe she's not home," Eric said, hunched against the cold.

"Maybe not. I thought it was strange when she didn't come out once the fire truck got here." But JJ still couldn't shake a nagging worry. "I'm going to call her just to make sure."

"It's two o'clock in the morning," Eric reminded her. "If she's out of town, you'll wake her and probably scare the hell out of her."

He was right. She nodded, sliding her phone back into her rear pocket. She'd have to wait until a decent hour to check on her friend. Even though she knew if Rhonda had been planning to go out of town, she would have asked JJ to keep an eye on her place.

Meanwhile, the water spray the firefighters had sent had frozen, making huge rivers of ice on the side of her house. As far as she could tell, the fire appeared to be out. A heavy lump of worry settled in her stomach.

Again moving together, they trudged back through the snow.

"I'm worried about the baby," she said. "I'm going to ask one of the firemen if you and Garth can sit in the cab of their truck. It's bound to be warmer."

"Wait." He grabbed her arm as she turned to go do exactly that. "What about you? You must be cold, too."

"I'll be fine," she said, gently pulling herself free. The dull chill that had settled in her bones had little to do with the temperature. "Until they tell me the fire is completely out, I'm not letting my house out of my sight. This is all I have in the world, my safe haven. I can't lose it. I simply can't."

Eric felt strange taking refuge in the warmth of the fire engine cab while JJ braved it out in the cold. He supposed he could go get his SUV and start that, but he really didn't want to leave the scene just yet. Plus he had his son to think of, and even though leaving a woman alone outside might not be gentlemanly or chivalrous, he was doing what was best for his baby.

Or so he repeatedly told himself, while he fidgeted inside the warm truck.

Finally, he couldn't take it any longer. Garth had fallen asleep, so Eric left him there, going to stand outside where he could see everything, but close to the door just in case.

JJ caught sight of him and hurried over.

"What's the word?" he asked.

"They don't think there was any structural damage." JJ sounded both relieved and anxious. "Lots of smoke and water damage, though." Her voice wavered and she looked down.

He realized she was fighting to keep from crying. Balling up his hands into fists to keep from touching her, he nodded. "What about the downstairs unit? My place."

The dullness in her gaze as she looked at him told

him she was operating on the last reserve of her waning strength. "I didn't think to ask," she finally admitted. "Since the fire didn't spread beyond the second floor…" Heaving a sigh, she blinked. "Let me go back and find the guy who said he was in charge." She hurried off.

When she returned a few minutes later, he saw the answer in her eyes. "Looks like we're both going to have to find a new place to stay for a little while." Panic flashed across her expression before she covered her face with her gloved hands. "I don't know what I'm going to do. I'm so sorry. I know you didn't plan on this."

"None of us did." Acting instinctively, he reached for her and pulled her close in a hug. "I'm sure Rhonda will let you stay with her," he said, hoping to reassure her. She smelled like smoke and water, completely different from her usual lavender scent.

"Maybe. I don't actually know her all that well." JJ looked up at him, frowning. "I wonder if she'd consider allowing you and Garth there, too. Even though she doesn't like babies, this is kind of an emergency."

"Kind of?" he teased, realizing he'd do just about anything to wipe the worry and stress out of her gaze. "Don't worry. Everything will work out."

Though her nod came slowly, at least she agreed. "Thank goodness your furniture hasn't arrived yet. I'd feel terrible if it had gotten damaged in the fire."

"It wasn't your fault," he said, then reconsidered. "Was it? Do they have any idea what caused the fire?"

"They're thinking an electrical short. Nothing that I did. Even though I had built a fire in the fireplace, that wasn't where the other fire originated." Shoulders slumped, she stepped away, out of his arms. He let her go.

Someone called to her and she hurried off without a backward glance.

Though standing around doing nothing went against his nature, there wasn't any way Eric could get closer to the hub of activity without endangering his son. So he stayed put, watching from a distance, and wishing he could offer more assurances and comfort to JJ. While he didn't know much about her personal circumstances, she didn't appear to have a good support system or many resources she could fall back on, being new in town. Of course, he was in a similar situation himself.

Wow. Just wow. When he'd planned on starting over, beginning a new life, he hadn't imagined anything like this. But he'd be okay, even if he had to tap into some of his savings to pay for another place to live.

It appeared that the fire department was wrapping things up. Eric checked on Garth, who, amazingly, continued to sleep. When one of the sooty firefighters came by, Eric questioned him. "How bad is the damage?" he asked.

The man shrugged, dragging his arm across his sooty face. "Lots of smoke and water damage. We had to cut a couple holes in the walls to check for flames. Maybe one or two in the roof, as well. Some of the windows were broken."

Eric nodded. "Is it safe to go inside?"

"Actually, we'd prefer you didn't."

"I have a three-month-old son." Gesturing at the truck cab, Eric frowned. "We lived in the downstairs unit. I just need to get his formula and diapers. Who do I need to talk to in order to get permission to do that?" Getting permission was only a formality. If they refused, Eric would simply wait until they left to go inside and grab his things.

"Talk to the chief." The firefighter pointed at another man, who was heading their way. "Good luck."

The chief listened while Eric repeated his request. "Fine," he said. "You can go. But only to grab what you absolutely need and get out. And you'll need to do it quickly.

The soot and dirty water might make you sick. Don't eat or drink anything. Oh, and you'll need a flashlight. We had to cut the utilities for safety. Too much chance of gas leaks or electric shorts that could have endangered my men or you. Do not attempt to turn them back on yourself."

Eric nodded. "When can we get a copy of the fire report?"

"It'll be ready in a few days. Just stop by the fire marshal's office."

"And after that?"

"You'll need to contact your insurance agent." The man peered at Eric. "You did have insurance, right?"

Since he could only assume so, Eric nodded. "Right. I mean, who doesn't have insurance?"

"Exactly. Once the insurance company comes out and takes a look, they'll hire a company to come in and do cleanup. I think they'll also make any and all repairs needed."

The firefighter caught sight of Garth. "Hey, is that your kid?"

"Yes. I put him in there to keep him out of the cold."

The man eyed him. "Good thinking. Listen, do you and your wife have someplace to go?"

"Oh, she's…" Eric swallowed. "I'm sure we'll figure something out," he said instead.

"Glad to hear it. If not, you can always contact the Red Cross or the Salvation Army. Now if you don't mind grabbing your baby, we've got to get back to the firehouse."

After retrieving Garth, Eric and JJ stood side by side and watched the fire engine pull away, the police car right behind it. A few of the neighbors—though not many, since the icy night wind still blew—had come out on their front porches to watch. One by one, they went inside. Aside from the lingering scent of charred wood and smoke, the neighborhood returned to the way it had been.

Chapter 10

"From this direction, the house still looks the same," JJ mused, her voice wobbly again. Eric put his arm around her, offering support. Though initially she stiffened, a second later she relaxed and leaned against him.

"They said we can go inside and get out what we need," he told her, repeating what the chief had said.

"Good." She shook her head. "I don't mind helping you, since we can't go to the top floor. I doubt anything of mine is going to be usable, anyway."

Keeping his son's carrier close again, Eric started for the front door. Garth had opened his eyes and appeared to be looking around, but hadn't started crying yet. They needed to get formula and diapers, as well as multiple changes of clothing.

When he realized JJ wasn't following, he stopped. "Aren't you coming?"

Still standing in the same place, she cut her gaze from him to the house. Finally, she swallowed hard. "I guess so. It's silly, but I'm afraid to see what's happened to the inside."

"Come on." He held out his free hand. "You might as well. You've got to face it eventually."

She searched his face and finally nodded. "You're right," she said, sliding her gloved fingers around his. He liked the way it felt, much more than he should have.

"Do you have a flashlight?" he asked as they climbed up on the porch. "They had to cut the power."

"I keep one in my kitchen, for when the electricity goes out. But that's upstairs."

Inside, the dank smoke smell was even worse. Eric repeated what the firefighter had said.

"So we have to get what you need and get out?" she asked. "And then what? Where can we go?"

"We'll figure that out," he assured her. "Right now, let's grab what we can. Once we're in my car, if you can point me to a motel, we'll get a room so we can all get some rest."

She opened her mouth and then closed it. "Okay," she finally said. "As long as we're here, I want to check out the damage upstairs. I'll meet you back here in ten minutes."

"I'm not sure it's safe," he told her.

"I'm just going to open my front door and peek inside. I might as well see how bad it is."

He hated letting her go upstairs alone, but there was no way he was taking Garth up there. "Are you sure you really need to? I can buy you some clothes or makeup or whatever else you need."

"It's okay," she said quietly. "I'll be careful. See you in the foyer in ten minutes." She paused. "Do you have a flashlight or do you need to borrow mine?"

"I've got one." He'd found one inside the drawer of a small curio cabinet near the door. All it had needed was new batteries and it worked perfectly.

Watching her as she climbed the stairs, he finally shook his head, picked up Garth's carrier and headed into his own space to gather what he needed. Inside his place, there was a lot of water damage and he thought maybe some smoke damage, too, though it was hard to tell, using the small beam of his flashlight.

One half-full box of diapers and a carton of formula, plus clothes for both himself and the baby. Unfortunately, he couldn't carry all this and Garth, too, so Eric moved as much as he could to just outside his front door. He'd get it in the car once he could ask JJ to keep an eye on Garth.

When he returned to the foyer, she was already waiting. She agreed to watch Garth in the SUV, so once he'd loaded the baby into his infant carrier and her duffel bag into the back, he went inside for his things.

She directed him to a small motel a few miles away. When they pulled up shortly after 4:00 a.m., he parked and turned to her. "I'm going to get us a room, okay?"

"I'll need my own," she told him, clearly exhausted. "I can pay."

"What if we have to stay here for a few days?" he asked. "Or even longer. I'm not trying to be nosy, but I don't know your financial situation."

"It's…fluid," she said, flashing him a quick, embarrassed smile. "Cash poor, right now. I've got a bit in savings, but I'll need some of it to meet the deductible on my policy. I'm going to call my insurance company in the morning," she continued, lifting her chin bravely. "After I get some rest, I'll figure out where exactly I'm going to live until everything is repaired. Hopefully, Rhonda will allow me to bunk on her couch or in her guest bedroom for a few weeks."

He nodded. "Sounds like a plan."

"But what about you? What will you do if this turns out to be some long, drawn-out thing?"

"I've been checking out some buildings online for my business. I'd planned to meet with a Realtor soon, so I'll do that. Maybe I can find one with a small apartment above the garage. That's not ideal for the long term, because I have to keep a clear separation between home and work, but maybe it'll do for now. At least until the house is repaired."

"Whew." A ghost of a smile flitted across her lips. "I was worried you'd say you and Garth were going back to California."

Surprised—and a bit touched that she even cared—he grimaced. "There's nothing back there for me."

After he'd paid the deposit and received a room key, he reconsidered. Maybe he *should* get her a separate room. But tonight, they were both so tired that all they wanted to do was sleep—if Garth would let them. Eric decided for tonight they'd share. If she wanted to change things up in the morning, he'd deal with it then. Most likely, she'd get ahold of her friend next door and go stay there.

Once they were inside the small room, she dropped her duffel on a bed and vanished into the bathroom. He changed Garth, thankful that he'd bathed him before he'd gone to bed, and warmed up some formula using the little hotplate he'd thought to bring along.

Once his son had been fed and burped, Eric carried him around the room, swaying softly and singing an old Norwegian lullaby he remembered his grandmother singing to his younger brother. They'd been born in the United States, but after their father's disappearance, their mother had taken both her sons to Norway and left them with her own mother, who'd raised them. Despite their young age— Eric had been three and Lars just eighteen months—they hadn't seen or heard from their mom again until they were teenagers. Then, both parents had shown up at their doorway and moved them all to California. It had been difficult for them to readjust to a family they'd never known, but they'd managed. Now, Eric could see why his parents had done what they did. What he couldn't understand was why, a day after Lars had turned eighteen, both Mom and Dad had vanished again. This time, they'd never come back.

Another reason Eric would never leave his son.

Once little Garth had fallen asleep, Eric set him in his portable crib—thank God for that thing—and stripped down to his boxers before climbing in between the sheets. He planned to only rest his eyes until JJ returned. He figured they'd talk a little and then they'd both catch some much-needed sleep.

After washing her face and hands, JJ grimaced at her image in the bathroom mirror. She felt grimy all over and her hair stank of smoke. Yawning, she knew she should take a quick shower, but she wasn't sure how much longer her wobbly legs would hold her upright. It'd have to wait until she got some sleep.

A sound from the other room… She strained to hear. When she realized what it was, she smiled. It sounded like Eric was singing some sort of lullaby to his son. When he stopped a moment later, she figured the baby had most likely fallen asleep.

Speaking of sleep. All she had left to do was brush her teeth and she could do the same.

When she'd finished, she opened the door slowly and quietly, not wanting to wake Garth. To her surprise, she saw Eric had climbed into one of the beds and dozed off.

This lessened the awkwardness somehow. Tiptoeing to the other bed, she turned out the light and pulled back the covers. About to get in between her sheets, still fully clothed, she hesitated. Her clothes smelled like smoke and soot. What about Eric? Had he stripped before getting into his bed? Peering over there, she judged by the little pile of clothes on the floor that he had.

Holding her breath and hoping he didn't wake, she hurriedly stripped down to her bra and panties. Then, at the last moment, she removed her bra. Much better. Once she'd gotten decently covered, she breathed a sigh of relief. And then found herself imagining his buff body naked against the sheets.

Ah, good thing she was so exhausted. Too tired to do more than briefly picture waking up next to him, she closed her eyes and willed herself to fall asleep.

An infant's cries startled her awake. She sat bolt upright, blinking. Sunlight sneaking from the sides of the curtains brought some light into the room. Enough to see Eric, wearing nothing but a pair of plaid boxer shorts, swinging his muscular legs over the side of his bed as he hurried to attend to his son.

She couldn't stop staring. She slid back under her sheets and watched through her eyelashes, hoping he'd think she still slept.

Muscles she hadn't even realized he possessed rippled along his back as he bent over to pick up the baby. The whole broad-shoulders-narrow-waist thing worked for him, too. Her entire body tingled.

More than that—watching the tenderness with which he treated his son, she wanted to melt. In her experience, men like him were rare. Shawn had cared about only his job and his status and himself. Oh, he'd known how badly she wanted her own family, and he'd dangled this possibility like a carrot in front of a starving rabbit. But after a while she'd come to realize he'd never meant a word of it. He'd made no secret of the way he despised children. The idea of him ever becoming a father was frightening.

The same way marrying him would have been.

Eric coughed, drawing her attention back to him. "Are you going to get up or just lie there and pretend to be sleeping?" he asked, his voice teasing.

She blushed—all over. "I was waiting for you to finish up first," she said, which wasn't entirely untrue. "I didn't want to hog the bathroom if you needed to use it."

"Oh, go ahead. I was up earlier and it's going to be a little while before I get done taking care of Garth."

Sitting up, she blinked and tugged the covers back to her chin. She'd completely forgotten she'd stripped down to her panties and nothing else.

Keeping the sheet wrapped tightly around her, she reached down and fumbled around on the floor until she'd located her bra and clothing. When she looked up, she saw Eric watching her with an amused expression.

"It's about to get even funnier," she told him, as she yanked the covers up and over her, making as big a tent as she could so she could dress.

"There." Triumphant, she threw back the covers and got up—only to realize she had her shirt on inside out and backward. At least she was covered. She marched off to the bathroom, knowing a hot shower would do wonders toward making her feel human again.

Later, she made some phone calls and watched the baby while Eric showered. He'd given his son a sponge bath earlier, which made little Garth all giggles. JJ had melted watching this, and had to resist the urge to ask if she could help.

Her insurance agent had already heard about the fire. He promised to put a rush on processing a claim, adding that he'd make sure and have someone out there quickly to take a look.

When Eric emerged from the bathroom, his hair still damp, he suggested they make a stop at the pancake house for breakfast and then check out her place. Though part of her dreaded seeing the damage in the stark light of day, she knew she needed to, so she agreed.

Breakfast was lovely, the three of them in a back booth, while JJ struggled to remind herself this wasn't her family, even if the waitress persisted in thinking they were. But this scene reminded her of what she'd wanted for so long. Shawn hadn't succeeded in killing that dream for her and she still had hope that someday she'd have a husband and child of her own. For now, she had too much reality to deal with.

The instant they pulled up in front of her house, her heart caught in her throat. Last night, after the firefighters and police had left, she'd seen the place only in darkness. Now, in the unforgiving light of day, she saw the soot staining the formerly white wood, the busted-out windows and the long, spiky icicles that had formed where the water had drained. Her pretty little house looked awful. Damaged and deserted, like something after a war.

"Oh," she said. Only it came out like something else entirely, a low, guttural sound as if from an animal in pain.

Eric looked at her. "It'll be okay, I promise. Once your insurance company gets started, they'll have this place looking as good as new."

Blinking back tears, she nodded. "My agent says the company will send a claims adjuster out here sometime this week. They also need to review the fire report. They told me I'd need to find another place to live for at least thirty days." Her voice broke and she took a deep breath, determined to steady it. "He also said it could even be longer."

Eric squeezed her shoulder. "I'm sorry. Hopefully, it won't be. Come on, let's go take a look. We just need to be very careful. At least now that it's not dark, we can find our way around, even without electricity."

"I'm worried about the pipes freezing," she said, as she pushed open the car door and stepped outside. She waited, shivering in the chilly air despite her warm jacket, while Eric unbuckled Garth's carrier. He'd dressed his son warmly, from a little knit cap to matching mittens and boots.

As she watched, the baby caught sight of her and grinned. Her heart stuttered in her chest. "He's so adorable," she said, unable to help herself.

"Thanks." Eric looked at her, his expression curious. "Are you okay with going inside?"

"Are you?" she countered. "I don't want to endanger Garth."

"I talked to the fire captain again this morning. The building is structurally safe and, since the utilities are still turned off, there's no danger from a gas leak or anything. He said it would be fine to go inside."

She shot Eric a cross look. "Why didn't you mention this to me until now?"

He shrugged, glancing at her. "Sorry. I figured you probably called, also. I heard you on the phone earlier."

"With my insurance company." She sighed. "I don't mean to be snippy. I apologize. This is very stressful. I didn't mean to take it out on you. I'm glad you called. Thank you."

"You're welcome." He hefted his son's carrier. "Come on. Let's go inside."

Once they entered, she stood in the foyer, undecided where to go first. "Let's check out your place before we see mine. That way I'll have some warning what to expect."

Since his would be in better shape than hers, she figured she could build up to the worst.

She waited just inside his living room with baby Garth while Eric went from room to room, assessing the damage. She imagined he was really grateful his personal belongings and furniture had been delayed. All this stuff had belonged to an old lady and wouldn't be even close to his taste.

Or hers, for that matter. But JJ had fled the city and her bad relationship with limited funds, and she'd been grateful for the gift of the house being fully furnished. She'd intended to use everything for as long as she could and gradually replace one item at a time.

Now, hopefully, the insurance would pay out enough for her to replace all the damaged furniture at once.

"Hey, there." Eric reappeared, carrying a large, black trash bag. "I grabbed some more clothes for both me and Garth. I think once I wash them, I can get the smoke smell out."

"Great." She couldn't help but glance apprehensively at the stairs.

Following her gaze with his own, he set his bag down near the door and picked up Garth. "Are you ready to go up?"

After taking a deep breath, she nodded. "As ready as I'm ever going to be, I guess."

"After you." He made a sweeping gesture with his free hand.

As she stared at him, there in the dim light of the sooty foyer, he looked dangerous for a moment. And unbelievably sexy.

Of course, she was only looking for a distraction. Something to take her mind off the mess her home would be in the cold light of day.

Chapter 11

As JJ opened her front door, the first thing that hit her was the smell. Smoke and soot and…ice. Shocked, she saw that her window had been broken and the cold outside air chilled the room.

"My pipes," she said, unable to take the steps that would carry her to the sink to open the cupboard doors.

Eric's hand came down on her shoulder, solid and reassuring. "It should be okay. They turned off the water when they cut the utilities."

Some of the tightness in her chest eased, though she fought the urge to lean into his touch. Slowly, she turned to look at her things. They were ruined. Every single item. Soot stained, water damaged… She didn't see how any amount of cleaning would be able to restore them. Her poor aunt would be turning over in her grave if she saw.

JJ felt as if she were wandering through the landscape of a bad dream. She went into her bedroom and stood, staring at the one piece of antique furniture she'd truly loved—the massive, four-poster bed.

Inching closer, she held her breath. While the comforter—and most likely the mattress—appeared unredeemable, she didn't see any real damage to the wood itself.

"I think the bed frame itself is all right," she breathed.

"I agree. And more stuff is probably salvageable than you think. They have restoration companies that specialize in this type of thing."

Numb, she headed toward her closet.

"Here. I got another trash bag so you could grab some more clothes."

Accepting it, she murmured a thank-you. She braced herself and slid the closet door open. To her surprise, all her clothing appeared untouched.

"Yeah, that's what I thought," Eric said, at her comment. "But smell it."

When she did, the acrid odor made her sneeze. "I wonder if any amount of washing will get that smell out."

"I don't know. All we can do is try."

Once she'd finished, she carried her bag down to the foyer. Her home, once cheery and slightly fussy, now looked grim and sad.

"At least no one was hurt," Eric said, almost as if he read her mind.

"True." She tried hard to push away the bleak feeling that had settled over her. "I'm sure as soon as the adjuster approves my claim and repairs are made, this place will look good as new."

She wasn't sure she really believed it.

Needing something to distract her, JJ glanced at the house next door. "I'm going to check in on Rhonda again," she said. "She must be out of town. There's no way she wouldn't have been out here already."

Sure enough, the ringing doorbell went unanswered,

even though she could hear the chimes echoing inside the house.

"Are you going to call her?" Eric asked, when she got back to his SUV.

"Yep." She already had her phone out. Punching the icon for Rhonda, she listened while the phone rang and rang. As it flipped over to voice mail, she left a quick and terse message, asking her friend to call her back.

"No luck?"

"Nope." JJ slid her phone back into her purse.

"That stinks." He grimaced. "Now there's even more bad news. The radio weather report says we're going to get another snowstorm. Come on, now. Are they serious? Does it ever end?"

Shaking her head, JJ shrugged. "I'm so sorry. This time, I'm with you. Normally, I love the snow. It always feels like a second chance. A new beginning. But there's too much going on. Right now I really could use a break, until my house is livable again."

"I like that," Eric said. "I never thought about snow that way before. A second chance. A new beginning. Which we all need."

"True. Just not right now. After my house is repaired and I can enjoy watching the snow fall from my living room, with a fire roaring in the fireplace, yes." She blinked, surprised to realize she was on the verge of tears.

"There's a lot of snow," he continued. "I take it this weather is worse than normal? The way the TV forecasters are acting, it's like the Armageddon of snow this winter."

"They're always like that. The weather people, I mean. Some years are worse than others. I imagine coming from sunny California, this must seem awful."

"No," he said thoughtfully, after a moment. "Not awful. Just different. It's been a long time since I lived in Norway, as a child. I remember the winters were long and snowy there, too."

Just then, a taxi pulled up, stopping at Rhonda's. Her neighbor emerged, gaping at JJ's house. She flung a few bills at the cab driver and ordered him to leave her luggage on the street by the mountain of snow on the curb. Rushing over, she enveloped JJ in a big hug.

"Oh, my gosh, what happened?"

Once she'd pulled herself free, JJ explained. "They still don't know how it started. As soon as my insurance adjuster gets out here, I can get started on making repairs."

"Of all the times for me to go to the city! I can't believe I wasn't here." Rhonda's gaze drifted from the house to JJ and past, settling on Eric. "Were both of you impacted?"

Slowly, Eric nodded. "Since the fire was upstairs, JJ's place got the worst of it. But mine still has smoke and water damage."

"Surely you're not staying there?" Hand to her throat, Rhonda looked from one to the other.

This time JJ answered. "No. The firefighters cut the utilities, so there's no electricity or heat. We're staying at the Innbrook Motel on Sixth Street."

"Well, go pack up and check out. You both can stay at my house. I have plenty of room."

Waving his chubby fists, Garth made a warbling sound, drawing her attention. A brief frown clouded her bright blue eyes, but a second later it cleared and she smiled again. "And the baby, too, of course."

Though this was what she'd hoped for in the beginning, now JJ hesitated. Something about the way Rhonda looked at Eric, as though she could eat him up for lunch, bothered her.

Telling herself to stop being ridiculous, JJ took a deep

breath. "Are you sure? It might be a few weeks or more, depending on how much work needs to be done."

"I'm positive." Beaming brightly, Rhonda turned on her heel and went to collect her bags. "Give me an hour to get everything ready and the beds made up. I can't tell you how happy I am to have company."

They both stared after her as she disappeared inside her house.

Eric had a bad feeling. For no good reason, but still… It sat on his shoulders like a heavy weight. Though he hadn't always, he was beginning to learn to trust his gut instincts. "I'm not sure about this," he said, turning to face JJ. "You go ahead and stay with your neighbor. As for me, I think I'd rather just remain in the motel."

"Seriously?" One corner of JJ's mouth quirked in amusement. "You're frightened of a tiny blonde woman?"

He had to chuckle at her choice of words. But then again, maybe she wasn't far off. "I wouldn't say frightened. Just…uncomfortable."

"Whatever." Plainly, she didn't believe him. "Now we just have to kill an hour. Maybe I should go back to the hotel and pack up my things."

He glanced at his watch, considering. "Come with me and look at commercial buildings for rent," he suggested, smiling at her startled expression. "It's something to take your mind off all this. I need to find somewhere to store my furniture. It should be here any day. And to be honest, I could use a second set of eyes."

"Don't you have a Realtor?"

"I do." He couldn't help but grimace. "His name is Greg Stenorio. I'm supposed to meet him in ten minutes. He's kind of pushy."

"I hate that."

"I do, too, but I have to deal with him. I'm meeting him downtown, so I need to get going. You're welcome to come."

She eyed little Garth, wide-awake and playing with his colored keys. "I guess I could. I can keep an eye on the baby while you look around the various places."

More pleased than he wanted to admit—or reveal—he nodded. "After we're done, I'll buy you lunch."

"You have a deal." Her smile stole his breath. "And while we eat, we can talk about why you really don't want to stay with me at Rhonda's."

He couldn't help but grin. "You're almost as pushy as my Realtor. The two of you should get along great."

In fact, once the real estate agent got a good look at JJ, with her lush curves, long mane of red hair and emerald eyes, he barely spared a glance for Eric. Normally, Eric would have found this amusing, but the quick, panicked looks JJ kept sending his way signaled that she was uncomfortable with the unwanted attention.

Greg wanted to use his car, but Eric didn't want to transfer the car seat, so insisted they go in his SUV. Greg wanted to ride in the back seat with JJ and the baby, despite her repeated declinations. Eric settled the issue by reminding the other man he was the client and would need help with directions.

Luckily, the Realtor took the hint.

They had three places lined up to look at, but the instant they pulled up in front of the first, Eric knew this was the one. In an older, yet restored part of town, the building had already been used as a body shop. It had been shut down when the owner died in a freak car accident, according to Greg. Even the signs remained.

"You could even keep the name if you wanted," he pointed out. "I'm sure there's some legal stuff you'd have to do, but it would save you a fortune on signs."

Eric didn't bother to tell the other man he'd use his own name, one he'd imagined back when he was a kid and had dreamed of building custom cars. Before he'd become a college professor, of all things, and relegated that dream to "someday."

After Garth's birth, he'd decided to make "someday" now.

"I want to make an offer on this one," he said, after they'd toured the inside. Both Greg and JJ looked at him in surprise.

"Let's at least take a look at the other two," the agent advised. "You never know."

"He's right," JJ interjected, coming up with Garth to stand next to him. "After you see the others, if you still want this one, then you'll know for sure."

He already did, but their logic seemed inescapable.

After viewing the other two places—one still operating as an oil change business and the other some sort of warehouse, Eric knew his first instinct had been correct.

"And I'll need to work out a lease agreement with them so I can store some belongings before closing," he added, after hammering out the terms of his offer with the Realtor.

Greg, who'd been staring at JJ, returned his attention to Eric and nodded. "I'll get right on it," he said. "I should have an answer by the end of the week."

"Perfect."

"Listen, JJ?" Greg touched her lower back, causing her to start. Almost flinch, Eric thought, concerned.

"Would you like to have dinner with me sometime?" the agent asked, the confidence in his tone letting her know he expected her answer to be yes.

"I'm sorry, but I'm not interested." Though she gave Greg a polite smile, Eric couldn't help but notice the flash of panic in her green eyes.

The Realtor opened his mouth, apparently intending to press his point, but Eric's hand on his shoulder stopped him. "She's with me," he said, surprising himself. And JJ, too, if her startled look was any indication.

"What?" The Realtor's face grew mottled. "Why didn't you say so?"

"Why would I have to?" Eric asked. "She and I met you together. She's made it clear she's not interested. And I'll be honest, your behavior is making me wonder if I need to find someone else to handle this real estate transaction."

Jaw tight, Greg shook his head. "My apologies." His stiff, formal tone let them both know he wasn't happy.

Eric didn't really care. He'd hired the guy to help him find a shop. Once that was accomplished, Greg could collect his commission and move on.

"Let's head to my office and write up the offer," Greg suggested, a patently false smile on his face. "It shouldn't take very long and then you two can be on your way. I'll call you when I hear something from the seller."

Once this was done, Eric and Greg shook hands. Noting the way the other man's gaze kept flicking toward JJ, Eric made a point of putting his arm around her and drawing her close. She held herself stiffly, though she managed to send him a grateful smile.

Once they were back in his SUV, Eric took a deep breath. "Are you all right?"

She nodded.

"What was wrong back there, when Greg asked you out?"

She wouldn't look at him.

"Come on, JJ. It's me. I saw how you flinched, how something about his invitation panicked you. What's going on?"

Her sigh seemed to come from deep inside her. "I told you I was involved with someone before I came here," she finally said. "It was a bad situation. I left the city to get away from him. Your real estate agent reminded me an awful lot of Shawn."

"Shawn." Eric let the name roll out of his mouth, disliking it. "Were you—are you—afraid of him?"

She still wouldn't meet his gaze. Her silent nod made his chest feel tight. He ached to hold her, but now he understood her unusual reticence. He wanted to tell her he'd never hurt her, wanted to promise her he'd protect her from any man who tried, but he hadn't earned the right to say those words, so he didn't.

"It's going to be all right," he promised, meaning it. "Now where would you like to eat lunch?"

Startled, she looked up, as if not entirely certain she'd heard correctly. One corner of her extremely kissable mouth quirked. "Thanks for that," she said. "Quite honestly I was bracing myself for a barrage of questions I didn't want to answer."

"I wouldn't do that to you," he stated.

"I know." Her smile widened. "And for lunch, there's the Home Cooking Café on Main Street I've been dying to try. Let's go there."

When they pulled up in front of the little café, Garth made a snuffling sound.

"That's his prelude to a full-out cry," Eric informed her. "It's time for him to eat. I warmed some formula in the motel microwave and put it in my YETI. It should still be the perfect temp."

As soon as they were shown their booth, he dug out a bottle from his bag, poured the formula from the stainless steel cup and offered it to his son. Garth latched on eagerly.

"He was hungry," JJ said, marveling. "Such a determined little face."

"We Mikkelsons like our grub." Eric grinned, gazing

down at his son with adoration shining from his handsome face. JJ's heart stuttered.

As if she'd heard, a waitress came by and took their drink orders. "I can give you a few minutes to look at the menu," she said. "Unless you already know what you want."

"I don't know about you," Eric said to JJ, "but I'm in the mood for a big bacon burger and fries."

Her mouth watered and her stomach growled at the thought. "Oh, that sounds amazing. That's what I want, too!"

The waitress grinned. "We have fantastic burgers. I think you'll both be pleased." She hurried away to turn in their order.

"I can't remember the last time I had a hamburger," JJ mused. "I try so hard to eat healthy, but every once in a while…"

Garth had finished his bottle. Lifting him to his shoulder, Eric began to burp him. "In California, just about everyone is obsessed with clean eating. I always felt like I had to sneak away when I wanted to eat red meat or fast food."

"Around here it's just the opposite," she told him. "Red meat is absolutely focused on." Because there were so many Pack members, though she didn't say that out loud.

Garth let out a healthy burp, chortling afterward, which made Eric smile. "That's a good boy." Pride rang in his voice.

The waitress brought them their drinks, cooing baby talk to Garth before straightening and promising them their food would be out soon.

Their meal arrived and, true to the waitress's word, the hamburgers were amazing. JJ ate slowly, trying to savor every bite, while Eric wolfed his down. Watching him, she hid her smile, enjoying the gusto with which he did most everything.

She had to wonder if that gusto extended to making love.

Chapter 12

As soon as JJ had the thought, accompanied with a vivid picture of him naked and on top of her, she pushed it away and focused on finishing her meal.

Having lunch with Eric relaxed her. The entire drive to the café, she'd been stressed. The way Greg had acted had unsettled her, to say the least. It had made her feel she'd stepped back into her old life, her old world.

Now, sitting across from Eric and Garth, she swore she could feel the tension draining out of her. The Realtor, though he looked nothing like Shawn, had acted just like her former boyfriend and most of his friends. If Eric hadn't been there, she knew darn good and well Greg would have kept on badgering her until she'd finally given in. It had been, after all, the same tactic Shawn had used.

Before Shawn—or BS, as she liked to think of it— she'd viewed herself as a reasonably confident person. In the three years she'd been with him, he'd managed to not only erode her confidence, but to somehow make her feel as if she *deserved* to be treated like dirt.

Now, she felt like herself again. "Thank you for lunch," she said, smiling.

"You're welcome. I think next I'll drop you off at Rhonda's and let her know I'm going to keep the motel room." Eric buckled little Garth back into his carrier.

JJ nodded. "I really wish you'd reconsider, but I understand why you'd rather not stay."

It wasn't long before they pulled up in front of Rhonda's. JJ couldn't help but glance next door at her house. Where before she'd thought the white frame structure looked cozy, it now looked damaged and sad.

Rhonda appeared at her front door the instant they got out of the car. "I was getting worried about you two," she said, smiling tightly.

"I'm sorry." JJ smiled back, uneasy again. "We met with Eric's Realtor and had lunch. I hope we didn't affect your plans or anything."

"Of course not." Rhonda hugged her, a quick, fierce movement more perfunctory than comforting. She turned to Eric, her smile wider. "I'm very excited to have you three staying with me. It gets lonely living by myself sometimes."

"About that…" Eric scratched the back of his neck. "I've decided Garth and I will continue to stay in the motel. I appreciate your kindness, but I really can't impose myself—and my baby—on someone I don't know."

"I wouldn't have offered if I thought it was an imposition." Rhonda's voice wavered. "Seriously, what kind of neighbor would I be if I didn't try to help you? Why waste money paying for a motel room when I have three perfectly good, empty bedrooms?"

Eric looked down.

As Rhonda stood there blinking at him, JJ realized the other woman was about to cry.

"It'll be okay, Eric," JJ told him. "If it doesn't work out or if Garth is too fussy, you can always go back to the motel."

Two against one. When Eric raised his face and met her gaze, JJ realized she should have stayed out of it. The expression in his eyes said he'd had her back with Greg, and she should have done something similar with Rhonda.

Except it wasn't the same situation. Rhonda was just trying to help, not force him to date her.

"I guess I can give it a shot," Eric finally said. "Let me go back to the motel and grab my stuff and check out."

Slowly, Rhonda nodded. "Only if you're sure," she sniffed. "I don't want you to do anything that makes you uncomfortable."

"I can watch Garth for you if you want," JJ offered.

He exhaled. "That'd probably work. Come on."

Following him to the SUV, she glanced back and saw Rhonda had gone inside.

"Look." JJ grabbed his arm. "I'm sorry. If you don't want to stay here, there's no reason you should. I should have done better to back you up."

The tightness in his jaw relaxed. Gazing down at her, his blue eyes crinkling at the corners, he smiled. For one skip of her heart, she thought he might actually kiss her, but then he looked away and the moment passed.

She raised her hand to her lips, unsurprised to realize they were trembling. As he unhooked Garth's infant carrier, she reached past him for the diaper bag.

"Thanks for this," he said, handing her the carrier. "I'll be back as quickly as I can."

Nodding, she turned and carried Garth to the front door, waiting until he'd driven away before going inside.

"Rhonda?" she called, standing in the foyer and feeling uncertain.

"In the kitchen," Rhonda said. "All the way back to your left."

JJ remembered. She hefted Garth's carrier and went to the large and bright kitchen. Sniffing appreciatively, she smiled. Rhonda had bread baking in a bread machine and a large pot of something that smelled like chili simmering on the stove.

"Do you want a glass of wine?" Rhonda asked as she turned around. Her smile faded as she took in the baby.

"No, thanks." JJ's chest felt tight again. Maybe Eric had been right to want to stay in the motel. "It smells amazing in here," she said. "I had no idea you liked to cook." Of course, she didn't actually know Rhonda very well at all.

"I love to cook." Rhonda sighed. "I thought I'd make a special meal to welcome you both to my home. But your tenant acts like it's going to be torture for him to stay here."

"Oh no, I'm sure he doesn't. He really just didn't want to impose. Babies are noisy and you're used to having peace and quiet…"

Rhonda motioned to one of the kitchen chairs. "Please, sit." She pulled out her own chair and dropped into it.

JJ took the seat across from her and began unbuckling little Garth to lift him out of his carrier. As she did, the baby started to cry.

Rhonda winced. "What does he need?" she asked. "Is he hungry? Thirsty? What can I do to help?"

Rocking him gently, JJ smiled. "I need to change his diaper, that's all. He ate when we did. Is there somewhere I can take him to do that?"

"Sure. Follow me." Rhonda led her down a hallway toward a bathroom. "This is the guest bathroom. You and Eric will be sharing it. Will this countertop work?"

"It will." Relieved and feeling more confident that everything would be all right, JJ smiled her thanks.

"I'll be in the kitchen when you're finished."

Once Rhonda had gone, JJ made short work of changing the baby's diaper and cleaning him up. Funny how she'd become almost expert at this, despite having known Eric and Garth only a couple weeks.

Still holding the little one, she picked up the carrier and made her way back to the kitchen. When she took a seat, she moved Garth to her shoulder so he could look around.

Rhonda poured two glasses of wine and brought them over, placing one in front of JJ, despite her earlier refusal. Amused, JJ restrained herself from shaking her head and simply smiled.

"Any word on what caused the fire?" Rhonda asked, taking a small sip of her own wine.

"They think electrical. My insurance company promises to have someone out tomorrow, and after that, I'm hoping I can get things to kick into gear fast. It's bad enough that I'm displaced, but poor Eric. His furniture is scheduled to arrive any day now."

Rhonda narrowed her eyes. "He has furniture? I sort of got the impression he was one of those drifter kind of men. You know, a free spirit, moving from town to town as the mood struck him."

Surprised, JJ shook her head. "No. He used to be a college professor. He took a leave of absence when his son was born."

"Seriously? He doesn't look…academic at all. I bet all his students had crushes on him."

"Probably." The subject made JJ uncomfortable. Mainly because she didn't like gossiping about someone she considered a friend. She decided to change the subject. "Did you do anything interesting when you went into the city?"

Rhonda crossed her arms. "Why?"

"Just making conversation," JJ retorted. "You've been acting weird ever since you returned. Is everything okay?"

"Just fine. And I'm not acting weird. It just scares me that my house could have caught on fire and I wouldn't have even known."

Such a strange comment. But then, maybe Rhonda had been homeless before. Who knew? One thing JJ firmly believed was never judge other people without knowing what they personally had gone through.

"I get it," JJ finally said.

The hard look on Rhonda's face faded. "Thank you. But I don't think you do. How could you? Actually, I got some bad news about a friend of mine while I was gone. They say she committed suicide, but I don't believe that. I think she might have been murdered." She looked down. "Anyway, I apologize if I was acting off. I've been trying to deal with the news the best I can."

Shocked, JJ stared. "I am so sorry. Now I feel awful."

"Don't." Rhonda shrugged. "I don't really want to talk about it anymore, so let's change the subject." Considering, she brightened. "Hey, I know we've discussed this before, but I thought I'd go ahead and double-check. Sort of like giving you a heads-up. If you're not interested in Eric, now that he'll be staying here I'm definitely going to make a play for him big time. So speak up now or have no regrets."

Horrified, JJ searched for the right words. If she didn't claim Eric as hers, then he'd definitely—and rightly—feel like she'd sold him down the river.

While Eric wasn't a hundred percent certain staying at Rhonda's was a good idea, he hated to let JJ down. Clearly, she'd really wanted him to stay. Not only did he have the absurd instinct that he should protect her, but the Rhonda who'd returned from her time away seemed a hell of a lot more tightly wound than the one whose driveway he'd shoveled a week ago.

Quite frankly, he had to wonder what had happened to her while she'd been gone. Not that it was any of his business, unless her behavior affected his son.

He shook his head. Worrying too much had always been one of his flaws. He'd hoped he'd left it behind when he'd traveled across the country, but maybe not.

After gathering up his and Garth's meager belongings from the motel room, he checked out and paid. With her attention focused on the television, the motel clerk barely acknowledged him. A quick glance revealed she was watching some kind of news conference.

"What's going on?" he asked.

"A burned and dismembered body was found near the performing arts center," she said. "And one of the college students has been missing. The police haven't identified the body yet, but everyone thinks it was her."

"Here?" he asked, still not understanding.

"Yes." Her tight lips, worried expression and the fear in her eyes told him this hit too close to home. "The girl that's missing…she was—is—my friend." Abruptly, she handed him his receipt and disappeared into the back room.

Once in his vehicle, he heard the rest of the story on the radio. Several small wild animals had been found, ripped apart but not eaten, as if they'd been killed just out of cruelty.

A chill snaked up his spine. As if on cue, his cell phone rang. When he saw caller ID, his stomach clenched.

"There are reports of a possible Berserker near you," Detective DeLeon said, his tone casual. Too casual. "You wouldn't happen to know anything about that, would you?"

"Of course not. I just learned about what happened. I'm as shocked as anyone else."

"Are you? What are the odds?" Instead of waiting for

an answer, the other man continued. "You remember I told you we didn't think Yolanda was acting alone. And since Jason's cell phone never turned up, there's a good chance one or more of these cult members has made their way to Forestwood looking for you and your boy. While we're investigating, I wanted to give you a heads-up. Watch your back and, especially, keep an eye on your son. We've got people in the area, but our resources are stretched too thin to offer you a protection detail."

"Thanks, Officer DeLeon."

"Frank. You can call me Frank." With that, the other man hung up. Heart pounding, Eric dropped his phone into the console and started the engine. Damn. The man had a point. And worse, Eric had left his son alone with a woman he'd known for only two weeks, and another woman he barely knew who'd been acting strange.

He made it back to Rhonda's house in half the time it would have taken if he'd driven the speed limit. Luckily, no police officer stopped him to give him a ticket.

After he pulled up in front of Rhonda's house, he slammed on his brakes, completely forgetting about the potential of icy patches. The rear of his truck fishtailed, which made him feel slightly foolish.

Still, he needed to calm his racing heart and then go inside and act as if nothing was wrong. Though he'd started to trust—and like—JJ, for now all bets were off. He'd watch her like a hawk. And make sure neither she nor Rhonda were ever alone with Garth again.

When he walked up to the front door, uncertain whether he should knock or just walk in, he heard the sound of the television and figured they were just learning about the girl's murder. Instead of interrupting, he opened the door and went in, making a mental note to talk to Rhonda about locking the place up.

Both women's gazes were glued to the television, though JJ waved a quick hello. She was holding Garth, rocking him back and forth gently. From the broad smile the baby wore, it was clear he loved it.

For a second, Eric felt bad for suspecting JJ. But then he reminded himself how he'd once trusted Yolanda, too. Until the cult members were caught, he could trust no one. Still, the attraction sizzling between them would be no less difficult to resist.

A commercial came on.

"Wow," Rhonda commented. "In our little town."

"Did you hear about this?" JJ asked him.

Before answering, he reached down and took Garth out of her arms.

"I saw a news report at the motel office when I was checking out, plus that's all they were talking about on the radio," he said. "It's awful. Just awful."

"Yes, it is." Rhonda bowed her head. "One of my friends in the city recently died. Too much death and suffering so close together."

He offered his apologies, understanding now why she'd been acting so strange. Maybe he had been overthinking things.

"Looks like you had a beautiful day to run errands." Smiling sadly, Rhonda changed the subject.

"It was nice," he replied. "I hope it stays this way for a few days longer. While I knew winters could be brutal in the Northeast, I hadn't expected to be slammed by one major snowstorm after another, with barely a break in between."

Rhonda laughed. "It's not usually like this." At his unconvinced expression, she laughed again. "You'll get used to it. Either that, or you'll go back to the West Coast, where it's always warm."

The West Coast? He tensed up. "How did you know where I'm from?" he asked, keeping his voice casual.

"JJ told me."

No doubt picking up on his distress, JJ flashed an apologetic smile. "I'm sorry, I didn't know it was a secret."

"It's not," he assured her. Then, addressing Rhonda, he managed to smile. "I have no intention of going anywhere, no matter how awful the winter becomes. I like having four seasons, which is one of the reasons I chose to move here. Cold, I can deal with. Snow, I usually enjoy as well, especially considering my ancestors are from Norway. I still have family there."

"Norway?" Rhonda asked, arching her brows. "Wow. That's pretty cool."

"More similarities to Thor," JJ chimed in, flashing a quiet, quirky grin that he found sexy as hell.

Though his heart flip-flopped, he ignored that. "I just need the movers to be able to get through, even though I'll have to store everything at my shop until the house is ready. Is that too much to ask?"

Apparently taking pity on him, she squeezed his shoulder. While the gesture had been meant to be friendly, her touch seared him. He fought the urge to pull her close for more.

Oblivious, she smiled. "It's going to be okay. They've revised the forecast. The arctic front went back up north. No more snow is predicted for the next week at least. I know they said it would only take a week, but the weather has managed to double it. Your stuff will be here before you know it."

He hoped she was right.

After a rather uneventful evening, Eric claimed exhaustion and went to bed early, letting Rhonda know Garth was an early riser. She smiled sweetly and told him not to worry, but he still sensed something off about her. JJ, too, though he knew his overactive imagination had probably kicked in.

In the morning, he woke to sunshine pouring through

his window. He jumped up and rushed to his window. Since the city had finally cleared the last of the snow dropped by the "storm of the century," Eric had been hoping Mother Nature would take a break for a while. Today, it appeared the skies would remain clear and sunny, with the weather cold, but dry.

Fortunately, he had a lot to do that would keep him out of the house. JJ informed him she had to stay there to meet the insurance adjuster.

He'd had Greg rush the closing, which was doable since it would be a cash deal. It was scheduled for that day, so he hadn't had to lease the space until the papers were signed. He'd be able to store most of his belongings there, until JJ's house was deemed livable again.

Last he'd heard, the moving truck with all his stuff on it had gotten stuck somewhere in Ohio. The nearly three thousand mile trip, originally projected to take a week, had already stretched into two weeks due to crazy winter weather all across the country. He made a quick phone call on the way to the closing, and the moving company promised him the truck would arrive tomorrow as long as the good weather held.

Luckily, all the forecasters continued to agree it would. He swore they sounded disappointed when they delivered the "no snow expected" forecast.

Relieved, Eric hummed as he drove. As if picking up his father's good mood, Garth waved his chubby fists and chortled from his carrier in the back seat, which made Eric smile. His son would never remember living in California, or experience the pain of knowing his mother had abandoned him. So far, no one but Frank DeLeon and his merry band of Pack Protectors knew Eric's story. And for at least right now, Eric planned to keep it that way.

This whole experience of moving East had been different than he'd expected. In so many ways.

Chapter 13

With Eric gone and the claims adjuster not scheduled to appear until that afternoon, JJ decided to take advantage of the good weather and roads and head into town herself. She climbed into her car, feeling odd when she realized she actually missed having a baby to fuss over in the back seat. Before starting the engine, she sat and looked next door at her poor house. Soon, she told herself. Soon repairs would begin and before too long everything would be back to normal.

While she was sitting in her car, her cell phone rang, startling her. When her mother's name came up on caller ID, she felt a nugget of worry. Just a tiny one, but it was there nonetheless. Her mother never called twice within a month, never mind within two weeks.

"Hello, Mom," JJ answered. "Is everything all right?"

"No, everything is not all right." Anita sounded both furious and afraid. "Shawn has been calling me. A lot. At all hours. I finally had to block him, but then he called from a different phone. I'm going to have to get a new number."

"I'm sorry."

"He's been threatening me," Anita continued, as if JJ hadn't spoken. "He says unless I tell him where you are, he's going to hire a hit man and have me killed."

Briefly, JJ closed her eyes. She knew Shawn, and sensed that while this was terrible, he'd only escalate it from here. Next he'd be talking dismemberment, and how he'd dispose of the body parts. She shuddered. How she'd ever thought she loved such a man astounded her now.

Of course, he hadn't revealed his crazy side until she'd been deeply involved in the relationship.

"Have you gone to the police?"

"Yes. And I'm going to have my number changed next. I'll make sure it's unlisted, if they do such a thing for cell phones."

JJ had no idea. "Mom, he's not going to hurt you. You're all the way over there in Australia. He's just using scare tactics to try to get information out of you."

"Well, it's working."

A shiver of foreboding skittered down her spine. "You didn't tell him where I was, did you?"

"Of course not." Anger vibrated in Anita's voice, pushing out the earlier fear. "I'm not an idiot. Judging from the horrible things he's been threatening, I'm really glad you got away from him. At first I thought you'd made a mistake. He seemed like the perfect man."

"I know. But that's all on the surface." Though she tried, JJ couldn't keep the shudder from her voice. "He's dangerous. I have no doubt that he'd eventually have killed me if I'd stayed with him."

Her mother went silent. When she spoke again, hurt rang in her voice. "Honey, why didn't you ever tell me? I'd have done what I could to help you. You could have flown here to Australia to live with me."

Which was probably what Shawn thought she'd done. Not wanting to frighten her mother, JJ kept this thought to herself. She wasn't even sure if she should mention the fire.

"Do you have a restraining order against him?" Anita asked shakily.

"I don't. Because if I did that, it would only make him angrier and more determined to make me pay. He considers me his belonging, not my own person. That's why I was so relieved to be left this house. I made sure to put the deed in my real name." Which wasn't Julia. Julia was her middle name. Her first name was actually Anabelle.

"He doesn't know your name?"

"Nope. He doesn't know a lot about me. That used to bother me, but now I'm just really grateful."

"Me, too." Anita's heartfelt response made JJ smile. "You know what? I'm glad you're not hiding stuff from me anymore. I can take it, you know. I think maybe I don't give you enough credit sometimes. You've gotten really good at handling whatever challenge life throws at you. I'm proud of you."

JJ winced, glad her mom couldn't see her. Now she had to tell her about the fire. "Uh, Mom?" she began, then hurried through the rest of the story.

Anita was silent for a few seconds after JJ finished. When she finally spoke, her voice was heavier. "Julia, you weren't going to mention any of that, were you?"

"I didn't want you to worry." Truth, but a pitiful excuse.

"I'm your mother. It's my job to worry about you." Anita stated the words matter-of-factly. "But it sounds like, once again, you have this under control."

"I do." And with a dawning sense of wonder, JJ knew that she did. "I was worried about my tenant, but he's worked out everything, too. Now all I need to do is get the place repaired so I can move back in."

"Good. I'll call you with my new phone number as soon as I have it."

"Okay. Stay safe, please. And, Mom? I love you."

"I love you, too."

After ending the call, JJ started the car and put it in Drive. She needed some retail therapy, though she couldn't spend too much money. Maybe a new top or a new pair of jeans. Or boots. She'd always loved boots.

As she drove slowly up Main Street, she tried to decide where to go first. The local bookstore, Nook of Books, caught her eye. There! She'd been planning to visit ever since she'd seen the place. There was nothing she loved better than perusing stacks of books looking for her next read. And she'd noticed an alarming absence of books in Rhonda's house. Maybe she could even get Rhonda reading. Heck, that was what friends were for, right?

After parking right in front, she killed the engine and, with her spirits up for the first time since the fire, went in. A little bell tinkled above the doorway, signifying her arrival.

Inside, the place even smelled like books. Paper and ink and…heaven. JJ stopped, turned in a circle and inhaled appreciatively.

"Can I help you find something?" An older woman, her silver hair arranged in a neat bun, approached. Her softly glowing aura proclaimed her a shifter. One thing JJ had noticed about this place was that just about everyone she met seemed to be. As far as she could tell, shifters outnumbered humans five to one.

JJ smiled. "No, thanks. Searching is half the fun."

The woman blinked. "You're new here. Are you visiting or…?"

"I just moved here. My aunt was Olivia Jacobs. I inherited her house."

"Oh, Olivia. We all loved her. I'm Gracie Cordell." She held out an elegant, long-fingered hand. "Welcome to Forestwood."

"I'm Julia Jacobs, but everyone calls me JJ." After shaking hands, JJ gestured at the well-stocked shelves. "I'm so glad to find an independent bookstore here. I didn't want to have to drive into Kingston and visit a chain store at a mall."

Gracie smiled and nodded. "Everyone's been really supportive of this place. We only opened up six months ago, but we're doing well. I'll leave you alone to browse," she said. "I'll be up front if you need anything."

"Thank you."

Time flew by. JJ couldn't believe the selection, which rivaled the big-box bookstore she used to visit in the city. By the time she headed to the cash register, she'd settled on two novels, one hardcover and one paperback. Though she hadn't read anything by the authors, the stories sounded interesting. A nonfiction, self-help book had also caught her eye, so she decided to get it, also since it was about making a career out of the things you loved doing. JJ figured she needed all the help she could get with that. While she'd truly enjoyed walking other people's dogs—and made quite a bit of money from it—that had been in the busy city. She wasn't sure there'd be a market for that in a small town. So she'd need to figure out some other way to earn a living, even though she'd have income from having a tenant.

"Good choices!" Gracie exclaimed as she rang up the two novels. When she got to the other book, she studied it for a second, before ringing it up and putting it in the bag. "Are you looking for work?"

Startled, JJ nodded. "Not actively, but I'll need to start soon. I'm just not sure what I want to do."

"I need a part-time clerk," Gracie told her. "I can't afford to pay too much, but it would give you spare time to look for something full-time."

"That's very kind of you. Working in a bookstore would be my dream job," JJ blurted, stunned. "Though I'd have to be careful not to spend all my paycheck on books."

"Then it's settled. I'll need you on Monday, Wednesday and Saturday, ten until six, with an hour for lunch. Will that work for you?"

"Of course." Though JJ knew she shouldn't look a gift horse in the mouth, she had to ask. "I'm wondering why, though. You don't even know me. How do you know whether I'd make a good employee?"

Gracie smiled. "I'm an excellent judge of character. Plus anyone who speaks about bookstores the way you do is meant to either work in one or own one. Since you can't do the latter, you might as well take the job."

"Thank you. I will." Bemused, JJ paid for her purchases and turned to go. "I'll be here at ten."

"Sounds good." Tilting her head, Gracie considered, her brown eyes sharp and assessing. "Every winter, one or two times when the weather permits, all of the Pack residents residing in Forestwood have a major hunt. I can see from your aura you're a shifter, though I don't know if you're Pack—nor do I want to know. But if you are, we're all meeting in the woods at the hill north of town on Saturday night. You're welcome to join us. It's a great way to get to know your neighbors."

JJ didn't bother to hide her shock. "Um, thank you?"

This made Gracie laugh. "I take it you're not used to people talking about what we are."

JJ couldn't help it; she looked around to make sure no one was listening. Since nobody else had entered the shop since her arrival, the two of them were still alone. "You're right. I'm not. It's just not done in the city. Though we can see the auras, we might nod in recognition, but it's never spoken of out loud."

"Well, Forestwood is not only small, but shifters out-number humans something like five to one. Most of us are Pack. Those that aren't, well, we don't know what they are and we don't ask." Continuing to smile, Gracie twisted an ornate, antique-looking ring on her index finger. "We do this several times a year. The solstices, for sure. And any time there's a full moon, you can always find a group putting together a hunt. We like the camaraderie. It brings us all closer together."

JJ nodded. A sense of community, something she'd always ached for... Longing filled her, though she took care to hide it. She couldn't imagine what it must be like to grow up in a place like this. Where she would have felt she belonged, rather than feeling like an outcast.

"I might be interested," she said. "My new tenant might want to go, as well. Is it okay if I mention it to him?"

"Of course." Grinning, Grace reached out and patted her hand. "The more the merrier."

All the way home, JJ couldn't stop smiling. Not only did she now have a job, but she had a communal hunt to look forward to. When she was a child, her mother used to regale her with stories of neighborhoods shifting and hunting in a community pack. JJ had always wondered what such a thing would be like. Now she'd get to find out for herself.

And maybe, just maybe, Eric would join her.

At the thought, she felt a shiver of longing. The sexual arousal after shape-shifting back to human was well known, and most times—unless by mutual agreement—politely ignored.

Being aroused around Eric was definitely not something she'd want to ignore. In fact, she could picture him, hard and huge and ready. Her being his friend, and available, might make him put his scruples aside and indulge in a moment of spontaneous passion.

And then she realized something else. Rhonda was also a shifter. If she attended the hunt, she'd be concentrating on staying close to Eric, JJ knew.

When she pulled up to Rhonda's house, she saw Eric's SUV parked out front. Rhonda's car was nowhere to be seen, which was probably a good thing, at least for Eric. Of course, JJ figured he could take care of himself. Guys who looked like him had to be used to being propositioned by women.

Making a mental note never to become one of those women, she went inside. Eric was in the living room with Garth. He was sitting on the couch, watching TV with the sound down really low and playing with his son.

Unable to contain her happiness, JJ greeted the baby, before showing Eric her purchases. She told him about her new job and also about the communal hunt.

"Anyway, I'd love it if we could go together," she finished, trying to ignore the way he'd lowered his brows in a thunderous frown.

"I'm sorry, I can't go." With that, he turned away, suddenly finding something fascinating in a brightly colored plastic baby toy. Garth's blue eyes followed the movement and he chortled.

Meanwhile, JJ struggled to process Eric's abrupt declination.

"I'm asking you as my friend. This will be my first time changing with a group of people I don't know." She wasn't begging, not quite. "It would really help to have a friend there with me among all the strangers."

"I can't go," he repeated, his voice hard, his expression closed off. "Can't. If I could I would. Believe me."

Perplexed, she eyed him. "Why not?" she finally asked, daring to push the limits of her courage. "What if you only stay for, like, an hour?"

"JJ." He rounded on her, his handsome face fierce and dark and something else, something that sent a shudder of raw need snaking up her spine. "I can't go. Because I'm not Pack."

After Eric's dramatic announcement, JJ hadn't known what to say. She'd mumbled something conciliatory, picked up her bag of books and hurried to her bedroom, closing the door quietly behind her. She sat down on the edge of the bed, wondering why she felt like crying.

She should have known. All along, she'd realized he was different. If he'd been Pack, she imagined his wolf would be larger than other men's, stronger, a better hunter. Beautiful, in the heavy, masculine way of him.

But since he'd stated definitively he was not Pack, not wolf, the question that begged to be answered was what? What form of beast did he become when he changed his shape?

She tried to picture him; she knew of many large feline shifters—panther and lion, tiger and cheetah. Most of them tended to avoid large settlings of Pack, and she couldn't imagine why Eric would want to live here rather than closer to others of his own kind.

But then she remembered what he'd said about the Drakkor. Their little town had gained a bit of notoriety when a female dragon shifter, or Drakkor, had been outed as living in a lakeside cabin and pretending to be their famed "lake monster" for many years. The entire town had embraced Libby, and her story had been published in several shifter periodicals.

Maybe he was Drakkor. That would explain his interest and his reasoning for moving here. Anyway, it didn't matter. Or it shouldn't. Because despite her best intentions, it seemed she had become one of those women who propositioned men. Even if only to ask him to hunt with her as a friend.

JJ's crestfallen expression tugged at Eric's heart. He'd given her the truth, trusted her with part of a secret he hadn't intended to reveal and managed to hurt her in the process.

He understood her request and wished he could have honored it. But the one thing he couldn't do was change with a bunch of wolves. He also couldn't reveal his true nature to JJ. No one except DeLeon and a few of his cronies knew what Eric was, and he intended for it to stay that way.

For centuries, his kind, his people, had been vilified and avoided, all because of a rare genetic mutation. Tests were unable to reveal it, and as a result, more and more bears had stopped having children. They were too afraid of bringing a monstrosity into the world. The bears' numbers had begun dwindling, and they tended to live in isolated communities, all of them in the North. Alaska, Canada, Russia, Norway and Sweden were the largest groupings. The farthest south Eric had heard of a settlement had been high in the Rocky Mountains.

When he'd been growing up, his grandparents and the rest of that family had been part of a group in Norway. But when one of the elders in the church, a kind and giving man, had been falsely accused of being Berserker by a small group of his detractors, his own friends had turned on him rather than defending him. Things had gotten so bad he'd feared for his family. He'd sent them to California to live, and once they were safely away, he'd hanged himself from the tallest tree in the village square.

The group had imploded after that, drawing up sides. Poisonous accusations, anger and eventually violence had flared. When, as if they'd known, Eric's parents had shown up to take them away, they'd all fled to California.

Now both his parents were truly gone. Eric and Lars had learned from a stranger that, a few years after they'd vanished from their sons' lives, they'd died in an airplane crash, slamming into the side of a mountain during a blizzard up in Alaska. The subsequent fire had been what actually killed them. Lars had gone back to Norway after that, leaving Eric with no family and only the company of the few other bear shifters he'd met. Yolanda had been one of them.

Living so far from others of his own kind wasn't easy. Eric envied the easy acceptance that Pack members enjoyed. The communal hunts, the knowledge that Protectors would always be there to have your back if you needed them... The freedom to mate and procreate when you wanted, without worrying about the consequences of a deadly gene mutation appearing one day without warning...

Eric didn't know what he'd do if it appeared in his son. He shook off the thought, refusing even to consider such a possibility.

Now, sitting alone in an unfamiliar bedroom in a virtual stranger's house, he acknowledged he may have made another major mistake. He'd allowed a petite and curvy redhead to get under his skin, to come too close. No one had ever said isolation would be easy. Maybe he should seriously think about finding somewhere else to live rather than waiting for JJ's place to be repaired.

Chapter 14

True to the company's word, the moving truck pulled into Forestwood at eight o'clock the next morning. The drivers called Eric once they were inside the city limits. He agreed to meet them at his shop, glad he'd already fed and bathed little Garth. He'd decided to store everything there until the house became livable again. The excitement of finally getting his familiar belongings, not to mention his car, had him moving fast.

After putting Garth's coat on him, Eric shrugged into his own parka, grabbed his keys and headed out. He didn't see either Rhonda or JJ, which was good, since he was too impatient for conversation or explanations.

He made it to his shop in ten minutes, glad for clear roads and good weather. Once he'd parked, he carried Garth inside the small office and set his carrier down on the massive wooden desk the previous owner had left.

Walking outside, Eric caught sight of the large moving truck rounding the corner. It was towing a trailer with the most precious cargo of all—his Camaro, still properly covered.

After winter had gone for good, that car would be the best advertisement for his fledgling business. He'd spent four years in his spare time restoring and customizing it, using only authentic parts. The time and love he'd put into making it absolutely perfect showed. He'd even entered it in a few custom car competitions, both times winning top prize. Anyone who wanted a car or truck restored would, after seeing his Camaro, know immediately that Eric was the man they wanted for the job. He was banking on that.

The first thing he had the movers do was unload his car. After they'd uncovered it, he inspected the exterior from front to back. Once he'd satisfied himself that the Camaro was still in perfect condition, he backed it into the first of the three bays and closed the door. The rest of his belongings would be stored in the middle bay. He'd purchased and installed security cameras, despite Rhonda shaking her head and claiming they were unnecessary. As if Forestwood had zero crime.

Once the men had finished unloading, Eric thanked them. He stood outside, holding Garth, and watched as the big truck lumbered away. He then closed all the doors and went back in. He planned to spend the rest of the day going through his things and taking out whatever he could use to make Garth's life—and his—easier.

The day of the community hunt, JJ half hoped Eric would ask her to come help him sift through more of his boxes. She would have agreed immediately, even though she had a meeting with a contractor at ten, and hoped to pin the man down on an actual date the repair of her house could start. But Eric didn't. In the kitchen, pouring herself another cup of coffee, she managed to smile at Rhonda as if nothing was wrong.

"Are you and Eric still having problems?" Her neighbor asked.

JJ shrugged. "I'm not sure. Why?"

"Because there's something I need to tell you." Rhonda looked around, as if afraid someone would hear her. "He's *wanted*, JJ." Her loud whisper came out both shocked and worried.

JJ crossed her arms. "Wanted for what? Where are you getting your information?"

"I have a friend who's a Pack Protector. Eric's ex-wife and best friend were both murdered under suspicious circumstances."

"What?" JJ couldn't help it; she gasped. "When? Where?"

"In California. I'm not sure when. But recently, like, within the last ten days."

Some of the tension drained from JJ's shoulders. "Well, Eric hasn't left. At all. If something happened in California, it couldn't have been him. He's been here longer than that."

Grimacing, Rhonda shrugged. "I could have the timeline wrong. Maybe it was before he got here. All I know is when I was in the city the night your house caught on fire, I met my friend for dinner. We were talking about fugitives and I asked him if the Protectors had their own top ten most wanted list. They do. He showed me on his phone. I saw all of their faces and their crimes. I recognized Eric immediately."

JJ swallowed. "Did you say anything to your friend?"

Rhonda gave her a calculating look. "No. Not yet. I don't know about you, but I confess, I'm intrigued. I like my men dangerous. It's so sexy."

Sexy? "That's crazy!" JJ gasped, the words bursting from her before she had time to reconsider.

Narrow-eyed, Rhonda pursed her lips. "Do you think

so?" Her silky voice carried a thread of anger. "Or are you just saying that because you want him for yourself?"

For a heartbeat JJ couldn't find any words. When she finally spoke, she took a deep breath first. "Rhonda, stop. Neither of us knows much about Eric, but I think we at least owe him a chance to explain himself. I, for one, don't find murderers or criminals sexy. Or appealing. Yet I've been around Eric for a good while. You've seen how great he is with that baby. I can't believe he could have done what you claim he has."

"*They* claim, not I." Rhonda shook her head. "And has it ever occurred to you he might have offed the kid's mother so he could get custody?"

Now JJ felt naive. And gullible. Yet even with that, she couldn't help but feel Rhonda's friend had the wrong information. "If they're Pack Protectors, you'd think they'd have been able to locate him. I mean, he hasn't tried to hide himself. He even registered his new business under his name. I know, because I saw the paperwork."

"I don't know." Seemingly unconcerned, Rhonda shrugged. "I guess just keep your eyes open. As for me…" She flashed a sly smile. "If I get a chance to get close to him, I'm taking it. So I might need you to make yourself scarce. Or better yet, take care of the baby while I take care of Eric."

"What are you two talking about?" Eric asked, walking into the room. JJ jumped, feeling her face heat. Rhonda just continued to smile, letting her gaze travel leisurely over Eric's body, as if she could undress him with her eyes.

"Why, you, of course," she purred. "I was hoping JJ would babysit little Garth tonight so I could take you out to dinner at my favorite Italian restaurant."

His quick—and alarmed—glance at JJ was almost comical. "JJ and I already have plans." His eyes begged her not to contradict him.

"Really?" Rhonda's disappointed pout seemed calculating. "Then how about tomorrow night?"

JJ barely kept from rolling her eyes. While she still liked Rhonda, and could understand her wanting Eric, her comments about criminals and murderers being sexy seemed creepy.

And no matter what Rhonda thought, no way was Eric either of those.

"I don't think so," he finally said, his voice kind. "I'm not really interested in dating anyone right now."

"Even JJ?" Rhonda asked, her hands on her hips and her color high. "Because it seems to me you and my friend there have been dating quite a bit."

"We're friends," JJ interjected, before Eric could comment. She actually felt sorry for Rhonda. While she didn't understand why Eric wasn't interested in a petite, curvy blonde, she was glad he wasn't.

"Yes, friends," Eric echoed.

"With benefits?" The bluntness of her neighbor's question shocked JJ. Again, her face heated. Just once she wished she didn't turn red every time she got embarrassed.

If he noticed, Eric gave no sign. "That's out of line, Rhonda. I think you owe JJ an apology."

She lifted her chin but said nothing.

Hurt, JJ lowered her head. She'd known all along that Rhonda had been interested in Eric, but hadn't thought they'd become enemies over it.

"Actually—" Rhonda finally spoke, giving JJ hope that this could all be smoothed over "—I think you're the one who owes JJ an apology. You didn't inform her she'd be harboring a criminal when she let you rent half her house."

Then, while both Eric and JJ gaped at her, she continued. "As a matter of fact, my suggestion is that you turn yourself in before she gets hurt."

It took a moment before Eric could speak. "Are you threatening me, Rhonda?"

Rhonda's perfectly shaped brows rose. "Of course not. Why would you think that?"

"Because that sounds like a threat." He crossed his arms. "I don't know where you're getting your information, but I'm not a criminal and I'm not wanted for anything."

"But—"

"No buts. I'm in constant communication with Pack Protectors. Believe me, if I were wanted for a crime, they'd know exactly where to find me." With that, he stalked from the room.

Rhonda remained silent for a few more seconds. "I don't know what to think," she said.

"Maybe you just looked at whatever you saw wrong. It sounds like the Pack Protectors are protecting him rather than hunting him."

"Maybe so. Either way, there he goes again." Rhonda jerked her head toward the window. Outside, Eric was buckling Garth into his infant seat. Briefly, JJ debated hurrying outside to talk to him, but then didn't move. Maybe they needed a little time and space before they could resume their friendship.

Friends. As if that was all she wanted. Deep down, she knew she longed for more, and she'd never been one to lie to herself. Clearly, since that would never happen, she needed to put it out of her mind. Right now, she wasn't even sure if their new friendship would survive.

Shortly before ten, she told Rhonda she'd be right back, and went next door to her own house to meet the contractor her insurance agent had recommended. Since he'd be dealing directly with the insurance company, he took a look around and promised to submit a quote to them. Once they'd agreed, he promised to start immediately. She considered that a win.

After that meeting, she went back to Rhonda's house. Needing something else to occupy herself until the hunt, she cleaned the kitchen and the bathroom. Then she ended up back in the kitchen, rummaging through the cupboards until she found enough ingredients to make a cake.

Rhonda wandered in as she was stirring the batter. "Sorry," JJ said. "I can't sit still. I'm a bundle of nerves."

"Why?"

"The group hunt tonight. I'm so stressed, I'm almost at the point of chickening out and changing my mind about going."

"Humph," Rhonda snorted. "If you want to fit in around here, you need to get to know people. That sounds like a good way to do it."

Pouring the batter into the cake pan, JJ nodded. "I know. That's why I'm telling myself that no matter what, I have to make my way to the woods tonight. Are you going? Maybe we could ride together."

To JJ's surprise, Rhonda shook her head. "I'm not. I've got way too much to do," she said vaguely, by way of explanation.

"Like what?" Though she knew she probably shouldn't, JJ pressed the point. When Rhonda wasn't at work, she did little other than watch TV and drift around the house.

"Fine. If you must know, quite honestly, I've never liked those things. Too much random togetherness."

JJ shrugged, not wanting to admit she'd never experienced it. She might end up feeling the same as Rhonda, but wouldn't know until she tried it. Or so she told herself.

When her phone rang, she answered, even though she

didn't recognize the number. It was her soon-to-be new boss, Gracie Cordell.

"Are you going tonight?" Gracie asked. JJ replied in the affirmative, though she was a little nervous.

Gracie chuckled. "It'll be fine. I tell you what—how about I meet you there? I'll watch for you. That way, at least you'll know someone. And then, when you start work at the bookstore on Monday, at least we'll have that shared experience between us. What do you say?"

Grateful, JJ thanked her. They agreed on a place to meet, and ended the call. Rhonda, who'd stayed in the kitchen, unabashedly listening to JJ's side of the conversation, shook her head and left the room.

JJ went back to making her cake. She was relieved by Gracie's friendliness, though she couldn't help but wish Eric was going. Which went to show how deluded she could be. He could no more change his species than she could.

What she hated more than that was the way Eric had been acting. He'd been remote and distant ever since telling her he wasn't Pack. He'd taken to spending a lot of time at his shop, and while she knew there was work to be done to get it ready, he didn't ask her to accompany him or even to watch Garth.

It hurt more than she wanted to think about. So she didn't. While her cake baked, she got busy making something else.

While Gracie had said the group was gathering at dusk at a spot deep inside the forest, she'd instructed JJ to meet her at the entrance to one of the hiking trails. Luckily, the weather had held. Even though cloudy and gray, the sky didn't even shed a single snow flurry. The temperatures hovered slightly above freezing. JJ dressed in layers, choosing each item of clothing by how easily it could be shed. The idea of stripping and changing in front of total strangers unnerved her, but she figured it would be pretty easy to find a bush or thicket to hide in for a few minutes.

The thought of hunting in a pack—a genuine pack of wolves—excited her.

Her enthusiasm warring with nerves, JJ arrived early. Since she'd never hiked a day in her life, she settled for pacing the parking lot. Relief flooded her when another car pulled up. The green four-door sedan parked next to JJ's car and Gracie waved from inside.

"Are you ready for the best hunt of your life?" she said in greeting as she exited her vehicle.

"Sure," JJ answered, aware she sounded anything but. "Listen, I'm wondering…for first-timers, is there a private area we can go to when it's time to strip off our clothes and shift?"

Gracie grinned. "You sound like you've never done this before. Don't worry, it'll be just like any other group hunt you've done, just with a bunch of different people."

Though she debated internally, JJ finally told her new boss the truth. "Actually, I've never done a group hunt."

"Never?"

"Nope. I've lived in the city among humans for most of my life."

Gracie shook her head. "Where did you go to change?"

"Central Park. I snuck out, usually in the middle of the night. Sometimes I could hear other shifters, but I never actually met up with one."

"You'll be fine." Patting her shoulder, Gracie pointed to where a small group of people had begun to gather near a huge oak tree. "Those are the organizers. Let me introduce you around."

Inwardly balking, JJ nodded and let her new boss lead her over. Two of the men swept their gazes over JJ appreciatively and openly, making her want to cross her arms in front of her in self-defense. Of course, soon everyone would let go of all human inhibitions, strip off their clothing and change into their wolf form. Then none of this would matter in the slightest.

At least not until the time came to shift back to human.

Maybe this had been one awful, huge mistake.

As the crowd of people grew, Gracie stayed by JJ's side. Finally, a tall man with a shock of gray hair blew a whistle. "It's time. Everyone move into the woods. We're going for the herd of deer that's been spotted on the other side of the ridge."

JJ's heart skipped a beat. She couldn't seem to make her feet move. As if she somehow understood, Gracie grabbed hold of her arm and tugged her.

"Come on. We'll find you a nice little private glade so you can change."

As they walked deeper into the woods, others already began yanking off their clothing. Impervious to the cold, several naked men dropped to the forest floor and began the process of becoming wolf.

JJ stared, fascinated. When Gracie tugged at her again, she wrenched her gaze away.

Ahead of them, several large wolves bounded off to begin the hunt.

"It's time." Excitement rang in Gracie's voice. JJ could see that her inner wolf obviously battled for release.

"You go ahead," JJ assured her. "I'm going to go that way and find a semiprivate place. I'll meet you on the hunt."

"Thank you." Her voice almost a growl, Gracie hurried away, shedding her clothing as she went.

JJ turned. All around her were people in various states of undress, and wolves. Lots of wolves—more than she'd ever seen in one place.

Growls and grunts and the occasional whine filled the air. Together in small groups, they loped off into the forest, joining larger groups. They'd hunt, working together, no doubt bringing down several deer. They'd feast on their kills, sharing equally. And when they were done, they'd return to this place and shift back to human.

After that, she could only imagine what would happen. Naked plus arousal equaled...

Panic jabbed her. She didn't want this. Not now. Not ever. She simply couldn't do it. Spinning on her heel, she took off at a dead run for the parking lot and her car.

Chapter 15

Eric couldn't stop thinking about JJ, stripping off her clothes to change in front of a bunch of strangers. Her smooth, pale, freckled skin, the lush curves her clothing only hinted at, on display for anyone and everyone to ogle. Another man would hold her close, breathe the slight sweetness of her lavender scent and run his hands over her curves. Eric didn't like it, not in the slightest, though he was well aware he didn't have a right to protest.

Though bears rarely hunted in groups like wolves, he'd done group hunts, too, though not recently. Not in years, in fact. Those had occurred only in his younger, more rowdy days. He well remembered the uninhibited group sex that always followed those things. He'd thought of mentioning this to JJ, but figured she had to know. Everyone—without exception—experienced sexual arousal after reassuming their human form.

His body stirred just thinking about it. Resolutely, he forced his thoughts away.

Because he hadn't wanted to be alone in the house with

Rhonda, he'd packed up Garth and headed to his shop. He'd been spending a lot of time there, setting up his tools and his office. All Garth's things were there, too: his playpen, stuffed animals and brightly colored toys. Eric had brought only a few things to Rhonda's place. He couldn't wait until JJ's house was fixed. Luckily, she'd said the contractor would be starting work on Monday.

He stayed at the shop until his growling stomach forced him to go in search of food. Most of downtown Forestwood appeared to be shut down—he guessed they were all at the hunt. Finally, he found a small Chinese restaurant and scarfed down some delicious sweet-and-sour chicken.

Since Garth had already eaten and had played most of the day, he slept through dinner. Eric suspected he'd lucked out with such a calm baby. He counted his blessing there.

When he finished up, he reluctantly went back to Rhonda's. He wished he'd kept the hotel room. With lights turned down low, she had several scented candles lit in the dim room, filling the air with something that smelled like pears. Watching TV in the living room, she offered him a beer and invited him to watch with her. Though tempted, he didn't want to have to fend off any advances, so he claimed exhaustion and retreated to his room. At least he had a good book to read. Settling back against his pillow to do so, he fell asleep almost immediately, waking later to shut off the light and climb in between the sheets.

The morning after JJ's communal hunt, Eric went to make coffee shortly after sunrise. He'd taken to rising early—Garth woke up at six, anyway—and showering, planning on having coffee and breakfast before anyone else got up. When JJ strolled into the kitchen midway through his first cup, he greeted her warily.

"Did you have a good time last night?" he asked, dividing his attention between her and his coffee mug.

"I did." Her sleepy smile made his man parts twinge. "At first, it was a bit weird," she continued, shaking her head. "Interesting, watching so many people so comfortable with themselves they could shift next to virtual strangers."

"Did you like it?" he asked, unable to help himself, the intensity in his voice revealing feelings better left hidden.

"Not really." She swallowed. "I finally realized it wasn't my cup of tea and left. I was too embarrassed to come back here, so I went into town and had a drink at a bar. Downtown was pretty deserted. Mostly only humans there, but it was all right. As for the hunt, I think they were planning to bring down a couple of deer."

Fierce joy bloomed inside him. She hadn't done it. He couldn't imagine her passing up the chance to take down a deer. The bear inside him woke at that, shaking off the last of his sleepiness with a rumbling yawn. He himself needed to change and hunt, the sooner the better. Except then he'd have to ask JJ to watch Garth. Part of him still balked at that.

Still a bit stunned, he wasn't sure what to say. Should he commiserate with her or congratulate her? He settled on simply nodding and saying nothing.

After fetching her own cup of coffee, she pulled out the chair across from him and sat. "I start my new job tomorrow. That is, if my new boss, Gracie, isn't mad at me for disappearing. The bookstore is a couple of blocks away from your new shop. Maybe we could have lunch together sometime?"

Her earnest expression made him smile. "I'd like that," he said. "Once you get settled in, we'll decide on a day and a place."

At his response, her entire body sagged with relief.

Surprised, he cocked his head. "Are you all right?"

"I am now. I've been worried about our friendship, especially after I asked you to hunt with me."

He swallowed hard. "Please don't mention that again."

Though her lovely green eyes widened, she nodded. "I won't. I just wanted you to know I'm glad we can still be friends."

Friends. He still wanted so much more. About to comment, he closed his mouth when Rhonda strolled into the kitchen.

"Morning, you two." Her cheery voice made him wince.

"Good morning," he and JJ answered in unison. Surprised, they looked at each other and laughed.

Rhonda stared. "Did I miss something?"

"No." Shaking her head, JJ continued smiling. "We were talking about me starting my new job tomorrow."

"In the bookstore, right?" Rhonda worked in the large bank downtown as a loan officer. She, too, worked close enough to have lunch with JJ. Though tempted to point this out, he held his tongue. If JJ wanted to invite her friend, she could do it herself.

Walking to the pot, Rhonda poured herself a cup of coffee and carried it to the table. After she'd taken a seat, she scooched her chair closer to Eric. It took every ounce of self-restraint he had to keep from moving away.

"Working in a bookstore sounds kind of boring," Rhonda commented.

Her expression shocked, JJ shook her head. "That's only because you don't like to read."

"How do you know?" Rhonda countered, taking a long drink of her coffee.

"Because you don't have a single book in the house, at least that I can tell."

Glancing back toward the living room, Eric realized JJ was right. He hadn't noticed, but not even a coffee table book graced the room.

Rhonda laughed. "I only read e-books."

"Oh." JJ's face turned pink. "I didn't think of that. I read e-books, too, but there's nothing like the feel of a real book in your hands."

When Rhonda shrugged, Eric changed the subject. "I finally have all my stuff stored in my shop until the house gets repaired. Do you have any idea how long that will take?"

Before she could answer, the front living room window shattered.

JJ screamed. Rhonda whirled, growling and baring her teeth. Eric leaped for the baby, aware only of the need to protect his son.

"A brick." Outrage in her voice, Rhonda stalked toward the window, her shoes crunching on shattered glass. She picked the brick up, holding it high as though she was considering lobbing it back out the window.

"There's a note or something tied to it." Still snarling, Rhonda jerked loose the small slip of white paper. "Freakin' cowards."

Eric raised his head, still sheltering his son with his body. He cursed, an unintelligible Norwegian word he remembered hearing his grandfather use.

"Get him out of here," JJ urged.

She was right, but he hated to leave both women unprotected. "JJ, you take him and go to the back. Please."

After a second's hesitation, she nodded. Crossing to him, she grabbed the baby carrier and hurried off toward her bedroom.

Frowning, Rhonda watched her go before handing the

note to him. "I don't understand what this means," she complained. "It doesn't make any sense."

Scrawled in red ink were three words. *Abomination. Valor.* And *Sacrifice.*

Only once the Forestwood PD arrived did JJ feel safe enough to venture from her bedroom with the baby. They took Rhonda's statement, and after handing Garth over to Eric, JJ helped her sweep up shards of glass. Rhonda passed her the note and together they puzzled over the meaning of the words.

The police left after taking the report and a photo of the note, promising to make sure to patrol the area more frequently. They'd also taken photos of the footprints in the snow out front, just in case. Meanwhile, the room had grown cold, with frigid air coming in through the broken pane.

"We'll need to nail plywood over that," Eric commented. Both JJ and Rhonda looked at him.

"I've got some in the garage," Rhonda said. "If you'll help nail it up, I'd appreciate it."

"How big is it?" he asked. "If you plan to nail it, it'll have to be big enough to cover the entire window."

"It is." Rhonda sounded surprisingly upbeat, considering someone had attacked her home.

"Sure. If JJ will agree to watch Garth for a few more minutes."

Tempted to tell Rhonda she'd help nail up the plywood, JJ took the baby instead. She watched as Eric followed Rhonda to the garage to retrieve the plywood. Though it took only a few minutes to locate it and move it into place, the interior temperature felt like it had dropped another twenty degrees. JJ had taken Garth into the bedroom and left him there. She'd closed the door to keep the heat in.

Finally, they had it up. When they came back inside, Rhonda was shivering, telling Eric in a wounded little voice how cold she felt.

If she'd been hinting at him in the hopes he'd warm her up, Eric didn't appear to notice. JJ read the note again, out loud this time.

"'Abomination, valor, sacrifice.' Does anyone have an idea what that means?"

Scowling, Rhonda shook her head. "No clue. But when I find out who's messing with me, they'd better be careful. I don't get mad, I get even."

JJ chanced a glance at Eric. A muscle worked in his jaw and the bleak, haunted fury in his eyes told her he might have an idea what those words meant. Clearly, she'd have to ask him privately.

His next words surprised her. "I think Garth and I need to move out."

Both JJ and Rhonda gaped at him. "Because of the brick?" Rhonda narrowed her eyes. "You know what the note means, don't you?"

Instead of answering, he took Garth from JJ and headed toward his room. "We'll pack immediately. Thanks for the hospitality. If you have a deductible or something, I'll be more than happy to pay it."

Once he'd gone, JJ looked at Rhonda.

"Do you know, too?" Rhonda asked.

"I have no idea." JJ's heart pounded and she took a deep breath. "But I'm going to try and find out."

Determined, she hurried down the hallway, hoping Rhonda wouldn't follow her. When she reached Eric's room, she knocked on the closed door.

He opened it a crack and peered out. "What?"

"Can I talk to you?"

"I don't want to discuss it," he replied, and started to close the door.

Surprising herself, she stuck her foot in the gap like she'd seen in the movies, keeping him from shutting it. "Please."

To her relief, he let her in. "Just you, no Rhonda, right?"

She glanced back over her shoulder to make sure. "Right."

He closed the door behind her and turned the lock. He had his duffel bag on the bed and had clearly been throwing in clothes.

"You're really leaving?"

Meeting her gaze, he nodded. "It's not safe here anymore. Garth's safety has to come before anything else."

"So the brick really was aimed at you? What's going on?"

"The less you know the better."

"No." She moved closer, until they were standing toe to toe. "I'm involved already, whether you like it or not. I can't help you if I'm not in the loop."

His eyes darkened as he gazed down at her. "It's a long story."

"I've got time."

Another heartbeat passed with their gazes locked. Finally, he exhaled. "Come for a drive with me."

"Where are you going?"

"My shop. I'm going to stay there. It's got a rudimentary kitchen and bathroom. The security is much better, too, since I installed cameras and an alarm system. I'll just need to find someplace to take showers."

"I'm sure you can use Rhonda's house," JJ offered.

He shook his head before she even finished speaking. "Not happening." His tone told her not to ask why.

Once he'd packed everything, he did a double check

of the room to make sure he hadn't left a single piece of clothing before putting on his parka. "Come on," he said.

"Okay." She followed him out into the hallway. As they went past the living room, Rhonda jumped up to intercept them. Her gaze immediately went to his loaded duffel bag.

"You're really leaving?" The alarm in her voice had JJ eyeing her.

"Yes."

"I wish you wouldn't." Somehow Rhonda managed to get in between them and the door. "If you go, you'll be leaving both JJ and me completely unprotected."

He froze, and then shook his head. "This attack wasn't about either of you. Once Garth and I are out of here, no one should bother you again."

Rhonda's eyes widened. She looked at JJ, who nodded. "Are you going, too?"

With all her heart, JJ suddenly wished she could say yes. "No. I'll be back."

Eric started moving again. When he opened the front door, he looked back over his shoulder at JJ and then continued walking away.

As JJ started after him, Rhonda grabbed her arm. "Don't go."

Jerking herself free, JJ snagged her coat off the rack and headed after Eric. "I'll be back, I promise."

Outside, she hurried to catch up with him. Buckling the baby into the infant carrier, he looked up and inclined his chin toward the passenger seat. She got in and clicked the seat belt.

As they pulled away, she watched him, waiting for him to speak. Instead, he stared straight ahead, hands tight on the wheel, silent. Most likely he wasn't entirely sure he wanted to involve her in any of this.

"Well?" she finally demanded, when he showed no sign of wanting to talk. "What was all that about?"

Jaw still tight, he barely glanced at her. "My son is in danger. The Pack Protectors want me to go into a sort of witness protection program with him."

She swallowed, shocked. Noting her reaction, he nodded. She couldn't believe how incredibly painful she found the idea of never seeing him again.

"Are you?" Clearing her throat, she tried once more. "Are you considering doing that?"

"I'd prefer not to," he admitted. "But I've got to consider what's best for Garth."

"What kind of danger? I assume the Protectors are looking for the person who's a threat to you two?"

"They are. But until then…" The bleakness in his tone told her he'd already considered the alternative.

"What did that note mean? Abomination, valor, sacrifice? It doesn't make sense."

"For reasons I can't go into, they consider Garth both an abomination and apparently full of valor. They want me to give him up, to sacrifice him to their cause."

"Sacrifice?" Horrified, she tried to comprehend. "I'm struggling to make sense of your words, but I can't. I just don't understand. The idea that anyone wants to kill a sweet, innocent baby? What kind of monster would do such a thing?"

"Oh, they don't want to kill him," he said. "They want to take him from me and eventually test him to see if he carries a particular gene mutation. If he does, they want to try and breed him, so they can get more of the same type of mutation."

His words puzzled her. "I'm afraid I don't understand," she began.

"They know where I am," he continued, as if he hadn't

heard her. "That's why I'm moving to the shop until I decide what to do. At least there I have security."

"What about your business?" she asked. "How can you run a business that's open to the public? Especially since you seem to have no idea what this person or people look like."

His expression disgusted, he shook his head. "Good point. I hadn't thought that far ahead. I might have to take the Protectors up on their offer, at least until they're able to contain the threat."

"But why?" She studied him. "Why are they willing to do this for you? It's not like you're a key witness to some horrific crime, are you?"

"No." He smiled. "I'm not."

"Then why? Can you at least tell me that? From what I know about the Pack Protectors, they'd need a darn good reason before offering you their assistance."

Her comment appeared to surprise him. But then again, she had no idea what kind of shifters he and Garth were. His answer reconfirmed that.

"Not only were they part of a dwindling number, but the Protectors wanted to keep a close eye on Garth to make sure he didn't develop into something dangerous. And I don't blame them, to be honest. While I completely discount the possibility, they also know I'd lay down my life to protect Garth. No matter what the circumstances."

Interesting. "What are they worried he might become?" she asked.

"Let's just say my baby is very unique and special," he told her.

"That's not a real answer," she protested.

"It is and it isn't. But I assure you, it's the truth."

She eyed him for another moment. Then she took a deep breath and touched his arm. "Let me go with you."

Chapter 16

Stunned, Eric nearly drove off the road. He gripped the wheel and corrected enough to get them back in their lane. Then he pushed back the leap of excitement he felt at her words. "What?"

"I want to go with you and Garth if you decide to go into hiding. I can help you with him. Plus, your cover story will be more convincing if you appear to be a family rather than a single dad with a baby. That's fairly unusual and might make you more noticeable."

She made sense. Instead of immediately discounting her offer, he let himself consider her words. "I don't have any idea how long it might be."

"That's fine. I don't know when my house will be livable again."

By then he'd pulled into the parking lot of his shop. He parked by the entrance and, instead of killing the engine, left it running. "Why?" he asked quietly. "You barely know me. Why would you want to give up your life and go into hiding with me?"

There were several different responses she could give to that question. He waited, interested to hear what she'd say.

"Why not?" she countered. "I have no home, at least until it's fixed. I'm staying with Rhonda, and I don't really know her, either."

Gaze steady, he continued to eye her.

"Look, I like you. And Garth. You rented a house from me and you'd barely moved in when it caught on fire. I owe you."

Frowning, he didn't bother to try and hide his disappointment. "You're saying you feel *obligated* to disappear with me, due to a fire? You had absolutely no control over that."

She lifted her chin. "True. But my life is kind of on hold right now. And honestly, I think you and Garth could both use my help."

While he pondered her words, she sat very still and quiet. In the back seat, Garth let out a wailing cry. "His hungry cry," she said, proving her point.

"Yes." Finally, Eric turned the key and shut off the motor. "You do pay attention. Come on, let's go inside and I'll see about getting my boy fed."

She climbed out and stood on the sidewalk, waiting while he unbuckled Garth. Eric could tell from the way she kept opening and closing her mouth that she wasn't sure if she should continue to press him for an answer. Good. After all, he hadn't even decided what course of action to take. Instinctively, she probably knew he'd much rather stay and fight. But he had more to consider than merely himself. His first priority had to be keeping Garth safe.

Though JJ had asked to go with Eric impulsively, the more she thought about it, the more she knew it was exactly what she needed to do. If he wanted her, that is.

Eric's cell phone rang. "It's the Pack Protector, calling me back. Would you keep an eye on Garth while I take it?"

She nodded. Eric turned away while he took the call. After answering, he went outside.

When he finished his phone call, he came back into the room. Expression serious, he stopped and studied his son before lifting his gaze to meet JJ's.

"I'm going to stay," he said quietly. "I've already done more running than I ever wanted to do in my lifetime. I can protect Garth. I'm not sure, however, that I can protect both of you."

Her heart skipped a beat. "You won't have to protect me," she told him. "I'm pretty damn good at protecting myself."

As she spoke the words, she knew with a sense of astonishment that they were true. When Shawn had first started his abuse, she'd been stunned and shell-shocked. While she hadn't defended herself due to the fact that the only way she could was to shift into wolf, she'd gotten out of the situation and started a new life. Looking back, she realized her experience had made her stronger.

At first, Eric didn't respond. Finally, he shook his head. "You know, I think it might be better if you stay away from me and Garth until this is over."

For whatever reason, this infuriated her. She'd been willing to go on the run with him, had offered to help him any way she could. And all he came up with was asking her to stay away?

"I don't accept that," she said, even if she didn't have the right. "How about you fill me in on what's going on? I can be much better prepared if I know what specific circumstances you're facing."

"I can't tell you," he answered, as she'd known he would. "It would go against Pack law."

And there he had her. If his statement was true, that is. "There aren't too many laws they're stringent on these days. So unless you shape-shifted and revealed yourself to a human, or hurt a human while in your other form, I'm thinking we're safe."

He wasn't able to hide the flash of surprise crossing his face at her words. "What about your job?"

The abrupt change of subject momentarily stumped her. "What about it?"

"You just took a job working in that bookstore. If we went on the run, you wouldn't be able to work there. And I doubt the store owner would hold it for you, especially since you'd be up and disappearing."

"I'm sure once I explained—" she began.

"No. You couldn't explain anything. That's what going into a protection program is like. You just go. There isn't time for explanations. You don't get to call anyone and let them know you're safe. You just disappear, like you never existed."

She hadn't really considered all of that, but in the end, she didn't mind. Because something inside her told her she had to be with Eric and Garth. While JJ hadn't known him very long, she felt as if she'd known him forever. She couldn't imagine life without him somewhere in it. Though she hated to disappoint Gracie, she'd do whatever she had to in order to keep Eric and Garth in her life. "I'd still go," she answered, lifting her chin stubbornly.

He eyed her. "Are we really that important to you?"

The question hung in the air. Admitting this might make her feel exposed and naked, but she didn't think she could respond any other way. "Yes," she answered. "Yes, you are."

He kissed her then. The kind of kiss that shook her all the way to her soul and made her want to melt into him.

His kiss promised more than any words could, and her response let him know she would welcome all of it.

When they broke apart, she could barely stand. Not bothering to hide her disappointment, she sighed. "I want—" she began, aching with need and unfulfilled desire.

"Shh." He smoothed her hair back away from her face. "I'm going to call them and tell them to come get us. We're going to go into the protection program."

Her heart stuttered. "Okay," she managed to reply. "I'll need to call Rhonda and let her know."

She realized what she'd said at the same time he did. They both laughed, more of a nervous chuckle, actually.

"I can't, can I?"

He shook his head. "No. And this will be your last opportunity to change your mind. Once I make that call, you're involved, whether you want to be or not."

Although she'd feel a lot better about her decision if she knew exactly what the danger was, she nodded. "I'm ready," she said. "But I don't have any clothes or makeup or anything. I'll need shampoo and deodorant and lotion, at least."

"I'm sure they'll provide it. I was told all I need to do is give them a list of what I want and they'll get it."

After that, things proceeded at a breathtaking pace. Less than thirty minutes after Eric made the call, a black sedan with tinted windows pulled up to the shop. Eric opened up the third bay and the vehicle drove in.

Once the door had closed, with the car inside, Eric hurriedly transferred several bags of baby provisions to the trunk. He also removed the infant carrier from his SUV and installed it in the back seat of the sedan.

After buckling little Garth inside, he crossed over to JJ and took her hand. "I'm going to sit up front until we're safely out of town. I want you to stay as close to my boy as possible."

Suddenly tongue-tied, she nodded. "That's fine. Where are we going? Do you have any idea?"

He shook his head. "No doubt they'll inform us once we're on the road."

She climbed into the back seat to be with the baby and Eric got into the front. The driver opened the bay, climbed into the car, and pulled out and parked, leaving the engine running. He then got out and went back to close everything up and lock it. Eric went with him, leaving Garth in the car with JJ.

Watching them, JJ felt a pang of misgiving, imagining Rhonda's worry when they didn't return. She had promised to go back, after all. Maybe she could sneak in one little phone call to reassure her neighbor. She could let Rhonda know they were safe, without revealing any pertinent information about their location.

Since she knew both Eric and the Protector would frown on this idea, maybe she could ask someone to at least get word to Rhonda and Gracie. The idea of being a no-show at the bookstore Monday turned her stomach. Not to mention her mother's worry when JJ appeared to drop off the face of the earth.

Had she made a mistake? Was she staking everything on a possibility that might never come to be?

Priorities, she told herself. Once all this—whatever *this* might be—was over, she'd be able to explain, and hoped they'd understand.

Once Eric had double-checked to make sure everything at his shop would be secure, he and the driver turned to head back to the car.

As they did, another vehicle came screeching around the corner. When she heard the first *pop-pop*, JJ realized they were under fire. Immediately, she went into protect-baby-Garth mode, ducking down and crawling over the seat to cover him with her body.

Heart pounding, and trembling as she was, her unusual action and utter terror communicated themselves to the baby. He began to wail. "Shh!" she told him, frantic to keep him quiet. "It's all right. Daddy will be back in a second. Please hush."

Of course, he understood none of this, and continued to cry.

More shots rang out. Someone shouted—was that Eric? When the car door opened, she prayed it was him. It wasn't.

She had one second to register that the man wore a black ski mask before he yanked her off Garth and tossed her to the pavement. Somehow, she lurched back up and went after him, with only one thought in her mind: *protect the baby*.

As she flung herself at her assailant, he turned and punched her. His fist connected with her jaw. She knew one instant of blazing pain before everything went dark.

When he came to, Eric rolled over, wincing from the pain of the wound in his leg. Belatedly, he saw that he'd been shot and was still bleeding. Next to him, the Pack Protector lay covered in blood. The dark sedan remained where they'd left it, engine running. The other vehicle was gone. Baby Garth. Where the hell was his son?

Pushing up, he tried to stand. The pain and loss of blood made him dizzy. Somehow, he got his scarf off and used it to tie a makeshift tourniquet around his leg. Then he crawled toward the Pack Protector, who didn't move. Eric checked him for a pulse. There wasn't one. The other man, whose name Eric hadn't even gotten, was dead.

JJ? Though the entire world tilted when he tried to

move, he managed to drag himself toward the sedan. He registered JJ lying on the cement next to the car, either unconscious or dead. The open back door revealed the seat was empty, infant carrier and all. Garth was gone.

Heart pumping, Eric could feel himself weakening. He couldn't pass out, not before he made it to JJ. His vision blurred as he reached her, but he summoned up every ounce of remaining strength he possessed to check her pulse. To his relief, the steady beat of her heart told him she lived. Unconscious, but the lack of blood meant she hadn't been shot. Good.

His phone. Dimly, he registered that his cell was in his pocket. Pulling it out slowly, wincing with every movement, he managed to type in 911. When the operator answered, he gave his location. After that, he let the blackness win and take him.

When he next opened his eyes, he found himself in a hospital bed. His leg had been bandaged and all around him machines beeped quietly. An IV had been placed in his arm.

As memory came flooding back to him, he sat up. "Garth!" Aching grief and worry and terror threatened to overcome him, but he pushed all that away. He had to focus on finding his son.

"Hey." JJ's voice. He swung his head in her direction. Anxiety that mirrored his own sparked in her eyes. "They took Garth," she said. "I tried to stop them, but I couldn't." Her voice wavered. "I'm so very, very sorry. I let you down. Worse, I let Garth down."

Somehow, despite the tubes and cords, he managed to put his arms around her. They held on to each other as if drowning. He drew strength from her, and suspected she might have felt the same way.

Someone cleared a throat from near the door. "Excuse me." A tall woman in a neat pantsuit entered the room. She had fashionable, horn-rimmed glasses and wore her dark hair in a tidy bun. "I'm Linda Felts and I'm with the Protectors," she said, keeping her voice low. "I know the human police will be here any moment to ask their questions, but our man was killed, so I needed to get in and go first."

JJ pulled away. Eric wanted to catch her arm and ask her to stay close, but he didn't. "Where's Frank DeLeon?" JJ started, though he wasn't sure why.

"He was assigned to meet you at the safe house. He's en route back here as we speak. For now, I'm in charge of this case."

Eric nodded. "What was his name, Linda?" he asked. "The agent who was killed. What was his name?"

"Dan Pendarki." She swallowed hard. "Thank you for asking. He was newly married, and he and his wife have a baby on the way."

Grief once again stabbed Eric. "He was the second Protector to die, because of my case."

"It's not your fault," she told him, her voice once again crisply professional. "They knew the danger when they signed up for this job." Her eyes watered, but she lifted her chin. "You weren't the one pulling the trigger. Now we've got to find out who did this and get them."

"And find my son," he declared, equally fierce. "I need to get out of here. Every second we waste is dangerous to him."

"We already have people searching." Linda looked from Eric to JJ before refocusing her gaze on him. "I've read the file. We have a pretty good idea who kidnapped your boy and why. What we don't know is where they are now. But we will find them. I assure you of that. We have people everywhere. And we're good. Damn good."

Worry for Garth clawed at him again. Aware he'd be absolutely useless unless he forced himself to focus, he pushed it away. His inner bear grumbled at that. Eric didn't blame him. After all, he couldn't just lie there and do nothing.

"The human police will put out an Amber Alert," JJ interjected.

"Yes, and that can be very helpful to us in locating them." Linda glanced back at the doorway as if expecting the human police to come in at any moment. "Any sightings will be relayed to us, as well as human law enforcement. We just need to make sure we get there before they do."

"I agree," Eric said. "As a matter of fact, I need out of here. The sooner I can start looking, the better."

JJ exhaled loudly, drawing both Eric's and Linda's attention. "Look, I'm embroiled in this now. Deeply. And I still don't know what's going on," she said. "Now that I've become involved, maybe it's time to fill me in? Starting with who is DeLeon?"

For the first time, Linda appeared flabbergasted. Her brows rose as she looked at Eric. "You didn't tell her?"

"We're not mated," he said. Everyone knew shifter law expressly forbade revealing too much about species unless the individuals were personally involved.

"You know I'm Pack," JJ said.

"Everyone's Pack," he retorted. "And I told you I wasn't."

"So I know that you're something else, but not what. Drakkor, maybe? And I assume Garth is the same. I'm going to also guess that's why the Protectors are involved, since the Drakkor are nearly extinct."

"Not Drakkor." That was as much of an answer as he wanted to give.

Pursing her lips in disapproval, Linda shook her head. "You need to fill her in," she said. "We've all got to be on the same page."

"Okay, so you know, too?" JJ's wounded tone matched her expression. "Everyone knows what Eric is but me?"

Jaw tight, Eric looked down. Though he dreaded telling JJ, he had no choice. He knew how she'd respond. After all, he'd seen how other shifters reacted to his kind. Too many times. Seeing that look of revulsion in JJ's beautiful green eyes would kill him.

But finding Garth mattered more. And if JJ could help, he'd give her all the truth she could handle.

"I'm Vedjorn," he said, using the Old Norse word. "A bear shifter. As is my son." Bracing himself for her reaction, he waited.

Chapter 17

Eric held his breath. JJ eyed him, her gaze thoughtful rather than condemning. "A bear, huh? I've never met one before. I didn't know there were any bear shifters in California."

"My family immigrated there when I was very young. Originally, we're from Norway." Which JJ already knew, but he figured maybe Linda Felts didn't.

"Okay, so you're a bear. Rare. I get it. And the Pack Protectors are helping you. What I don't understand is why did someone kidnap Garth? He's just a baby. He can't even crawl yet." The anguish in JJ's voice mirrored Eric's own feelings, making him realize JJ loved Garth, too. "Does this have something to do with those three words that were written on the paper attached to that brick that came through Rhonda's window?"

"Yes." Linda answered for him. "There are a group of people, a cult, actually, who want you to offer the baby to them as your sacrifice, we think. They want to raise him, until they can see if he'll become Berserker."

"We know that already. What we don't know is what they'd plan to do if he doesn't," Eric said.

Linda continued on as if she hadn't heard him. "What we do know is these people appear to worship the Berserkers. They seem to be an odd mixture of many disillusioned shifters. We're not sure if they already have a Berserker in their midst or if they're merely hoping to breed one." She swallowed hard, glancing sideways at Eric before continuing. "Since Garth's mother might have been Berserker, you are aware that there's a good chance the baby will be one, as well."

"He won't," Eric insisted, his tone fierce. "And Yolanda wasn't. She was crazy, yes. Strung out on drugs and alcohol. But I shifted with her many times, and she wasn't a Berserker. Garth will be fine."

"You won't know that until he's old enough to shapeshift," Linda said smoothly. "But I agree, it's not something we need to worry about now. What we do need to worry about is his safety."

"Agreed." Again Eric tried to sit up. Dizziness made him freeze. Hoping no one had noticed, he eased his head back onto the pillow and willed his strength to return.

JJ looked sick. "What do they want to do to him? He's only three months old. Surely they won't hurt him?"

"Hopefully not," Linda interjected, her tone soothing. "We don't know exactly what they want to do with him."

"Even the possibility of anything happening is unacceptable." JJ glared at Linda before turning to Eric. "We've got to find them. And him. Now." She grabbed Eric's arm. Startled, he winced.

"Sorry." Releasing him, she took a deep breath. "Are you strong enough to leave? Because we need to save Garth. We have a better chance than anyone. No one else cares about him like we do."

"I know." He spoke with grim certainty as he ripped out his IV, an action that hurt like hell. "Help me get out of here. I need to find my clothes."

"They had to cut your pants off you," Linda told him. "And you need to stay put, at least until you've answered the human police's questions."

He was about to argue, but closed his mouth as a nurse appeared, no doubt alerted by the frantic beeping of the machine. "You pulled out your IV?" She shook her head. "Now we'll have to start a new one in your other arm."

Though his entire body vibrated with impatience, he managed to nod. "Sorry. I got a little bit agitated."

She bustled out, promising to be back in a minute with the supplies she needed.

"We don't have much time," Linda said, speaking in a low, urgent voice. "The police will be here at any moment. Right now, you just need to claim ignorance. You have no idea why anyone would abduct your son. As far as you know, it could be totally random."

"I feel like all this is just wasting time," he grumbled. "I need to *do* something."

"Our people are on it, I promise. And we need the help of all the human law enforcement agencies, so you've got to cooperate."

Though he didn't like it, he could see her point.

True to Linda's predictions, both the Forestwood police and the FBI came by and questioned him. Since there'd been a kidnapping and Garth was so young, not only had an Amber Alert been issued, but the FBI had assigned extra people to the case.

Eric stuck to a limited version of the truth. After all, it was no lie that he frantically wanted his son back. And though he—along with the Pack Protectors—had a theory, in reality he wasn't sure why anyone would want to go to such lengths to snatch a three-month-old infant.

Both the local law enforcement and the FBI agent promised to do everything within their power to bring Garth home.

After they left, Linda returned. "If you're ready to go, we've got a car out back." She handed him a pair of men's black slacks. "You're probably going to have to cut a slit in these so they'll fit over your bandage."

Accepting them, he thanked her. He motioned for JJ to close the curtain around his bed and wait on the other side of it with Linda. It was a struggle, but he managed to get the slacks on. "What about a shirt?" he asked. "I think mine should be around here somewhere."

"I brought another one." Linda stuck her hand inside the curtain and tossed a red sweatshirt on the bed. "It should fit you."

It did.

"Are you ready?" Linda asked.

When he answered in the affirmative, she yanked back the curtain. "Then let's get out of here."

"Don't we have to wait for the doctor to discharge him?" JJ asked.

"We'll handle that." Linda pursed her lips. "Just follow me and do exactly what I say."

While Eric felt he and JJ would do better on their own, for now he knew he had to trust the Pack Protectors to help. "Okay. Where are we headed?"

"The two of you need to go back home—to that woman's house where you are staying. Act like everything is normal—"

"That's impossible," JJ interrupted. "Rhonda's going to notice we're missing the baby."

Linda shot her a quelling look. "As I was saying, go

there. Go straight to your room and gather up whatever belongings you want to bring with you. I will send a vehicle for you half an hour after you're dropped off."

Eric nodded. "We'll have to stall Rhonda. Maybe we'll luck out and she won't be there."

"But what if she is?" JJ sounded doubtful.

"Then you distract her long enough for me to get to my room and close the door. If she sees my leg…"

Eyes wide, JJ looked at him. "What exactly do you want me to tell her?"

"Anything but the truth," Linda stated. "No civilians need to know anything about this, understand? We keep this to ourselves."

Which made sense, he supposed. Especially since they had absolutely no idea who they could trust.

As they drove back to his shop, both Eric and JJ were silent. He couldn't stop worrying about his son. The mental images that kept flooding him were the stuff of horror movies. He had to forcibly expel them from his head.

Instead, he tried to concentrate on what he'd do to the bastards who'd kidnapped Garth. In this, he thought like his bear self, because he wanted to rip them apart with his bare hands.

When they pulled up in front of his shop to retrieve his SUV, the first thing he saw was the bullet-ridden sedan, still parked where he'd last seen it. His gut twisted and bile rose in his throat.

"Why is that still here?" JJ wondered out loud.

"Right now, it's still evidence," Linda answered. "All the law enforcement agencies are going over it with a fine-toothed comb. It'll stay until they're finished with it."

"Who's it registered to?" Eric looked away from the car. The last time he'd seen his son had been when Garth had been securely strapped in his infant carrier in the back seat. "Surely the FBI will want an explanation of why we were even in that car instead of my SUV." He frowned. "I'm surprised they didn't ask me. Or did they?"

"They already did," Linda said. "You were kind of in and out, so JJ answered for you."

The mention of her name brought JJ out of whatever deep reverie she'd gotten lost in. She blinked. "What?"

"We were talking about that car." Linda pointed. "Eric was wondering what we told the Feds."

"Oh. I told them we were going on vacation with a friend. Exactly like you said."

"Vacation?" Eric needed to know how well thought out the Protectors had gone with their story. "Where?"

"Tybee Island, Georgia," JJ promptly replied.

"Good job." Linda flashed an approving smile before she turned back to look at Eric. "Now, I want you both to go back to Rhonda's and try to act normal. If she sees the leg, tell her you got hurt at the shop."

"I still think she's going to notice we don't have the baby." JJ's voice broke midway through her statement.

"Make something up. Remember, you have thirty minutes before we come back for you. Pack what you need."

JJ sighed. "Fine."

"Half an hour, people." Linda looked from one to the other. "Surely you can stall this Rhonda person for that long."

Eric nodded. "We'll figure something out."

"We will," JJ echoed.

"Good." Drumming her fingers on the steering wheel, Linda considered them both. "I'll pick you up around the corner. The two of you will have to pretend to be going for a walk or a drive or something. Just don't tell anyone anything."

Eric nodded. "I'd prefer to take my own vehicle."

"You can't."

"I'm not leaving it parked in her driveway. How about we meet you back at the shop?"

"I like that idea," JJ agreed. "As long as I drive."

After a moment of silence, Linda finally nodded. "Fine. Half an hour. Don't be late. I don't want to have to come looking for you."

Eric wondered if she knew she sounded like a mother chiding her two small children. The quick glance JJ shot his way told him she was thinking the same thing.

"Understood," he said. "We'll meet you at the shop in one hour."

"See you then." Linda started to walk away. She looked back over her shoulder and sent them both a casual wave.

"Right." He nodded, clenching his jaw. Actually, he had no intention of meeting anyone. He planned on heading out immediately to find his son. JJ would be welcome to come with him if she wanted. If not, he'd tell her he understood.

Rhonda met them at the front door when they walked in. "What happened to you?" she asked, eyeing his bandaged leg.

He muttered something about an accident with a piece of machinery at the shop, and hurried away to his room. Once he'd closed the door behind him, he listened while JJ attempted to make small talk with Rhonda. After a few moments, he heard her coming down the hall and closing the door to her own room.

His cell phone pinged, indicating a text. Checking, he saw it was JJ, wondering how much longer she had. He texted back, asking her if she could be ready in ten minutes rather than thirty.

She replied in the affirmative, saying she'd meet him outside. He wondered if she had an inkling of his plans. He rather hoped she did. Together, he and JJ made a pretty good team.

* * *

As she hurriedly tossed random bits and pieces of her remaining clothes onto her sheet, as Eric had suggested, JJ wondered what he was up to. Asking to meet earlier could mean he simply wanted out of the house, was eager to get started…or he had another plan in mind. Whatever it might be, she'd be on board with it.

Because the most important thing in all of this was saving Garth. Still, the surname of DeLeon was one she'd hoped never to hear again. Surely it was only a coincidence. She'd ask again, as soon as they were safely away from here.

Once she had enough to wear for a week, she tied the sheet up as best she could. Now the trick would be getting out of the house. Rhonda had a nose for intrigue and she'd soon sense that something was up, even though she hadn't yet noticed baby Garth's absence. That would only be a matter of time. JJ didn't want to involve her neighbor if she could help it. Rhonda had already done more than enough to help.

Her phone pinged. Another text from Eric. Go out the window. Great idea.

After lifting the sash, she tossed her makeshift bag out before climbing over the sill.

Once outside, she prayed Rhonda wouldn't glance at the yard and see her. She hurried to Eric's SUV, relieved to see he was already inside, in the passenger seat, with the engine running. She gave one last glance over her shoulder before climbing into the driver's seat. No sign of Rhonda. Good. The less she knew, the better, especially in this situation.

"What's your plan?" she asked. "I know you must be up to something, since you wanted to leave much earlier."

As she pulled out of the driveway, he didn't answer at

first. Instead, he directed her down the street and around the corner before asking her to pull over to the shoulder and park. "Look," he said, turning in his seat to face her. "You have a choice here. What I'm about to do might be wrong, but I feel in my gut it's what I have to do."

Somehow she knew what he would say before he said it. "You want to search for Garth alone."

One brow rose. "Exactly. I think I'll have a better chance if I don't have to play by the same rules law enforcement does. Plus they'll keep looking, with or without me, so there'll be double the chance to locate my son."

Slowly, she nodded. "You know they'll be furious."

"Yes. And they'll expend time and resources to locate us, because they'll think we know something we didn't tell them."

She liked that he included her by saying *us*. As if he knew she was with him, no matter what. "Do you not trust them?"

"Right now, I don't trust anyone." He shook his head. "Except you. I appreciate you being in my corner and wanting to help, despite barely knowing me."

Deciding to be honest, she gave him her truth. "I feel like I've know you forever."

When he grinned, she couldn't help but notice the attractive way the corners of his eyes crinkled. "Exactly. I'm not sure why that is, but I'm awfully glad we're friends."

Friends. Talk about quickly deflating her ego. Still, in a way, she knew he was right. The attraction remained, simmering beneath the surface, but they were definitely friends.

"Are you with me?" he asked. "Because we need to put as much distance between us and Forestwood as we can before they realize we're not going to show."

Feeling a low thrum of excitement in her belly, she nodded. "Let's go."

As she was about to shift into Drive and pull back into the street, Eric covered her hand with his. "Thank you," he said. "I don't know what I'd do without your support. I can't stop worrying about him. I'm praying he's safe. If they so much as touch one single hair on that baby's head…"

"They won't." She squeezed his hand hard. "Don't even allow yourself to think it. They clearly need him for breeding or something."

He exhaled. "Thanks again. I needed to hear that." He took another deep breath. "I need to drive."

"No. You have a wounded leg and you just got out of the hospital."

"I don't drive with my left leg." His grin showed he knew she'd give in. "And I know where I'm going. Please."

The please did it. With a sigh, she got out and switched places with him.

"Thank you," he said. Pulling out into the street, he headed east. "I'm going to pick up 87 and go south."

Surprised, she eyed him. "Where are we heading?"

"Poughkeepsie. My ex-wife has family there. I figure I'll start with them."

"Why? I don't understand. You said she gave up all rights to Garth shortly after he was born."

"She did." His grim expression told her there was more. "But then, after a month went by, Yolanda changed her mind. But she was unstable, using drugs, and when I refused to cooperate she began harassing me. She made horrible accusations, trying to get me arrested and thrown in jail. All so she could get her hands on our son."

"Is that why you traveled clear across the country to Forestwood?"

"Yes."

"And you think your ex is behind Garth's kidnapping?"

He exhaled. "Yolanda was killed shortly after I got here. She attacked a Pack Protector and shot him, then turned the gun on herself. She didn't die, but vanished from the hospital, and they found her body in an exploded car a few miles away. At least, that's what they think. No one has actually given me verification on that."

Struggling to absorb this information, JJ shook her head. "That sounds like the plot from an action-adventure movie. What happened to the Pack Protector?"

"Unfortunately, he died, too. He was one of my friends."

"I'm sorry." Staring, JJ didn't know what else to say. The craziness Eric had been living with since his son was born seemed unimaginable.

"Who's DeLeon?" she asked, trying to sound casual.

"One of the Pack Protectors assigned to the case."

Immediately, relief filled her. Shawn was human. He might share the same last name, but no way could he be the same DeLeon Eric knew.

"Why?" Eric queried.

"I used to know someone with that last name," she said. "My ex, actually. But he's human, so they're not related. Which is what I expected, but still…"

"With all the crazy things happening to me, you never know. Anyway," Eric continued, "before I left California, Yolanda's mother and sister were making noises about wanting to see the baby. It's entirely possible one of them might have been behind this."

"But they live here in New York?"

"Her mom does," he admitted. "But they've been estranged since before we married. I have no idea where the sister lives."

"Yet you still moved here?"

He sighed. "To be honest, I didn't even consider her mother when I chose Forestwood. I'd almost completely forgotten about her. It wasn't until Garth was kidnapped and I started racking my brain that I remembered."

The thought that his ex's estranged mother might have taken his son seemed staggering, but JJ guessed the reality of Eric's life made it a very real possibility. "Do you really think…" She couldn't finish.

"I do." His grim tone matched the tenseness in his jawline. "Especially if they're even half as crazy as Yolanda was. At the very least, it's a possibility I don't want to discount. So we're going to Poughkeepsie to pay them a visit."

Chapter 18

They were a few miles south of Kingston when JJ's cell phone rang. "It's Rhonda," she said, frowning. "I feel terrible sneaking out of her house like that. I should tell her something."

"Don't answer," he urged. "We'll fill her in later."

Though her stomach churned, she let the call go to voice mail. "She's going to worry, you know. And she's been a good friend."

"How long have you known her?"

"Not long. I met her when I moved to Forestwood a little over a month ago." She glanced sideways at him, just as her phone beeped to tell her Rhonda had left a message. "Why?"

He shrugged. "Just making conversation. Rhonda's been great. She seems like a nice woman. A bit flirty, but nice. But I promise you, the less she knows, the better. In about an hour, Linda Felts and the others are going to descend on her, wanting to know where we are and if she's heard from us."

"Which is going to confuse her."

"True. But how much better if she doesn't feel compelled to lie?"

He had a point.

"I left a message for my new boss, explaining I was going to have to pass up on the job. I told her I was sorry and that I'd try to come by and explain later. At least that way she won't be expecting me."

"Good idea."

They stopped for gas in New Paltz. After filling up, Eric typed an address into his GPS. Once he'd finished, his cell rang. "It's Linda Felts. I'm going to have to ditch my phone. As a matter of fact, you should, too."

Wondering if he might have gone a little crazy, she eyed him. "What? Why?"

"Because they can track our phones. They don't even need a warrant." He cruised to a stop on the shoulder and got out. When he climbed back in, he smiled. "I put my phone under the front tire. When I go forward, the car will crush it. Let me have yours." He held out his hand.

"No. I'm kind of attached to this one." She cradled it protectively. "It's new. I just got it when I moved to Forestwood."

"I'll buy you a new one."

She didn't like the idea of being without a phone. "But all my numbers are in here."

"I'll take out your SIM card. When you get a new one, we'll use that card to retrieve all your info."

Reluctantly, she handed over her cell. Again, he stepped outside, and walked around to the other front tire. When he returned, he squeezed her shoulder. "It's going to be okay."

Though she nodded, she couldn't help but wonder if she'd made a huge mistake.

When he put the vehicle in Drive and pulled forward,

she covered her ears with her hands. Childish, maybe, but she didn't want to hear the awful crunching sound when her iPhone was destroyed.

As they continued on, following the directions given by the dashboard GPS, JJ tried to relax.

"You're really attached to your phone, aren't you?" he asked.

She shrugged. "I am. I like knowing if I get in trouble, I have a way to reach help."

"Look inside the glove box," he said. "There are two budget cell phones in there. Pick one. And yes, it's only temporary. For now, it will have to do."

After doing as he asked, she removed the plastic case from one of the phones. "When did you get these?"

"Before I left Cali. You never know when something like that might come in handy."

Finally, they pulled up in front of a modest raised ranch. The robotic voice of the GPS announced they had arrived at their destination.

Suddenly nervous, JJ eyed the house. "Now what?"

"This is where Yolanda's mom lives. I'm going to ring the bell and, once she answers, introduce myself."

"Do you think she has Garth?"

Grim-faced, he shrugged. "I don't know. But I figure I'll be able to tell from her reaction."

"Just in case, do you want me to go around to the back and scope things out?" Her stomach might have twisted at the idea, but if Eric thought she should, she'd do it.

"Not yet. I don't know who all lives here. Just wait here and keep an eye out."

"Okay." She watched as he made his way to the front door. More than anything, she hoped little Garth would be found safe. Here in the arms of his misguided but loving grandmother rather than with some demented cult intent on doing him harm.

The front door opened, though Eric didn't go inside. As he stood conversing with whoever had answered his knock, JJ guessed from the tense set of his shoulders that it wasn't going well. A moment later, the door closed and Eric made his way back to the SUV.

"Yolanda's mother, Sophia, answered, but she didn't even recognize me," he said as he climbed into the driver's seat. "Of course, we've only met once. Another woman who claimed to be her caregiver told me Sophia has dementia. If that's true—and I believe it is—there's zero chance she was the one who came after Garth."

"I'm sorry." JJ squeezed his shoulder. "I know this is disheartening. What do you want to do next?"

He blinked. "I'm not sure. I was so convinced she had Garth, and now…" Her heart squeezed as he hung his head and took a deep breath.

"You're tired and not thinking straight," she said. "Maybe you should get some rest. Things might appear clearer in the morning."

"I'd like to find a place to change," he said, surprising her. "This area has lots of woods and thickets. Sometimes being my other self brings clarity to my mind. Let's find a motel to stay for the night. Maybe one near a restaurant, so we can grab supper before dark. I don't want to hunt on an empty stomach. I'm apt to kill too many small animals, and that would be noticed."

Heart pounding, she took a deep breath. "Would you mind if I changed and hunted with you?"

Among her kind, this was a completely ordinary request. Wolves were by nature pack animals, and the more the merrier. She wasn't sure how that was among bears.

It seemed to her that, in nature, they were much more solitary.

Eric appeared to be thinking while he drove. Though he didn't answer her right away, she had a feeling she'd crossed some forbidden boundary she'd known nothing about. Hurt stabbed her, swift and sharp, but she squashed it quickly. She had no right to expect him to do things just because her species considered it normal.

"Or do the Vedjorn not do that sort of thing?" she asked, more to give him an easy way out.

"Not usually," he admitted. "Though it's been a long time since I left Norway. In California, I mostly hunted alone. My ex came with me a time or two, but since our kind are few and far between, we'd both grown used to shifting by ourselves."

Hiding her disappointment, JJ managed a friendly smile. "It's okay. I understand. I guess you can go change, and then when you come back, I'll go out and do my thing."

Jaw tight, he shot a quick glance at her. "I actually wouldn't mind your company."

Her breath caught. "Okay. Sounds good then. Let's change before we find a motel and get dinner. After we hunt, we might not need to eat again."

Though he jerked his head in a nod, he didn't look at her. "Are you certain you…"

Since he let his words trail off, she tried to guess what he was asking. "Won't be intimidated because a bear and a wolf aren't normally running buddies? Of course not."

Now he glanced at her quickly, before returning his gaze to the road. "I was thinking more along the lines of won't find me repulsive. Believe me, I'm well aware of how the Pack regards my people."

"The Pack is a group of individuals," she pointed out.

"Not every single one thinks the same way as all the others. You know that."

At first he didn't respond. Finally, he gave a small nod. "Perhaps you're right." But his tone indicated he didn't believe her.

"Look," she said. "I've never met a bear shifter. But I've never been one of those who feel wolves are the best. Yes, there are more of us, but I recognize the others. Lion, tiger, panther, all the big cats—I'd love to meet one. And even though our town is well-known for harboring a Drakkor, I never witnessed her changing into a dragon."

His half smile made her heart do a quick flip-flop. Though still a long way from appearing happy, this was the best she'd seen him since Garth had been taken. "What are you trying to say?" he asked wryly.

"That my experience is limited, that's all. Heck, I've never even changed with other wolves before. Well, except for my mother. I have to admit that I'm very interested to see what it's like when you shift into bear."

"Probably much the same as when you become wolf." His expression grew serious. "You do know what happens after we change back to human, right?"

A tiny thrill went through her, settling into her core. "Yes," she answered, her face heating. "I'm aware." More than aware, actually. She actively hoped they could act on the fierce stab of desire they were sure to feel. As if she hadn't been fantasizing about doing just that.

"Don't worry, I can control myself," he said, dashing her hopes. "I won't touch you."

She wished she had the nerve to speak, to let him know she wanted him to touch her, aching for him with every fiber of her being. It had become a constant companion, this need for him.

They both were quiet as they drove to a large, wooded

park they'd passed earlier. Inside, JJ's heart pounded and she felt jittery, though she tried to seem calm and composed. She had no idea what Eric was thinking, whether he regretted whatever impulse had led him to agree to hunt with her.

They pulled into the deserted parking lot. At this time of the year, the woods were empty.

"Good," he said, sounding satisfied as he parked and killed the engine. "We have the place to ourselves."

Struck by a sudden attack of nerves, she opened her door and got out. "Let's do this," she said, sounding much more confident than she felt as she strode off into the woods. In the cold night air, her breath made little puffs ahead of her. Luckily, the waning moon provided enough light that they were able to make their way as humans. Once they became their beasts, their animal eyes would adjust much more quickly to the darkness.

He hurried to catch up to her. "You don't have to, you know. I won't think less of you if you want to back out."

"I get it." Slowing her pace, she exhaled. "If I seem a bit nervous, it's because of me, not you. I've never let anyone besides my mother see me shape-shift."

"Again, you don't have to. We can go our separate ways and meet up at a designated place when we're done, if you want."

"No." She stopped and turned to face him. "Let me have this experience, please. I consider you a friend and I'm looking forward to this." As she spoke, she felt a rush of expectation. Her words were true. Even if she wished Eric was more than a friend, at least she had that.

"Okay." He pointed to a narrow, apparently less used trail that veered off from the main one. "Let's try that way."

Suppressing a shiver, she did as he suggested. The cold had begun to seep through the soles of her shoes, chilling her bones. But that wouldn't last for long. Once she became wolf, her heavy winter fur would protect her.

Inside, her wolf paced. Already awake, her beast knew she would soon be let out to run. Anticipation overrode the last of JJ's human nerves.

Next to her, she sensed Eric's beast doing the same.

He caught her looking and nodded. "Raring to go. How about you?"

"The same." If only she could slow her racing heart.

Finally, they came to a small clearing and stopped. A large fallen tree off to one side would be the perfect place to stash their clothing. All around them were the faint sounds of nocturnal nature.

"Do you want to go first or shall I?" he asked.

The idea of stripping off her clothes in front of him and changing to wolf while he watched made her feel dizzy. "You, please. I want to see what happens when you become bear."

He stared at her hard, his face expressionless. "Okay. Whatever you do, don't let fear get the best of you. As bear, I'm pretty large and threatening, but I won't hurt you."

"I'll be fine."

At her response, he shrugged. "All right then. But don't say I didn't warn you."

Without waiting for her to respond, he peeled off his coat and placed it on the fallen tree. When he next proceeded to undo his belt, her mouth went dry. While a more polite person would have looked away, she kept her gaze trained on him, unwilling to miss a single second of this. For once, she wished for more light and less darkness, though she counted herself lucky that she was able to see him at all.

Next he removed his shirt, his skin gleaming in the moonlight. His muscles rippled with each movement, making her long to touch him. Luckily, her feet felt rooted in place as she waited for him to take off the rest of his clothes.

He stepped out of his shoes and socks without looking up. Now his jeans and underwear were all that remained. She held her breath, the anticipation building in her, even as her wolf snarled with impatience.

The jeans went and then, while she shamelessly ogled him, he dropped the boxers. She gulped and blinked. She had a few seconds' impression of him, impossibly large and already incredibly aroused, before he dropped to all fours on the forest floor and initiated his change.

Instead of the sparkling lights that surrounded a wolf shifting, she saw ripples of energy. Which made sense, because the change from human to bear had to be more powerful than human to wolf. While she watched, his perfect masculine body contorted. His bones stretched and elongated, and fur began to appear on his previously smooth skin.

And then, so suddenly she jumped back in surprise, a large brown bear reared up in front of her. Powerful, strong and breathtaking. It—he—eyed her for a moment before lumbering off into the underbrush.

Damn. Heart racing, JJ felt her fingers tremble as she fumbled to rid herself of her clothes. Finally, they were off, the frigid air bringing goose bumps to her naked skin. Like Eric had done, she also got down on her hands and knees, loving the feel of the damp earth and rustling leaves under her.

Once more she inhaled deeply, and she, too, began to change. Around her, the usual sparkling lights reassured her, even as she grimaced at the mild discomfort while bones lengthened and changed shape. For her, becoming wolf always felt like this, slightly painful and also invigorating. Though much smaller in body, she wasn't as fast as Eric, though once she gave herself over to her wolf she lost all sense of chronological time. As wolf, she lived in the moment.

Finally, her change complete, she lifted her muzzle to the wind to locate Eric's scent. Tangy and sharp as it was, she quickly located it, and loped off after him. When she caught him, he playfully rolled, inviting her to tag him with her nose. Once she had, she did the same, leaping and spinning in a manner more like a pup than a full grown she-wolf. It had been years since she'd felt this carefree and playful. Overjoyed, she grinned.

They played tag for a good while. Though he outweighed her by twice as much, Eric was gentle with her, careful of his massive claws and sharp teeth. For her part, she tried to do the same, though a couple times she nipped him in her excitement. He never protested or retaliated, making her wonder if he even felt anything through his thick fur coat.

If anyone had been watching, the sight of a massive bear and a good-sized wolf running together might have seemed like something miraculous. Or at least unusual. But as they chased each other and played, a deep happiness filled JJ's wolf self, a joyful contentment that even overrode her need to hunt. Once or twice, as a very young wolf pup, she'd played with similar abandon, until her mother had ended the hunt. She'd never thought she would feel this way again.

Her stomach growled, reminding her she hadn't eaten. She needed to hunt. Yet she was having too much fun to break it off, at least just yet. Her hunger pangs would have to wait.

Though not for long. A quick whiff of a scent had her turning, just in time to catch the flash of gray as a rabbit raced past. Without a second thought, she took off after it, leaving Eric to bring up the rear. Unlike wolves, bears were omnivores, she knew, just as comfortable eating roots and berries as meat. The need to hunt might not be as ingrained in Eric, but JJ felt compelled to follow the tantalizing scent of her natural prey.

Without heed to direction or distance, she crashed through the brush, running low to the ground. Eventually, she lost scent of the rabbit, raising her head to find she had no idea where she might be. Again, she lifted her snout and scented the wind. Nothing. Odd, since Eric's bear smell had been strong, almost overpowering.

Thinking hard, she remembered where the moon had been positioned, and took off in the direction from which she'd hopefully come. Several times she stopped and sniffed, slightly worried that she still could not locate Eric.

Just as she felt confident that she'd almost reached the clearing, she came across the same large boulder she'd passed a few minutes earlier. Which meant she'd been traveling in a circle. While wolves didn't get lost, as far as she knew, her bad sense of direction as human had translated to tonight's change.

No scent of bear reached her, but in the distance she heard a crashing sound. Something big, moving fast. Bear Eric? Or someone else? Instinct had her staying hidden, low to the ground, at least until she ascertained whether it was friend or foe.

The scent reached her at the same time as the snuffling sounds. Bear. Eric. With a joyous woof, she ran toward him, head-butting him hard enough that he staggered. Instinctively, he let out a startled snarl, which, had she not known him, would have scared the heck out of her.

Her stomach growled again, loudly this time. Panting, she wondered if Eric would object to one more hunt, a productive one this time. But no, he shook his massive head, and then moved off, looking back at her as if asking her to follow him.

After a few minutes, they arrived back in the clearing where they'd left their clothes. Eric stopped, eyeing her. She knew he wanted to know if she wanted to change back to human first, or should he.

Sitting back on her haunches, she considered. She had no way to communicate other than by body movement, so she couldn't tell him she thought they should both shift at the same time. She dipped her head at him, aware he'd take the gesture to mean he should begin.

A second later, he did.

Inhaling sharply, she initiated her own change. This time, going back to her natural state, the pain seemed far less and was over much more quickly.

Just like that, she found herself lying in her human form, stark naked on the cold, damp forest floor.

Restless and stimulated, she stretched once, her nipples pebbling from the cold, and pushed herself to her feet. Anticipation making her heart pound, she looked around for Eric, eager to see the force of his own arousal, hoping it would match hers.

Chapter 19

To JJ's disappointment, Eric stood with his back to her, already stepping into his clothes.

"Wait," she rasped. "Not yet." Her quiet plea reverberated with longing. Slowly, he turned, holding his shirt over the part of him that she most ached to see.

"JJ, we discussed this." He shook his head, almost as if by doing so he could shake off the primal urge of his body's desire. "Friends don't take advantage of friends."

"Friends don't make friends beg." The words slipped out before she had time to consider them. Once said, she couldn't call them back, so she decided she might as well run with it. "You know I want you. And I'm aware you want me, too. What could be the harm?"

Turning away, he continued dressing, as if he hadn't heard her. While she stood shivering, naked and aching, refusing to let the sting of his rejection win.

Finally, he faced her again. Now fully dressed, even in the shadowy forest he couldn't hide the desire blazing from his eyes. "Put some clothes on, please." He sounded as if he'd swallowed a mouthful of rusty nails. "You know I want you, JJ. But if and when we ever come together, it won't be because we've just shape-shifted. I want it to mean more than that."

Stunned, she lowered her gaze. How could she argue with that? Even though she knew coupling after shape-shifting was as natural as breathing.

No matter what words he used, she couldn't keep from feeling inadequate. As though her naked female form hadn't been enough to make him want her.

Dressing quickly, her movements wooden, she wondered how she'd ever face him again.

He must have sensed this. For whatever reason, Eric seemed unusually attuned to her emotions. But as soon as she'd finished dressing, pulling on her winter parka, he strode off, barking out a quick order to follow him.

If they hadn't been in an unfamiliar area, she would have done the opposite. Anything to keep from facing him and making herself realize he didn't need her, at least not in the way she did him.

Finally, they emerged from the trail into the parking lot. His SUV still sat there, under a streetlight. She kept as far away from him as possible. Once he'd used the key fob to unlock the doors, she climbed up into the passenger seat and turned her face toward the window.

Silent as well, he turned the key and started the motor. "The heat will take some time to come on," he said, his tone casual.

Small talk. She refused to acknowledge his comment, but continued to stare out at the dark parking lot and wait for him to put the SUV into Drive.

Instead, he reached out and squeezed her shoulder. Despite herself, she jumped.

"Come on, JJ. I don't break my word. Not if I can help it."

This got her attention. "Your word?"

"Yes. I promised not to touch you. No matter what.

We discussed this, well in advance of what we both knew would happen."

She closed her eyes. She hadn't had the nerve to tell him earlier how much she would have welcomed his touch, and after what had just happened in the woods, she didn't know, either. "It's okay," she said, pleased her voice came out steady. "We're friends, nothing more. I was just overcome after shifting. It happens. It's all gone now." A tiny white lie, but completely necessary.

With his gaze shuttered, he nodded. "All right. Now let's find a motel and bunk down for the night. We'll head back home early in the morning."

Her stomach chose that moment to loudly protest. "I need to eat," she said. "I didn't have much luck hunting earlier."

"You know what?" His remote expression relaxed. "I do, too. Let's find a place to grab a late dinner."

By the time they'd located a restaurant and taken a seat in a booth near the back, JJ felt better. "Listen," she began, gathering up her courage to tell him the truth. "I—"

"Can I get you two something to drink?" the waitress asked, interrupting. JJ ordered a glass of wine and Eric a beer. Once the woman had hurried off to get their drinks, JJ opened the menu and studied it.

"You were saying?" Eric asked.

Suddenly glad she hadn't spilled her guts, JJ shrugged. "I don't remember. Whatever it was, it mustn't have been important. Now to decide what I want to eat. Everything looks so good."

Eric nodded, taking one more glance at his menu before closing it. "I'm in the mood for steak," he said, studying her. "How about you?"

She thought of the rabbit she'd been chasing in the woods and her mouth watered. "Since rabbit isn't a choice on the menu, I'm going with chicken."

After bringing their drinks and taking their orders, the waitress promised their food would be ready soon and took off again.

"I'm sorry," Eric said, reaching across the table for JJ's hand. "I didn't mean to insult you."

Though she had a fleeting urge to cover her embarrassment with a flip remark, JJ decided if he could be honest, so could she. "I'm trying not to take it personally, but it's difficult. It's just…" She gave a helpless shrug. "It's just what we do."

He nodded. "I'll be honest with you, JJ. I want you. But right now, with Garth missing, I can't focus on anything else. And if you and I—when you and I—ever get together, I want to be able to give you my undivided attention."

Though warmth flooded her at his words, she hoped she didn't show it. "You're good, I'll give you that."

His puzzled frown didn't seem feigned. "Good?"

"At sweet-talking." She flashed him what she hoped was a careful smile. "Thanks. And know this. We will get Garth back."

"Yes. We will." Because the alternative was not only unacceptable, but unthinkable.

Their food arrived and they each dug in. JJ had to pace herself, feeling she could have shoved the entire meal in her face and inhaled it. Even so, she cleaned her plate in record time. But looking up at Eric, she saw that he, too, had finished.

"I wonder if we set a new record?" She kept her tone light, though the fact that she had to stifle a yawn before she'd finished might have ruined it.

"Maybe so."

After paying the bill, they drove down the street and checked into a single-story motel. The room they were given was small but clean, with two double beds.

"Are you going to be okay with this?" Eric watched her closely. She couldn't help but wonder what he'd do if she said no. Offer to sleep in the car? Of course, the knowledge that he wouldn't be touching her would make any woman feel at ease, right? Even if she still, despite everything, wanted more, she'd get over it. She had to.

"I'll be fine." Another yawn. "I'm so tired I don't care where I sleep. I just need a place to lay my head."

Despite her exhaustion, falling asleep seemed impossible. Her body craved rest, but she couldn't shut off her mind. She'd made sure to slip in between the sheets well before Eric came out of the bathroom, and yet the heat suffusing her had her fighting the urge to kick away the covers.

He'd emerged from the bathroom fully dressed, clicking off the lights before divesting himself of his jeans. Every movement, every rustle, had her imagining him naked beneath his covers. She couldn't help but wonder what he'd do if she crossed the space between their beds and joined him there.

Sometime after, she dozed. She woke to a sound she didn't recognize, the faintest noise, muffled. Listening, she pushed herself up on her elbows, wondering if she should alert Eric, just in case. As her eyes adjusted to the dim light, she realized Eric had gotten out of bed and taken a seat in one of the armchairs near the window. She could barely make out his outline, but he appeared to be doubled over, hunched in pain. And then, with growing worry, she realized what she'd heard had been him, trying hard to silence the sounds of his anguish.

Her heart broke. Without a second thought, she hurried from her bed and went to him. Kneeling in front of him, she saw he'd covered his face with his hands, and his shoulders shook with the force of his silent emotion.

What else could she do but gather him close to her? "It's all right," she soothed. "I promise, it's going to be okay."

The instant she touched him, he froze. As she gently peeled his hands away from his face, she wasn't surprised to see the gleam of moisture in his eyes.

"I'm sorry," he muttered, his voice breaking. "I'm just worried sick about my baby boy."

She kissed him then, aware she could do little to ease his pain other than offer herself. As a distraction, maybe, or in sympathy… Either way, she knew her desire, her need, could help make him feel better, if only temporarily. As for herself, well, maybe he could heal her, too.

As their lips touched, the jolt of the connection sent warmth through her. Opening her mouth to him, she let her tongue spar with his, finding the taste of him intoxicating and arousing. She knew he claimed he couldn't want her, but she also knew he needed something to take away the sharpest edges of his pain. She was willing to be that distraction, giving them both what they desired.

He turned, she shifted, and then she found herself straddling him. A bit shocked as she settled herself over his arousal—Shawn had never allowed this—JJ found she quite liked it. The fact that she wore only thin panties, while Eric had on boxer shorts, made the contact almost as good as if they were naked.

He stroked her with his fingers. Already wet, her body became slicker. She moaned, unable to keep from clenching herself around him as he pressed inside her. At her fevered response, he arched himself, thrusting up.

"That's it," he growled. "The clothing has to go. I need you naked, touching me skin to skin."

Hooking one finger into the waistband of her panties, he tugged them down over her hips. She lifted herself, stepping out of them as he hurriedly divested himself of his cotton boxers. His body, hard and thick, rose to meet her hungry gaze.

Heart racing, she couldn't resist touching him. As she closed her hand around his shaft, he groaned. His body throbbed. Frantic, she rose, settled over him again, then lowered herself slowly, until she'd sheathed him deep inside her. The feeling of fullness, of completion, so stunned her that she froze, unable to move, unable to breathe.

And then, beneath her, he brought himself up, going even deeper. She gasped, and rocked in response. Together, they danced the age-old movements of mating. As the pleasure built nearly to the point of explosion, he went still.

"Don't. Move." He sounded as if he spoke through gritted teeth.

Though the order had been clear, she could no more resist moving than she could stop her heart from beating. Though she tried to go slow, the frenzied need built inside her. This time, he didn't try to stop her. Instead, he let himself go along for the ride.

When her desire finally peaked, she shuddered again and again, as pleasure rippled through her in waves. A second later, he groaned and pushed himself even deeper inside her, his body pulsing with his own release.

As they held each other, sweat-slickened bodies gradually cooling, she realized they hadn't used protection. Their lovemaking had been too spontaneous for either of them to think about such a precaution. Foolish, but even worse, she wasn't on contraceptives. Though with Shawn she'd always vigilantly taken her birth control pills, she hadn't refilled the prescription last month, after she'd run out. She hadn't thought she'd need them, with no man on the horizon.

Keeping her concerns to herself, because Eric definitely had enough on his mind, she finally rolled away and headed to the bathroom. When she returned, she went to her own bed, feeling slightly awkward, a whole lot sore and way more satisfied than she probably should.

He got up slowly and, on his way to the bathroom, stopped and kissed her cheek. While she lay there dazed and ridiculously pleased, he continued on, closing the door quietly behind him.

Turning on her side, she shut her eyes and tried to will herself to sleep.

The next morning, Eric wasn't sure whether to be angry with himself over his shocking lack of self-control or to push it to the side until he had the strength of mind to deal with it. Right now, worry and fear for Garth consumed him, though JJ with her generous spirit and earthy sensuality had managed to make him forget temporarily. Despite what he'd told her earlier, turning away from her splendidly naked body in the forest had been one of the hardest things he'd ever done. Only the knowledge that giving in to a moment's intense desire could ruin their friendship had stopped him. He didn't know what he'd do without JJ's help and support. He could only hope the previous night's lovemaking hadn't managed to wreck everything.

After cleaning up in the bathroom, he'd walked past JJ and gone to sleep in his own bed, though he would have liked nothing better than to crawl in next to her and hold her. But while he knew he would have drawn comfort from the simple touch of her, doing such a thing might hint at promises he wouldn't be able to keep. Not now, maybe not ever. He refused to do that to her. In his mind, that would be an even worse betrayal than what had already occurred.

Somehow, despite his inner turmoil, he'd managed to sleep. When he next opened his eyes, sunlight spilled around the edges of the light-blocking curtains. In the other bed, JJ sat up and stretched, glancing over at him while he lay motionless and watched her through half-closed eyes.

When she got up and headed to the bathroom, he stayed in bed a few minutes longer, trying to calm his instantly roiling gut. If Garth had been here, Eric would have been the first one up, changing his son's diaper and warming a bottle. The thought made him ache all over.

JJ emerged a few minutes later. He tried to smile at her, aware his weak attempt probably resembled a grimace.

"Your turn," she said, her voice brisk. "Do you want first shower, or shall I?"

Grateful that she didn't want to talk about what had happened between them, he exhaled. "Do you mind if I go first?" he asked quietly. As usual, worry and fear continued to simmer within him, but he refused to give in to it again, as he had last night. "It'll just take me a few minutes and then the place is all yours."

"Okay." She seemed unusually shy. "I'm going to turn the TV on and see if there's anything interesting on the morning shows. Maybe I can catch the local news."

He took his shower the way he always did—hot and quick and furious. Once he'd toweled off, he felt at least fairly ready to face the day. While JJ showered, he planned to try and firm up his plans to find his son.

After he'd dressed, he emerged to find her standing motionless in front of the television. Something in her posture alerted him.

"What's up?" he asked.

"Come here," she said. The panicked undertone in her voice had him hurrying. "Look. We're on the news."

"On the news? That doesn't make sense. We haven't done anything wrong." He moved closer.

"The authorities are looking for these two missing people," the announcer said, flashing both his and JJ's photos on the screen. And then, to Eric's disbelief and shock, a video began, showing the recovery of a missing infant supposedly tied to the two of them. The baby had been found with a woman who was apparently trying to cross the international border, into Canada. Her name was not mentioned. The newscaster finished up with the news that the baby was safe.

Garth. It had to be.

For a second, Eric couldn't force a single word past the lump in his throat.

"Garth," he said, staring at the screen, not quite certain he could believe his ears. "They found him."

JJ nodded. When she turned her face to his, tears were streaming in silver tracks down her cheeks. "He's all right," she sobbed, her voice catching.

"Come here." Emotion made his own sound rough. He held out his arms. With a choked sob, she launched herself at him, wrapping him in a fierce hug. He held on to her, feeling as if he'd been drowning and had gone under for the third and final time before being thrown a life raft.

"He's okay, he's okay," JJ kept repeating. And then she stiffened and pulled away. "Eric, we've got to find out where he is. We need to go get him."

"Exactly. And we will. Get ready, as quickly as you can."

After sending her off to the shower, he dialed Linda Felts. Her voice mail picked up, so he left a message with his new number. He figured right now she was in the middle of a heck of a lot of craziness. He began packing up both his and JJ's belongings in preparation for checking out.

When JJ reappeared, her long hair still damp, she hurried over. "Well?" she asked. "What did they say?"

"I left a message. Let's grab breakfast on the road. I fig-

ure we'll head back to Rhonda's house and make it easy
for them to find us."

They got food at a drive-through and ate while he drove.

They pulled up in front of Rhonda's shortly before
eleven. The construction crews were busy working on JJ's
house. She bit her lip, looking from her place to Rhonda's.
"I think I'm going to go over and check on them," she said.
"Want to join me?"

With impatience thrumming through his blood, he managed to nod, not wanting to have to make explanations
to Rhonda alone. He kept his phone in his hand, silently
willing Felts—or someone, anyone—to call back. If he
didn't hear from her in the next half hour, he would make
a repeat phone call.

JJ held out her hand and he took it.

Inside, the workers had made tremendous progress. The
front entrance and hall looked completely repaired. It had
even been repainted. The soggy smoke smell had vanished,
also. The workers all seemed to be upstairs. He wasn't sure
if that was a good thing or bad. Maybe that meant they'd
finished repairing the downstairs.

"Wow." Eyes wide, JJ was turning in a slow circle.
"Amazing."

His cell phone rang. He started, his heart pounding.

JJ froze. "Answer it," she said.

As if he needed urging. He already had it out of his
pocket and his password typed in.

"Where the hell are you?" Linda Felts demanded once
he'd answered. "We've wasted valuable resources searching for you and—"

He cut her off. "Where's Garth? I saw on the news that
you found him. I want my son."

Silence. Then she sighed. "That's a long story."

His gut clenched at her ambiguous words. "I don't care.

You can tell me the story later. Not right now. Just let me know where I can go to pick up my boy."

"We'll bring him to you," she said. "Eventually. We've got some questions we're hoping you can answer first."

Unease coiled in the pit of his stomach. "Is this some kind of a trick?"

"Of course not. There's simply a lot more than meets the eye. We need to talk in person rather than on the phone."

"After." He snarled the word. "After I have my son, then we'll talk. Not before. Do you understand?"

"We'll be there in half an hour," she said, and then ended the call.

Dazed, he stared at his phone for a second.

"What the heck was that?" JJ asked. "Is everything all right?"

"I don't know." Pushing away his despair, he shook his head. "That entire conversation was strange. I'm beginning to wonder if that video was fake."

"What?" JJ gasped. "Why would they do something like that? It makes no sense."

"I don't know."

Coming closer, JJ laid her hand on his shoulder. "Linda is a Pack Protector, and as such, is held to a higher ethical standard. She—they—wouldn't trick you. They're on your side."

"Are they?" He couldn't keep the bitterness from his voice. "She never definitely said they had Garth. Though she did say they'd bring him to me, eventually."

JJ cussed, a rarity for her. "Hand me your phone. I'm about to call that woman and give her a piece of my mind."

"It's okay," he said, even though it wasn't. Not even remotely. "I don't want to risk antagonizing her. She'll be here in thirty minutes. You can tell her in person."

Chapter 20

Rather than dealing with explanations to Rhonda, they elected to wait at JJ's house. Eric insisted they complete the inspection, forcing himself to care that the downstairs area—his living space—appeared completely finished. There was even electricity again. And water. "I wonder if this means Garth and I can move in again. Once I have him back, that is."

Though a shadow crossed her face, she nodded. "It probably does. I confess, I'm almost afraid to go upstairs and see my place."

Which right now was the last thing he wanted to do. He couldn't keep from checking his watch, dismayed to see only ten minutes had passed since Felts's call. "We've got time," he said grimly. Actually, he wanted to start pacing, outside, where he could see the Protector's car pull up. Waiting infuriated and worried him. Especially since he didn't know if they were really bringing Garth or not.

Judging from the nervous apprehension on JJ's face, she needed a distraction almost as badly as he did. "Let's at least go take a look. Then we'll wait outside on the front porch."

She didn't move. "I'd rather just go outside now. I can't take the suspense, the not knowing."

This he understood. But he also knew it would be worse if they just stood there staring at the street, waiting for the vehicle to appear. "Come on," he urged. "Upstairs. Let's take a look. We'll hurry."

Reluctantly, she followed him up the stairs. They'd just reached the landing outside her living space when the downstairs front door flew open, hitting the wall with a thud.

"Freeze," a male voice shouted. "No one move. We've got this place surrounded. Eric Mikkelson and Julia Jacobs, you're under arrest."

Eric's first instinct was to shield JJ with his body. He wasn't sure what kind of game the Protectors were playing, but he didn't want her risking her life for his mess.

"We're here," he shouted. "Upstairs, on the landing." The hammering in JJ's living area stopped, which meant the contractors had heard him. Perfect. It never hurt to have witnesses.

"Come down with your hands up," Felts ordered. Good, at least he wouldn't be dealing with a total stranger.

He glanced back at JJ. Her petrified expression warred with the outrage in her eyes. "Put your hands up," he told her quietly. "And don't lower them until they say you can, no matter what."

She nodded. "But why?"

"I have no idea." Turning, he raised his hands and began making his way, step by step, slowly down the stairs. "Stay behind me."

When they turned the corner, he saw Linda Felts, her

weapon drawn, flanked by two others who, judging by the auras, were also Protectors.

"Where's my son?" he demanded, shooting her a hard look.

"He's safe." Her own hard glare infuriated him. "But we have a few questions for the two of you."

He'd already started shaking his head before she'd finished speaking. "Not until I have my boy."

"Are we being charged with something?" JJ asked, stepping out from behind him, in complete disregard of his instructions. "If so, you'd better charge us. And I'll be contacting an attorney, so if you do charge us with something, I'll be wanting to speak with her first."

After a quick, startled look, Felts shook her head and laughed. "Honey, we're Protectors. You know that. We are definitely *not* human law-enforcement. As Pack, we operate by our own rules, not the ones the human police and FBI have in place. You're under Pack law now. You don't get an attorney."

JJ swallowed, but to her credit, her expression remained undaunted. "I still have the right to know the accusations being made against me."

"Hello?" Rhonda was coming up the porch steps. "JJ, is everything okay in here? I saw you and Eric come back and then—" She stopped short as she entered the foyer and saw Linda Felts and her two armed agents. Fear flashed across her face, though she quickly hid it. "What exactly is going on here?" she demanded.

"That's what I want to know," JJ replied. "These people just showed up and claimed they're arresting us, but they won't say what the charges are. Not only that, but Eric's baby has gone missing and these people supposedly found him, but won't give him back to us. I think you need to call 911."

Involving the humans. Exactly the last thing the Pack Protectors would want. They'd really have a difficult time making explanations, since they couldn't tell humans the truth.

"Pack Protectors?" Her expression grim, Rhonda looked from one to the other. Linda Felts jerked her head in a grudging nod. She could tell by Rhonda's aura that she, too, was a shape-shifter.

"I thought your job was to uphold the law," Rhonda continued sternly. "Not break it. Stealing this man's child and now threatening to arrest them without good cause doesn't sound like the Pack Protectors we all know and love."

Wow. Even Eric was impressed by Rhonda's confident and authoritative tone. He saw the way Felts blanched, but the Protector stuck to her guns.

"This is none of your concern," she said coolly. "I suggest you simply turn around and march right back to wherever you came from. Unless you want to be arrested, too."

Instead of appearing worried by the threat, Rhonda laughed. "Just try it," she said. "I'm sure even corrupt Pack Protectors have to draw the line at cold-blooded murder."

JJ gasped. Clearly, the thought of being killed hadn't occurred to her. It had to Eric, though. And he knew he couldn't allow it to happen, because Garth needed his father.

"I'm not going anywhere," Rhonda declared, crossing her arms. "Not until I'm certain my friends here are safe."

Felts made a sound of disgust and holstered her weapon. "Stand down," she ordered, and the other agents did the same. Jerking her thumb toward Rhonda, she met Eric's gaze. "Who is this woman?"

"JJ's next-door neighbor. The three of us have been living with her while JJ's house is repaired."

"From the fire," Rhonda added helpfully. "Now I'm wondering if you Protectors had anything to do with setting that?"

JJ gasped again. "This is a mess" she managed to mutter.

"Isn't it?" Rhonda's voice was a mixture of gleeful and disgusted. She still seemed poised to attack at the slightest provocation. Inside, Eric's bear reacted to the hostility emanating from her and reared up, massive head cocked in interest. The urge to change, right then, right there, rocked Eric, but he managed to wrestle his other self quickly back into submission.

When he looked up, Rhonda was watching him with what he could only describe as a satisfied gleam in her eye.

"I don't understand any of this," JJ said quietly. "We were going to a safe house with your agent. Someone attacked us and—"

"Our agent was killed." Felts looked from JJ to Eric, her expression cold. "This is the second agent we lost while working with Eric. This time, we've received reputable intel that you two knew this was going to happen."

"That's ridiculous." Now furious, Eric glared at the Protector. "Explain our motives, please. And identify the source of this so-called reputable information. Because from where I stand, that is nonsense. It defies all logic. Not only was JJ knocked out, but I was injured in the shootout, and my baby was taken. How could you—how could anyone—possibly think I'd be okay with that?"

"It's not you we're concerned about." Felts swung her gaze around and pinned JJ with it. "It's her. One of the suspects we have in custody has told us Julia Jacobs did this in a twisted plot to gain control of your child."

Stunned into silence, Eric struggled to make sense of her words. JJ appeared equally shocked, already shaking her head. He waited for her to deny the accusations, but she remained silent. Even Rhonda now eyed her friend with suspicion and doubt in her gaze.

He thought about his ex-wife and how completely

Yolanda had fooled him. Was it possible that he'd been tricked again, this time by a warm and giving redhead?

No. "I don't believe it," he declared, earning a grateful look from JJ. "If she wanted Garth, she'd had numerous opportunities to take him. She's been my friend and his, and she'd never in a million years do something like this."

"Thank you." JJ finally found her voice, gratitude and something else resonating in it. "He's right. I don't know what's wrong with you people, but I'm not the bad guy in this situation. I'm also a victim here."

"What have you lost?" Felts asked, her tone skeptical.

JJ stared at the other woman. "My home, for starters. Is it true? Were the Protectors behind the fire?"

"No." Of this Felts appeared certain. "You never even came onto our radar until you decided to tag along with Eric and his son."

"Speaking of my son," Eric interjected. "Do you really have him safe or was that a ruse to get us to come in? Because so help me, if he's still out there somewhere, in danger from a bunch of religious fanatics, I'll—"

"Garth is fine. He's being looked after by our people."

Eric sagged with relief. Meanwhile, Felts continued holding his gaze. "We've arrested two people for his kidnapping. Your ex-mother-in-law and her nurse."

"What?" He blinked. "I visited my ex-mother-in-law yesterday. There's no way she could have been involved. She has dementia."

"There is some cognitive impairment," Felts conceded. "But she's still largely functional. We're still questioning her and the nurse. There are several more people involved in this. Julia Jacobs was specifically mentioned as one of them."

"By whom?"

"Does it matter?" Felts barked. "Why aren't you

more concerned that your supposed friend apparently betrayed you?"

"Because I don't believe it." Deliberately, he reached out and gathered JJ close. "And you still haven't explained to me exactly why you do."

Clearly frustrated, the Protector grimaced. "There are other things in play that we aren't at liberty to reveal yet. When the time is right, we will."

"But my son is safe, right?" Even though they'd already said he was, Eric wanted to hear it again.

"Yes."

"Then why won't you let me have him back?"

"We have to deal with all threats first." Felts dipped her head toward JJ. "There's no way we're letting him around anyone who might mean him harm."

While he appreciated their concern, he didn't understand why Garth was suddenly so important to them. Something wasn't right with their story.

Aware now, more than ever, that he had to be careful, Eric swallowed. "Was there ever even a real cult who wanted him? Or was that some bizarre story you cooked up for whatever reason?"

Again Felts glanced at Rhonda, who watched the exchange with avid interest. "I'm not comfortable with discussing this in front of your neighbor."

He agreed. "Rhonda, you should go. JJ and I will fill you in later."

"Are you sure you two will be okay?" Rhonda asked.

"Yes. Please leave. The sooner I can get through this nonsense, the faster I can see my son."

Though she huffed, Rhonda turned and went out the front door. "I'll be in my kitchen if anyone needs me," she called. "Just shout. I've got really good hearing."

Once she was gone, Felts sighed. "Your ex-wife might not be dead."

Convinced he must have heard incorrectly, Eric asked her to repeat herself.

"I said we believe Yolanda is still alive. And she's behind the attempt to steal Garth. She wants her son, according to her mother. And she'll stop at nothing to get him."

He shook his head in denial. "But you found her body, with Jason's, remember? A positive ID was made, or so I was told."

"And you still haven't explained why you think I'm involved in all of this," JJ added, her arms crossed and her expression tight. "I didn't even know Eric until he rented the bottom floor of my house."

"Do you know a Shawn DeLeon?"

JJ's expression froze. "Yes." Her clipped response seemed at odds with the stark look of fear in her eyes. "What about him?"

"He has friends who are Pack Protectors," Felts began. "Actually, his older brother, Frank, is assigned to Eric's case."

"Brother?" JJ frowned. "How is that possible? Shawn is human and Frank is Pack."

"Shawn is Frank's adoptive brother. It turns out that his parents took him in when Shawn's mother was killed in a subway accident."

"Frank DeLeon is related to Shawn," JJ repeated, as if she didn't believe it. "The Pack Protector who is helping Eric with his case."

"Exactly." Now Felts sounded bored. "And if you have a problem with that, you'll need to take it up with Frank."

"If you want to, JJ, we will. I keep waiting for him to make a reappearance," Eric stated. "I'm sure he could help you sort through everything. Frank DeLeon's a good guy."

"Maybe so." JJ cleared her throat. "His brother, Shawn, is not."

Eric looked from her to the Protector. "What does De-Leon's brother have to do with any of this?"

"He asked his brother to help him locate you," Felts said, eyeing JJ. "He also gave us some information that led us to believe you are more involved in this case than you let on."

"I'd be careful of believing anything Shawn DeLeon has to say." JJ sounded brittle, as if made of glass and about to shatter at any moment.

Still not understanding, Eric caught JJ's arm. "Was he your former boyfriend?"

Swallowing hard, JJ held his gaze. "Yes."

"He said fiancé," Felts corrected.

"No. We lived together, but were never engaged. And I broke it off a couple of months ago."

"Again, not according to him." It almost sounded as if Felts was enjoying herself. "He said when he refused to allow you to get pregnant, you ran off. And that you are so desperate for a baby, he's worried you planned to steal one. Is that what happened here, with Garth?"

"No." Keeping her chin up, JJ swayed slightly. Then she squared her shoulders and met Felts's gaze. "He's not only a liar, but he's dangerous. I'm sure he's furious that I dared to leave him. After all, he regards me as his property. Please don't let him know how to find me."

Felts cocked her head. "I'm sorry to say it's a bit too late for that. He already knows."

Eric caught JJ as she slid silently to the floor.

When JJ opened her eyes again, a jolt of sheer terror made her gasp. She sat up, her head pounding and her mouth so dry it might have been full of cotton.

"Hey." Eric's voice.

Blinking, she tried to focus, finally succeeding as he moved closer, into her line of vision. She saw that they were still inside her house, downstairs in Eric's living room. He'd evidently carried her there and placed her on his sofa.

"You've got to get me out of here." She didn't bother to try and hide the panic in her voice. "If Shawn comes after me, I'm as good as dead."

"Are you serious, or...?"

"Or what? Being dramatic? I can't tell you how many times he's threatened to kill me if I ever left him."

"Is he human or Pack?"

"Human."

Eric shook his head. "Then you were never in any real danger. Any wolves can defend themselves against a mere human."

"What?" She couldn't help but stare at him in rising horror. "You know the edict. I can't harm a human while in my wolf form. I'd be hunted down by the Protectors."

"Not if it was in self-defense." He seemed too calm, his voice flat and rational, she realized. Almost as if he was humoring her.

Then she remembered the lie Shawn had told the Protectors. A falsehood Eric apparently believed. That stung, but then again, she wasn't sure she wouldn't wonder which was the truth if their situations had been reversed.

"I would never hurt Garth," she said. "And I promise you, I had nothing to do with his abduction."

Chapter 21

JJ held her breath while Eric studied her. Finally, his expression softened. "I know you didn't. I'm just puzzled as to why Felts thinks you did. I've got a call in to Frank DeLeon to see if I can get this cleared up."

She winced. "If Shawn is his brother, it won't matter what you or I say. Blood runs thick. He'll help him."

"I wouldn't be too sure of that. Frank takes his job seriously. And this Shawn person sounds like an all-around bad guy."

"He's a stockbroker. Well respected among his peers."

After pulling out a chair next to the couch, Eric took her hand. "How about you fill me in? I had no idea you were in an abusive relationship."

To her horror, her eyes filled with tears. Swiping at them with the back of her hand, she took a moment to gather her composure. "I didn't know," she finally said. "I grew up in the city, and met him right after college. I wasn't sure what I wanted to do, and since my degree was in business, I took a receptionist job at the finance company he worked for. He was tall and handsome and sure of himself. Everything I wasn't. He drew me in the way a bright light attracts a moth."

Saying nothing, Eric waited.

"It started with small things at first. He didn't like my outfit, or the way I fixed my hair. Soon I was scrambling to please him, because he was always so right, and I wanted him to love me."

Now that she heard herself speaking the truth of their life, she could only wonder how she hadn't seen it sooner.

"The first time he hit me, he apologized. But he also said it was all my fault. If I'd been better, prettier, less *me*, it would never have happened." She gave a self-deprecating laugh. "And I don't know why, but I believed him."

"Until one day you didn't."

She nodded. "Exactly. Until one day I didn't." Swallowing hard to get past the lump in her throat, she shrugged. "And now I'm here. My great-aunt passed away and left me the house in Forestwood. I made sure Shawn didn't find out, and I left when he was at work. I didn't take anything that wasn't mine, because I sure didn't want to be accused of stealing."

"Did you have a car?"

"No. I took the train." Thinking about it made her smile. "When I got here, I had to take a driving class and get my license. After I had that, I purchased my car used. My mother was so impressed."

"Your mother?" Gaze sharp, he watched her. "What about your mother? Did she know? Couldn't she help you?"

"Oh, she knows. And she tries, but since she lives in Australia, there's not a lot she can do from so far away. We talk once or twice a month on the phone."

"Well, at least Shawn couldn't threaten her."

"True." Try as she might, JJ couldn't manage to produce a second smile. "That's one advantage to not having her close, I supposed. But even so, the distance didn't stop Shawn from repeatedly calling and harassing her. The last time I talked to her, she was changing her phone number so he couldn't keep phoning her."

"Come here." Eric pulled JJ into his arms. "It's all going to be fine, I promise. I'll get Garth back, and I'll make sure Shawn leaves you—us—alone."

With his muscular arms around her, she could almost believe him. She'd been strong for so long, and though she'd settled into her new life in her new town, in the back of her mind she felt like she'd been on the run. And damn if she wasn't tired of running.

"I'd like that." She sighed. "What happens next? Where did Felts and her people go?"

"They had no concrete evidence and couldn't arrest you, so I asked them to leave. I'm still waiting to hear back from Frank DeLeon."

"What about Garth?" JJ searched Eric's face. "When can you go get him, or are they bringing him to you?"

"I'm still trying to get confirmation on that." He grimaced. "But Felts did let me see video of him, which proves he's all right."

Relieved, she nodded. "Good. As for me, I really don't want to hang around here and wait for Shawn to show up."

"I agree." Smoothing a few wayward strands of hair from her face, he followed up with a quick kiss on her forehead. "Are you strong enough to walk?"

"I think so." To prove it, she sat up and swung her legs over the side of the sofa. She waited, but everything remained in focus. "I'm not even dizzy. I'm not sure why I fainted, but I've heard shock will do that to you sometimes."

Despite that, he took her arm. "Come on."

Walking with him to the door, she resisted the urge to lean into him. Though she would enjoy it, she didn't want him to think her weak or unsteady. "Where are we going?"

"To Rhonda's. If Shawn DeLeon comes looking for you, no doubt he'll go directly to your house. We can see everything from Rhonda's, and we should be safe there."

He had a point. Plus she wanted to thank Rhonda for standing up for them the way she had earlier.

Once they reached Rhonda's house, they found the door locked. "I can't say I blame her," Eric commented. "Things have been a little crazy lately." Lifting his fist, he knocked three times sharply.

They heard the sound of Rhonda's heels as she hurried to answer. "Come on in," she said, peering around them as she ushered them past her. "Where's your police escort?"

JJ waited to answer until they'd reached the kitchen. As usual, the warm yellow walls and bright artwork cheered her. "They couldn't actually charge me with anything, so Eric made them go." She climbed up on her usual bar stool. Rhonda went around to the other side of the island, fiddling with a mixing bowl full of what looked like cookie dough.

"Oatmeal cookies," she said, smiling faintly. "I tend to bake when I get upset. It soothes me."

"Those are my favorite." Eric took a seat next to JJ, taking her hand in his.

"Listen, Rhonda," JJ began. "I wanted to thank you for standing up for us earlier. You haven't known me that long, but I appreciate your faith in me more than I can express."

Rhonda looked down, appearing almost shy. "You're a friend. Both of you. I don't let anyone talk that way about people I care about."

"Thank you for that." Eric echoed JJ's words. "And if you need someone to help you dispose of those oatmeal cookies, I'm your man."

They all had a quiet chuckle at that. Rhonda began dropping dough by the spoonful onto a baking sheet. Once it was full, she slid it into the oven and set a timer. "In just a few minutes, you're welcome to have as many as you want."

As the delectable scent of oatmeal cookies baking filled the room, Eric inhaled. "I'll definitely take you up on that," he said.

"Good." Smiling, Rhonda filled a second cookie sheet to put in once the first came out. "Eric, I'm really glad they found your son. I'm sorry I didn't even notice he was missing. When are you supposed to get him back?"

"No worries." Eric checked his watch. "As a matter of fact, I'm waiting to find out when I will get him back. Actually, I'm tired of waiting." He stood, phone in hand. "If you ladies will excuse me, I need to make a call."

Both JJ and Rhonda fell silent, watching as Eric walked outside to the front porch. Once he'd gone, JJ filled Rhonda in on everything that had transpired after the other woman had left.

"A crazy ex-boyfriend?" Rhonda's brows rose. "Wow, I never would have guessed it. I'm glad you found the courage to get out of that situation. A lot of people don't."

JJ studied Rhonda's carefully neutral expression. "You sound as if you speak from experience," she said.

"Actually, I do." Rhonda grimaced. "I know exactly where you're coming from."

Before JJ could ask her to explain, several gunshots went off outside, one right after the other.

"Eric!" Jumping up, JJ ran for the door. Behind her, she heard Rhonda's oven timer sound.

"Wait!" her neighbor yelled. "What if it's Shawn? Don't go outside until you know what's going on."

Almost to the front door, JJ skidded to a stop. She turned as Rhonda rushed up behind her. "Eric's out there."

"I know." Shouldering in front of her, Rhonda pushed her back. "I'm an uninvolved third party. Let me go check things out. You hang back until I give you the all clear."

Before JJ could speak, Rhonda went out the front door. Stunned, JJ hesitated for all of three seconds before going after her. No way was she leaving Eric out there to fend for himself, not to mention letting her friend put herself in danger.

Heart pounding, JJ at first didn't see anything, squinting as she was into the bright winter sunlight. Rhonda's front yard was empty. Next door, though, at JJ's place, a small crowd of people had gathered. She spotted Rhonda's fuchsia sweater on the fringes and ran over to join them.

Rhonda turned as JJ reached her. "It wasn't a gunshot," she said, her voice relieved. "One of the construction workers had an accident with one of the nail guns. He's hurt and an ambulance is on the way."

"I'm so sorry." Feeling bad for the worker, JJ nonetheless couldn't help searching the area for Eric. Sirens grew closer and an ambulance pulled up, lights flashing. As the paramedics got out and began administering first aid to the wounded man, most of the neighbors dispersed, heading back to their homes. And still no sign of Eric.

"Rhonda?" JJ caught her friend's arm. "Have you seen Eric? I know he came outside to make that call."

Rhonda frowned. "No. But his SUV is still here. Maybe he went inside to his own place."

Breathing a sigh of relief, JJ nodded. "You're probably right. I'm going to go check on him."

"I think you should leave him alone. He's going through an awful lot right now." Rhonda's tone sounded a tiny bit sharp. "Give him his space. He'll come back when he's ready."

Maybe Rhonda was right. After all, Eric had wanted to talk in private. JJ didn't want to intrude by barging in on him. Still…she couldn't shake the feeling that something might be off. She wasn't sure what or how, but even as she turned to follow Rhonda back to her house, she questioned whether or not she was doing the right thing.

"Come on," Rhonda urged. "Those oatmeal cookies might still be warm. And if they're not, I've got another batch ready to put into the oven."

Eating cookies was the furthest thing from JJ's mind, but she managed to smile and nod. "I'm game," she said.

As she followed Rhonda down the hall toward the kitchen, she wished she could shake the ominous feeling that something was very, very wrong.

Once Eric had informed Frank DeLeon's assistant that he'd hold until the Protector was located, the woman took him up on his offer to do exactly that. He held, listening to tinned Muzak, and held, and held, until he wanted to throw the phone against the wall in a fit of anger.

After the first fifteen minutes, about to hang up and dial again, he heard a commotion outside. A nail gun, maybe. Then sirens indicating an ambulance. Curious, he went to the window to check it out, just in time to see one of the construction workers loaded up to be taken to the hospital.

Then Frank came on the line. "What's up?" he barked, his voice stressed.

Immediately, Eric tensed. "I'm calling to get an ETA on my son's arrival," he retorted. "Infants his age don't do well away from their parent for too long."

The silence on the other end stretched on for the space

of several heartbeats. "Uh, yeah," Frank finally said. "We're working on that. It'll be soon, that's all I know."

"This is ridiculous." Letting his frustration show, Eric muttered a curse. "Damn it, I just want to see my boy."

"Look, I've got company here. I'll have to call you back." And the Protector hung up the phone.

Eric cursed. While normal social niceties might demand he wait to hear back from the other man, this was not a normal situation. He punched Redial, listening as the phone rang and rang. Finally, voice mail picked up.

Well, two could play that game. He punched Redial again. Voice mail. And he tried once more. Voice mail. Whatever the hell DeLeon was up to pissed Eric off. And worried him. Until he had Garth back, he couldn't take anything for granted.

Just as he was about to try calling again, his phone rang. "What the hell, DeLeon?" Eric snarled. "Now is not the time to play games."

"I just had a visitor," DeLeon began.

The hair on the back of Eric's neck stood up. "Your brother?" he asked. "Shawn?"

"How do you...? Never mind. Yes, Shawn. We've got a major problem. There's a bit of a situation."

"Involving Julia Jacobs? Because Felts and her crew already questioned her. Your brother has a personal vendetta against her and his intel can't be trusted."

"I know." Exhaustion and strain warred with each other in DeLeon's voice. "That fact has recently been hammered home. This is my adoptive brother, damn it. But what he's done this time... Listen, I might as well level with you. I had one of my people drop Garth off here so I could personally return him to you. Shawn tied me up and took off with the baby. My assistant walked in and just freed me."

"Took off with... Why?" Feeling his heart drop, Eric

struggled to make sense of it all. "What the hell does your brother want with my son?"

"That's just it. He doesn't want Garth at all. He says he'll exchange the baby for the girl."

At first Eric didn't understand. "The girl?" Then, as he realized what Shawn DeLeon wanted, horror filled him. "You mean JJ?"

"Yes. And he wants it to go down in an hour, right after dark. At the crossroads of Fifth and Elm, near the cemetery. He says if we don't do what he asks, the baby is as good as dead."

And if JJ went to Shawn, he'd kill her. Rage filled Eric. He muttered something along the lines of he'd call DeLeon back later. Jamming the phone into his pocket, he ran outside and hurried next door to Rhonda's house.

"JJ!" he called, rushing up the steps, inside and down the hallway. "JJ, where are you?"

He found her in the kitchen with Rhonda. Both women looked up as he ran in. "I need to talk to you privately," he said, grabbing her arm. "Sorry, Rhonda."

"It's okay." JJ shook off his hand. "Rhonda's on our side. You can talk in front of her. What's going on?"

Breathing hard, he took a second to catch his breath. Then he told her what DeLeon had said. "And he wants you in exchange for Garth. He's demanded we meet tonight, near the cemetery at Fifth and Elm. In less than an hour. It's already dark outside."

Eyes narrowed, Rhonda stepped in front of JJ as if to protect her. "You're not seriously thinking of doing this, are you?"

At first he didn't answer.

"You are, aren't you?" Rhonda shook her head. "Men. You're all alike."

JJ moved around in front of the other woman. "It's

okay," she said. "Actually, I think Eric needs our help to come up with another plan."

Relieved, he nodded. "Exactly. And that's why I wanted to talk to you alone."

"I'm glad you didn't." Rhonda came around the other side of the island, a heavy cast-iron skillet in her hand. "Because now I know what I have to do."

She swung. He felt an instant of blazing, red-hot pain before he fell.

JJ jumped back, her heart pounding as Rhonda slammed her skillet into the back of Eric's head. He went down like a bowling pin hit by a heavy ball. As she rushed to Eric's side to check on him, she cradled his head in her hands and checked for a pulse. His heart beat steady and strong, despite the egg-sized knot coming up on the back of his head. "Rhonda!" She glared up at her friend. "You didn't have to do that. He wasn't going to overpower me and drag me to the cemetery."

"No, he wasn't." Something in Rhonda's tone made everything inside JJ tighten. "But I will."

JJ saw Rhonda swing the skillet right before it hit her.

Chapter 22

When JJ came to, her head aching, she was in the back seat of a car. Trussed and tied like a Thanksgiving turkey, she could barely move. But she was able to lift her head just enough to see Rhonda in the driver's seat.

"I don't understand," JJ managed to say. "Rhonda, please. Tell me what's going on."

They made a right turn and Rhonda slowed, finally pulling over. "We're at Fifth and Elm," she said, her voice an odd mixture of both sad and satisfied. "I'm bringing you here to exchange you for Eric's baby."

Once again, her friend had managed to surprise her. "You knocked both me and Eric out to *help* him?"

"No." Rhonda sighed. "I'm not exchanging you for Garth to get the baby back to Eric. The baby's mother—a lovely woman named Yolanda—contacted me shortly after Eric moved into your house. After listening to her story, I agreed to help her. Whatever wrongs she might have done, whatever mistakes she made, those don't give him the right to deny her access to her own child. She's been broken up about this."

"You're helping Yolanda, someone you barely know?" JJ struggled to understand. "I considered you a friend."

"I am your friend," Rhonda said decisively. "Believe me, you'll thank me when this is over."

"Thank you? For delivering me to a man who's surely going to kill me? For taking an infant away from a father who loves him? How could you possibly think I'd thank you for that?"

Rhonda sighed. "Because there's a lot more going on here than you know. I know you've heard the term *Berserker*, but are you aware what it really means?"

Slowly, JJ tried to shake her head, wincing at the pain. "Crazy killer, is my guess," she said. "Though Eric insists Yolanda wasn't one."

"Berserkers stem from an affliction among bear shifters. When they change, they become a focused killing machine. Nothing can stop them. Nothing except death. Little Garth is believed by his own mother to be a Berserker. Of course, no one will know until he's old enough to shapeshift, but he must be safeguarded until then. Yolanda will protect him."

Still struggling to make sense of Rhonda's words, JJ swallowed. "Protect him from what? And if you have no way of knowing whether or not such a tiny infant is going to become this Berserker, how can you possibly hold it against him until he's a teenager? I believe bears are just like the rest of us. Children can't change their form until they're in their teens."

"This child is different. Yolanda said she'd seen him start to shift. She knows they'll kill him once they learn what he is. She's only trying to save her son."

"Yolanda is lying. I've spent a good bit of time with

Garth. Not once did he ever act like anything other than a normal, three-month-old baby. He certainly isn't shape-shifting."

As she stared down at her silently, Rhonda's expression told JJ she didn't believe her.

"Please don't do this." JJ let her fear and worry sound in her voice. "Please, Rhonda. I'm begging you." There had to be something more, something she was missing. Because otherwise, Rhonda's desire to help a woman she barely knew made absolutely no sense. "What is it you're not telling me? There has to be more to this than you're saying. Otherwise, I don't understand what you're doing. Help me understand." Even talking hurt. She wondered if Rhonda's skillet had dislocated her jaw.

Rhonda went silent for so long JJ feared she wouldn't answer. "I've been there," she finally said. "Where Yolanda is now. But my ex took my daughter overseas. I never saw her again. She'd be a teenager now." She sighed, the sound heavy. "So I couldn't let another woman go through what I did. Eric seems like a nice guy, but what he's doing is wrong."

"Except you don't know all the facts, do you? All you're going on is what Yolanda told you. You've never discussed any of this with Eric. You don't have his side of things. He's told me a little about all of this, and Yolanda was doing drugs and partying. She got involved with a group of people that sound like a cult. They're wanting little Garth—our sacrifice for their greater good, as they see it. Remember that brick that came through your window? The note read 'Abomination, valor and sacrifice.' That was from them."

For a moment, Rhonda appeared torn. "How do you know this? Are you a hundred percent certain?"

"The Pack Protectors are involved. They're trying to

protect Garth. Eric, Garth and I were on our way to a safe house when someone attacked us and one of the Protectors was killed."

Rhonda closed her eyes. "Now I'm not sure. Everything seemed so clear. Listening to you has done nothing but confuse me. You've gone and muddied the waters."

This gave JJ hope. Maybe, just maybe, Rhonda would change her mind before handing her over to Shawn. She shuddered, well aware of how powerful his need for revenge would be. Still, she'd gladly walk into the bowels of hell if by doing so she could save Garth.

"Maybe I should reconsider." A note of panic had crept into Rhonda's voice and she rubbed her temples. "I need a little more time to think about this."

A sharp rap at the window made her jump. Heart pounding, JJ saw Shawn's face pressed against the glass. When he spotted her, a slow smile spread across his patrician features. "Good. You tied her up for me. Thank you. And you're early. Come with me and I'll take you to the baby."

"Don't do it, Rhonda," JJ urged in a low voice. "Once he gets you outside alone, he won't honor his bargain."

"That's where you're wrong," Rhonda said. Her smile chilled JJ's blood. "Because he has no idea what he's dealing with."

Eric came to, his head throbbing. He sat up too quickly as he remembered what Rhonda had done. Everything spun. She'd knocked him out. But why? Pushing to his feet, he held on to the kitchen counter until the room stopped moving. Moving as fast as he could, he checked out every room. No sign of either Rhonda or JJ. Which could mean only one thing. Rhonda had taken JJ to the cemetery to make the exchange. He'd have to figure out the why of it all later. For now, he had to get out there now.

Though it felt as if a sledgehammer relentlessly slammed into his head with every step, he ran to his SUV. Jumped in, found his keys and sped toward the cemetery. Once there, he figured he'd play it by ear. If worst came to worst, he'd shape-shift and let his bear self deal with Shawn DeLeon. The human wouldn't know how to react to a massive grizzly looming over him.

Traffic was light and he made it to the corner of Fifth and Elm in record time, turning on Elm to pull into the first entrance and park. The cemetery took up two blocks on Elm, stretching all the way to Third. This time of the year after dark, the place was deserted, which no doubt was why Shawn DeLeon had chosen it.

Now Eric had to find Rhonda, JJ, and hopefully Shawn and Garth.

Getting out of his car, he considered his next move. JJ had seen him as bear, so she wouldn't be alarmed. He figured shifting would only be to his advantage.

He stepped behind a huge oak, stripped off his clothes, dropped to the ground and initiated the change. He pushed his body to shift as quickly as possible.

Slam. It hurt like hell, especially with his still-aching skull, but he did it. Then, using his powerful bear nose, he lifted his massive head to the wind and tried to catch a whiff of anyone's scent.

Nothing. Just damp earth, decaying leaves and a bite of winter. Disappointed, he began moving, aware they had to be here somewhere. He hadn't been unconscious long enough for Rhonda to have already handed JJ over to Shawn.

A sound reached his ear, a faint wail that seemed to come from underground. It was almost unearthly, if he hadn't been so familiar with the cry. His heart skipped a beat. Garth. On all fours, Eric raced in that direction, keeping all his animal senses on high alert.

As of yet, he saw no sign of any of the others. While Garth was his first priority, no way was he letting Shawn DeLeon get his hands on JJ if there was anything he could do to stop it. And Rhonda. He had no idea how she was involved, but she had gotten in the middle of a mess.

The eerie sight of so many tombstones and trees, along with fading mementos left by loved ones, would have been spooky to a human, stumbling along in the dark night without a flashlight to guide his way. The waning moon provided little light, especially with the cloud cover. Luckily, his bear eyes could see better in the dark than when human. Again, he heard Garth cry. He went utterly still, moving only his gaze across the desolate landscape, trying to get a bead on the cry. Again, the sound seemed to come from under the ground. Had Garth been buried alive? If Shawn DeLeon had harmed that baby in any way, laws be damned. Eric would rip him apart, limb from limb.

Someone screamed, distracting him. Male or female, he couldn't tell, though part of him hoped it had been Shawn. JJ might have been captured. Rhonda, too. But JJ had one distinct advantage over any human. If she'd use it.

Another scream sounded, softer this time. At least he'd been able to pinpoint the direction. He started off, moving swiftly on all fours, keeping as low to the ground as possible.

Scent reached him first—the overwhelming musky smell that always signified humans. Then a light floral odor that he recognized as JJ. Rhonda, too, along with a masculine, too-heavy cologne that had to be Shawn. The one scent he most wanted to detect—the baby powder and milk of Garth—seemed oddly absent.

As Eric drew closer, their words drifted to him on the

breeze. They were arguing. And when they finally came into focus, he saw Rhonda facing off against a tall, slender man who must be Shawn. JJ, who was either tied up or unconscious, lay on the damp earth in front of him.

"Look, you promised me the baby," Rhonda said, her voice low and furious. "I brought your ex-girlfriend, now give me the kid."

"I promised you nothing," the man sneered. "I made a deal with my adoptive brother, not you. If you chose to go around behind his back, that's your problem. I'm not turning the baby over to you."

Rhonda growled, the low and guttural sound a warning Eric well recognized. Shawn even stepped back, his eyes widening. Though he no doubt had no idea what that growl could mean, he knew enough to be aware it wasn't good.

JJ struggled to sit up. "Rhonda, don't." Her sharp voice told him she knew what Rhonda meant to do. "Shawn, I'm not going back with you until I know Garth is safe."

"You don't have a choice." Just like that, his confidence returned. "You're tied up, with no way to escape. So it's safe to say you'll go wherever I want you to."

This time JJ snarled. Eric knew if he didn't act fast, she'd shift to wolf and attack. And if she did, Shawn wouldn't reveal where he'd hidden little Garth.

With a roar, Eric reared up to his full height and lumbered into the midst of them.

Rhonda jumped back, clearly startled. Shawn froze, his mind apparently struggling to process what had appeared right in front of him. And JJ, looking up at him, started to laugh. "My knight in shining armor," she said, her words clear enough to let him know she hadn't been seriously injured. "If not a bear, he'd have been facing a wolf any second now."

Eric moved over and placed himself between her and

Shawn. Shawn moved backward so quickly he tripped over his own feet and nearly fell.

As Eric opened his mouth to issue another threatening growl, Garth cried out again, his hungry cry. This time, Eric could tell the sound seemed to be coming from a few feet away, but *below* them. He bared his teeth.

"Where's the baby, Shawn?" JJ demanded, pushing herself up awkwardly into a standing position. Even with her hands still tied behind her, she faced the other man with her chin up. "Bring out the baby or I'll have the bear attack you."

Shawn's eyes darted from her to Eric. Unbelievably, he appeared undecided as to what course of action to take.

Rhonda chose that moment to step into the fray, grabbing JJ and spinning her around. "Is that Eric?" she demanded, jerking her thumb toward him. "Because if so, you need to be extremely careful what you ask him to do."

"You think?" JJ glared at her neighbor. "Considering you knocked both of us out so you could meet my ex here at the cemetery and become party to abducting a baby, maybe you aren't the one to be offering advice."

Garth's cries went from whimpers to out-and-out wailing, which meant he wanted a bottle *right now*. Glancing at JJ, who understood and nodded, Eric dropped to all fours and moved rapidly in the direction of his son's cries.

"Stop him," Shawn ordered. "Don't let your pet maul the kid."

As he got closer and closer to Garth, Eric was able to pinpoint where the cries were coming from—a massive stone crypt, ancient and covered with dying moss. Circling it, he used his shoulder to push on the door to see if it would open. It did not.

Spinning around, he gave a furious roar.

"He wants you to open up that crypt," JJ said to Shawn.

"And Rhonda, do you think maybe you could untie my hands now?"

Instead of rushing over, Shawn began to edge away in the opposite direction.

"Hold on," Rhonda shouted, rushing to block his exit. "You're not going anywhere, buddy."

Even as bear, Eric could have predicted what would happen next. Shawn swung at her, clearly having no qualms about striking a woman. With moves worthy of a professional boxer, Rhonda arched away, narrowly missing his blow.

And then, with a furious snarl, Rhonda dropped to all fours, still fully clothed, and began to initiate a change.

JJ reacted from pure instinct. "No!" she shouted, slamming herself into Rhonda before she could shape-shift. Changing in front of a human who wasn't one's mate was a crime punishable by imprisonment or even death.

Surprised, Rhonda rolled. "What the hell was that for?" she demanded, launching herself to her feet, fists up, looking as if she wanted to go a few rounds in a boxing ring.

"You know." JJ glared right back. "Now untie me so we can go rescue the baby."

To her surprise, Rhonda did as she asked. Once her wrists were free, JJ shook them to try and get the circulation going again.

"You know if you go into the crypt, he's going to lock you inside with that baby," Rhonda said. "Which is why I'm not going in there."

"Maybe." JJ shot her ex a disparaging look. Next to Eric as grizzly, Shawn didn't seem nearly as intimidating. "Or you will. I'm not an idiot. Which is why Eric there is going to make sure that doesn't happen."

Nodding his huge head in agreement, Eric crossed the

space between them and the crypt, taking a position next to Shawn.

"Thanks," JJ said. Then, in case he hadn't figured everything out yet, she jerked her head toward Rhonda. "She tried to exchange me for Garth, just so you know. Apparently, she and Yolanda worked out some sort of agreement. Yolanda wants her son back. Rumors of her death appear to have been greatly exaggerated."

Eric's bear blinked, which she guessed was his way of letting her know he understood. Meanwhile, poor little Garth had worked himself up into a frenzy, hiccuping in between frantic cries. Her stomach knotted. They needed to hurry up before the air ran out.

"Now, Shawn, show me how to get into the crypt," JJ barked. She couldn't help but notice the way he gave a little start before shooting the bear a worried glance.

Reluctantly, and moving slowly enough that JJ suspected he was working on an alternate plan, Shawn shuffled over to the crypt. He reached behind a stone marker and twisted something—obviously some sort of hidden lever—and the massive door began to slide slowly open. As it did, Garth's cries sounded clearer and much closer.

It took every ounce of self-discipline she had to keep from rushing inside the crypt for the baby.

"How did you find out about that?" Rhonda asked, the admiration in her voice infuriating JJ.

Shooting Eric yet another assessing glance, Shawn shrugged. "I watched a documentary on old graveyards. They featured a crypt similar to this one. When I arrived here early, I couldn't figure out where to put the kid. So I checked out a couple of crypts. This one had the gears to open it up. Perfect place to stash him."

"Yeah, until he ran out of air," JJ said. Shawn's frown told her he hadn't even considered that horrifying possibility. "Then you would have been guilty of murder in addition to kidnapping."

"I'll be fine," Shawn retorted. "My adoptive brother is in law enforcement. FBI, I think. He'll take care of me. He always does."

"Not this time." JJ took great pleasure in saying those words. The crypt was finally open. "Eric, I'm going in," she said. "Watch my back."

Chapter 23

The giant grizzly nodded. As JJ took a deep breath and stepped into the dank darkness, little Garth stopped crying. She froze, uncertain now which direction to move. She didn't know what she'd do if she bumped into a skeletal body or a coffin or whatever they put inside these things.

"Garth?" she called out, using the singsong voice he always responded to. "Where's my little Garthy-poo?"

He made that little snuffling sound, with his small fist in his mouth, that she loved so much. Which was enough for her to judge how close he was. Had Shawn placed him on the frigid ground or on, heaven forbid, a cement ledge, shelf or a casket?

Taking a deep breath, she tried not to think about where she was or how awful it would feel to get locked in this place. Luckily, little Garth had no idea—all he knew was cold and darkness.

Hands in front of her, moving slowly, she called the baby's name again. This time, apparently still hungry and most likely wondering why she wasn't feeding him, Garth let loose with his impressive lungs.

Perfect. Crossing the space between them, she focused on the sound. "Here you are." Picking him up, she clutched him to her. At least he'd been bundled into his coat, though his tiny hands were icy cold.

She turned around and carefully made her way toward the opening. "I've got him," she called as she stepped out of the darkness. To her shock, Shawn had vanished.

The instant JJ disappeared inside the crypt, Shawn took off, sprinting toward the parking lot as if he truly believed he could outrun a grizzly bear. Except in this case, Eric had no plans to chase him. No way was he leaving JJ and Garth alone with Rhonda. Since she'd admitted to attempting to help Yolanda get Garth back, he figured he knew exactly what she'd do. Attack JJ and steal the baby.

He glanced at her, to find her watching him with a half smile on her face. "You need to change back," she said. "Before the authorities get here. I know you've got Pack Protectors helping you, but they just might send the human police or FBI. You know there's no way you can explain a grizzly bear in the cemetery."

Just then, JJ emerged from the crypt holding a quiet Garth. Eric immediately forgot everything besides getting to his son.

"Here he is," JJ announced.

Immediately, Eric knew he needed to change back to human so he could hold his little boy. But his clothes were a good way off, and the last thing he wanted was both Rhonda and JJ there to witness the expected arousal that always came with the change.

JJ seemed to understand the problem immediately. "We'll walk to where you left your clothing," she said, shooting a hard look at Rhonda. "While you change, I'll make sure she doesn't try anything foolish."

"Really?" Rhonda drawled, apparently unable to resist. "And how, exactly, are you planning to do that?"

"Tie you up, of course," JJ responded sweetly, as she reached down and picked up the rope previously used to bind her.

"That's not really necessary," Rhonda began.

But JJ shook her head. Carefully placing little Garth at Eric's furry feet, she walked over to Rhonda. "Hands behind your back," she ordered. "And count yourself lucky I don't hit you upside the head and knock you out."

Once Rhonda's hands were secured and JJ had picked up Garth again, Eric led the way back to the place where he'd changed. His discarded clothing remained in a pile at the base of a tree.

With a quick jerk of his head, he indicated JJ should stand with Garth on the other side of him, away from Rhonda. Even though her hands were bound, he didn't entirely trust her not to try something. She was a shifter also, and could easily change to escape her ties.

Of necessity, he planned to make this the fastest shift back to human he'd ever done.

Dropping to all fours, he initiated the change, pushing his body hard. Pain knifed through him. Ignoring it, he continued. As soon as he'd regained his human form, he turned his back to the two women and grabbed his clothes.

"You know, you and I are more alike than you realize," Rhonda said. "I didn't put two and two together until you appeared in your bear self here, but now I understand much better. I thought Garth got his nature from Yolanda, but if both of you are Vedjorn, the chance of him becoming Berserker is that much more likely. You know this, which is why you went on the run."

"I went on the run, as you put it, to protect my son. And what do you mean, like you?" Though he suspected he knew. Hoped it wasn't so, but figured Rhonda would tell him.

Still moving fast, he yanked up his jeans to cover his arousal. He winced as he tried to close the zipper. There'd been other times in the past when he'd wished there was a way to turn off this particular occurrence, but never more than right now.

Rhonda didn't answer, which could be good or bad, depending.

Once he'd donned his shirt and his parka, he yanked on his gloves before he finally turned to face her. Holding Garth, JJ remained on his other side. "Are you planning to answer?" he asked. His breath made plumes in the frigid night air.

"A bear." All bundled up herself, she came closer. "I saw you shift back to human. And I know what happens after that. I'm available," she purred. "If you want to slake your body's need."

Though his arousal stirred, he didn't move. "No, thank you," he began, before the rest of her words dawned on him. "You're a bear shifter, too?"

"Yes. I came here five years ago to hide out." She licked her lips, not a wise move in this kind of cold. "My father was put to death for being a Berserker. And you know how they feel that trait is hereditary, so my mother packed me up and shipped me off. She wanted to protect me, the same way you think you can protect your child."

She took another step, her gaze fixed on his somehow still conspicuous bulge. He yanked his parka down over it.

"Come here," she urged him, her voice seductive, despite the fact that she knew JJ stood right behind him. "I know all too well that burning need. You're as aware as I am of what we have to do."

"No." He straightened up, drawing all his strength and willpower into himself. While to any other man her offer might have been tempting, the only woman he wanted was JJ. This realization so astounded him, he froze.

Which turned out to be a huge mistake. With her hands still tied, Rhonda barreled into him, knocking him down into the damp leaves. On top of him, she bared her teeth as if she meant to bite him. When he recoiled, she began fumbling with his clothes.

Eric pushed. Hard. He might have used a lot of his energy changing and hunting, but he still had enough strength to move a determined woman off him. She flew backward, landing on her behind in the snow.

"No," he said again, loud and clear, just in case she'd somehow missed it the last time. He pushed himself to his feet, glaring at her. She bowed her head, finally acquiescing.

Behind him, little Garth began to cry, his hunger pangs unabated.

Watching Rhonda carefully, JJ brought the baby to him. "He wants his daddy."

Relief and love flooded through him.

"Is he all right?" he asked, taking Garth from her and kissing his baby boy's forehead. "He looks okay."

"He seems fine. His hands are a little cold, but Shawn knew enough to put him in his winter coat and hat. He just forgot the gloves."

Eric carefully examined Garth's small fingers. Luckily, the sleeves of his jacket were long enough to keep them semiwarm. Though the dim light made it difficult to see, blood flow appeared good. He saw no sign of frostbite.

While he did all this, Rhonda stood stock-still, her head

back up, her eyes glittering, watching. "You really love that little guy, don't you?" she asked, a note of wonder in her voice. "Maybe I was wrong to believe everything your ex-wife told me."

He wouldn't have put it past her to lie in the hopes of getting away with what she'd done. Or worse, attempting to trick them so she could make a move to grab Garth. Over his dead body. Right now, dealing with Rhonda was the least of his priorities.

"Let's get out of here," he told JJ. "I want to get Garth home so I can check him over and get him fed."

"What about her?" JJ asked, eyeing Rhonda. "I'm guessing we should bring her with us. We can't leave her here."

Which actually would be what he preferred to do. But JJ was right. "We'll let the Protectors deal with her once we're back home."

"Let me take Garth," JJ offered. "That way your hands will be free to handle anything else that might happen." She meant Rhonda, who turned to grimace at her.

Because JJ was right, he handed over Garth. Ordering Rhonda to walk ahead of them so he could keep her in his eyesight at all times, they began to make their way back to the car.

Rocking the baby as she walked, JJ sighed. "I still can't believe Shawn found me. I'm not sure I can ever feel safe again."

"It'll be okay. He's probably looking at some jail time, since he faces human charges of kidnapping and attempted murder. Both Protectors and human law-enforcement will be looking for him. I'm pretty sure he won't do anything that might reveal his location right now."

"I wouldn't be so sure of that," Rhonda interjected, her voice smug. "I don't know how you feel about your ex-wife, but that woman can be very persuasive when she wants to be."

He grimaced. It was true that Yolanda had a raw, animalistic sex appeal, at least when one didn't know she was crazy. No doubt someone like Shawn would be susceptible to her wiles.

"What about you?" he asked, more from curiosity than anything else. "Does Yolanda appeal to you, as well?"

"Not in that way." Her response came immediately. "Though I have to admit, *you* do."

JJ snorted. "Keep dreaming."

Staring directly at Eric, Rhonda ignored her. "Eric, you know you have a duty to our kind, don't you?"

The cold had begun to seep through his clothes, making him concerned for his son. They'd almost reached his SUV. Using his key fob, he unlocked it and then handed the keys to JJ. "Go ahead and get him inside and start the engine so the heat can warm him up. His car seat is still in the back."

JJ nodded, glancing from him to Rhonda before accepting the keys and hurrying to the car. He waited until she and Garth were both inside, with the motor running, before turning to face Rhonda. "I'm going to press charges," he said. "And I'll be urging JJ to do the same."

"For what?" Her indignant tone seemed to indicate she didn't feel she'd done anything wrong. "This is a Vedjorn matter, and as such, not subject to external laws."

Did she just make up her own rules as she went along? "We'll let the Pack Protectors decide about that."

"What is *wrong* with you?" she asked. With her hands still tied behind her back, she thrust her chest out. "I know I'm attractive. There are not very many of us here in the United States. How is it that you aren't even interested in mating with me?"

Inwardly wincing at her complete absence of self-respect, he shook his head. "I'm not interested in mating with anyone right now."

"Right," she sneered. "You sure seem interested in JJ. Of course, you're aware that's not allowed."

"It's allowed," he said, before he thought better of it. "Just frowned upon. There's a difference."

"Forbidden," she insisted, glaring at him. "I know. I met a really nice wolf shifter a few years ago, but once he learned I was bear, he told me he got visited by the Pack Protectors."

"You revealed your true nature?"

"I can do what I want. Plus I thought he should know, since we were about to have sex together."

More wrongness, but what Rhonda did was not his concern. The Pack Protectors might decide otherwise. He took a deep breath. "Rhonda, you need to let this go. There will never be anything between you and me."

For a split second, he thought she might agree. But then she narrowed her eyes and advanced on him. "I claim you as mate," she declared. "You cannot refuse me. Join with me, now."

Eric stared in disbelief. That wasn't how it worked and she had to know it. Shaking his head, he gestured toward his SUV. "Get in. We're going back to the house. The Protectors will most likely be waiting for us there."

As he turned toward the vehicle, Rhonda let out a guttural roar. Full of rage and fury and something else: madness. Damn. Heart pounding, he realized she'd begun making the change to bear. Though her hands were tied, they wouldn't be for long. Since she still wore her human clothing, her jacket tore and her jeans ripped.

Not wanting any part of this, Eric began to sprint for

the car. Surely she wouldn't attack him from behind, bear against human. Surely not.

He grabbed the driver's side door handle, yanked it open and jumped inside, locking the doors behind him. Since the engine was already running, he shifted into Drive and hit the accelerator, making the wheels spin.

"She's coming at us!" JJ exclaimed. "I think she's going to ram the side."

As they pulled away, he looked back. A large brown bear, grizzly just like him, stood at the edge of the cemetery watching them go.

"I hate that she's getting away, too," JJ said, her voice shaky. "Now both she and Shawn are out there, free. And they could get together again with Yolanda."

Eric slowed so he could make the corner. Rhonda roared, the rage-filled sound reverberating around the cemetery and down the street. Loud enough to wake the dead.

One more backward glance and he kept going, his heart pounding in his chest. A word lurked at the edge of his consciousness, one he didn't want to even allow himself to think. Not now. Not yet.

And then…incredibly, the bear launched herself toward them, running full-out. Luckily, her top speed was only around 35 mph. Deadly for anyone on foot, but easily beatable in a car.

Still, despite having to know catching them would be impossible, Rhonda kept coming. Unbelievably gaining, until Eric accelerated and left her behind.

"She's crazy." JJ sounded both shocked and sad.

"No wonder she and Yolanda get along." He would mention this episode to Frank DeLeon and Felts for sure. Because he seriously wondered if it was possible Rhonda might be Berserker. And determined to make his innocent son one of them, too.

* * *

As they drove, JJ eyed the back of Eric's head and wondered when she'd fallen so deeply in love with him. She'd chosen to stay in the back with Garth, figuring he'd put a tied-up Rhonda up front.

Rhonda. A Vedjorn. No wonder she hadn't wanted to participate in the town Pack hunt. Thinking back to how often she and Garth had been alone with Rhonda, JJ considered it quite a miracle that something awful hadn't happened sooner.

"I can't believe your ex-wife contacted Rhonda and got her to turn against us," JJ mused. "But then again, if they're both bears, I guess that would automatically convey a sense of solidarity."

"It shouldn't," he said. "I regret the day I met Yolanda." The dejection in his voice made JJ ache to comfort him. "But then you wouldn't have this beautiful baby boy. You know, I really think this is all going to work out in the end. Wait and see."

Though she'd really been offering that hope to cheer him up, after uttering the words she felt better.

They pulled up in front of her house. The construction workers were long gone, though they'd left her front porch light on. Next door, Rhonda's house sat dark. JJ wondered if the other woman would be going back home, or if she'd meet up with Shawn and Yolanda somewhere and begin plotting a second attempt.

The thought turned her stomach. "Eric?" Leaning forward, she squeezed his shoulder. "I'm thinking it might be better if you took Garth and went somewhere else. At least until they catch the three of them."

"We tried that, remember? Besides, I'm not going anywhere without you."

His words had her heart skipping a beat. Still… "Keeping Garth safe is first priority."

"Of course." He got out of the car and opened the back door, unbuckling a remarkably silent Garth from his car seat. "Right now, getting him fed is what needs to happen. After that, we'll deal with anything else."

But once they were inside Eric's living space and he'd heated a bottle of formula, the baby wouldn't take it. He moved his head from side to side, his mouth tightly closed.

"He looks kind of pink," JJ pointed out. She placed the back of her hand against Garth's forehead. "He's burning up. You need to take his temperature."

Looking worried, Eric did as she suggested. "He's got a fever of 104 and he's breathing fast. It's probably a result of being kept for who knows how long inside that crypt. We'd better get him to the ER."

They bundled him back up and headed outside. Midway between the house and the car, the tiny baby shuddered and went limp.

Eric froze, panicked. "Is he…?"

Chapter 24

JJ snatched Garth out of Eric's arms. "He can't be," she said, insistent in her belief. Then, as she lifted him, completely unsure of what action to take, Garth inhaled a deep, shuddering breath and began to cry. Even his voice seemed off, broken and weak.

"Let's go," Eric ordered. "Right now, before something else happens."

They made it to the hospital in record time. Eric pulled up in front of the ER and jumped from the SUV to help JJ and little Garth out of the back seat. They left the vehicle there and hurried in to the triage desk. As soon as the nurse heard what had happened, she sent for an aide, who promptly showed them to a room.

"A nurse will be in to take his vitals," she said. "And then a doctor will visit."

After that, things moved surprisingly fast. The nurse arrived, took Garth's temperature and blood pressure, and before she'd even finished making notations in her computer, a white-coated doctor arrived.

"You have a very sick baby," he said, looking from JJ to Eric and back again. "We think he might have bacterial pneumonia. He's going to need antibiotics and we're going to be admitting him."

"Pneumonia?" Eric frowned. "Would that have caused him to lose consciousness?"

"No. Are you sure you didn't imagine that?"

JJ bristled at the doctor's insinuation. But something about the way Eric was watching the man caused her to pay attention and keep her thoughts to herself.

Just as the thought occurred to her, several men in dark suits came into the room. A look of recognition flashed over Eric's face at the sight of one of them. "DeLeon," he said. "It's about time you got here."

Unable to help herself, JJ took a long look at the Protector. So this was Shawn's adoptive brother. Odd how Shawn had never mentioned him, not once in all the time they'd been together. But then that was Shawn, completely absorbed only in himself.

Another man, taller and heavier than the others, stepped forward. "I'm afraid we need to speak to you privately," he said, his voice deep and sonorous. "I have to ask you both to please come with us, right now."

"No." Eric didn't even have to think about his answer. "I'm not leaving my son."

DeLeon nodded as if he understood, but one of the other men grunted. He looked out of sorts in his rumpled, navy blue suit and tie. "Don't make us arrest you."

What the... Eric stood his ground. "On what charges?"

"Assault and battery," the other man said. "A Ms. Rhonda Descart is pressing charges against you."

JJ gasped, but Eric could only stare. "Descart? Are you sure that's her last name?"

"Yes. Why?"

They all watched him now. Even JJ, her eyes wide and still full of shock. "Because I know that name. I've heard Yolanda mention it. Descart is the last name of one of her best friends. A woman who moved away before Yolanda and I married, so I never met her."

"Rhonda?" DeLeon asked. "Was Rhonda your ex-wife's friend before moving here?"

He struggled to remember. "No, her first name wasn't Rhonda. It was something weird, like a seasoning. Sage. That was it. Sage."

He saw he now had everyone's full attention. "What?" he asked, directing his question to DeLeon. "What did I say?"

"Sage is Rhonda's middle name," DeLeon explained. "It's extremely likely Rhonda actually was—or is—Yolanda's best friend."

Which would explain a lot.

"There's more," Eric said, bracing himself for their reactions. "I suspect Rhonda might be Berserker."

DeLeon and the others all exchanged looks. "That's a weighty word to throw around," the Protector said. Then asked, "Are you telling us that Rhonda is also Vedjorn?"

"Yes."

"As is Yolanda," JJ offered.

"We know."

DeLeon's sharp reply didn't appear to faze her. "Do you still have to arrest him?" she asked. "Because I was there the entire time and Eric never assaulted Rhonda."

No one immediately answered.

Finally, the same agent who'd threatened to arrest Eric spoke. "Excuse us a moment. We need to talk privately." At his gesture, the other agents followed him out of the room.

Except DeLeon. "I'm sorry about all this," he said, his

expression miserable. "I'm glad you got your son back, though. I hope he's going to be all right."

"Me, too." Eric frowned. "He's got pneumonia, no doubt because Shawn stuck him in a crypt, with little protection from the damp and the cold. I have no idea how long my son was kept there, but evidently long enough to make him seriously ill."

"I'm sorry." Apologizing again, DeLeon heaved a sigh. "This is a mess. I'm not really sure how my brother got involved in this, but I hate that he's on the run now." He eyed Eric. "Why didn't you call and fill me in? I had no idea you even had your son back until Rhonda showed up, wanting to press charges."

"No time." Glancing toward the doorway, Eric spoke quickly, telling DeLeon everything that had happened since they'd last spoken.

When he finished, the other man stared, scratching his head. "You couldn't make this stuff up. Geez."

"I know."

"Let me get this straight. You're telling me Rhonda clobbered you, and then knocked out JJ? Using a...frying pan?"

"Cast-iron skillet," JJ corrected. "It's much heavier. In fact, I think we need to press charges against *her*."

For the first time since arriving at the hospital, DeLeon smiled. "You know what? That might work. At least it would shut those other guys down." He jerked his head toward the door. "They aren't real sure what to do right now."

"Who do they work for?" Eric asked. "I know they're shifters, from their auras. I thought they were Protectors like you. That's why I mentioned the possibility that Rhonda is a Berserker."

"FBI." DeLeon sounded glum. "The child abduction got them involved. Dealing with that agency can be a pain in the ass sometimes. At least we have enough contacts there to ensure they didn't send human agents to investigate."

Eric shook his head, returning his attention to Garth, who was still far too motionless. At least the machines hooked up to his tiny body showed that his heart still beat. That, and the steady rise and fall of his chest, reassured Eric that his son still lived. "I'm not leaving him," he repeated. "Not without a fight."

"Me, either." JJ came and stood next to him. "The only thing that matters right now is Garth. Once he's better, we can focus on catching Shawn and dealing with Rhonda."

"Actually, that's my job," DeLeon stated with a twisted smile. "Though they've asked me to step down from the case due to family being involved, so I should say that's the Pack Protection Agency's job."

"Can you do anything to keep Eric from being arrested?" JJ asked. She stood near enough to him that their hips bumped. He put his arm around her and pulled her even closer. When he looked back at DeLeon, the other man gave him a nod of approval.

"He won't be arrested now. If they push it, all you have to do is claim Rhonda assaulted you."

"It's the truth."

"I know." DeLeon sighed. "Let me go find them and see if we can work something out. You two focus on getting your baby well. I'll talk to you later."

Neither DeLeon nor the FBI guys ever came back.

Later, after Garth had been admitted and they'd moved him to a room on the pediatric floor, Eric gestured toward a recliner near the large window. "It's late," he said to JJ. "Why don't you try to get some rest and I'll watch over Garth."

"First shift?" She attempted to smile, but exhaustion

tugged the corners of her mouth down. "I sleep for four hours and then you wake me so you can get some sleep."

Though he didn't plan to close his eyes until he knew for certain his son was out of the woods, he nodded as if he agreed. "Sounds like a plan," he said, taking the hard-backed visitor's chair next to the bed.

Wearily, JJ climbed into the recliner, pulling up the extra blanket a nurse had found. Within seconds, she'd fallen fast asleep.

Eric contented himself alternating between watching her and watching Garth. Staying awake was going to be a challenge, but he'd do it. He wished he'd had the foresight to grab a cup of coffee before JJ went to sleep.

DeLeon texted ninety minutes later.

All charges dropped. Though we had Rhonda in custody, we had to let her go. Let me know if either of you are serious about pressing charges against her. Right now, with both Shawn and Yolanda on the loose, I think it's better if we let her go. She might lead us to them.

Eric sent back his agreement. For now, he'd leave Rhonda alone. But if she came anywhere near him or his family—including JJ—all bets were off.

Sometime during the night he must have dozed off. He woke up with JJ gently shaking his shoulder. "Time to switch out," she whispered.

"What time is it?" he whispered back. He stood and stretched, trying to ease some of the kinks in his back.

"A little after three." She pointed toward the recliner. "Go rest. I'll try to watch him."

Though he hated to leave Garth's side, Eric knew he needed to catch a few hours' sleep if he hoped to have a prayer of being at his best later. And he trusted JJ to keep a good watch over his son.

Gratitude filled him. It had been a long time since he'd trusted anyone but himself.

With a thankful nod, he kissed JJ on the cheek and crawled into the recliner. He figured he'd be out like a light as soon as he closed his eyes.

His assumption must have been correct, because the next thing he knew, a too-cheerful nurse entered the room, warbling out a bright "good morning" as she flipped on the lights. Both he and JJ started. Garth still lay quietly, but his eyes were open and he appeared to be tracking the nurse's every move.

"I've got his bottle here," the woman said with a smile. "After I take his temperature, would Mommy or Daddy like to give it to him?"

Too tired to correct the misconception, Eric pushed to his feet. "I'll do it."

She handed him the bottle. Using a digital thermometer, she put it under Garth's arm and waited. "Perfect," she said, when it beeped. "His fever is gone. I'll let the doctor know. Let's see if he wants his bottle, shall we?"

To Eric's relief, when he offered, Garth latched on and drank hungrily.

"Wonderful!" the nurse exclaimed. "I bet if he keeps improving, the doctor might let him go home this afternoon."

Eric blinked away the sudden rush of moisture to his eyes. "He's going to be okay?"

"Of course he is," she chided. "The antibiotics are doing their job. Call me if you need anything."

Once she'd gone, JJ hurried over and wrapped her arms around Eric's waist. They stood together while Garth finished his bottle. When he had, Eric carefully lifted him up and burped him.

"He needs a diaper change," JJ pointed out. She located a stack of disposable diapers and handed him one.

Contentment and joy filled Eric as he changed his son. Reluctant to let him go, he sat on the edge of the bed and simply held him.

The nurse had been correct. After the doctor made his rounds, he informed Eric he'd be sending Garth home with antibiotics. He gave instructions that they were to follow up with a family physician, unaware that they'd need to locate one first since they hadn't been in town long enough to have one.

By the time they left the hospital, both Eric and JJ were starving. She'd made a quick run earlier to the hospital coffee shop and gotten them each coffee and a sweet roll, but he went to a drive-through on the way home and picked up a box of fried chicken, along with two sides.

JJ realized something once they'd arrived back at her house and were comfortably ensconced in his warm kitchen. This was how it felt to be a family.

After they'd eaten and Eric had given his son his afternoon bottle, Garth went down for a nap. Eric joined JJ in the living room. "You know you're staying here until your place is livable," he said. "No arguments."

"There won't be." Tight-lipped, she glanced out the window at Rhonda's house. "I have nowhere else to go."

"I wonder if she went home," Eric mused. "Since no one filed any charges."

"I doubt it. She's probably with Shawn and Yolanda, plotting their next move." JJ took a deep breath. "Don't you think it's odd that both our exes are working together against us? Even though they both want different things, it's crazy."

"Extremely odd. It's even weirder that your ex happens to be related to the Pack Protector assigned to my case."

She tried for a smile, though she had the feeling it looked more like a grimace. "One of those instances where truth is stranger than fiction. You couldn't make this stuff up."

He agreed. "I just want it to be over, so we can all get back to normal."

Normal. Eric had no idea how much she'd hoped moving to Forestwood would give her that. She'd started down that road, too—settled in to her house, even found a job. And while she'd never intended to fall for her handsome tenant and his adorable infant, she had. She could only hope once all this craziness ended, normal would still be a possibility for them all.

That night, JJ slept on the couch. Eric tried to offer her his bed, but she insisted he stay close to his son. In the morning, she got up first and made a pot of coffee.

Since he'd had to throw away everything in his refrigerator when the power had been cut off, she rummaged through the cupboard to see if there was anything she could make for breakfast. She found some pancake mix, the kind that needed only water added, and an unopened container of maple syrup. They wouldn't have butter, but this would be better than nothing.

After breakfast, she showered, then watched over Garth so Eric could do the same. Once he emerged, his blond hair still damp, she took a quick trip to buy groceries. Even though Eric asked if she wanted to help him bathe Garth, she felt she needed to get out of the house to reclaim her equilibrium. This sudden enforced coziness had the potential of causing great emotional distress if she allowed herself to get too comfortable.

Because Eric—and Garth—were everything she'd ever yearned for, everything she'd ever dreamed of. The shining possibility of a future with them made her dizzy with longing.

At the store, she loaded up on meat and produce, plus essentials like milk and butter and cheese. Trying not to wince at the total, she paid and wheeled the cart with her bagged groceries outside. Of necessity, she took extra precautions—scoping out the entire parking lot before she went too far, car keys in hand, and being vigilant about checking out her surroundings. But she didn't relax until she had everything loaded in her trunk, cart put away, and her doors locked with the engine running. Now to drive home.

Home. Even though her floor still wasn't finished, staying with Eric felt the same as being home. Except better.

When she got back, Eric came out and helped her bring in the groceries. Catching sight of the receipt, he handed her two hundred-dollar bills. "Thank you," he said, ignoring her weak attempts to refuse. "This should stock us up for a little while."

Over the next few days, they settled into a sort of domestic routine. Mundane, actually, but one JJ found satisfying. The only thing that would have made it better would be if Eric would welcome her into his bed. They'd shied away from any kind of intimacy since that night in the motel room. Often, she found herself watching him, aching with suppressed desire and need, and wondering if he felt it, too.

Eric kept in touch with Frank DeLeon. So far, five days in, no trace had been found of Rhonda, Yolanda or Shawn. JJ wondered about Shawn's job—he'd been zealously dedicated and well compensated there. His brother informed her that Shawn had taken two weeks' vacation, and as of yet, his position wasn't in any danger. Of course, that would all change once he returned. The Protectors were watching and waiting for that to happen.

"We just need to be careful not to get lulled into a sense of false security," Eric told her over dinner.

About to take a bite of the fried chicken she'd prepared, JJ nodded. The construction company had given her a ten-day estimate of when they figured the work would be done in her place. Once everything passed inspection, she'd be able to move back in. She and Eric hadn't discussed this yet, mostly because she was hoping all the craziness would be over by then. Surely, the Protectors would be able to close Rhonda and the others down.

"You'd think," Eric agreed, when she mentioned this to him. "The main problem seems to be that they've gone into hiding. Until they make a move or someone spots them, we're kind of stuck in this limbo. DeLeon assures me that they're working every lead. There's a lot we're not privy to going on behind the scenes."

She nodded. His restlessness that evening was a new thing and made her feel jittery. Eric insisted on cleaning up after their meal, since she'd cooked, so she let him, but afterward he prowled around the small living room like a wild animal confined to too small of a space.

"Are you all right?" she finally asked, as she realized what might be his problem. "I can watch Garth for a few hours tonight if you need to change."

The grateful look he shot her made her smile. "How did you know?"

Secretly pleased, she shrugged. "How could I not know? You're acting like a grizzly trapped in a cage. Go hunt. Garth and I will be fine."

Brows lowered, Eric stopped his pacing long enough to consider her words. "I don't know," he hedged. "I'm still afraid to leave you and Garth unprotected. And I can't take you with me, because the last thing he needs is to be outside in the cold while he's recovering."

"We'll be fine." She smiled at him. "I'll lock the place up after you leave and won't sleep until you get back. Remember, I always have my own secret weapon. Wolves have sharp teeth and claws. Besides, unless they're watching us, they'll have no way of knowing you're gone."

Still he hesitated. Full of love, she couldn't keep herself from going to him and wrapping her arms around his waist. Eric stiffened for an instant, but then relaxed enough to hug her back.

They stood that way for the space of a few heartbeats, while she battled a surge of desire. About to look up and pull him close for a kiss, she instead stifled her disappointment when he pulled away.

Chapter 25

Some of JJ's disappointment must have shown in her face.

"Do you have any idea how much I want you?" Eric asked, his voice low and rough. When she shook her head, he grimaced and dragged his hand through his hair. "I haven't stopped wanting you since that night. Hell, the truth is, I've desired you since the first moment we met."

Speechless, she stared at him, her heart racing while a slow heat built inside her.

"But," he continued, "I want to do things right with you. Get to know you without all this evil hanging over our heads. Hunt with you, run with you, have a picnic in the park in the spring, go on a real date, all the things a man should do to court a woman."

"Court?" She liked the old-fashioned word.

"Yes." He came closer, his gaze intense. For a second, she could have sworn she saw a hint of his bear self in his eyes.

When he stopped less than six inches from her, she swallowed hard. Her entire body tingled with anticipation.

"I could tell you everything I want to do to you, starting with my mouth on your lips, but I won't. My bear is already agitated. But I can promise you this—once all the danger is past and those crazies are safely locked up, if you're game, we'll begin our courtship."

Courtship. She liked that. The way he said it sounded as if he meant for them to have a real shot at a future together. "I'm game," she told him, smiling. "Now go and let your bear out to play. I'll be here once you get back."

He did kiss her then, a light, lingering kiss that he broke off too soon. "I won't be gone long," he promised. "I'll go right after I put Garth down for the night."

Though her wolf stirred at the thought of hunting, she knew she could wait a few more days before she'd need to change. The idea of shape-shifting with Eric, hunting and running as they'd done once before, filled her entire being with longing.

Someday, she told herself. Someday.

Finally, after bathing and feeding Garth, Eric had him settled in his crib. The baby fussed for a moment or two, but eventually drifted off to sleep.

Though Eric practically vibrated with impatience, still he hovered. "Are you sure about this?"

"Yes." She gave him a small shove. "Just go. Run. Hunt. Let your beast out to play."

Finally, he nodded. "All right. But JJ, stay vigilant, just in case."

"I will."

He kissed her on the cheek, a chaste kiss that plainly showed his worry. Once she heard the front door close, she went to the bedroom window and watched as he hurried across the frozen field toward the woods.

Before she settled down with her book, she went from room to room, checking every window and door, making sure no lock had been left unfastened. Once she was satisfied, she settled in the rocking chair next to Garth's crib to read.

A loud roar startled her from a restless doze. She picked up her book from the floor where it had fallen and listened. Nothing.

Had she dreamed it? First she checked on the baby, relieved to see his chest rising and falling with deep, even breaths as he slept. Padding to the window, she looked out, barely able to make out the dark outline of a man crossing the field toward the house. Eric! On his way back.

Her soft smile became a frown as she saw him stop. He turned back to look at the woods. Or something at the edge of the trees. As she tried to make out what it might be, the thing moved into the clearing and roared again.

Now she saw it. A giant bear lumbered a few steps toward Eric and stopped, eyeing him. Her heart skipped a beat. She remembered what Eric had called Rhonda, and whispered it to herself, hoping against hope that he'd been wrong.

Berserker.

If Eric's suspicions were reality, then he was in great danger.

Indecision froze her. She should call someone, except 911 was clearly out and she didn't have Felts's or DeLeon's number. JJ knew objectively that Eric was capable of defending himself, though she wanted to help him if at all possible. But how?

As she watched, the giant beast circled around Eric, as if sizing him up. His best chance would be to change into his own bear self. Except she knew he had already done that earlier, and like all shifters, he'd have little energy to do so again. Shifting a second time so soon after the first wasn't always possible. There were only a few rare individuals strong enough.

Her heart pounded as she watched. She couldn't just stand here and let him be cut down. Which meant she would have to save him.

After another quick glance at the sleeping infant, JJ decided. Garth would be fine left alone, as long as she made sure the place was locked up. For his sake—and hers—she couldn't let Eric be killed. Garth needed his father. And she needed Eric, too.

Shedding clothes as she went, she ran out through the door and locked it. When the outside air hit her skin with a blast of icy cold, she began the change, faster than she'd ever done before. She was wolf before her paws even left the cement.

And she ran. Blasting through the snow, past a startled Eric, who had turned to face the charging bear. He'd crouched low and had his arms up, as if he thought his human strength would be enough to deflect the blow.

JJ snarled, drawing the huge beast's attention. The bear skidded to a stop and swung its huge, shaggy head from her to Eric and back again. As wolf, JJ knew she wasn't huge, but she still made a threatening figure. She'd become a skilled hunter and would fight to the death to defend someone she loved.

Like Eric.

Of course she loved him. She filed this bit of astounding information away. Now was not the time to philosophize. She had to either frighten the bear away or fight it. Right now, she thought savagely, she was good with either choice.

Planting herself in front of Eric, JJ bared her teeth and made it clear she would defend him. The bear tossed its head and grunted. It was either Yolanda or Rhonda, but JJ couldn't tell which one.

"Rhonda, please stop," Eric said, speaking directly to the beast. "You don't have to do this."

Rhonda. Okay. JJ cut her gaze from Eric to the bear. So Rhonda had returned and taken the shape of her beast. Did that mean Yolanda and Shawn were somewhere nearby?

While she struggled to assimilate this information, the bear—Rhonda—roared again. Another roar came from deeper in the trees, and then a second bear emerged. JJ's heart sank. As wolf, she had strength and skill, but against two bears?

"Yolanda," Eric said, his voice resigned. "I'd recognize her anywhere. Damn."

In response, JJ crouched low, preparing to spring at her, and snarled, letting him know she'd fight with him.

"Where's Garth?" Eric asked her, low-voiced.

Since she couldn't answer in words, she cut her eyes back toward the house, where she'd left the baby asleep in his crib. And then she realized what she'd done in her mad rush to help Eric. She'd left his son unprotected. The doors were locked, but with Rhonda and Yolanda this close, surely Shawn wasn't far behind.

"Go. Now." Eric kept his voice calm. "I can deal with the two of them."

Since she could run much faster as a wolf, JJ kept her shape and spun around. The instant she did, the wild-eyed first bear charged, heading directly for her.

Bracing herself, JJ readied for the moment of impact. Crouching low, she'd slash up with her teeth, going for the vulnerable belly and throat.

Just before the beast was upon her, a shot rang out. The bear fell backward, almost in slow motion, clawing at the air and then at its bloody throat.

Disbelieving, but aware Garth had to be her first priority, JJ jumped up and raced off again. She took a final glance back. Eric stood frozen, one arm extended, his hand holding a pistol. He stared in sorrow and shock at the downed bear, which didn't move. As they watched, the bear began to shimmer. Slowly, it turned back to its human form. Rhonda.

Though the shot had given the second bear pause, after watching Rhonda fall, it resumed racing toward them.

Eric shook his head, his anguish plain to see even from this distance.

JJ swallowed, her heart pumping. She hated that Rhonda had died, and she definitely didn't like leaving Eric alone to face Yolanda in her possibly Berserker form. But Garth needed her now, especially since the third member of the trio—Shawn—hadn't shown up. For all she knew, he could be in the house right now, snatching Garth from his crib.

In the end, she did the only thing she could. She tucked her body as low as possible and sprinted for the house. She would change back to human once she got there, and then she'd make sure the baby was safe.

Facing Yolanda as bear, Eric kept his pistol up, finger near the trigger. Both he and Yolanda watched as the wolf took off, running low to the ground, across the field toward the house, as fast as the snow would let her.

JJ. His heart swelled. He'd recognized her immediately. She'd come out here to try and save him. He knew she wouldn't have left Garth if she had thought there was any alternative. Now, he could only pray she got back in time. Once he dealt with Yolanda, he hoped he'd be able to help JJ against Shawn, who probably wasn't far behind.

Yolanda growled, her eyes glinting red. Berserker? Most likely. If so, once she launched an attack, nothing would stop her but death. He had loaded silver bullets and he'd already killed Rhonda. He hoped like hell he wasn't forced to shoot his ex-wife, as well.

Across the clearing, Yolanda paced, sizing him up, her massive body vibrating with rage. She seethed with hatred, yet something held her back. He suspected she understood what his pistol would do. Either that, or she was waiting for Shawn to appear with Garth.

Luckily, Eric considered himself an excellent shot. While he couldn't and wouldn't kill her outright, in cold blood, self-defense was a different matter entirely.

In his pants pocket, his phone vibrated, indicating a text. DeLeon had called right after Eric had changed, and left a voice mail warning him that the trio was on the move, most likely in his direction. He'd been glad then that he'd packed his pistol and the silver bullets. Better safe than sorry.

Across the clearing, the massive bear continued to pace at the edge of the trees. The third time she swung her head toward the house, he knew.

Furious, he raised his weapon. While he was an excellent marksman, hitting her from such a distance would be a stretch. But since he had no other choice, he squeezed off a shot.

Yolanda jerked back and he knew he'd hit her. She roared, this time the sound more of a cry of pain than a belligerent threat. Dropping to all fours, she disappeared into the woods. He knew if he wanted to track her, a trail of blood would lead him right to her.

Instead, he turned away and holstered his pistol. As he passed the dead woman lying naked in the snow, he reached for her shredded and tattered clothes and covered her the best he could. His bullet had hit her right between her eyes.

Then he headed off at a jog for what truly mattered now—his son and the woman he loved. Though he wanted to run, the best Eric could manage was a series of short sprints. The earlier change and subsequent hunt had zapped his energy.

On the way, he dug his cell from his pocket and jabbed the call back button for DeLeon. The call went straight to voice mail.

Running as if the devil nipped at her heels, JJ didn't slow down until she reached her house. Since without opposable thumbs she couldn't open her front door, she'd need to change back to human.

So she did, right there on her back doorstep, under her porch light, praying no one saw her. As soon as she'd become human again, she fumbled with the doorknob and let herself in. Moving quickly, she yanked her previously discarded clothes on piece by piece, following the trail she'd left earlier, all the way to Garth's room.

Taking a deep breath, she stepped inside. To her infinite relief, the baby still slept in his crib. Unbothered and safe. Thank goodness for locked doors and windows.

Exhausted, she wished she could drop into the rocking chair next to the crib and exhale in relief. Instead, she crossed over to the window to see how Eric was faring with the other bear.

As she squinted to see what was going on out in the field, she saw Eric and his ex-wife had apparently reached a standoff. The massive bear circled at the edge of the field, keeping her distance. Eric still had his gun at the ready, careful not to let down his guard. She watched him bring his pistol up and fire off a shot.

Clearly, he'd hit his target. While his bullet didn't take Yolanda out, the huge bear went to all fours before disappearing into the trees.

Hand to her throat, JJ watched as Eric holstered his gun and began running for the house.

"There you are."

A shudder went through her and she froze, her heart stuttering in her chest. It was a voice she knew intimately, and one she'd hoped never to hear again. Shawn. How long had he been there? Had he seen her shape-shift from wolf to human? And if needed, did she have enough strength to change again? Her life might depend on her being able to do it.

Of course, Eric would be here in a few minutes. Clearly, he was armed and wasn't afraid to use his pistol. Even Shawn would have to respect that.

Until Eric arrived, she'd have to try and stall Shawn. And keep him the hell away from baby Garth.

Turning slowly, despite her racing heart, she managed a completely fake smile. "Hey, there," she said calmly, as if terror hadn't immediately turned her blood to ice. "Shawn. What are you doing here?"

Casual, casual. Even though they'd already faced each other down, in his arrogance and narcissistic pride, Shawn wouldn't have considered her lost to him. In the time they'd spent together, she'd come to know him well. He considered himself a shark of a man, an alpha male hunter, even though he was only human and she the true huntress. The bitter irony in that had never been lost on her. At least right now, she had a small advantage. A larger one, once Eric reached them.

Except as she stared at Shawn, she noticed he, too, had a gun. A black, dangerous-looking pistol, pointed at her. She wondered if he knew how to use it, but figured he'd probably taken the time to learn. She prayed the baby wouldn't wake, wouldn't make a sound. Shawn knew her well enough to know if he threatened an innocent infant, she'd do whatever he wanted.

"I've been looking for you," he said, the grimness in his voice matching his expression. "You really didn't think I'd let you go so easily, did you?"

"Why?" Though she already knew. He'd never actually understood that she was a person with real hopes and needs and desires. To him, she'd been his possession. Something to do with as he pleased. And when she'd fled, he'd been infuriated, as if she'd tried to steal herself away from him.

"Because you're mine. And you're coming with me," he declared. "Right this instant."

"No." Lifting her chin, she met his gaze to let him know even though her response had been quiet, she meant it. "I'm not. This is my home now."

He hadn't been expecting this; she could tell from the way he cocked his head and narrowed his eyes. "You're different," he finally said, his tone hard with fury. "Impertinent. I don't like it."

"I really don't care what you like."

"Bitch." He hit her. Hard, an uppercut fist under the chin. She went down like a rock, fighting to stay conscious, swallowing back the nausea and pain. She'd bitten her tongue, she figured, tasting blood. And maybe lost a tooth or two. The coppery taste woke her wolf. Inside, the beast rose, less exhausted now, alert once again. And dangerous. After all, she hadn't let her beast hunt.

"Get up."

Blinking up at him, she tried to focus, but everything had gone blurry. Still, she could make out the black outline of his weapon. *Garth*, she thought. She had to keep Garth safe.

"Get up," he repeated, spraying her with spittle.

Moving carefully, she somehow managed to push herself to her feet. She had to get him outside, away from the house and the baby. She couldn't risk anything happening to Garth. Though Eric had been heading this way, he'd been moving relatively slowly, attesting to his fatigue. She figured there was a fifty-fifty chance he'd show up in time to save her. Therefore, she'd need to save herself. She'd come a long way in the months since she'd freed herself from Shawn. She could do this.

Chapter 26

Once she'd made it to her feet, using one hand to hold on to the wall, she eyed him. If she appeared overeager to get outside, he'd suspect something might be up. Instead, she had to appear to *not* want to leave the house.

"I refuse to go anywhere with you," she declared, her voice shaky and breathless. "If you're going to kill me, you might as well do it here and now." He had no way of knowing a bullet wouldn't kill her. Not unless it was made of silver. Her kind could die only from a silver bullet or fire. But she'd keep that information under wraps for now.

Her statement had the desired effect. "Outside," he growled, prodding her with the gun. "Now."

Since outside was exactly where she wanted to go, she didn't put up too much of a struggle. She wouldn't have been able to resist too much, anyway, with her head throbbing from the blow she'd taken. Dragging her hand across her mouth, she found her fingers came back smeared with blood. Again, just the taste of it infuriated her inner beast.

Pacing, her inner wolf snarled. She pushed it back,

drawing strength from the sure knowledge that she—with her razor-sharp teeth and massive wolf claws—could take him down and rip out his throat easily, even after being shot.

Pack law declared she'd have to be careful. While wolf, she could attack a human only in self-defense, and then only if her life was seriously threatened. She couldn't do such a thing lightly, and she'd prefer not to have to do it at all. She'd rather have him arrested and sent to jail.

For now, Shawn appeared to have forgotten about the baby. Good. The longer she could keep his focus on her, the better.

"Yolanda is taking care of your new boyfriend, you whore," Shawn spat. "After she's done with him, I'm going to let her work you over, too. We'll see how defiant you are after that."

Now he had her wondering how much he really knew. "Umm, Shawn? Do you have any idea what Yolanda can become?"

"Of course I do. Why do you think I'm helping her?" Eyes wild, he gestured widely. "She has a special gift—a superpower. And if I continue to help her, eventually she'll let me have it, too. Once she does, I'll be unstoppable. Just wait, you'll see."

Oh, brother. JJ knew better than to roll her eyes, but she really wanted to. With each second that ticked past, she felt herself grow stronger.

Downstairs, she heard the sound of the front door crashing open. Though Eric knew better than to call her name, he made a lot of noise as he rushed up the steps.

Shawn swung his pistol from left to right, covering her and then the doorway, making her wonder if he actually knew how to use it. If he accidentally squeezed the trigger while aiming at the crib, Garth could get shot. This helped her make her decision.

The next time Shawn had his gun pointed at the doorway, she sprang up, launching herself at him. A second after she did, Eric came rushing in the front door.

The gun went off. No silver bullet, but Eric jerked back and fell. He'd been hit. The echo of the gunshot woke Garth, who let out a frightened cry.

Outside, sirens sounded in the distance. The Pack Protectors to the rescue, she supposed. It appeared they would arrive too late.

Somehow, Eric struggled to his feet. Grinning, Shawn grabbed JJ and held the gun to her throat. "First her, and then the kid," he gloated. "You might as well watch."

Garth had been through so much already with his pneumonia. Babies' bodies hadn't yet built up the strength adult shifters had. In his weakened state, it was entirely possible a gunshot wound might kill him. If not, he'd surely suffer.

JJ could see that Eric was fading fast. While she knew he wouldn't die, seeing him in such a state terrified her. Blood seeped from the new wound in his leg and he swayed as he tried to reach them.

With his arm around her throat, Shawn could see it, too. Tightening his hold, he dragged JJ over to the crib. "Such a cute little baby," he mocked. "Wonder how adorable he'll look with a big ole bullet hole right through his forehead."

"No," JJ protested, struggling to get the words out while choking. Her vision went gray and she nearly fell, causing Shawn to loosen his grip so that she could breathe. "Leave the baby alone!"

Shawn only laughed in response.

Eric roared. The inhuman sound alerted JJ to the unbelievable. He had changed. Somehow, Eric had shapeshifted back to bear in a furious instant, tearing his clothes.

He attacked Shawn, saving his son, saving her. As Eric slammed into Shawn, he pushed her aside hard enough that she hit the side of the crib, jostling Garth.

This, as well as Shawn's pain-filled screams, frightened the baby, who began to wail. One swipe of Eric's powerful claws and Shawn went down. JJ grabbed Garth, startled to see the baby appeared to be shimmering in between a human and a bear. No way. Shifters couldn't actually shape-shift until they were in their teens.

Trying to process this, she ran for the door. Behind her, the two wrestled—man and bear—in a fight most certainly to the death.

She heard the report of the gunshot at the exact same instant she felt the flash of pain in her back. Somehow, she kept going, aware she couldn't fall while carrying the baby. Once she reached the living room, she managed to place Garth carefully on the sofa before her legs gave out and she crumpled to the floor.

When Shawn shot JJ in the back, Eric relinquished his tenuous grip on restraint and let himself go. With one hard swipe of his mighty paw, he whacked at Shawn. He meant to only knock the other man unconscious, but he must have hit him in such a way as to break his neck. He knew instantly, looking at the awful angle Shawn lay, that he was dead.

Full of worry and remorse, he eased himself to the floor, light-headed from the loss of blood. He'd need to shape-shift back to human so he could call 911. To do that, he'd have to find the strength from somewhere.

Initiating the change, he couldn't keep from crying out as the pain sliced through him. Once he was man, he wrapped a baby blanket around his wound in an attempt to stop the bleeding, and crawled into the living room, to find JJ unconscious and Garth unharmed.

He checked her pulse, relieved to find her heart still beating. And then, because he had no strength for anything else, he picked up the phone and dialed 911, just as DeLeon and his crew burst through the door.

They came for him at sunset. Three men, grim-faced and silent. They put the steel handcuffs on without a word and led him to their car. Eric didn't resist. They didn't bother reading him his rights. Because of his crime, he had none.

He went willingly, glad JJ didn't have to witness this. His heart ached, already missing her and Garth. He'd saved her, protected her and himself both, and for what? The crime of killing a human in his bear form was punishable by death. Unless he could prove it wasn't him or that it had been self-defense. Unfortunately, he had no proof. Only his and JJ's word. Once again, he wished he'd had a camera.

"Get in the car," the tallest man ordered.

Unable to help himself, he glanced back once at JJ's house, foolishly hoping for a final glimpse of her before the Protectors took him away. He imagined there'd be a trial, a mock hearing at best, giving him a chance to explain himself before they killed him. Meanwhile, people would be working behind the scenes to mess up the forensic reports, to make sure nothing showed the dead man had been attacked and killed by a large bear. Among his kind, humans finding out about their existence was considered the worst of all threats.

And for nearly revealing this, someone would have to pay. The Protectors seemed determined to ensure that someone would be him.

Heart racing, Eric opened his eyes, momentarily disoriented. Instead of being cuffed in the back of a government-issue sedan, he lay prone in a hospital bed, hooked up to machines. His heartbeat slowed as he realized his arrest had been only a dream. Hopefully, not a premonition.

Garth. Suddenly, everything came crashing back to him. JJ hit in the back, finding her on the floor, Garth unhurt. Was JJ all right? And where was his son?

He located the call button and pressed it. When no one immediately answered, he pressed it again. And again. Until finally an annoyed feminine voice asked how she could help him.

"My son," he croaked. "I need to know who has my son."

"I do," DeLeon said, as he walked into the room. "And JJ is recovering in the room next door."

Briefly, Eric wondered if he was dreaming again. "What do you mean? Do you really have Garth?"

DeLeon ducked his head as if embarrassed. "Well, actually, my wife is babysitting him while the two of you recover. Seemed like the least I could do after what happened with my brother."

His brother. Shawn. Eric swallowed. "I'm sorry about your loss, Frank. Please know that I never intended to—"

"Stop." Gently, the Protector placed a hand on Eric's shoulder. "It was very clear what occurred. You did what you had to do in order to protect your family. I'm just glad Shawn didn't manage to kill anyone before you took him out."

"Still, I know how difficult it is to lose a family member, especially a brother."

A shadow crossed the other man's face. "My mother is taking it hard. But we'll get through it. Rhonda's and Yolanda's deaths were a bit more difficult to explain. Sadly, we made Shawn the scapegoat there, too, at least publically."

Inwardly wincing, Eric nodded. He couldn't help but wonder if DeLeon would casually add that, oh, by the way, Eric was under arrest.

Instead, the Protector released him. "Your prognosis is good. They got the bullet out and it doesn't appear to have done any serious nerve or muscle damage. You both were lucky he didn't know to use silver bullets."

"I'll say." Eric thought of his own weapon, and what he'd loaded. He'd known if he was going to shoot, he'd have to shoot to kill. He'd hoped he wouldn't have to, but Garth had to be protected and kept safe. "What about JJ?" he asked. "She was shot in the back."

And while she might not die, she could still end up paralyzed. For a shifter, that would be a special sort of hell. Trapped in a nonworking body, unable to die.

DeLeon looked down. "The good news is that the bullet didn't go anywhere near her spinal cord. The bad news is she hasn't regained consciousness yet. The doctors don't understand why not."

"I want to go see her." Eric pushed himself up, using his elbows. "Please. Can you take me to her?"

"I don't think you can walk." DeLeon appeared uncertain. "Maybe you should wait until you're better."

"What about a wheelchair? Surely you can ask the nurse. Wait, I'll do it." Eric pressed the call button again. This time, the voice said someone would be with him in a moment.

When the nurse arrived, she seemed surprisingly amendable to locating a wheelchair and helping get Eric to the room next door. She paged someone else and a few minutes later an orderly came in with a chair. The nurse and the aide helped Eric out of bed and got him settled, hanging his IV pole on a bar on the wheelchair.

"I'll take him," DeLeon said, stepping forward. "I'll call you when he's ready to get back in his bed."

Once the nurse had gone, Eric drew a deep breath. "Let's go," he said.

Though the Protector placed his hands on the chair handles, he didn't push it forward yet. "I should warn you that she looks pretty bad."

Eric nodded. "And I should tell you that she'll always be beautiful to me, no matter what shape she's in."

His comment made the other man smile. "Let's go," he said, and wheeled him out of the room.

JJ felt light, as if she could float along without the heaviness of her earthly body weighing her down. The sense of calmness and peace felt so profoundly beautiful that she wanted to weep. At first, she'd struggled to remember, to ground herself back where she knew she needed to be, but the effort seemed too much, so she let it go. She knew there had been turmoil and violence. Bloodshed even. But there'd also been love.

She needed to focus on the love. But doing that was so difficult, she didn't. So much easier to simply let herself float.

A familiar voice called her name. Not once, but twice, lingering lovingly over each letter. She wanted to respond, goodness knows she even tried, but she couldn't summon up the necessary strength.

With silence came abject disappointment. Had the voice gone? Suddenly, desperately, she wanted it to stay. Moisture filled her eyes. But then—then—he spoke again, so close to her ear she felt the tickle of his warm breath. Her heart gave a little skip of joy as the voice surrounded her with love, gently and firmly grounding her.

"Come back," he pleaded. "We've got too much of a future for you to go away now. Garth needs you. I need you."

Still, though she understood the sentiment, the context of the words didn't quite make sense. Who was he, the man behind the love? His name... Still frozen, still trapped in that strange sort of space between asleep and awake, she struggled to remember the name of who the deep, masculine voice belonged to. Somehow she sensed doing so would be vitally important.

Eric. It finally came to her. *Eric Mikkelson*.

And just like that, she remembered everything. Him, his baby Garth and the love that filled her heart. Still.

But with love came fear. Terror. Shawn and his pistol. She remembered nothing after he'd shot her in the back.

She struggled to open her eyes. But the ethereal, unfocused self she'd become had no control over anything. Especially her earthly body. Yet she could feel a tear track moisture down her frozen cheek. And when his calloused finger softly brushed it away, she knew he remained at her side.

"Don't go," she said silently, hoping against hope that Eric somehow heard and understood. "Keep talking to me. Stay."

As if he heard her, he did.

"My brave little wolf," he said, tenderness and love making his voice rough. "You've been through so much. But that's over now. We're safe. You're safe. And the future—our future—looks so bright, you gotta wear shades."

This last comment made her smile. More than smile—laugh. She felt the joyful sound bubble up inside her and was actually able to open her mouth to let the laughter out.

"JJ?" Sounding stunned and joyous, Eric took her hand.

"Are you back, sweetheart? Squeeze my fingers if you can hear me."

With her strength returning, JJ did better than that. She opened her eyes.

Later, when the astounded doctors had finished examining her, after all the multiple tests were completed and she'd been brought back to her room, she and Eric were finally alone again.

Exhausted and relieved, JJ smiled at him. "Thanks for sticking with me," she said softly. "Hearing your voice felt like a lifeline, keeping me grounded, keeping me here. I'm not sure what would have happened if you hadn't started talking to me."

He kissed her again, this time on the cheek. "I'm not letting you go anywhere."

Smiling at his comment, she wished she had enough strength to turn her face so his kiss landed on her mouth. "Where's Garth?" she asked. "Since you're not worried, I know he's somewhere safe."

"He's with Frank DeLeon."

Shocked, she could only stare. "The Pack Protector? Shawn's brother?"

"Yes. And he's perfectly safe." Eric pulled out his phone. "Frank's been sending me videos. Apparently, his wife works in a neonatal unit in a hospital and loves taking care of infants. Look."

Rapt, JJ watched as a woman with long, slender fingers dangled a set of bright plastic keys in front of Garth, letting him play with them.

"He looks good," she mused.

"Yes, he does."

Though part of her didn't want to know, she had to ask. "Is Shawn…?"

Eric knew what she was asking without her having to say the words. "Dead? Yes. He is. I killed him."

Considering his words, she realized she felt nothing. Not joy, not sorrow, just a huge blankness. "How?" Selfishly, part of her wanted to know.

"Vedjorn claws and teeth," he whispered. "I was worried the Protectors would arrest me, but since it so clearly was self-defense..."

Closing her eyes as relief flooded her, she nodded. "So it's really over? All of it?"

"Yes."

Her gaze drifted to the window. Outside, she saw it had begun to snow.

"To new beginnings," he said, following her gaze with his own.

She smiled, glad that he'd remembered her words about how snow made her feel. "To new beginnings," she repeated.

Gently, carefully, he gathered her in his arms and held her close. "Now you just need to focus on getting well so we can go home."

Home. The word had never sounded so beautiful.

* * * * *

Sharon Ashwood is a novelist, desk jockey and enthusiast for the weird and spooky. She has an English literature degree but works as a finance geek. Interests include growing her to-be-read pile and playing with the toy graveyard on her desk. Sharon is the winner of the 2011 RITA® Award for Best Paranormal Romance. She lives in the Pacific Northwest and is owned by the Demon Lord of Kitty Badness.

Books by Sharon Ashwood

Harlequin Nocturne

Possessed by a Warrior
Possessed by an Immortal
Possessed by a Wolf
Possessed by the Fallen
Enchanted Warrior
Enchanted Guardian
Royal Enchantment

Visit the Author Profile page
at Harlequin.com for more titles.

ROYAL
ENCHANTMENT
Sharon Ashwood

For all the princesses who wanted the sword *and* the frilly dress—and maybe the horse and the dragon, too. Why not?

Prologue

Once upon a time, King Arthur of Camelot made an alliance with the fae and the witches to keep the mortal realms safe for all the free peoples. The world back then was filled with peril, with dragons and ogres and much, much worse lurking in the dark places. The greatest danger came from the demons who roamed the earth, causing suffering wherever they went. With the help of the enchanter, Merlin the Wise, the allies waged war upon the demons and succeeded in casting them back into the abyss.

At least, that's what Queen Guinevere was told. Stuck in the castle with her ladies-in-waiting, all she heard was gossip and rumors and thirdhand accounts of how mighty Sir So-and-So had been that day. As a royal princess, her value was measured by the children she'd bear, not the strength of her sword arm—and certainly not by anything she had to say.

So she missed how Merlin's final battle spells had

stripped the fae of their souls—and how the Faery people blamed Camelot for the disaster—until an enraged party of wounded fae burst into the castle threatening to crush humanity to dust. That's when fear rose from the soles of Guinevere's slippers, creeping up her body in chill waves of foreboding. Something had gone horribly wrong for her husband and his friends—but, as usual, Arthur had failed to send her word, and so there was nothing Guinevere could do.

In the end, it was Merlin who gave her a full account of the disaster. He came to her sitting room, dusty and disheveled from the road and with his dark face tight with worry. She set down her embroidery and stood, feeling as if she needed to be on her feet for whatever he had to say.

And then he told her. The fae would indeed carry out their threat against the mortal realms, but no one knew which day, year or even century their attack would come. So Merlin had put the king and his knights into an enchanted sleep and, when the fae returned, the heroes of Camelot would arise once more. As Merlin spoke, the mighty warriors of the Round Table were already stretched out upon empty tombs, trapped as effigies made of stone. In that form they would wait out the ages. They had sacrificed everything—fame, wealth and their very futures to stand guard over humankind.

But Guinevere had been left behind. Again.

Chapter 1

"Is this where you saw the beast?" asked Arthur Pendragon, High King of the Britons, as he slowed the Chevy SUV into the gravel beside a remote highway.

"Yes, about a half hour's walk off the road." His passenger was the dark-haired Scottish knight, Sir Gawain. "That's a wee bit close for comfort."

They were miles from civilization, but both men knew that meant nothing. A determined monster could find a town and crush it in the matter of an afternoon. Arthur parked and got out, a cold drop of rain making him look up. The October sky was baggy with clouds, promising a downpour.

Sir Gawain slammed the passenger door and walked around the front of the vehicle to stand beside him. The two men gazed toward the wild landscape of the inlet, a forest of cedars to their backs. Arthur glimpsed a distant sliver of water crowned with the ghostly outline of

hills. The raw beauty of the place only darkened his mood.
"Let's gear up."

They pulled weapons from the back of the SUV—
swords, guns and knives—and buckled them on. Once
armed, Gawain loped toward the forest at a speed that said
much about the urgency of their hunt. He'd shrugged a
leather jacket over a fleece hoodie and looked more like a
local than a knight of Camelot. On the whole, he'd adapted
to the twenty-first century with enviable ease.

Arthur followed, his heavy-soled boots sinking into
the soft loam. Unlike Gawain, he'd spent his entire life
as a king or preparing to be one, and blending in hadn't
been a necessary skill. Until now, anyway. Waking up in
the modern world had changed more things than he could
count—but not his duty to guard the mortal realms.

As they crossed the swath of scruffy grass between
the road and the trees, Arthur saw the tracks. He immediately dropped to one knee. "Blood and thunder," he cursed
softly. The print was enormous, as big as a platter with
three clawed toes pointed forward and a fourth behind.
"Not to ask the obvious question, but what is a dragon
doing in Washington State?"

"What's Camelot doing here?" Gawain countered with
a shrug.

"Are you saying there's a connection?"

Gawain didn't answer, and Arthur didn't blame him.
Sometimes there was no easy way to tell enchantment from
sheer bad luck. As a case in point, after Merlin had sent
the Knights of the Round Table into an enchanted sleep,
an entrepreneur had moved the church and its contents—
knights included—to the small town of Carlyle, Washington, to form the central feature of the Medievaland Theme
Park. Arthur had gone to sleep in the south of England and
awakened nearly a thousand years later as part of a tour-

ist attraction in the US of A. After that, a fire-breathing monster hardly surprised him.

Arthur rose, dusting grit and pine needles from his hands. "A dragon can't cross into the mortal realms on its own. It doesn't have that kind of magic."

"Then it had help," Gawain muttered. "I suspect that's your connection."

Arthur shifted uneasily, the wind catching at the long skirts of his heavy leather coat. "So do we have a new enemy or an old one we've overlooked?" There were too many choices.

Gawain grabbed his arm in a bruising grip. "There!" He pointed, his hand steady but his face losing color.

Arthur sucked in his breath as a ripple of movement stirred the undergrowth. He reached for the hilt of his sword, Excalibur, but his fingers froze as the beast reared from the shaggy treetops. He was forced to tip his head back, and then tip it more as he looked up into a nightmare. "Bloody hell."

The dragon's green head was long and narrow with extravagant whiskers. Huge topaz eyes flared with menace, the slitted pupils widened as the beast caught sight of the two men. The eager expression in that gaze reminded Arthur of a cat spotting a wounded bird.

"I told you it was big," said Gawain helpfully.

Arthur's thoughts jammed like a rusted crossbow. The dragon was close enough that he could make out its scent— an odd mix of musk and cinders. Through the screen of trees, he could see a bony ridge of spikes descending from its humped back onto a long muscular tail that twitched with impatience. Or hunger.

"Ideas?" Gawain asked under his breath.

Arthur repressed a desperate urge to run. "Be charming. Maybe it will listen to reason."

Gawain gave a strangled curse.

"Hello, mortal fleas," the dragon boomed, its deep voice resonant with unpleasant amusement.

Arthur grasped Excalibur's hilt and drew the long sword with a hiss. It should have made him feel better, but fewer knights than dragons walked away from a fight. He adopted his most courteous tone. "Sir Dragon, pray tell us what brings you to this realm?"

"Are there only two of you?" The dragon's tufted ears cupped forward with curiosity as he pointedly ignored Arthur's question. "What happened to your armies, little king?"

Arthur flinched with annoyance. After transporting Camelot's resting place to Washington State, Medievaland's founder had sold off most of the stone knights as a fund-raising effort. As a result, Camelot's warriors now resided in museums and private collections, and there they would stay until awakened with magic. Counting Arthur, Camelot had exactly eight knights awake out of the one hundred and fifty that had gone into the stone sleep and no one knew where the rest of them were. Arthur was hunting his missing men one by one, but it was slow going.

There was no way he was sharing those details. "I don't need an army to say that this place offers you no welcome. The mortal realms have forgotten the old ways, and dragons are no more than myths. Not even the fae reveal themselves to the humans here."

The dragon snorted, twin puffs of smoke curling up from its cavernous nostrils. "And what does this world make of you, High King of the Britons?"

Arthur held Excalibur loosely in one hand, the tip resting between his feet. It was a posture meant to look relaxed, but he was balanced and ready to strike. "To my great sorrow, Camelot is forgotten. I keep my true name to myself."

Amused, the dragon rumbled with a sound like crashing boulders. "But you still tell me to go? You would risk a thankless death for the ignorant rabble who live here?"

"Yes," Arthur replied with outward calm.

Like a preening cat, the dragon stroked a huge, taloned forepaw over its whiskers. It looked casual, but Arthur detected something else in the dragon's manner. Anger or sorrow or even disappointment.

"You amaze me, little king," said the creature. "Once, your Pendragon forefathers held the deep respect of my kind. Now you can do no more than shoo me away as if I were a stray cat."

"This time is different."

"Is that why you left the mistress of your forgotten realm a widow?"

Arthur clenched his jaw. *Guinevere.* The memory of her made him ache with a mix of fury and regret. "That is not your affair."

"A shame." There was a dragonish, smoky sigh. "The minstrels of my world still sing of the Queen of Camelot's beauty. A dragon would have kept his mate close."

Arthur ground his teeth. Leaving his queen was the only thing he'd done right in their marriage. Back then, even the image of her delicate face and graceful hands had burned like acid crumbling his bones. He'd desired her so much, and yet they'd been so utterly mismatched. His crown and sword, his title and lands—none of it had meant a thing to her. All she'd wanted was—he wasn't even certain what she'd wanted. He prayed she'd found happiness in the end.

"Don't speak of my queen," Arthur growled, all pretense of civility gone. "I ask you again, dragon, why are you here?"

"Ask me rather what I want." The dragon arched its neck to angle one huge yellow eye at Arthur.

His words echoed Arthur's thoughts with almost-sinister precision. "Fine. What do you want?"

"It has been long years since I made humans tremble behind their flimsy doors. I was once a destroyer of cities, a fiery death that rained from the skies. The name of Rukon Shadow Wing was the refrain of minstrels' songs."

None that Arthur had heard, but he kept that to himself. "Our cities are not your playthings."

"They are if I make them so, and this mortal realm is ripe for plucking. My name shall be whispered in terror once again."

"Humans have weapons far greater than my sword," Arthur said, his voice hard. "You won't survive."

"But there your logic breaks down, little king. You don't have an army, and by your own admission, modern mortals think me a myth." The dragon gave a sly smile that was horribly full of teeth. "It will be too late by the time the modern generals gather their wits for an attack."

"I will stop you."

"Assuming you could find the men to do so, every accord with the hidden world, including the witches and even the fae, decrees that the magical realm must stay hidden. Breaking that trust means war with the few allies you have left, and you can't afford that."

Arthur said nothing. Unfortunately, the creature was right.

The dragon chuckled, smoke rolling from its muzzle. "Poor king. Even if you could convince the human world that I am real, the rules won't let you say a word. What will you do, I wonder? Stand aside and watch me rampage through the countryside, or try to stop me all by yourself?"

Arthur finally lost his temper, gripping Excalibur's hilt, but the dragon still wasn't done.

"That would be the finest song of all," the beast said with a growling purr. "Rukon Shadow Wing defeating the mighty King of Camelot. You see, at the end of it all, that is what I want the most. The trophy of your head in my lair."

"I will not play the games of a delusional lizard!" Arthur roared, his gut burning. "I will see you dead first."

The creature's gaze flashed. "Foolish and rude. An unfortunate move, little king." And it bared its scythe-like fangs, saliva dripping from their points.

Arthur heard Gawain's breath hiss with alarm. His friend had been so still, Arthur had all but forgotten his presence. Now, with quicksilver speed, Gawain drew his gun and fired, grazing the long, weaving neck.

The dragon stretched its head high and snarled. White flame shot toward the sky, the heart of it a blue as pale and clear as gemstones. Terror shot down Arthur's spine, making his heart pound so hard he barely heard the branches shatter as the dragon crashed through the trees. It was coming toward them at a deliberate jog, tail lashing in its wake.

Gawain and Arthur fell back step by step, keeping just enough distance to avoid the wicked jaws. The creature was perhaps eight feet high at the shoulder, but three times that from nose to tail. The huge head bobbed on the snake-like neck, jaws gaping to show its flickering tongue. But despite the danger, Arthur's thoughts turned to crystalline calm as he tracked its every motion. This kind of impossible fight was what Arthur of Camelot had trained for.

They reached the grassy ground beyond the trees and used the room to run, drawing the monster into the open. Gawain fired again just as the dragon's shoulders pushed out of the forest. The weak sunlight shimmered along its scales as it twisted away from the shot, but this time the beast wasn't so lucky. Chips of scale flew as the bullet hit its side. It was no more than a flesh wound, but the dragon bellowed with fury, the sound so loud it was a physical blow.

The beast bounded forward and snatched up Gawain, quick as a heron plucking fish from the water. The knight's howl of surprise shut off as the dragon's jaws clamped around his chest. The gun flew from Gawain's hand as the long neck reeled him skyward. One burst of flame, and he would be cooked.

Arthur swung Excalibur, his only thought to save his friend. Rukon reared up as Arthur attacked, the long belly flashing creamy white. Arthur lunged for one of the pale gaps between scales. It was a suicidal move, but a man defended his brothers, and a king spilled his blood for them. Arthur felt his blade connect, the shock of the blow jolting his shoulder before he spun away. Blood spilled but Excalibur's edge did not slide far into the flesh. The beast seemed to be made of iron. Still, Arthur bolted in again, refusing to give up.

The next second Rukon's whiplike tail whirled through the air, hammering Arthur so hard he flew back into the forest. Branches crackled and clawed at his face, turning the world into a mosaic of green and golden leaves—but not before he saw the dragon toss Gawain into the air with a disgusted flick. Gawain spun, arms outstretched, and dropped into the bushes with a mighty crash.

Arthur scrambled to Gawain's side, dreading what he would find. Just as Arthur reached him, the dragon roared again, then thrust its head through the trees toward Arthur. He scrabbled for Excalibur, but it wasn't needed. The dragon simply wanted to mock them now.

"This match goes to me. Have a worthy army waiting

for my return, and bring reporters so that they can sing the song of my victory."

"Reporters?" Arthur repeated the word with confusion. What did a dragon know about the human press?

He didn't get a reply. With a huff of smoke, the dragon drew its head out of the trees and turned its back to the forest. Then it broke into a thundering run across the grass and unfurled huge leathery wings, each spine tipped with a glittering claw. The wingspan was enormous, blotting out the light. With a thunderous flap, Rukon Shadow Wing sprang into the sky, beating hard until the long, twisting form soared above the wild landscape.

As it rose higher and higher, a bright spiral of light appeared in the clouds. It was no bigger than a coin to Arthur's sight, but he knew it was a rift into another realm—a doorway no dragon should have been able to create. Rukon dived through it, and the light winked out. The sky was suddenly empty of anything but the coming rain.

Gawain moaned and rolled onto his back. "Did I ever mention dragon breath smells like old barbecue?"

"How badly are you hurt?" Arthur asked, helping Gawain as he struggled to sit up.

The knight paused before answering, as if doing a mental check of his bruises. "Hitting the bushes hurt the worst." He peered at the sleeve of his leather jacket. The fabric was scarred by the dragon's fangs, but not torn. For some reason, Rukon had spared him.

Arthur clapped his friend on the shoulder, unable to speak. Relief had closed his throat with a burning ache. They had survived, but he had a feeling their good luck had just run out. Too much didn't make sense. How was the dragon traveling between realms? Was Rukon really so hungry for glory—for the chance to kill Arthur before the cameras of the human media—that it was willing to risk starting a war with every magical creature that preferred to hide from human eyes? And why hadn't it butchered Gawain?

"Have you ever heard of Rukon Shadow Wing?" Gawain asked.

"No," Arthur replied, getting to his feet. "And I'd remember if we'd met."

Arthur picked up Excalibur and scowled at the blade. The strike against the dragon's scales had dulled the edge. He slammed the sword back into its scabbard and paced the loamy ground, anger and confusion prickling along his nerves. What was going on and, more to the point, how could he stop it?

Both men jumped when Gawain's phone rang with the sound of a tiny fanfare. The knight was still sitting on the ground, but he unzipped his pocket and extracted the smartphone in its shockproof case. "Hello?"

Arthur watched his friend's face pucker in confusion. He knew most of Gawain's trademark scowls, but this was different. The knight held out the phone with a faintly dazed expression. "It's your wife."

The clouds picked that moment to unlock their downpour.

Chapter 2

Minutes later, Guinevere handed the phone back to Merlin the Wise. They sat in his workshop, the light dim and the details of the room lost in shadow. It didn't bother her that she couldn't see much. Her mind was already far too crowded.

"That voice," she said, the words faint. "That was his voice."

She'd heard her husband speak through a tiny square of a slippery, unfamiliar material called plastic. Impossible. Disorienting. A bone-deep queasiness made her clutch the edge of her chair.

"What about Arthur's voice?" Merlin asked gently.

She wasn't sure what to say. That hearing Arthur speak had made the blood rush to her cheeks? That she'd thought him lost to her forever? That hearing his words—she could barely recall what those were, she'd been so flustered—brought back bitter disappointment that Arthur had left her behind?

No, she'd never reveal that much vulnerability to Merlin. He was too arrogant and too manipulative for trust. She had no wish to be a pawn on his chessboard.

"Has Arthur changed?" she asked instead. Despite the unfamiliar form of communication, she'd recognized the force of Arthur's personality through his shock. There had been something different, more grim.

"Yes, he's had to change. This is a new world," Merlin said, offering no details as he pocketed the phone. "And, no, he's the same as he always was. That's the strength and the curse of Arthur."

"He left you behind, as well," she said, suddenly putting things together. "That must have been a blow."

"There is no need to concern yourself with that. I am here with Arthur now, and so are you." The enchanter's eyes were an odd amber color that reminded her of a hawk. She had no idea how old he was, but he appeared to be a man in his thirties, lean and dark and with the air of someone too smart for his own good. He watched her now as if afraid she'd turn hysterical. Maybe she would.

Her eyes strayed to the tomb at the center of the gloomy workshop. On top of it was an elegant effigy made of white marble, every fold of cloth expertly carved. She would have admired its beauty, except the face on that statue was hers. *She* was that stone woman with the budding rose in her folded hands—and that Gwen was dead. It was a tomb for her, and it was very old. So why was she alive?

She tried to swallow, but her mouth was as dry as the grave. "Tell me again how I woke up inside that statue?"

"Magic," he said with an airy wave. "I cast the same spell on you as I did on the knights of Camelot. While you were part of the stone, you slept. No age or disease touched you. But now you are awake and fully mortal again. Your life picks up exactly where you left off."

"Oh." She didn't sound enthusiastic even to herself.

Had she asked for this? She couldn't remember Merlin's spell, much less discussing it beforehand—and yet somehow that seemed the least of her problems. "Does this mean I shall continue as Arthur's wife and the Queen of Camelot?"

Merlin gave an affirmative nod.

"Why?" The word came out before she could stop it.

"Why?" He tilted his head. "I brought you here because Camelot requires a queen." He said it casually, the way someone might say Camelot required a gate or a carpet or new furniture in the reception hall. She was an object taken out of storage.

Gwen had always done what was required of her, but a hot nugget of anger was coming to life, as if emerging from its own block of stone. She hadn't asked to be abandoned, but she hadn't asked to be turned into a gigantic paperweight, either. Of course, there was only one man who was ultimately responsible for anything that happened in Camelot. "I want to speak to Arthur. Take me to him."

Merlin gave a sly smile and bowed low. "At once, my queen."

Merlin's obedience was about as reliable as a cat's but, for the moment, she was at his mercy. She watched with unease while he sketched an arc in the air with his hand. Where his fingertips passed, a bright, tremulous light followed, as if he'd opened a seam in reality. Gwen blinked and stepped back in alarm as the golden luminescence dripped across the air like honey from a spoon. She'd seen many of Merlin's tricks, but this was new. She swallowed hard, trying to look as if this sort of thing happened every day.

When the light had filled in the impromptu doorway, he bowed again and reached for her hand. Stiffly, she allowed him to take it, and they stepped through the brilliance. A buzzing sensation rippled across her skin and, in the time it took Gwen to gasp, they emerged into a long hallway punctuated with closed doors. Merlin began walking, Gwen trailing after him. When she twisted her head to look behind her, the arc of golden light had vanished.

"Where is this place?" Gwen asked.

Merlin stopped before a plain and very unmagical-looking door at the end of the hallway. "The king's dwelling, as you desired."

The enchanter put one long-fingered hand around the doorknob and spoke a word. Pale light flared around the brass knob, and a series of clicks followed. Gwen guessed that was the sound of the locks surrendering.

"Why not simply knock?" Gwen asked, suspecting Merlin was just showing off now.

"Arthur's not home, so we'll let ourselves in."

"I may have hurtled through centuries," Gwen said under her breath, "but I can't imagine any reality in which my royal husband welcomes uninvited guests."

"We're not guests," Merlin said smoothly. "This is your home as much as his."

He pushed the door open with a flourish. Gwen stood on the threshold, suddenly uncertain if she wanted to step inside. "This is Arthur's home? Where is his castle?"

The enchanter gave a nervous cough. "Things work slightly differently in this day and age. This is my lord's apartment, which he rents. These rooms are his, but not the entire building."

On one level, Gwen understood the concept. Merlin's enchantment had given her information about the modern world, but the tumult of facts had come too fast for her to grasp them all. Not yet, and what she had absorbed seemed random. Modern clothes were a blank, but she was certain the standard measurements for an entry door like this were thirty-six by eighty inches.

Merlin was waiting for her to react, a concerned frown creeping onto his face. She stepped inside, reminding herself she was queen of this domain. Ahead was a large room with a balcony beyond tall glass doors. There were dark leather couches suitable for sprawling males. There was a bowl of something on a low table she assumed was food, although it was nothing that she recognized.

She continued her inspection, keeping emotion from her face. She didn't need Merlin to see her mounting distress. The function of the other rooms—a kitchen, bathroom and bedroom—were clear, although they lacked warmth or interest or personality or the slightest hint of being a home. Even the grand castle at Camelot, with hundreds of inhabitants, said more about its king than this sad place. Arthur was utterly absent. Gwen bit her lip. Come to think of it, absent was rather his style.

She turned back to Merlin. "Is this everything? Where do the servants sleep?"

"There's an office." He pointed to the one door she hadn't opened yet. "No servants."

"No servants?" That explained the dirty dishes in the kitchen sink and the crumbs around the bowl of whatever it was on the table. Words formed on the tip of her tongue, hot and burning. This was an insult. Royalty had men and maids to do their bidding. Gwen curled her fingers, indignation sharp in her chest. Then she swallowed it down. Arthur, for all his flaws, did everything for a reason. There had to be an explanation.

"Will I have my own chambers?" she asked, quieting her voice. "Will there be ladies to tend me?"

Merlin actually shuffled his feet like an embarrassed

squire. "That's a conversation you should have with Arthur."

Which meant she wouldn't like the answer.

"Very well." She walked to the nearest couch and sat down, folding her hands in her lap. "When will the king arrive?"

Merlin gave a slight shrug. "Not long. He's meeting with his men."

"I understand," she said with a touch of acid. "His wife returning from the grave is a small matter compared to his knights."

The enchanter winced. "There was a dragon."

"Oh?" She raised a brow. "This is not the Forest Sauvage. How did a dragon get here?"

"We don't know. That's half the problem."

"And the other half?"

Merlin opened his mouth, and then closed it. "Arthur will tell you."

Which meant Arthur had asked Merlin not to say more. This, at least, was familiar territory. Battling monsters was a man's business. Never mind that it was the women, left at home, who had the most face time with whatever horror was tearing the village apart. They typically had the beastie on the run by the time Sir Whatever showed up to poke it with a sword.

Gwen paused, wondering at her thoughts. Merlin's spell had introduced a lot of unfamiliar—and usefully sarcastic—words and phrases. She rather liked that.

"I can wait. There's always a dragon. Or a troll. Or a quest." Closing her eyes, Gwen leaned back against the squishy cushions, discovering the ugly piece of furniture was actually comfortable. "While we wait, you can tell me why Camelot needs a queen."

Merlin's voice was soft. "That's also something Arthur needs to say."

Gwen sighed. She considered trying out one of the useful modern phrases, but when she looked up again, Merlin had disappeared. The only thing left was a faint curl of smoke drifting toward the spackled ceiling.

Gwen huffed. *Coward.* It was Merlin's fault she was here. She hadn't asked to be dragged forward in time.

She rose, too nervous to stay still. The prospect of seeing Arthur turned her insides cold. She was angry with him, of course, but there were other emotions, too—ones that she really didn't want to examine. Fear, maybe? Shame? Anytime she'd tried to fix things between them, it had all gone wrong. They were just too different. And then there was the fact she'd never done the one thing required of a queen—she'd failed to give him an heir.

She drifted around the space, picking things up and putting them down again. The circuit didn't take long. To the left was an alcove with table and chairs, but she couldn't imagine it had ever seen a dinner party. The kitchen was filled with marvelous devices, but little food. She avoided the bedroom.

The office door beckoned. Why was it closed when every other room was open for inspection? There was no lock, however, and in a moment she was inside. She froze before she'd taken two steps.

Now she understood the closed door. This was the room where Arthur lived. It was not large, but there was a substantial desk in the corner covered with papers. The clutter had the feel of determination and excitement, of boundless enthusiasm colliding with rigorous organization. She approached it, her hands at her sides, touching nothing.

A map hung on the wall, poked full of colored pins. Gwen studied it, not sure what it signified but recognizing the hand of the high king who had made a conquest of Britain. He'd been barely more than a child when the lesser rulers had bowed to his sword. Give Arthur something to conquer, and he was in his element.

Once upon a time, that confidence, that strength of purpose had stopped her heart. Who wouldn't revere a man who could pluck kingdoms like ripe fruit and make them his own? But she might as well have loved the sea or a range of mountains. Great works of nature had no time for mortal women. She had been a clause in a treaty between Arthur and her father, King Leodegranz. Marriage had been the price of peace, and her dowry had been the famous Round Table.

The table had got more of Arthur's attention. Gwen frowned and turned away from the map.

There was a computer on the desk, and she experimentally touched a key. The black screen jumped to life, displaying words and pictures. She bent closer to look, her brain catching up to the spell that made it possible for her to read the modern text. Once she began, Gwen lost all awareness of the room around her. She pushed the arrow buttons, making the lines of type move. The novelty of it intrigued her.

So did the words themselves. It was a report of mysterious destruction outside the town. Was this the dragon Merlin had mentioned? Her pulse quickened.

A thickly muscled arm caught her around the waist. Deep in thought, Gwen jerked away from the desk, surprise quickly turning to alarm. The grip tightened, pulling her back against a wall of chest. And then she knew him. She knew the scent, the feel of his body.

"Arthur." She put both hands on his confining arm, but he didn't release her.

"What are you doing in here?"

He'd spoken to her on the phone, but the device had done his voice an injustice. Up close, the deep, rich sound was something touchable, like warm fur. Gwen closed her eyes, wishing it didn't enchant her quite so thoroughly. He'd left her behind. That said enough about his true feelings.

"Shouldn't you be asking why I'm here at all?" She put an edge in her voice out of reflex, as if that would hold his magnetic effect at bay.

"You forget I spoke to Merlin. I know how you arrived." His tone was carefully neutral.

His coolness burned her. "And no more needs to be said?"

"What would you have me say?"

"You could begin with hello. I am your wife."

He relaxed his grip enough that she could turn and pull away. She took a step back, looking up into his face. Her breath hitched then. The encounter with the dragon hadn't been gentle. His left cheekbone was purpling over raw scrapes that said he'd skidded on hard ground. Without thinking, she reached up and cupped his wounded face. "How badly are you hurt?"

"Gawain got the worst of it, but he walked away."

Arthur's clear blue eyes finally met hers. Their expression made it plain that he was unsettled to see her. That made everything worse. His anger was easier to fight.

Gwen dropped her hand, her mouth gone dry. The bruises did nothing to hide the clean, strong symmetry of his face. He was eight years older than she was, but that only put him in his early thirties. His neatly trimmed beard had not changed, but his hair was longer. There was something lionlike about the shaggy mass—it was no one color, but a wealth of autumn shades from gold to dark auburn. She yearned to touch it.

He was dressed strangely in what she assumed was the modern style. Her hands fisted in her skirts—the same ones she'd slept in for centuries. The clothes made the gulf between them seem even wider.

They stared at each other for a long moment, teetering at the edge of…something. Could it be he was glad to see her? There was so much unsaid, so many hurts and so many things she didn't understand.

In all their years together, she'd never come to grips with what drove him. Most of all, she'd never known what drove him away, exactly, beyond the fact that she wouldn't sit still and say nothing for years on end.

All Gwen's unspoken questions rose up, almost a physical pressure under her ribs. At times—though not often enough—she would have swallowed her questions back, bowed her head and retreated. But she'd been ripped from her century and dumped here without permission, and she was done with silent obedience.

"Why am I here?" she demanded.

Chapter 3

Once, Guinevere hadn't been bold enough to hold Arthur's gaze, but she did so now. He could see her irises were not the perfect blue that minstrels described. Rays of green and gold gave them an iridescent depth. In a similar way, Guinevere was never just one thing. Arthur's life would have been so much more predictable if she were.

He took a step back, taking in her tall, slim form. By all the saints, she was lovely. Her golden beauty cut him to the quick, reminding him why he had tried so hard to wipe it from his thoughts.

"Why, Arthur? Why bring me here?" Guinevere asked again, her voice shaking.

Why had he brought her here? He'd done no such thing, but he wasn't ready to admit that. Not until he knew more. "Why are you rifling through my private space?" he countered.

"Your private space? Is there something here the

Queen of Camelot cannot see?" Her color was rising to an angry pink.

"There are confidential matters that I would keep to myself." Such as the many places he believed stone knights might be languishing. If his research fell into enemy hands, their lives might not be safe.

Gwen clenched her fists. "You're not content unless I'm locked in a tower, deaf and blind to the dangers at our door!"

"You meddle," he growled. "You have from the first day you set foot in my realm."

That wasn't exactly true. Their disagreements had grown with time. At first, he'd been conquering a realm and far too busy for his young wife. After the first few years, they'd begun to get along. But then she'd been ill, and then trouble had started: the scandal with Lancelot. She'd always claimed he was just a friend, and Arthur believed her now. But that hadn't always been the case, especially after the incident with the Mercian prince. Then there had been their endless fights. In the end, he'd ridden off to war as often as he could. They couldn't make each other unhappy if they were miles apart.

Her eyes flashed. "The realm is not just your business, husband. I am the queen. These are my people, as well."

The air between them sang with frustration. Within seconds, they'd picked up the threads of their old argument. Arthur cleared his throat, cursing his anger. Her stubborn will ignited his temper at every turn.

"It's dangerous in this time," he said softly. "Even worse than before. This world is deceptive in its illusion of order and safety."

"And you would protect me through ignorance? I'm not a child."

His chest burned. "Remember the prince of Mercia."

The man had been rotten through and through—young, handsome, a good dancer and witty conversationalist. He'd flattered Gwen when she'd first come to court, and later that flirtation had grown more serious. In the end he'd coaxed information out of her that broke a treaty and all but started a war. Gwen hadn't even suspected trickery until it was too late. By then, both Gwen and Arthur looked like fools. It was plain he had no control over his wife—and any weakness in a king made their enemies bold.

"I know better now," she said through clenched teeth. "I've said a thousand times how I learned my lesson."

Anger made his voice cold. "Self-knowledge is good. Trusting you to stay out of the kingdom's affairs is another matter."

"When will you trust me?"

"I would take that chance if I was an ordinary husband with an ordinary life. I'm not that man."

She visibly flinched. "And what would you have me do?"

"I would have you at my side." He reached out, cupping her cheek and hoping to take some of the sting from his words. "As you say, you are the queen. A queen has a household to run and official duties to discharge. You make guests welcome, smile at our subjects and grace my arm at official functions."

She lifted her chin, the movement breaking contact with his hand. "In other words, you want me to sit quietly like a good little mouse."

It was a harsh statement but true. He didn't want her involved in matters of state. Guinevere's intentions were good, but she had always underestimated schemers. And now? Nothing had changed. Enemy fae were skulking around every corner. Many foes would try to attack him through his curious, trusting wife, and that meant neither of them were safe with her here. But here she was, his greatest vulnerability wrapped in an exquisite female form.

Arthur released the breath he'd been holding. She hadn't moved—her arms still folded as if to protect her vital organs. Sadness took him then, an ache for the gulf that forever yawned between them. He reached out, taking one of her hands and unwinding that closed posture.

"Come sit down," he said, with all the gentleness he could muster. "We need to talk."

She frowned. "Why does no one say that for a happy reason?"

Despite himself, Arthur gave a rueful chuckle. "I don't know, but you're right." He led her from the office and closed the door firmly behind them. He hadn't been in the apartment long enough to invest in a lock for his office, but clearly it was time.

Arthur led Guinevere to the black leather couch and guided her to a seat beside him. The familiar swish of her long skirts stirred memories. At every step, a fresh storm of emotion ran through him—regret, desire and a strong conviction that she would bring nothing but trouble.

And yet...

This was Guinevere, the queen who made hardened warriors stand gaping like witless boys. Her beauty wasn't just flesh and features, but a lively kindness that burned like a lantern through a winter night. It was her forthright ease with strangers, her wit in conversation and the charm that had turned his warrior's castle into a shining court. In a small, secret corner of his heart, he was in awe of her. She made people love her with a smile. He'd needed an army before anyone would spare him a glance.

They sat and regarded each other for a long moment, as if neither knew how to begin. What was there to say? They'd faced the same problems so many times before: her independence and his need to rule, her curiosity and his protectiveness. There would be a fight, and usually he'd end it by leaving.

But what about reconciliation after the storm? That was the one consolation of their relationship, and he would rather begin again with sweetness than fury. Perhaps if he tried harder this time, maybe, just maybe he could make her accept his rule.

Arthur picked up her hand from where it lay on the black leather and kissed it. He lingered over the act, feeling her soft warmth. Her fingers were long and delicate, the palms slender and graceful. They smelled of scented oils and, beneath that, the richness of her skin.

When Arthur finally looked up, there was a flush high on her cheekbones. He felt a surge of pride that he had the power to stir her blood. But instead of smiling, the corners of her lush mouth turned down. "It has been a long while since you did that, my lord."

"Too long." He tasted her warmth on his lips, and it awakened old hungers. "An unforgivable oversight."

"You left for battle and never came home again."

He looked away, back into a battlefield strewn with carnage. "The fae swore to destroy Camelot, and then all the mortal realms. We just never knew when or how. We had to come up with a plan."

"Merlin told me," she replied. "You went into the stone sleep and woke up here. The fae have returned to carry out their threat."

He nodded. "Morgan LaFaye is their queen now, but she is in a magical prison. It should hold her long enough for Camelot to strengthen its forces."

Guinevere's eyes were intent. "How will you accomplish that?"

This was information she'd find out anyhow. There was

no harm in answering. "The knights were scattered during the stone sleep, and I've had to locate them one by one. I've only found a handful of my warriors so far, but I will keep searching."

"Where did they go?" Guinevere's brows furrowed.

"The tombs have turned up in museums and private collections." Arthur was still holding her hand, but his grip had tightened. He released Guinevere, afraid of crushing her bones. Suddenly weary, he released a sigh. "I had to buy Percival at auction."

A smile twitched the corners of her mouth. "I hope you didn't overpay. That would surely go to his head."

For the first time since she'd arrived, they laughed together. Merriment was scant in his life. Female company was even rarer. For all their difficulties, he'd been faithful to his wife, and having her near stirred heated memories. Arthur's heart gave an odd skip at the thought of Guinevere's sleepy face in the pale light of early morning. They'd had their moments.

He snapped himself back to the present. "I shouldn't be troubling you with unpleasant tidings."

"Trouble me," she said. "How did you come out of the stone sleep?"

"Not easily. Gawain found my tomb in the Forest Sauvage."

"And then?"

"There was a battle. It's a long story."

"I want to hear it."

"Why?"

"First, you are my husband." She said it with a bittersweet smile that speared his heart. "And I'm part of Camelot, too."

She was more than that. Guinevere was royalty, but noble birth meant little in these modern times. A difficult truth struck him. With no skills, no occupation, how would she survive? Whatever he'd done in the past to protect her—and he would lay down his life in an instant—he had to keep her close now. Without him, Guinevere was alone. The thought filled him with an odd mix of dread and desire.

Her expression was expectant, waiting for him to say more. He smiled, feeling the bruises on his cheek and jaw. "I promise I'll regale you with the entire story, every last dull detail of it. But right now I'd rather tell you what this modern age has to offer."

Her eyes widened with interest. "All right. Please do."

"This is a strange world, filled with extremes. Most obvious is the wealth of information and experience. Books are readily available, and travel is breathtakingly fast."

"Really? And who are the books for?"

It was a reasonable question. They'd been born in a time when relatively few learned to read. "Schools are available to everyone, rich or poor."

"Do women go to school, as well?"

"Yes, they are regarded as equals here."

Guinevere said nothing, but her breath had quickened, a sure sign of emotion. An uneasy feeling crept down Arthur's spine—had he just opened Pandora's box?—but then she put a gentle hand on his knee. The unexpected touch sent a flood of heat up his thigh. Without quite knowing what he did, he leaned forward, needing to be closer.

"Then perhaps things can be different," she said. "We can live as the modern people do."

Her words did not quite sink in—other sensations were elbowing their way to the fore. Enchanted, he reached over, touching the slight cleft of her chin. The skin there was like satin, beckoning him to explore further. She stilled, growing watchful again. Only the muscles of her long, graceful throat moved as she swallowed.

Arthur was mesmerized. Her scent enveloped him, the space between them growing warm. All his earlier reservations melted, and he didn't care that he was dropping his guard. Right then all that mattered was Guinevere. His Gwen. She should be at his side, where he could touch her silken skin whenever he liked.

"Things will be different," he said, believing it for a heady moment. "Things will finally be right." He would rule Camelot, and she would be at his side, bonded together in this strange new time. The challenge of finding their way in the modern world would give them the common ground they'd always lacked. An image formed in his mind's eye of them seated before the assembled knights, hand in hand and finally united. They looked deliriously happy.

"Right?" she asked softly.

"As they always should have been. As I always meant them to be."

His daydream faded when she rose with a sigh, crossing to the balcony door to look outside. Rain splattered the glass, blurring the lights outside. At some point, dusk had fallen.

"How do I know we want the same thing?" The question was hesitant.

A familiar knot of confusion made Arthur frown. He never understood exactly how her mind worked. It was as if tiny demons lived inside her skull, coming up with ways to torment him. "How could it be otherwise? You're my queen."

She turned from the window, her expression defiant. "You didn't ask me to follow you into the future."

Arthur got to his feet, wary of her mood now. "The fae

had sworn vengeance on me. I was the one they wanted, so it was safer for you to remain in Camelot. With danger gone, I believed you'd find happiness."

"Happiness?" She gave a mirthless laugh that fired his skin with shame. "You left me alone."

His anger rose in self-defense, but he held it in check as she lifted her hands in a helpless gesture. "Never mind the past," she said. "What am I supposed to do now?"

Arthur took a deep breath, then let it out slowly. A moment ago, he'd been certain everything would be fine. He wanted to recapture that mood. "You're wondering if there's a role for you here, in this world?"

"Precisely." She looked ghostly in the soft light, twilight deepening behind her silhouette.

He covered the distance between them in a single stride. The energy of their argument prickled beneath his skin, and it made his hands rough as he grasped her slender waist. She went rigid at his touch, resisting until he ran a hand down her spine. Yes, she needed comfort. Another long stroke and she arched into him, her body remembering his. The skirts of her dress floated around her as he pulled her close.

Relief made him ache as he realized there was still a welcome for him in her arms. Arthur bent his head, murmuring into her ear. "Let me reassure you that there is no one else I would consider as my queen."

Lashes veiled her eyes, with a hint of mischief lurking beneath her sadness. "And why is that?"

"I wanted you the moment I saw you dancing in your father's garden. You were everything I was not."

Her lips quirked. "A girl, you mean?"

He buried his nose in the cloud of her hair, her scent filling his soul. "You knew nothing of the ills of the world. You were innocent."

She pulled back to search his face. "No one stays that pure. That ignorant."

"Not when you become a wife," he said, letting desire sharpen his smile. Then he kissed her.

He was forced to bend while she rose on tiptoe. They flowed into the embrace naturally, her arms winding around his neck. His hands inched down her ribs and over her hips, reclaiming her curves. Desire, already invading his thoughts, pushed its way to the fore.

He kissed her hard, reminding her that he was the master, and yet leaving coaxing nips behind. When they were together like this, there had never been a question about the spark between them. Her mouth opened, welcoming his exploration, letting their tongues twist and mingle. The gentle swell of her breasts pressed into his chest, demanding to be stroked and when he obeyed—even a sovereign sometimes obeyed—a sound of pleasure escaped her throat. Heat tore through his body, making him drive her back against the cool glass door. He held her head, gentle and yet not, as he plundered her mouth. Her fingers twined with his, her body arching up, straining to meet him.

How long the kiss lasted was impossible to know, but the sky was fully dark when they were done. The lights of the city shone behind his Gwen as if this new age had fashioned a celestial crown for his queen. Arthur ached with desire, eager to put his seal on this conquest. It was a healing, yes, and a reunion, but he also wanted her to know beyond doubt that she was his.

He took her hand, pulling her with him until he paused at the door of his bedroom. He touched a switch and a soft light bloomed from the bedside lamp. Praise all the saints that the room was acceptably tidy. He placed his hands on her shoulders, turning her to face him.

Guinevere's eyes were soft and dazed. "That was quite the kiss, my lord."

Satisfaction sprawled within him. "There is no need for it to end."

Her posture shifted. It was a slight thing, but it seemed to put her worlds away. "I think there is."

Arthur blinked. His need for her was a runaway stallion. Hauling it back took effort. "There is?"

"You want me as your queen. I understand that."

"And?" Arthur was confused. What more was there to add?

"Is that what I want now, in this new world? Did you ever think to ask?"

She waited, but he had no answer to give. That said enough, and they both knew it. He felt his temper begin to fray beneath the sting of awkwardness. Why should he ask? He was king and she had made her vows when she was little more than a girl.

Then again, was it fair to ask her to keep them when so much had changed?

"You left me behind—not just once, but over and over again." Guinevere shut her eyes a moment, then met his gaze without retreat. "I know you believed you were doing the right thing. You saw my desire to participate fully in your reign as naive and dangerous because of the fae and magic and the kings who hated the fact you'd conquered them."

She was completely right. "And?" he asked.

"And nothing, not even an apology, makes up for being considered invisible—dispensable—for so long. I don't want to be that woman anymore."

None of what she'd just said made sense to him. He'd never thought of her that way—not in the fashion she meant. "So what is it that you *do* want?"

"I've been in this world for only hours, but what you've said intrigues me. You say women have access to education? That they have equality? I'd like to find out what that means."

"How does that matter? You're the Queen of Camelot. What more could you desire?"

Gwen caught her breath, as if he'd slapped her. "There is a whole new world in which to answer that question."

She stepped into the bedroom and closed the door. "Good night." The words were muffled and very final.

"Gwen!" Chagrined, he pressed his palm against the hard barrier. He'd said the wrong thing. He'd known it the moment the words left his lips. *Stupid.*

And now the door was firmly closed. Arthur could easily break it down, but that was no answer. Reason demanded that they both cool off before the argument escalated to a fight, but his temper didn't want to listen. Self-discipline alone made him back away from the blank, infuriating blockade.

Right then, the dragon problem looked simple.

Chapter 4

Gwen's eyes snapped open. Bright sun streamed in the window, pooling on the carpet. Her eyes, sore and sandy from crying herself to sleep, protested against the glare. Squinting, she sat up, mind scrambling to reassemble yesterday's events. Statue. Merlin. Arthur. Gwen pressed a hand to her head, as if the memories might shatter her skull.

She'd shut Arthur out of his own bedroom. He was her husband. He was the *king*. What had she been thinking?

Gwen sagged back to the pillows. That was the whole point—she'd been *trying* to think, and with Arthur charming her, that was hard. He'd kissed her, and the heat of it still simmered under her skin. But bed sport, however delicious, wasn't the only thing she desired from her husband. She'd pushed him away, but she'd done it in hopes he would consider everything she'd said. If their marriage was to get better, someone had to make the first move.

She wanted Arthur's conversation, his confidence and his trust. She needed the same respect he gave to his knights. No, she demanded more. He should love her, Guinevere, and not just the idea of a wife or queen.

Gwen clawed her way out from under the covers. It was a large, soft bed, and it took her a moment to put her feet on the floor. When she finally stood, shivering slightly in her thin chemise, she could see the streets beyond the apartment window. She was high up, higher than the tallest towers of Camelot, and the men and women below seemed tiny. How on earth had these people built so many enormously tall buildings, with so much glass and so little stone?

She took a step closer, momentarily hypnotized. Merlin had said the name of this city was Carlyle, Washington. The streets ran in perfect lines, brightly colored vehicles speeding along them like ambitious beetles. Merlin's spell provided the proper words for what she saw—trucks, cars, buses and stoplights. But the knowledge had little meaning. She had no experience of any of it.

A sudden need to sit down put her back on the bed. Gwen pressed her face into her palms, willing her thudding heart to slow down. All the bizarre things that had happened yesterday were still true. She'd half expected to wake up in her own chambers far, far in the past.

She dropped her hands to her lap. She had to find courage. After all, this wasn't the first time her life had changed utterly from one sunrise to the next. One day, her mother had died. One day, she'd been betrothed. One day, she'd left the only home she'd known for Camelot. She would face this trouble like every other, even if she'd been catapulted centuries into the future. What other choice was there?

As she sat, she slowly became aware of the world around her. There were deep, rumbling voices sounding through

the walls—Arthur's definitely, and perhaps Gawain's
brogue, and then others she couldn't name. The last thing
she wanted to do was to face the knights on her first day
here, when everything was unfamiliar and awkward. But
again, what choice did she have?

She padded into the tiny bathroom that adjoined the
chamber. Merlin's spell had been helpful here, but the sight
of water appearing without pumps or buckets—hot water,
no less—was still fascinating. And oddly overwhelming.
Taking a breath, she turned a tap over the sink. She must
have turned too hard, because the water hit the porce-
lain with so much force that it bounced back, blinding
her with the spray. She jerked it off again, panting with
the surprise. An impulse to cry rolled over her—to cry
and be comforted and told everything would be fine. But
that was a weakness she couldn't afford if she was ever
to earn respect.

Grimly, she washed and pulled on her gown, wishing
for her ladies-in-waiting. They would have made sure her
hair was perfect and her dress free of dust or wrinkles.
Most of all, they would have distracted her with gossip
and silly jokes. They had been her friends, and now she
had none. She was alone.

Once Gwen had tidied herself, she stepped into the
rest of the bland, spare apartment. The living room was
crowded with big men draped over the black leather furniture. Arthur saw her first and looked up. As if that were
a signal, everyone fell silent and rose to their feet, then,
as one, they bowed.

"Be at your ease," she said, the words made automatic
from long habit.

There was a rustle as they straightened, every face
turned her way. She paused, frozen by the weight of their
stares. She recognized the knights: Gawain, Beaumains,

Percival and Palomedes. There was also a young woman
she did not know, with short fair hair and a smartphone in
her hand. Gwen scanned the young woman's clothes and
the confident way she carried herself. There was no question she was from the modern age.

Gwen forced herself to take another step into the room
until she faced Arthur, and then sank into a deep curtsy.
"My lord."

"We're not so formal here," he said. "Please rise."

She did, feeling an unaccustomed shyness. She'd at least
been able to count on her manners, but even that was different here.

"I'm glad to see you awake," said Arthur. "I trust you
slept well." He, on the other hand, had dark circles under
his eyes. Gwen wondered if he'd slept at all.

"Well enough." She barely noticed what she said, for
she was studying her husband with care. The warmth of
the night before had been replaced by a more impersonal
friendliness. She knew it of old—the mask of Arthur the
King, friendly, jovial and utterly impenetrable. It was as
if they hadn't kissed or touched or had a real conversation.
Disappointment throbbed like something wedged under
her breastbone.

Gwen swallowed hard. Had she destroyed everything
by pushing him? For asking for a voice in their marriage?
She wanted to talk everything through, but now was not
the time. As always, the business of court pushed her needs
aside. She was aware of the others, staring as if she were an
exotic beast. Her breath hitched, but she found her voice.

"How long did I sleep?" she asked with complete casu-
alness. "It must have been some time, judging by the light."

"My lady," said Beaumains, who was Gawain's younger
brother and her favorite among the courtiers. "We all crash
when we first come out of the stone sleep."

"Crash?" The word confused her.

"Sleep for a long time," explained the woman, who was standing beside Gawain. "Don't be surprised if you feel disoriented at first. Everyone's reaction on waking is different. Arthur held my sister at sword point for the first few minutes after he regained consciousness."

The king gave the young woman a pained look. "I'm not a morning person."

"You were in a paranoid delirium."

"That's something like your resting state, isn't it?" Gawain quipped, giving Arthur a sidelong glance.

The banter didn't hide the tension in the room. Gwen looked quickly from face to face. The young knights—the ones she considered friends—were subdued. Gawain, on the other hand, scowled at Gwen. She groaned inwardly. He had always blamed her for making Arthur unhappy, and clearly that hadn't changed.

Well, she would just have to work around him. She gave a confident nod to the room. "I did not mean to disturb your conversation, but here I am." She approached an empty chair next to Arthur. "What were you discussing?"

"Nothing of importance." Arthur waved a dismissive hand. "By your leave, my lady, I have summoned a friend to take you into town. You need clothes."

Gwen stopped in her tracks. Arthur was close enough to touch, but she kept her hands by her sides. "My lord," she began quietly, "by your own account there is a dragon marauding through the countryside, and fae armies threaten Camelot's welfare. Surely my wardrobe can wait?"

Arthur met her gaze and held it with his own. Despite his smile, the warning in his eyes was clear—he would not tolerate defiance in front of his men. "You need appropriate dress," he replied, his voice reasonable. "You don't need to remain here. There is nothing you can do."

The urge to protest rose up, but something made her look at the others in the room. Their expressions were carefully blank, but she could read the discomfort in their eyes. That made her back down. They didn't need to witness a fight.

"I'm sorry," she said quickly, turning to the young blonde woman. "We have not been introduced."

"My name is Clary Greene," she said. She had a pretty, triangular face and bright green eyes. "I'm one of the new kids in Camelot."

Gwen marveled. Clary's manner was quick and assured, as if certain she was the equal of the knights. If this was what living in the modern age meant, Gwen craved it with her entire being.

She smiled at Clary, plans already forming in her thoughts. "I trust you will show me everything. There is a great deal I want to learn."

Shortly after, the two women left. The scene Gwen had viewed from the apartment window was twice as frantic once she stepped onto the streets. Perhaps she should have been frightened, but there was too much to know where to start. Cars—including the old Camry Clary drove— intrigued her, but those tall buildings entranced. So did the more modest buildings, the houses and malls and gas stations. There was a dull sameness to many of the structures, but every one of them was airy and light compared to Gwen's old home. As they drove to Carlyle's downtown shopping district, Gwen tried to figure out how the seemingly flimsy walls held together.

"So what do you need to get?" Clary asked as she parked by the side of a teeming road.

"I don't know," Gwen confessed.

"What do you have?"

"What I'm wearing."

Clary grinned, green eyes filling with mischief. "We're going to have some fun, girlfriend."

Gwen narrowed her eyes. "Who are you?"

"My big sister, Tamsin, is Gawain's sweetheart." Clary made a gagging noise, which said everything about being a younger sibling. "She and Dad went back home to the East Coast to see the family, and I came out here to keep an eye on things."

"What for?"

Clary shrugged, gathering up the phone that seemed to be part of her hand. "Camelot needs a witch on hand to thaw out any stone knights they find. Merlin's not always around. Plus, a modern guide comes in handy when a medieval queen needs to go shopping." With that, she got out of the car and waited while Gwen figured out how to do the same.

Shopping in the modern era was a revelation. Gwen had always been required to select a fabric and design, and then wait for a seamstress—or herself—to make a new gown by hand. Now she could try on as many outfits as she liked, then walk out the door with her purchase in hand. And the choices!

"I want some trews like you're wearing." Gwen had worn boy's clothes when running about the farms as a child. As much as she loved miles of swishing skirts, the option to choose something else once in a while was attractive.

"We call them pants," Clary corrected her. "Or slacks. They're on the list. So is lingerie."

The lingerie was intriguing, the pants marvelous and the three-way mirrors hateful. She dressed and undressed more times in a single afternoon than she had during her entire life. And there were so many colors and shapes of footwear! Every shoe had a personality, and Gwen saw a slice of herself in each—feminine, adventurous, bold or hardworking. Picking a pair—or several—was almost impossible.

Nowhere, not even in Camelot's greatest markets, had she seen so many goods for sale. The abundance was dazzling at first, but after a few hours of rambling from store to store, it became overwhelming.

"I need to stop," Gwen finally admitted. "Surely I have enough shoes."

She was wearing her latest purchase, low ankle boots of maroon leather. According to Clary, they paired perfectly with Gwen's new black skinny jeans and turquoise silk sweater. Compared to the gown that was now packed away in the trunk of the car, the clothes felt tight but almost weightless.

"It's not possible to possess enough shoes," Clary said, threading her arm around Gwen's. "Trust me on this. I'm an expert, and you have the king's credit card. I won't be happy until it melts."

"I need to sit down," Gwen moaned. "My new boots are pinching my feet."

The restaurant Clary chose was cheerful, with large windows overlooking the street. They crammed a mountain of shopping bags in beside them as they squeezed into a booth. A moment later, menus sat open before them, promising an abundance of treats. It was sunny, and the golden light felt good on Gwen's skin. She turned her face toward it for a moment, soaking in the warmth.

Her companion typed on her phone, engaged in a world as ephemeral to Gwen as the Faery kingdom. Over the course of the day, Gwen had learned Clary and Tamsin were Sir Hector's daughters, though they had been born in modern times. The circumstances of it all formed a convoluted tale she'd have to hear again before she understood it. It was enough to know the young woman was part of Camelot's extended family. Finally, Clary closed the case of her device.

"We've been talking nonstop all afternoon, but it's mostly been about clothes. I'm sure you have more questions about this time," Clary said. "Feel free to ask whatever you like."

Gwen didn't hesitate. "What is a woman's life in this time like? Surely you don't go shopping like this often?"

"Not often," Clary said. "Arthur doesn't usually loan out his charge card."

He probably never would again, judging by the number of shopping bags they'd accumulated. They gave their order to the waitress as Gwen smothered her guilt about everything she'd bought that day. She liked nice things, but had no desire to empty the treasury. "But what else makes up your daily routine?"

Clary played with her napkin. "I'm not sure a witch is the best person to ask about the average experience."

"Because you used your power three times this afternoon to summon clerks to help us?"

Clary shrugged. "In some department stores, it's the only way to get service. It helps with finding parking spaces, too."

Coffee and blackberry pie arrived, the sturdy dishes filling up the table of the booth. Gwen was hungry, and the pie wasn't that different from what she was used to, so she ate it with relish. The coffee was hot, but bitter and she spooned a lot of sugar into it before she could get it down.

"Then again, maybe I'm wrong. I don't think magic makes us all that different from other women," Clary said once the first few bites were savored. "We go to work and pay our bills just like everyone else."

"What do you work at?" Gwen asked.

"Computers." Clary shrugged. "I'm bored with the job I'm in and looking around for something else. While I've been visiting in Carlyle, I went for a few interviews. I'd like to get into social media marketing."

"And you can find employment wherever you wish?"

"Pretty much. I have good skills."

Gwen pondered that. Such independence! She'd never earned money herself.

No wonder she felt invisible. How was she supposed to be equal to someone who paid for everything she ate or wore? "How did you learn your skills?" Gwen asked, suddenly aware this was important.

"I went to school," said Clary. "That's normally how people learn their trade."

That fit with what Arthur had said.

Gwen chewed her lip. *Could I study at a school?* Maybe she could learn how the great, towering buildings of this time were made. "I've always had a knack for constructing things—fences and sheds and even my father's war machines. I understand siege towers and catapults better than most soldiers."

Clary looked impressed. "You're an engineer at heart?"

"I don't know," Gwen said. "Some people carry a tune or bake perfect bread. I know what makes things stand up or fall down. Is there a school for that?"

"Yes." Clary nodded. "People pay well for that expertise. It's a long course of study, though."

Gwen didn't say more. This was a ridiculous conversation. She hadn't been in this world for a day, so any plans she made were castles in the air, without foundation or substance. And yet, the idea intrigued her. She'd always envied the monks their great libraries. Here, she could read her fill and become whatever she liked.

Or could she? What would Arthur do if she spent her

days with her nose in a book, too busy to meddle with Camelot's affairs? Would he be grateful to be rid of her, or would he consider it disloyalty?

Sudden doubt seized her, and she stared down into her coffee cup. The drink was half-gone, for all she disliked it. Sugar only masked some of the taste, but the bitterness lingered. She'd swallowed it because it was expected of her, just like she did most things.

"Is there something wrong?" Clary asked.

"I'm sorry," Gwen said. "I don't think I like coffee."

"Then try something else," Clary said with a laugh. "There's lots to choose from on the menu."

Would it be that easy, Gwen wondered, *to place an order for a completely different life?*

Chapter 5

Swords rang and whistled in an elaborate dance, splashing shards of light on the walls. Tall windows opened onto a vista of wind-tossed trees, but inside the long fencing gallery, all was pristine order. Except, of course, for the deadly dance of the fae.

Talvaric executed an expert feint, swinging in a circle to cut high. His step was light, barely making any sound—though the force of his blow sang against his opponent's saber. Barto, Lord of Fareen, was almost his equal, which was saying something. Though of insignificant lineage, Talvaric had made his fortune as a professional.

Barto doubled his attack, striking over and over in a pattern that should have brought Talvaric to his knees. For an uneasy moment, Talvaric retreated. Fear needled through him, exhilarating and rich. It was said the fae had no souls—not since Merlin's spells had stripped them away at the end of the demon wars. It was also common knowledge that the lack of a soul meant a lack of feelings. That was and was not true. Fae were immortal, but they could be killed. The desire to survive and the fear of defeat remained. That was why Talvaric had taken up the sword as his life. It was a splash of red against an otherwise-eternal gray.

With a pounding heart, he let Barto drive him back another step, then twisted away. He went low this time, aiming for his opponent's legs. It was a move of cool precision, but Barto escaped with a backward leap. It didn't matter. With a turn of the wrist, Talvaric changed direction, sweeping the blade upward until it pricked Barto's chin.

There he stopped, his control of the weapon absolute. Talvaric held Barto's gaze, waiting for acknowledgment. Talvaric could have taken his head with ease. Slowly, Barto nodded, the gesture releasing a drop of scarlet blood where the sword tip pierced his skin. Talvaric waited until the trickle reached Barto's collar before he withdrew. They were both panting hard.

"A good match," Barto conceded. He wiped his neck and looked at his blood-streaked hand with clinical interest.

Waiting servants—two of the many dryads Talvaric kept as slaves—hurried to attend the two males, taking their weapons and handing them soft white towels. Barto wiped his face. Like all the fae, like Talvaric himself, Barto was tall and slender, with dark olive skin and hair so pale it was almost white. The coloring made a startling contrast to the brilliant green of fae eyes.

"You are a worthy opponent," Talvaric returned, compliment for compliment. "I fought for many years at the pleasure of the queen and rarely saw the like."

Barto bowed and finished mopping his face. When he

dropped his towel to the floor, a servant dashed forward and gathered it up.

"I appreciate the compliment," Barto said. "I would like to fight in the palace games this winter. There is no better preparation than practicing against our foremost swordsman. Will you compete?"

"Perhaps."

Barto shrugged. "You have won several times. I suppose the honor of victory begins to pale."

"Not really. But I wonder if the games will go forward in the queen's absence."

"Good point," Barto sighed. "This business with La-Faye is tiresome."

Queen Morgan LaFaye was under lock and key, captured by the allies of King Arthur of Camelot. That left an interesting vacancy on the throne, but none had immediately jumped to fill it. If the queen ever got free, she would not welcome a usurper.

"It's a pity I could not cross swords with Arthur," Barto said lightly. "He is said to be almost your equal."

Talvaric narrowed his eyes. "I doubt it's a fair comparison. His blade is enchanted by the Lady of the Lake. Excalibur has magic enough to cut through even Morgan's spells."

Which was why the queen feared it. Excalibur was the only real weapon the mortals had against a fae invasion. Morgan had been on the cusp of attacking the mortal realms when she'd been captured. Now hostilities were suspended while the leaderless fae milled about like sheep.

"I suppose you're right." Barto wandered over to the rack of swords suspended on the wall. He fingered one hilt, then another. "Is this the weapon you used in the last contest?"

"The same."

"And this?"

"I used that one in the match against the Giant of Trevayne."

"That was quite the contest. I wagered on you and won."

Contests? Talvaric felt a twinge of impatience. Who cared about sports when the whole of the mortal realms were ripe for plucking? But Talvaric knew better than to blurt that out. Barto was Lord of Fareen, and Talvaric was a commoner with no right to an opinion. Yet.

"Would you care to see my other collection?" he asked.

Barto looked up, curious. "Your beasts? Yes, I would."

Talvaric led the way through his manor. It wasn't a palace or a castle, but it sprawled through an endless maze of corridors and wings. Although his property sat far from the fashionable cities, the inconvenience was made up for by privacy. Soon they were traversing a long passageway lined with cages on either side.

The rooms were bright, with plenty of windows, and clean. The steel of the bars was polished, the floors of the cages always strewn with fresh straw. The pristine conditions weren't due to Talvaric's love for animals; it was simply that his collection was expensive and hard to replace.

Each cage held something unusual. Barto's gaze whipped from side to side, his eyes wide with wonder. "Wyvern. Manticore. Pixie. I'm not even certain what that is. How do you control them?"

"A variety of methods. The dragons are hardest to manage, but I've found a way."

"Dragons?"

Talvaric gave a careless wave. "It's always easy to impress your friends when you have dragons."

Barto's expression hardened, but he said nothing.

"There is a great deal of power here." Talvaric tapped on the bars of a particularly large cage. "Any magical beast can be a weapon if you know how to control it. And the study and acquisition of such creatures is never dull."

Barto said more nothing, but peered into the cage. It contained a large black dog with red eyes and shaggy dark fur. It smelled like something dead. "A barguest?" The question was sharp—not quite fear, but recognition of something dangerous. Barguests were best known for devouring lone travelers, especially after dark.

"Yes."

"How long have you been building this collection?"

"Hundreds of years." About the same amount of time as his ambition had been growing. The two were closely intertwined.

Barto straightened, his eyes cautious now. "You call these creatures weapons. That makes this manor a vast armory. Why have you gathered all this?"

Talvaric was forced to concede Barto was smarter than expected. Talvaric could all but taste the tang of his anxiety, and liked it. "I occasionally send my beasts abroad to deal with annoyances."

"Annoyances?" Barto really was starting to sound like a parrot.

"The goblins of the Crystal Mountains developed an irritating attitude. I sent them a gift. A troll."

Barto blinked in surprise. "On whose authority? The fae trade with King Zorath's people! This could start a war we don't need."

Talvaric almost wanted to laugh. "Trust me, the goblins are too busy for that at the moment."

Barto's mouth dropped open a moment before he snapped it shut. "That's unbelievably irresponsible."

Talvaric lifted a brow. "Are you actually angry?"

After Morgan's capture, some fae seemed to be regaining scraps of their souls. That raised some interesting questions, especially since many fae, including Talvaric, now regarded emotion as a weakness.

"No." Barto flushed, proving his denial a lie. "But I think it's time for me to leave."

"Come now, won't you stay and drink wine with me? I never like to see a guest depart without showing him the best hospitality I can offer."

"I—no." Barto had gone stiff, his shoulders rigid. "I have other commitments to attend to."

Talvaric didn't argue. If he'd had the capacity, he would have been amused. The servants showed Barto the door, because no one ever found the door in Talvaric's manor unless he wanted them to.

Talvaric poured himself a glass of ruby wine, made from the wild snowberries that grew high on the Crystal Mountains' peaks. That's where he'd found his dragons and formulated his plans. Rukon had performed his first task well and Arthur had received the message. Talvaric hadn't been sure the dragon would cooperate, but his added controls had worked. Of course, the message had only been the first step in a long progression of calculated mayhem, but one thing at a time.

Talvaric watched from an upstairs window as his erstwhile guest mounted a fine gray stallion and galloped off across the manor's rolling lawns. A minute later, he returned to his collection and unlocked the barguest's cage. The huge, black nightmare backed to the far corner of its cage, cowering like a terrified puppy. Talvaric felt a knot of something warm and tingling in his gut. This display of subservience was the best part of mastering his beasts.

"That male I was with has annoyed me, and I believe he might just squeal to the council about the troll. I trust you have his scent?"

With a nod of its huge head, the creature crouched still more, its nose almost resting on its paws.

"Dispose of him, but bring the horse back unharmed. It looked valuable."

In a rush of fetid air, the barguest vanished to do his bidding. Talvaric finished his wine and dreamed of what he would do next.

Morgan's throne was vacant, and someone had to fill it—someone with courage enough to seize the opportunity and brave the consequences. Why not Talvaric? The titled fae might look down their noses at an upstart commoner—but not if he could prove, very publicly, that he was the most powerful of their number.

Talvaric would succeed where Morgan had failed, and destroy the fae's greatest enemy, Arthur of Camelot. And, he would do it in a way no one could ignore.

"See?" Clary turned her cell phone toward Gwen. "Wedding dresses look like cakes. Wedding cakes look like dresses. There's a kind of weird symmetry involving layers and fluff."

They'd been talking forever, still sitting in the coffee shop. They were becoming fast friends in a matter of hours, and Gwen was thoroughly enjoying the process. "So when will Sir Gawain and your sister wed?"

"When she's done planning, which could be never." Clary shrugged. "Tamsin wants what she wants, and Gawain lets her have her way."

"That hardly sounds like the same man," Gwen said, shaking her head. "The knight I knew was gruff, to say the least."

"That hasn't changed. If he was a dog, they'd say he was unsuitable for adoption."

"Except for Tamsin?"

"Yeah." Clary sounded unimpressed. "Meanwhile, it's all wedding, all the time. Plus, she's a historian, which means a medieval wedding has to be accurate to the period."

"Why?" Gwen wondered. "What's the point of that?"

"It's a thing historians do. So what was a real medieval wedding like, anyway?"

"Mine was—it was not at all what I had expected for myself." Gwen had switched to tea and held the cup in her hands, warming her fingers. She hadn't been cold until a moment ago, but memory changed everything.

Gwen recalled standing at the window with her nurse, looking out on the summer-green hills. Below, the sound of saws and hammers broke the morning peace. Growing bored, she leaned on the wide stone sill, her chin in her hands. "What are they making?" she asked.

"A great wooden table, I'm told." Nurse smoothed Gwen's hair. She was a plump, homely woman who had been with Gwen since infancy. She'd fed and bathed her as a baby and been a mother when the lady of the castle died and Gwen had just turned eight. "The table will be your dowry."

"A table?" Gwen said with disgust. "That's a silly thing for a dowry."

"A special round table," Nurse said, "so all the knights who sit there will be equals. It will be grand, large enough to seat all of your Arthur's mightiest warriors, and he has many and more champions, let me tell you. It will fill the whole of his feast hall."

"That's a stupid idea," said Gwen with all the certainty of her sixteen years. "I'll go down in history as the queen with the silly table."

"You mustn't call your father's gift stupid, chickling. Men don't like that."

"It's my dowry, and it's a poor design if it's going to fill up a whole banquet hall. They should build the table like a ring. If they did it in sections, the servants could serve the food from inside the circle. It will take less wood that way."

"What a clever girl you are," Nurse said, but she sounded sad. "Don't tell your father."

Gwen didn't understand why, but the wisdom of her nurse's advice became clear once she went ahead and shared her idea with King Leodegranz. Her father saw the advantages of her design at once, and the round table was built her way. Gwen was delighted until he told everyone the innovation was his own. The world of men had no place for young girls with ideas.

By the time she married Arthur, the table had been finished and delivered to Camelot and Guinevere had turned seventeen. The wedding itself was a dream—or a nightmare. Camelot was far larger than her father's lands, the castle grander and filled with strangers. Gwen was expected to be a fine lady, fit to rule at her new husband's side. She felt like an utter fraud.

It was easy to stand tall and proud during the wedding and the feast afterward. Her gown was so stiff with gold embroidery it might have stood on its own. Her handsome new husband was all merriment, drinking and dancing with everyone. He danced with her of course, but only a few times. Gwen knew that was proper, that the host had to make sure everyone had a little bit of his attention, but she selfishly wanted more. She hardly knew anyone there, after all.

That was when she first met the Mercian prince, who told her she was a beautiful bride and saw to it that her wine cup was filled and filled again. For a lonely young country girl, that kind of attention was balm to her nerves. She hadn't yet learned to smell betrayal.

If only Arthur had known how naive she was—but he'd been a king since he'd pulled that sword from a stone as a child. He'd won wars, conquered tyrants and had an enchanter at his beck and call. She was good with chickens.

At the end of the long feast, he'd taken her to his bed. Nurse had told her—or tried to tell her—what would happen. Gwen had all but died of embarrassment and covered her ears. But in that moment, after her ladies had put her in her nightgown and brushed out her hair so that it lay like a shining cape almost to her knees, she wished she'd let Nurse speak. Gwen shook like an aspen leaf.

When he came to the queen's bedchamber, Arthur wore only his shirt. One would have thought removing his fine clothes and crown would have made him seem smaller, but the opposite was true. She could see the deep chest and the hard muscles of a swordsman's arms.

"Don't be frightened," he said, leading her to sit on the edge of the bed. "I'll make this as pleasant as I can."

Gwen bit her lips, stifling a nervous giggle.

"What?" he asked with a frown.

"Nurse says that before giving me medicine. She at least gives me a spoonful of honey to wash it down."

Arthur's expression went strangely blank. "You don't believe in sparing a man's pride, do you?"

"I'm sure you have enough to spare." She regretted her tartness almost at once, but she couldn't help herself. Her claws came out when she was afraid.

Arthur paced a few steps to the door and back again. Was he nervous? That was utterly impossible, of course, because he was the mighty King Arthur. He finally came and knelt before her. "I will give you sweetness," he said.

She had a good idea of what he meant. Despite her father's watchful eye, she'd kissed one or two of the younger knights at the last Yuletide feast, and at least one squire had sworn undying love. But the look in her husband's eyes had nothing to do with a youngster's flirtations. He was a man of five and twenty.

I will give you sweetness. With effort, she marshaled her thoughts and formed a word. "How?"

He held her hands, just that, and leaned forward, brushing her lips with his. "A little at a time," he said, and then did it again.

Gwen raised her eyes from her cup, meeting Clary's. "My wedding didn't start well, but in the end it was a very fine event."

Chapter 6

As the last knight left Camelot's council about the dragon—Sir Gawain with the last slice of pizza in one hand—Arthur stifled a jaw-cracking yawn. They'd been talking since the morning, examining every theory about where Rukon had come from and why. Now it was nearly four o'clock and they'd talked the matter of the dragon to death. Merlin had been invited, but, as usual, was never there when he could actually be useful.

After Gawain's footsteps retreated toward the elevator, Arthur shut the door and turned the dead bolt, relieved to be alone with his exhaustion. Sleep had been impossible last night, with Guinevere in his bedroom and him not.

Anger had slowly spiraled around and around his gut as the clock had ticked toward dawn. A lesser man might have raged and demanded, but Arthur had his pride. He'd reacted the only way he knew how—by being the king.

And so he had summoned a council to deal with Camelot's problems and pushed his own away.

Not that he'd accomplished much. There wasn't enough information to track the creature to its lair. They were at a dead end until it appeared again. With a frustrated grunt, Arthur returned to the living room, stacked the empty pizza boxes and carried them to the recycling bin.

Basic cleanup complete, he poured himself a mug of coffee and went to his office. Immediately, a feminine scent distracted him. There was no mistaking the light floral musk of Guinevere's perfume, left over from her invasion of his space. It was faint, but his senses were attuned to its sweetness. Arthur set down his mug and scanned the papers on the desk, seeking any evidence that she'd disturbed his methodical chaos. Finding no signs of meddling, he woke his computer and saw the screen was just as he'd left it. Clearly, she hadn't had time to wreak her usual havoc.

Not like the time she tried to play peacemaker between the dwarves and goblins and nearly started a war, or the time she amended the peace treaty with Cumbria by giving away a forest or two because it seemed fairer that way. She'd been utterly sincere when she'd tried to make a match between a fae noble and the elven Queen of the Isles. Arthur closed his eyes, almost smiling despite the memory of drawn swords and angry oaths. No, as a newly minted queen, Guinevere had never stood aside when she thought she could make things better. Disaster after disaster had kept things…interesting. It would have been amusing if the kingdom hadn't been on the constant brink of war.

To be fair, she had learned her lesson after the prince of Mercia had played her for a fool. Arthur had been relieved but strangely sad, and a voice had nagged at him to say none of it would have happened if he'd been a mentor instead of consigning her to a life of embroidery and love poems. But politics was a bloody game, and he'd wanted her to be safe. Somehow, that never worked with Gwen.

Stifling another yawn, he sat down at the desk, determined to put in another few hours of work despite the need for sleep. There was no time for rest. The knights supported themselves by staging tournaments and feasts at Medievaland, Carlyle's medieval theme park, and there were schedules to make up and special events to plan. And then there were missing knights to find and fae to battle and... Arthur rubbed his eyes and willed himself to focus. Kings didn't get to take naps.

He opened his email program, his sword-calloused hands feeling clumsy on the tiny keys. He used the computer because that's what the modern world required, but he didn't relish the confined world of screen and desk and keyboard. This would be Guinevere's domain, once she discovered it—a place with more information than even her boundless curiosity could devour.

There was the usual slew of unread emails waiting, most of them routine items related to business at Medievaland. He scanned for something from Merlin, but there was nothing. However, one unfamiliar sender caught his eye: BeastMaster13@spellbound.com. A fan? Someone selling sword polish? Or another fellow with a make-believe quest? Medievaland attracted some very odd people, even by the standards of a time traveler with a magic sword.

With mild trepidation, King Arthur opened the message. It had only a single line, written in capital letters.

YOUR QUEEN IS BEAUTIFUL.

Arthur stared at the words, cold spreading from his core as if melting ice were trickling into his veins. Who knew his Gwen was here? Although the words were nothing, Arthur could read the threat beneath. Gwen had caught BeastMaster13's notice.

He jumped up from his chair and paced the tiny room. His logical side—the one that had been trained from boyhood to understand the ways of war—told him not to react. Threats were sent to goad. But his imagination conjured a thousand dangers—madmen, evil fae, sorcerers and demons. Logic didn't help when the enemy came this close to home. All he wanted was to find his queen and guard her with his own sword—and he wanted it with a fury that made him shudder.

Arthur took a deep breath. He knew better than to reply, but that was as far as his discipline went. Guinevere was out of his sight, wandering around the city without a care. She was his beautiful wife, and as the Queen of Camelot, she was also a symbol of his power. Harming her would hurt Arthur on several fronts—not just as a man, but as a king.

This was his fault. He had carelessly allowed Guinevere to run loose. That had to end at once.

Gwen noticed Clary looking toward the door and followed the woman's gaze. Arthur was striding toward them with a thunderous expression, and every thought about her future evaporated with an almost-audible pop. His mood radiated outward, clearing a broad path on all sides. Although the people of Carlyle had no king, they recognized his absolute authority as if by instinct. Arthur wore a long coat that hid Excalibur, but he may as well have been holding it in one of his massive hands. Everything about the commanding giant said he was a warrior king on a mission.

From the force of long habit, Gwen rose as he entered and barely stopped herself from dropping into a low curtsy.

The gesture had the unintended consequence of showing off her new clothes. Arthur stopped a few feet away, his gaze lingering on her soft sweater before sliding over the curves of her tight black jeans. Gwen knew she looked good, and his expression sparked a glow of satisfaction. Unfortunately, it wasn't destined to last.

"May I join you?" he said in a tone that wasn't really a question.

Gwen sat down again and he slid into the booth beside her, waving away the waitress before she could offer to take his order. "What brings you here?" Gwen asked.

"I came to ensure you were well," he said in a quiet voice that didn't carry beyond their table. "I am not positive, but I think the enemy may be aware that you are in Carlyle. I received an email that concerned me. I did not recognize the sender's name."

Gwen stared. Arthur rarely shared information in such a straightforward manner. The fact that he'd bothered to explain himself meant he wanted her to understand. She nodded slowly, feeling the weight of his clear blue gaze. It seemed to pierce through to her bones, as if gauging her response at the deepest level. "Thank you for the warning," she said.

Irritation flickered in his expression. He'd been expecting more. "It was a simple matter to find you. You're sitting in the window in full public view." He gave her another look up and down, as if he found her dress slightly indecent.

"Are you telling me to go back to your apartment now?" she asked, although she was sure that was exactly what he meant.

To Gwen's surprise, it was Clary who spoke up. "We're not without our defenses, my lord." Her look was polite but full of meaning. "I've spun a few battle spells."

His brows lowered. "I don't know who this enemy is or if he wields a gun or a pack of wolves. I would not be overconfident."

"Are you saying that there is danger here, in the full view of all these people?" Gwen aimed the question at both of them.

"Based on what's happened since yesterday," Arthur replied, "I'd assume nothing."

Clary toyed with her phone. "But as I said, my lord, you can trust me to get Gwen home safely."

Arthur's nod was stiff, as if he didn't want to agree but knew he was being unreasonable. He turned stormy eyes on Gwen, their expression possessive. "Very well, but I will assign guards to accompany you in the future. I will not have you walking the streets alone."

The words were roughly spoken, almost rasping. It was as close to emotion as Arthur would show in so public a place. Gwen stared, hating what she was hearing. Guards?

He rose with seeming reluctance. "When will you be home?"

Clary looked as if she was about to say something, but Gwen put a hand over hers. "Soon. We have one more stop to make." Gwen had no idea what that would be, but she was grateful for a moment to think.

Arthur hesitated a moment, but then bent and kissed Gwen's cheek. "Hurry home, wife."

"Of course," she said, suddenly awkward, but he was already halfway to the door. He never seemed to hurry, but his stride ate the distance at a pace few could match.

Silence fell over the two women, all their previous lightness gone. Gwen's thoughts of the future, of an expanding world unfolding before her shriveled to nothing. Cold nausea weighed in her stomach, but she sucked in a deep breath, doing her best to dispel it. "I don't want guards. I had them in Camelot, and I felt like a nuisance—or a prisoner—every time I wanted to go for a walk."

Clary stared at her, no doubt hearing the strain—and the uncertainty—in her voice. "Seriously? He's done this before?"

"He's worried," Gwen said, trying and failing to bury her bitterness. "I had a talent for trouble when I was younger. Years have gone by, but he's never forgotten." *And he's never trusted me.*

Gwen knew she'd said too much. She began gathering her parcels, the rattle of shopping bags hiding her confusion. Clary followed suit.

As they left, Gwen walked two paces behind Clary, her thoughts slowed to a dead crawl. She knew how to make drawbridges and catapults work, but not her marriage. An all-too-familiar confusion dragged at her like quicksand. A wife's first duty was to please her husband, a subject's first duty was to serve her king, and yet Arthur was a puzzle she'd never solved.

Once they reached the street, Gwen's fortitude ran out. She stopped walking, unable to push on. The cycle of unhappiness that was her marriage had started all over again. "I can't go home. I don't want to do what I'm told anymore. I can't be invisible, and I can't be a precious object always under guard. It's too much."

Clary turned and walked back to Gwen, coming to stand at her side. Clary's lips were thin with anger, but it clearly wasn't aimed at Gwen.

"What do you want to do?" Clary asked. "I won't take you anyplace you don't want to go."

The witch held Gwen's gaze with her own, her expression gentle. It was oddly unsettling, for Gwen had never had many female friends, especially after becoming queen. She wasn't sure how to respond. "Merlin has to send me back."

A car honked, and all at once Gwen was aware of the busy street around them. Vehicles swooshed past at unimaginable speeds. Pedestrians pushed by, arguing into their little squares of plastic. All around was color, sound, signs and a thundering bounty of objects and ideas. Gwen wanted it all with a sharpness that made her want to weep.

"I doubt Merlin has that power," Clary mused. "Even if he did, are you sure that's what you want?"

Gwen gripped the handles of her bags, feeling the weight of the pretty, bright clothes that should be part of a new freedom. She blinked hard, refusing the impulse to cry. "No, but where else would I go?"

"I don't understand," Clary said flatly.

Gwen sucked in her breath, letting it out in a heavy sigh. She wasn't allowed in Arthur's office, but couldn't leave their rooms without a guard. Arthur didn't trust her to take part in Camelot's councils, and yet he wanted to keep her close. She was too naive and impulsive to let roam free, and yet he didn't want her in his private business. He judged everything she did, and he judged it harshly. "I was far less trouble as a piece of history."

Clary made a rude noise. "Sister, this world is full of opportunity. Forget Arthur and his chain mail boy band."

Clary slipped an arm around Gwen's shoulders, pulling her close. "You're in our time now. You get to decide what you want to do, and I think Arthur needs to know that."

Gwen's mind went blank, a hollow sensation stealing over her. It took her a moment to recognize it as a species of fear. "This is going to cause trouble."

They began walking again, drifting in the direction of Clary's car. "You don't need to decide everything at once," said Clary. "In fact, you shouldn't. You need time to breathe and clear your head, and so does he."

"But where?"

"You can stay with me at my hotel," Clary suggested, warming to the plan. "I have a double room, and we've got all your clothes right here. It's as if this was meant to be."

It made sense. It made *perfect* sense, and Gwen's instincts grabbed at the offer. Yet, old habits died hard. "What do I tell Arthur?"

"That there is one more thing you need to buy," Clary replied. "Every independent woman needs a suitcase."

Chapter 7

The king pushed his way out of the café and strode down the street, his temper steaming. Other pedestrians cleared a path, pulling dogs and children to safety. He was aware of it all, but barely, as he stormed down the sidewalk with no sense of direction or purpose.

Arthur had reassured himself that Guinevere was safe, but he was far from satisfied. There had been a few moments when he'd seen her before she'd noticed him, and those moments had been a revelation. She'd glowed from within, as if a long-forgotten hope was awakening. It was a glimpse of the girl he'd first met, the one he'd wanted for himself before danger and politics and arguments had crushed that light out of her. And then, of course, there had been the modern clothes, with those tight black jeans caressing her thighs. He had witnessed many unanticipated marvels in his lifetime, but those legs had pride of place at the top of the list.

And then he'd seen the life die out of her the moment he'd opened his mouth. It was one thing to believe she was better off without him, and quite another to see the evidence with his own eyes.

Arthur crossed the street, dimly aware of the bustle around him as he grimly replayed the scene in the café. The image of Guinevere's soft curves, so evident in those modern clothes, tangled his thoughts badly enough that he almost didn't hear his phone ringing. He pulled it from his jacket pocket, finding a quiet doorway before he answered. "Yes?"

"Pendragon?"

"Who is this?" One more misgiving crowded into Arthur's mind. The male voice was unfamiliar, and no one addressed him by his surname. It was always "my lord" or "Your Majesty" or simply "Arthur."

"We haven't met, but you encountered my associate in the woods."

The statement cleared Arthur's head in an instant. This was about the dragon. "You mean your associate with the fiery temper?" Arthur asked drily.

"The same. I assume you got my email?"

Arthur cast a quick look around the street, just in case he spotted someone else talking into a phone. There was nothing but the usual busy street under a fitful sky. "What do you want?"

"I'm curious."

"About what?"

"I'm conducting an experiment."

The voice was rough, but the timbre and accent suggested it belonged to a fae. That was enough to make the skin at his nape prickle with foreboding. Still, Arthur let the moment stretch on. As a king, he'd learned the power of silence long ago.

Finally, with a quick sigh, the fae spoke again. "I'm standing at the gas station on the west side of town. Do you know it?"

"Yes." It was on a busy highway a few miles from the medieval theme park where the knights worked.

"If I tell you my dragon is about to burn it down, what will you do?"

"Find you and kill you like I do every other psychotic fae," Arthur replied without emotion. "That's why I took a long nap in a stone suit."

"You have a high opinion of yourself."

"The modern term is *badass*. I'm the one with the big, shiny sword not even your queen can survive."

"And I'm the one with the dragon. You don't have much time to get here before the show."

The line went dead.

Arthur swore as he put the phone away. A wave of unreality stole over him as the pedestrians swept by him, laughing or talking or hurrying with heads down in thought. They were ordinary humans with no idea what the enemy could do. He'd seen the soulless fae steal human lives for the sake of pleasure, drinking their life essence like a drug. It was Arthur's job to stop the fae from making these people their slaves.

If the dragon was in partnership with a fae, that changed everything. This wasn't just a large, scaly bully in need of a fire hose. With another oath, Arthur strode down the street, shouldering his way past a knot of idling boys. Was this threat a trap? Probably. But a warrior king took his share of risks to save the people in his charge. Anything less wasn't worthy of Camelot.

Pete's Pay and Go sat on the corner where a six-lane truck route crossed paths with the four-lane artery that ran into Carlyle. There was nothing remarkable or attractive about the place. It had gas, groceries and a fast-food drive-through that sold a chemical approximation of burgers and fries. As usual, there was road construction because the highways department never dug a hole unless they could tie up traffic for months at a time.

Arthur dodged the traffic cones and pulled into the last parking spot. When he got out, the first thing he saw was a van decorated with the call letters of the local news station and a cluster of equipment mounted on top. Whatever happened next would be beamed to every TV in town. Arthur's stomach went cold. Magic was a secret kept from ordinary mortals, but this fae ignored that rule.

Arthur wheeled, looking for explanations. Instead, he saw one of Camelot's knights getting out of a battered pickup. Sir Owen of the Beasts walked across the parking lot, pushing wavy brown hair out of his eyes and glowering at the highway traffic. Like the animals he befriended, the tall, young Welshman was happiest in the wilds. He hadn't been at their council earlier, but on his way back from a weekend in the woods.

"Sir Gawain texted me as I was driving back into town," Owen said in his soft, lilting voice. "He will be here presently but suffered an unforeseen delay."

Gawain hadn't mentioned anything when Arthur had phoned him en route, but Owen's careful courtesy discouraged questions. Arthur forged ahead. "You missed some excitement while you were gone. I'm expecting a dragon."

Owen's expression was eager. "Well, that will be something. I've only ever seen a wyvern up close. It was quite fond of dried salmon."

"Rukon Shadow Wing isn't friendly."

"That isn't unusual," the Welsh knight replied, his enthusiasm firmly in place. "Dragons are touchy and intolerable braggarts to be sure."

Arthur nodded to the news van. "This one seems to want an interview. We should look around for any sign of his fae friend."

Owen fell into step beside him. "I don't understand why the dragon came here. They don't typically travel beyond their own domain."

Arthur grunted agreement. "If he's in league with a fae, no doubt the idea came from Queen Morgan's court."

"Of course, sire, that's quite possible, but I've heard of Rukon Shadow Wing. He lives in the Crystal Mountains."

Surprise made Arthur pause. Not that Owen had information on Rukon—if something had four legs, chances are Owen of the Beasts knew about it—but the mountains were deep in goblin country. Goblin and fae didn't mix. Ever. So how did Rukon cross paths with a fae? "That poses some interesting questions."

"Indeed, sire." Owen frowned in apology, as if he were somehow responsible.

Arthur didn't get a chance to reply. A young brunette with high heels and a microphone bore down on them with a predator's determination. "I'm Megan Dutton, Nighthawk News. I know you fine gentlemen are from the Medievaland jousting tournaments. Arthur Pendragon, isn't it? And you?"

She turned to Owen with a look Arthur recognized. The knight charmed more than just puppies and wounded fawns. "Owen Powys, mistress."

The reporter blinked rapidly, as if dazzled. "Yes, well, our newsroom received a tip regarding an imminent attack by fire-breathing dragons. Isn't that why you gentlemen are here? As part of a promotional event for Medievaland?"

She plowed on before Arthur could think of an answer. "And aren't you afraid that this kind of stunt might cause panic among the population? Care to comment on this irresponsible action by Medievaland's management?"

She thrust the mic toward him like a badly handled blade. Behind her, a minion with a camera edged closer. As one of the primary performers at the theme park, Arthur had some experience with press doing puff pieces for the tourist season, but Megan Dutton was after controversy.

He didn't have time for this. The longer she had him trapped, the less time he had to stop whatever was about to happen. "I'm sure I speak for the management of the Medievaland Theme Park when I assure you that there is no intention to panic the citizens of Carlyle."

"Then what are your intentions, Mr. Pendragon? What are we about to see?"

There was no opportunity to say anything more. Owen pointed to the sky, and then Arthur became a far less interesting part of the story. The camera swung away and Arthur followed the knight's pointing finger, squinting against the sun. Far, far up was a scrap of black with a long tail and it was spiraling downward in erratic loops. It was so distant one might have mistaken it for a child's kite if not for the long, sinuous neck.

Arthur watched, calculating where the beast was going to land. The wings were spread, but the creature was struggling to control its descent. Something was wrong.

"That's not Rukon—that's a female," said Owen softly. "Look at the slender shape of her head."

Arthur couldn't tell the difference. It was still the size of a truck and falling from the sky right over moving traffic. Whatever was beneath the dragon would be crushed. He spun to the reporter and her cameraman, putting the snap of authority into his voice. "Do something useful! Get everyone back."

He turned to Owen. "Help me clear the road."

With that, he bolted for the intersection, holding up a hand to stop the steady stream of cars. Owen was on his heels, intercepting the other lanes. It was foolhardy, but the dragon's shadow was steadily spreading as seconds ticked by. He looked up, estimating one more time where she'd land. She'd stopped trying to fly and was hurtling for the highway.

A truck started to turn and gave a furious honk as Arthur sprang in front of it, waving his arms. He danced back as a sudden wave of heat and fumes washed over him. His hands went out, slamming against the hot grille, but it stopped. He looked up expecting to see the driver's scowl, but the man gazed skyward, transfixed.

No one was moving now. Eerie silence muffled the scene. Arthur turned, putting his back to the vehicle, and felt his jaw go slack. The creature was still falling, close enough now to make out more detail. *Ten seconds until it hits the earth.* For an instant, he could see the dragon's iridescent blue hide and the slender taper of her wings. *Eight.* She seemed to shudder, as if heaving her last breath. It was then he saw the weave of golden magic tangling her wings, like a dog wound in its own leash. Whoever controlled her had bungled things, and now she couldn't fly. *Five.* Arthur watched, appalled as the dragon struggled, then loosed her fire. She blazed like a falling star, the thin membranes of her wings a corona of blinding white. She was trying to burn the chains of magic away. His gorge began to rise in pure, unadulterated horror as she roared in agony. *Zero.*

She vanished. Utter silence reigned.

Arthur's heart pounded. He'd expected a crash, a crumpled mass of bone and flesh, but there was nothing but the charcoal stink of dragon flame and spent magic. Arthur buried his nose in his sleeve as he backed away. He'd guessed the dragon's landing site correctly—if it had actually landed. A little bit more to the left, and the gas station would have been alight.

And yet none of that mattered now because the creature was gone, yanked back to her own world before her chains could break. Whatever the fae had wanted to do here, he'd failed.

Owen appeared at Arthur's elbow, his face white. "The dragon burned herself trying to get free."

The fae, whoever he was, was about to be dead meat. Arthur swore it in the depths of his heart.

The howl of sirens broke through his stunned dismay. Emergency lights flashed as a fire truck and ambulance pulled into the parking lot. A policeman was shooing the crowd back. Megan Dutton was still there, yelling into her mic about heroes and disaster and mysteries.

Arthur shot a glance at the reporter, and then at Owen. "Let's go before she starts asking us questions."

They slipped through the crowd to the parking lot. There, they found Gawain waiting, worry creasing his face. "What happened?" he asked. "Someone said a flaming cow dropped out of an airplane. Is Merlin involved?"

Arthur heaved a sigh, half in relief and half in irritation. *Flaming cow?* People only saw what they expected to see. "A dragon was supposed to destroy the gas station, but something went wrong."

Gawain looked at the Pay and Go, which was clearly not burning. "Wrong in what way?"

"We don't know," Arthur said. "At least no one was hurt."

"Except the dragon," Owen put in. "How could she possibly have survived that fall, regardless of what world she was in?"

"Right." The beautiful, agonized dragon. Arthur closed his eyes, fighting back a rage so large he could barely breathe. They still didn't know anything, but Owen had a solid point. "Spread out and search this place. No doubt the fae is watching. He didn't orchestrate all this without a front-row seat."

Owen nodded and strode away, face thunderous. Arthur moved to follow, but Gawain caught his arm. "I'll take over here. You're needed at home—or rather, at Clary's hotel."

"Why?"

Gawain grimaced. "That's where Guinevere is sleeping tonight."

"What?" Blood rushed to Arthur's head. This wasn't the time for Gwen's antics, not with fae and burning dragons and reporters crawling all over Carlyle. And the Crystal Mountains—what was a fae doing crossing the goblins' lands? There were too many questions. He couldn't deal with another distraction. "There are no guards at the hotel. She's not protected."

"I think that might be the point." Gawain's face was carefully neutral.

"Doesn't she understand what's going on?" snapped Arthur.

Gawain raised his hands in a gesture of surrender. "Ask her, not me."

"After all the problems she's caused over the years, has she learned nothing?"

No sooner did Arthur say it than he snapped his jaw shut, remembering the light going out of Gwen's eyes when he'd approached her in the restaurant. She'd learned he was willing to walk away and leave her in the past for her own protection. Was that what he still wanted? Had he really just thought of her as a distraction?

Is it any wonder she wants her freedom?

So what was he going to do about it?

Chapter 8

Gwen had never dated and therefore needed advice.

Clary's first move had been to search the internet for tips on planning a romantic evening with an estranged spouse. This involved answering a number of quizzes and the application of Smoking Surrender Coral nail polish. Clary had then bullied Gwen into a dainty black dress and sent her to the hotel bar in time to meet Arthur for drinks. The two women had agreed a public place was a good choice, at least to begin the conversation. Finally, Clary had gone out, leaving the room unoccupied until at least midnight.

Gwen should have been pleased. For once, she was in control of the situation and Arthur was the one asking for attention. It took a lot for him to bend. Clary had attributed that to shutting the bedroom door last night, but Gwen wasn't sure his reasons were that straightforward. The King of Camelot was a complicated man.

She wondered if he'd ever loved her.

Guinevere took the elevator up to the cocktail lounge on the top floor. She'd been told the room rotated slowly, so that diners got a view of the entire city skyline by the time the night was done. To someone born in a stone castle that seemed both wondrous and enormously silly. What was the point when it took far less effort to simply walk around the room?

She pushed the thought out of her mind as soon as she entered the lounge. Arthur sat near the far wall, but he rose as she stepped into view. He'd been watching for her. He hadn't done that for a long time.

The space between them suddenly seemed enormous, as if she had to cross a vast plain in her high heels instead of a little bit of carpet. She wasn't used to the shoes, and her ankles wobbled slightly, but she kept her chin high and her bare arms relaxed at her sides. The only way to face Arthur, ever, was with courage.

The dress Clary had made her buy was a backless halter style with a tight waist and a skirt that flared just above the knee. The black satin whispered as she walked to Arthur's table by the tall glass window. He continued to stand, a frozen look on his face that she couldn't quite read. He'd dressed, too, in a well-cut suit and plain white shirt that showed off the taper from his broad shoulders to trim waist. He wore no tie, the casual touch somehow putting him above the formal crowd. Nothing marked him as a king, and yet the whole lounge seemed to acknowledge his status. Waitstaff hovered, and every other male had chosen a table far away.

Courage, she repeated to herself as she drew closer. She could see his eyes now, the heat in that bright blue like the fire of diamonds. The hunger in them was a physical touch, a hot lick from her ankles upward to the low plunge of her bodice. There was no pretense of manners in that look, just raw male appreciation. A sword-swinging warrior's appetite, despite what the costly suit implied. For that alone, she wanted to thank Clary for insisting on the dress. She needed confidence now.

He took a few steps, meeting her before she finally reached the table. He placed a hand at the small of her back, guiding her forward. "You look amazing," he said, bending to murmur in her ear.

That close, she could smell soap and skin. The scent and his nearness brought memories of lying beside him, exploring the landscape of his hard body. She snatched her mind back to the present, needing to keep her wits about her.

"Thank you," she said with a cool nod as he held the chair for her. She sat carefully, the short skirt making her feel exposed. She noticed a long black bag beneath the table and guessed Excalibur was inside. The sword never went far from Arthur's side.

A beat of silence followed, filled with questions and an undercurrent of hurt. It didn't show on their faces—they were both too skilled at court politics for that—but Gwen felt it like fingers along her skin. He was edgy, filled with nervous energy. Arthur took his seat and signaled a waiter with a flick of fingers. The man quickly returned with an ice bucket, champagne and delicate glasses.

If there had been any doubt before, Arthur was trying to impress her. By the rules they'd grown up with that meant showing his wealth and status. He might not have a castle here, but he wasn't a pauper. According to Clary, Medievaland was doing extremely well since the knights had arrived, and the management of the theme park had given them generous contracts. They were, in fact, becoming local celebrities with a dedicated fan base.

The waiter poured the champagne and retreated on silent feet. Arthur raised his glass. "We haven't had a chance to drink to your arrival. Be welcome, my lady."

Gwen tasted the bubbling liquid, decided she liked it and set it aside. Again, she wanted a clear head. It would be too easy to surrender to Arthur simply because he asked. She'd only imagined a path of her own choosing for a few hours, and she was unsure of herself.

"The lights are very beautiful," she said, looking out the window because it was easier than looking at him. "What is that ring in the sky?"

"A Ferris wheel," he said. "Those colored lights belong to Medievaland."

"Oh." She looked more closely, actually interested now.

"Did you find everything you required at the stores?" he asked, gaze intent on her.

"Everything to wear and to groom myself," she replied. "And a phone. Clary insisted I need one, although I'm not sure of all its uses yet."

"Give it to me," he said, holding out a hand.

She hesitated, fingers tightening on the black silk clutch purse she held in her lap. "Why?"

"I want your number."

She slowly handed it over. She'd chosen a green leather case painted with exotic birds, but he barely noticed it as he thumbed the screen to life and began tapping in numbers. Once, he said he'd been trained to ignore distraction on pain of a beating. She believed the story. It said as much about him as his great victories.

He handed her phone back. "I put my number in. Now you can phone me."

"Thank you." She closed the case and put it away in her purse.

"How did you spend the rest of the day?" he asked, his tone forced now.

She noticed the tight lines of his face, a sure sign of strain. She wondered what he'd been doing in the hours since she'd seen him last. "Reading. I borrowed Clary's laptop and just looked and looked. There's so much to know about this time. So many marvels." She'd searched for schools, too, falling in love with the idea of being a student. But that dream belonged to a new Guinevere that Arthur hadn't met yet. She wasn't ready to expose that vulnerable piece of herself to the man across from her. Not until she had a chance to find her feet.

Arthur looked down at his hands, clearly gathering his thoughts. The brief awkwardness of small talk was over. "Why are you staying here and not at home?"

"I—"

He fixed her with the piercing blue gaze that had made kings and sorcerers quail. "What do you want that you can't have beneath my roof?"

You, she thought, but knew he wouldn't understand. "Me," she replied instead. "I'm not there."

It was plain to see he didn't understand that, either. His brow furrowed in irritation. "Please explain."

Gwen cast a furtive look at her champagne glass, suddenly wishing she'd drunk more. Even liquor-induced courage was something, and he clearly thought her a spoiled child. "I don't know if I can."

"If you don't try, then we will achieve nothing."

As if this was just another project to be tackled and conquered. She felt the heat rise to her face and looked away, staring at the bubbles floating in her glass.

"Clary told me what has gone on here." Her body was rigid. "She said Gawain held her sister at knifepoint when they first met. The night Nimueh and Lancelot found each other again, they battled the Queen of Faery's assassin.

That they both nearly died before all was over. And here we sit in a hotel lounge."

"Is that what you want? Knives and violence instead of this?" Arthur waved a hand at the half-darkened room. "I didn't take you for a warrior queen."

Gwen flinched. "You know I'm not." It would have been easier if she had been, but she preferred building things to killing.

"Then what is your point?" An edge of frustration crept into his voice. Not quite sarcasm, but its cousin.

She gave him a hard look. "Those men and women have passion between them."

"So do we."

She flushed. "There is a difference between passion and pleasure. Passion involves the heart and mind as well as the flesh."

The corners of Arthur's lips turned down. "You are frank, my lady."

"I am saving us pain. We had six years of doubt. Do we need a seventh? An eighth?"

The flush of temper crept up his neck. "Yes, I doubted you. After your illness, you kept company with Lancelot and Lionel and any of the other young knights who would sit at your feet and adore you. What was I to think?"

Agitated, she picked up the tiny paper napkin the waiter had placed under her drink and began tearing it to bits. After her illness, Arthur had kept her confined. She'd been depressed already and his overprotectiveness had made everything so much worse. "You left me alone, day after day. I was lonely and very young."

"And so you let them court you under my nose?"

"Yes, I did." She lifted her chin. "Did you ever stop to think why?"

"A girl's game." He said it with contempt, probably because her ploy had worked. She knew he'd been jealous and still felt guilty about it. And yet, what tools did a girl that age have?

Gwen met his eyes. "Perhaps I wanted you to fight for my affection. I was dazzled by you when we wed, and then you put me in your castle and rode away. I was no more to you than a chair or a tapestry. If I'd been a dog, at least you would have had a use for me."

They stared at each other, gazes hot with resentment. She'd never been so blunt before now. Arthur had to visibly unclench his teeth before he could speak. "Did those men ever touch you?"

She made a strangled noise, resentment bubbling up like a fresh wound. "No. They were my friends, not my lovers. And you've asked that a thousand times before."

He fell back in his chair with a hiss of breath. "I know. You have no idea how well that arrow flew."

"Then why did you never change?" It was a simple question, but she'd never dared to ask it. Now, though, there was no chance of retreat. She'd already shown too many cards.

Arthur glanced from side to side, fingers fidgeting on the tablecloth. Another couple was sitting down at a nearby table, close enough to overhear. "Is there another place we could go?"

"My room. Clary will be gone for hours."

He nodded, rising at once and ordering the champagne to be delivered. Arthur led the way to the elevator, not touching her and not offering a word. He held the bag with his sword instead, gripping the handle in a white-knuckled fist. Gwen didn't attempt to break the silence, but pushed the elevator button and waited stiffly. This standoff lasted until the hotel-room door clacked shut behind them.

The champagne arrived barely a minute after, and the fuss of delivery and tipping stalled the conversation further. Gwen kicked off her shoes, feeling more secure in the refuge Clary had offered her. The room was large, with a comfortable sitting area. Compared to Arthur's apartment, it was pretty, decorated in blue and yellow. Nevertheless, the place seemed smaller with Arthur in it. Gwen sat down in one of the overstuffed chairs, purposefully avoiding the intimacy of the couch.

He went to stand at the window, looking out with his hands clasped behind his back. "I knew you turned to others for friendship. I never understood why you didn't trust me. I did everything to protect you, whether or not you appreciated my methods. It was my duty and desire to keep you safe."

When she didn't answer, he released a noisy breath. "I suppose you still want an answer to your question."

"I do."

"I didn't change because there was never time."

It made sense, up to a point. There was always a war, a fire, crop failure or some other emergency. Good kings barely had a private life, and Arthur had taken his duty to heart. Gwen had never found fault with his care of Camelot's citizens—just with his care for her. She breathed a sigh, but it did nothing to expel the tension jangling inside her. She snatched up the champagne and filled her glass, drinking it down.

"And now?" she asked quietly. "Is there time for us now?"

He turned from the window. "Is that what you want? Time? Passion? Lazy afternoons to share our thoughts?"

Gwen sucked in a breath. "Yes."

He frowned. "What else?"

She set down the glass, pulling her thoughts into order. She might only get one chance to say what she needed to say. "I will not live the way I did before."

He actually looked shocked. "You do not wish to be queen?"

"A queen rules by her husband's side. I can't do that if I'm, um, if I…" She stumbled, wanting to say that she wanted him very much, but that wasn't the sum and total of who and what she was.

"Gwen?"

"I want to matter," she finally said. It sounded selfish, though she didn't mean it that way.

"You do matter. I want you at my side," he said, but she couldn't decipher his tone.

"Do you really? A real queen would be involved with the running of whatever kingdom you establish here. Otherwise, I have no purpose in Camelot."

And if she had no reason to stay, there were other places she could go. All the rules governing women and marriage had changed over the centuries. She finally had choices.

By the look on Arthur's face, he knew that, too. Time seemed to stop. So did Gwen's breath.

"You were indeed very young when we wed," he said.

"I'm old enough now, my lord. I've learned much about the responsibilities of the throne."

Something shifted in his expression. "So you have, my lady."

Was this the reassurance she'd been waiting for? Uncertain, Gwen rose from her chair, her bare feet sinking into the soft carpet. "Then tell me what's going on with the dragon. If you want me at your side, I need to understand what Camelot is facing."

For an instant, Arthur's composure slipped and she saw a flash of unexpected sadness. He turned back to the window before she could fully read his expression. "There is more than one dragon involved. I may well have seen one die today, after I left you and the witch. She was a female of breeding age, I think."

"Where?" Gwen demanded, perplexed. One beast finding its way into the world was an unhappy accident. More than one spelled a plot.

"Are you certain you want to know? It is not a pleasant tale."

"Trust me, I do."

So he told her about what he'd seen at the gas station and about the fight with Rukon Shadow Wing. Gwen listened carefully and didn't interrupt. He was making an effort to restore peace between them.

"There is a fae involved," he said as he finished, "but I'm not certain how."

"There are dragons in the Faery Realms."

"But Rukon Shadow Wing lives in the Crystal Mountains, deep in goblin territory. No fae would dare set foot there."

Guinevere shook her head. "In our time, that was true, but centuries have passed while we slept. Perhaps the fae have made peace with the goblin king."

"That's possible." He rubbed his eyes. "I can't get the image of that unfortunate creature out of my head. I have fought many of her kind, but nothing deserves that suffering. Why are they coming here?"

The sadness in his words moved her. "Perhaps she had no choice."

He reached out, his fingers tracing her cheek until she caught his hand. A spark of angry confusion streaked through her. "How could you sit drinking wine with this fresh in your mind?"

"We needed to talk."

Gwen closed her eyes, exasperated and grateful at the same time. "How can you block something like that out?"

"I don't feel it any less, but there are many terrible things, all wanting attention." He freed his hand from hers, and then ran his fingers down the length of her hair. "I wished to contemplate beauty for a time."

She couldn't help but smile, although it was bittersweet. "Have you borrowed a poet's tongue for the night?"

"I always speak the truth. Once in a long while I do it well."

They were standing close together now, sharing the same breath. Her arms and face tingled as if he gave off an electric charge, but it was just his presence. It was always like this, the anticipation of touch a kind of fire beneath her skin. She lowered her gaze, hoping her need for him didn't appear as naked as it felt. She gave a light sigh, and then met his blue, blue eyes. "Can we make this work?"

Chapter 9

Arthur didn't respond—not in words. Instead, he slid an arm around her waist, stepping into her embrace as smoothly as a dancer. Or a swordsman. He had a deadly grace Gwen had seen in no other man and it left her dry-mouthed and hungry in places no decent woman would name.

Her hands were around his neck, though she did not remember reaching for him, or when they'd started to kiss. When the times were peaceful between them, making love came naturally, needing no thought or will, nothing but instinct. As easy as breathing, and as necessary. Maybe that was why the last years had been so hard—he'd been gone, and in the empty, loveless halls of the castle, she'd been fighting for air.

Her fingers eased beneath his jacket, finding the satin lining warm with his heat. He shrugged off the coat, letting it fall, and pulled her close. His mouth was on her lips, her jaw, the sensitive place just below her ear. Everywhere, and each lingering touch was more inviting than the last. It was like being pulled into the ocean, the current too strong to resist. A reckless part of Gwen yearned to be swept under. Love—or whatever it was Arthur offered when he was in this mood—wasn't about caution. Her response was the hunger of a flower for the sun.

His hands found the bare skin beneath the fall of her hair and caressed it lightly, trailing his fingers down to her waist. Gwen shivered, but kept her attention on the buttons of his shirt. They weren't what she was used to—shirts in her mind pulled over the head, with strings to pull the neckline closed. This was like a puzzle box, each little fastening revealing a few more inches of masculine skin. The process was tantalizing but slow.

And Arthur wouldn't stand still for it. He was kissing down her throat, his tongue leaving hot licks as he progressed toward the low neckline of her dress. Gwen arched into it, feeling the brush of his hair as he bent his head, the beard a coarser sensation against her sensitized skin. Her nipples ached, wanting the hot wetness of his mouth on them. If she could have torn the dress away, she would have, but she'd lost command of her limbs.

He looked up, revealing a man who had abandoned any pretense of civilization. Appetite dominated his gaze, the raw need of possession. These moments were as close as she ever got to reaching his soul. She ran her palms up the delicious planes the open shirt now revealed—the hard stomach, the swell of his chest, the thickness of his shoulders. Finally, Gwen took his face between her hands and kissed him full on the mouth, her tongue meeting his and tasting sweet champagne beneath the richness of the man. He returned her ardor, demanding more. Gwen gasped as he lifted her, the sudden weightlessness adding to her sense of abandon. She hooked her legs around his waist and let him carry her to the bed.

He laid her down with exquisite care, everything in his manner declaring her a rare prize. "You are so beautiful," he rumbled, pressing his lips to the base of her throat. That nearly undid her, right then and there. She had no more will than warm candle wax, ready to be coaxed into any shape he desired.

And she could tell he was eager to do it, the swell of him plain against her belly. Her hands went to his belt, finding a new challenge—but also something passing strange. "My lord, you are vibrating."

Arthur pulled the phone from his pocket with a colorful oath, and tossed it onto the bedside table. That only made the insistent buzzing worse. He snatched it up again, glaring as if looks alone could make the phone burst into flames. He jabbed the screen to silence, only to have it burble a moment later as a text message popped into view.

"By Saint Sebastian's bleeding arrows," he snarled, tossing the phone to the coverlet.

He jammed both hands into his tousled hair. From Gwen's vantage point on the bed, the gesture did interesting things to his chest muscles.

"What is it?" she asked, sitting up.

His eyes were wild. "There's another dragon. It's at the park."

"Medievaland?"

He nodded. "I'm sorry. I need to go."

"Of course you do," she said, and meant it. This was serious.

As she watched, his frantic expression vanished bit by bit, as if a series of walls slammed into place. One moment he was filled with emotion—desire and distress— and the next he was all icy control. Watching the change sobered her faster than any cold shower. She sat up and slid off the bed.

"Wait a moment and I'll change," she said, padding to the closet.

"Why?"

"Because I'm going with you." She pulled out the jeans she'd worn earlier. Surely they'd be practical enough if she had to run or climb.

"No, you're not." His voice was a whip crack.

She spun, all her anger pouncing on his words. "What did you say?"

"Dragons are dangerous, Gwen. I can't let you walk into that." He buttoned up his shirt with brisk movements, erasing all her careful work before retrieving his jacket from the floor. "You're my wife. It's up to me to protect you."

"How can you protect me when I'm here and you're at Medievaland?"

"I'll call for one of the men to guard you. I already told you I'd do that."

If he was reverting to the plans already in place, nothing she'd said that night had mattered. Frustration exploded inside her, a huge and unreasoning beast. She tossed the jeans at him, but they only flopped to the bed in a defeated sprawl. "What happened to having me at your side? What happened to me being a grown woman? Don't you think I have a right to serve our people, too?"

His expression hardened. "I don't have time to argue about this now. We'll talk when I get back."

"If I'm here," she snapped.

Annoyance twisted his features, settling into the angry scowl she knew too well. "That is, of course, entirely your decision." He jammed his phone into his jacket pocket, picked up his sword and strode toward the door.

With that, he left her alone.

* * *

Arthur bolted from the hotel, furious with Guinevere. She thought she'd join the dragon hunt? That was pure insanity. The one time he allowed her to march with his army—during a simple, dragon-free engagement—she'd nearly died from a fever that ran through the ranks like wildfire. And she'd caught it because she wouldn't listen to him and keep safe in her tent but insisted on nursing the sick and dying.

How would she fare against a monster that had nearly killed a seasoned warrior like Gawain?

The notion of Gwen anywhere near a fire-breathing monster brought a prickling sweat to his skin. If something happened to her… He couldn't find an end to the statement. There was no room for that possibility. Why couldn't she understand that always, always he'd been doing his best to protect her? Yes, sometimes that meant leaving her behind, but wasn't that better than death?

He pulled out of the hotel parking lot at breakneck speed, sailing down the main drag that would take him out of the downtown. Three blocks later he ran a red light and only after that forced himself to slow down. The witches—mostly Tamsin and Clary's family—had shepherded the knights through the labyrinthine process of establishing fake identification. The last thing he needed to do was risk it all for a traffic violation.

Or at least that was what the reasonable part of his brain insisted. There was a burning pit beneath his breastbone that bubbled with frustrated lust and wounded pride. Anger urged him to be reckless, but he was a king. Royalty didn't have the luxury of emotion—not when they had a realm to protect.

Arthur swung into Medievaland's parking lot and barely stopped the SUV before jumping out and running for the gates. The theme park re-created the Middle Ages, complete with jousts, banquets, artisans and costumed minstrels. There was also a midway and rides guaranteed to curdle the hardiest stomach. For the knights of Camelot, it was the one place they could exist in the modern world without completely abandoning who they were. They couldn't afford to lose it to a dragon.

The workers at the gates knew him by sight and he ran past without comment. The familiar mechanical whirs and bells of the midway assaulted him, while the aromas of fried onions and popcorn were sharp in the chilly air. Jugglers roamed the pathways, tossing clubs that glowed in the dark while far above, lights from the roller coaster swirled through the starlit sky. As it was close to ten o'clock and a half hour away from the winter closing time, the crowd was thinning out.

Arthur charged ahead, seeking any sign of fire or panic, but all seemed normal. He stopped beside the life-size statue of a pink unicorn to get his bearings. The text message that had called him to the theme park had come from Gawain. He dialed the Scottish knight's phone. "I'm here. Where is it?" he demanded the instant Gawain picked up.

"Look above the church."

The Church of the Holy Well was the only truly medieval item in the park. It had once housed the sleeping knights of Camelot and had been transplanted from England decades ago when Medievaland was built. Arthur's gaze found it easily among the theme park's structures and he obediently studied the roofline. "I don't see anything."

"Keep watching."

Impatient, Arthur paced, the phone still to his ear. What was Gwen doing? Was there any chance of returning to her hotel room that night? His anger was still a live thing, flaring if his thoughts touched it, but hers had been just as hot. Would that make a reunion impossible, or delectable?

His reverie lasted only seconds before he saw a dark shape gliding above the whirling lights of the rides. It was as if a scrap of nothingness flitted across the sky, but he knew what that absence of light meant. "I see it."

"It's been circling for the last half hour," said Gawain. "We've gathered at the tourney grounds."

"Ready my gear," Arthur ordered.

He sprinted to the complex where the jousting took place. The games themselves were held in an amphitheater, while the stables and equipment rooms were in low buildings behind. When the white wooden structure came into view, Arthur put on a last burst of speed. Gawain, already clad in his red armor, waited outside the locker-room door. He turned as Arthur approached, silently leading him inside.

The space where they donned their equipment was much like any locker room, with sinks and showers. Beaumains had Arthur's white-and-blue armor already spread out on a bench. This was not the gear they used for jousting, though much of it looked similar. This was battle-scarred and shaped to personal taste, often sacrificing coverage for ease of movement. Jousting was inherently dangerous, but it was nothing compared to true warfare, where speed could save one's life.

"We don't know if the dragon will even land," Gawain said, buckling Arthur's breastplate in place. His fingers flew with the urgency of one well used to donning battle gear on the fly. "This preparation may be for nothing."

"I would rather not meet the beast's teeth unprotected," Arthur replied, "though armor never did much against a dragon's flame." Unhelpfully, his imagination pictured a potato in tinfoil, ready for the barbecue.

"Perhaps there's a modern material that would help," Beaumains suggested, fastening the metal vambraces that protected Arthur's forearms. "Maybe asbestos?"

Gawain gave an eye roll only an older brother could produce. "Perhaps we could put a sprinkler system in our helms and spout like fountains. Go help Owen with the horses."

Beaumains bowed and left, giving a cheeky grin. Arthur took Excalibur from Gawain and fastened the sword belt in place.

"I'm sorry this happened tonight of all nights," said Gawain. "I know you went to see the queen."

No doubt Clary had told him. There was nothing worse than being the object of gossip. Arthur shifted from foot to foot, his armor clanking softly. "The queen understands the urgency," he said in a tone that didn't invite conversation.

Gawain studied him, but said nothing more on the subject. He simply handed Arthur his shield, with its three golden crowns against a field of blue. These were the great kite-shaped shields rather than the smaller, round bucklers—clumsier, but they offered better protection from flame. Arthur took it, and they marched toward the door. Just as Arthur's mailed fist touched the door handle, he heard the scream of horses.

As the door opened, Rukon Shadow Wing landed at Medievaland's heart in a gout of flame. This time, Arthur knew, the dragon had come to kill them.

Chapter 10

Only the dragon's breath was visible in the unlit amphitheater. Scraps of flame picked out pieces from the shadow it cast—a shoulder, a curl of tail, a flare of amber eyes. In contrast, the men of the Round Table stood in the pool of light cast by the building, their shields defiantly bright with color. Beaumains and Percival had readied their horses and were struggling with their mounts' bridles. The terrified animals were stamping and tossing their heads, nostrils flaring at the unfamiliar scent. They were good, brave mounts, but they weren't trained for dragons.

"Get the horses back in the stables," Arthur ordered. "We're doing this on foot."

"What's your plan?" Gawain asked, as the younger knights hurried to obey.

Arthur heard the blare of sirens—fire and police, no doubt. This was just getting worse. There was no hiding a flapping, talking dragon from the human authorities.

"I've tried polite reason. Now it's time to make our scaly friend leave."

"I'm right beside you," said Gawain. Putting action to words, he drew his sword and stood at Arthur's right.

"I never thought I'd have the chance to fight a dragon." Percival stretched his limbs, hiding his eagerness with a show of preparation.

"I've battled one before," Palomedes replied, sounding less enthusiastic. "I can't say I wanted a rematch, but here we are."

The dragon was moving now, advancing at a steady pace that said it had an agenda. At the same time, Arthur was aware of the other knights clustering around him, shields up to present an unbreakable wall of courage. Every knight who could be was there. With five mighty warriors against one dragon, the odds were almost even. All the same, it was going to be a bloodbath.

Rukon folded his wings and bellowed, the pale underside of his neck a stripe against the inky sky. A second later, a dozen camera flashes bleached the darkness. Reporters, Arthur realized with a sinking stomach. The hidden world would be in the headlines by breakfast—unless Rukon made the press his late-night snack.

If Arthur had been a glory seeker, a horseback charge with lance and shining armor would have set social media aflame—right along with Medievaland. As King of Camelot and protector of the mortal realms, Arthur had to put an end to this drama before it began. "No hashtag for me," he muttered under his breath as he drew Excalibur.

"Stay here," he ordered his men, his voice brooking no argument. "I go in first. If he attacks, I'll keep him busy while you move in."

"You're buying us a chance," Gawain said darkly.

"A king spends the lives of his men as carefully as he can."

"What about your own?"

"Give my regards to the late-night news. Now, do as I ask."

While he heard armor clank and feet scuffle, the knights knew better than to protest. Discipline had been hard-won among these fighters, but Arthur had enforced his will through respect and occasional bravado. Just the same, when he strode forward their watchfulness prickled along his spine. He was protecting his men, but they had his back. In moments like this, he loved them fiercely.

As always, the prospect of battle heightened his senses. Night robbed the world of color and precise edges—the amphitheater had no lighting for after-dark events. But he could smell the fairground's tapestry of scents—horses, food, exhaust, dust and, over it all, the thick musk of dragon. The last clogged his nose and throat worse than it had in the forest, or maybe his chest was tight because the fight was on his ground now. Here, he had far more to lose.

He stopped halfway down the field. Walking in armor was noisy, and only now could he hear the profound silence surrounding him. No one spoke, no car doors slammed. All attention was fixed on the king and the dragon. As if on cue, the clock tower at the Church of the Holy Well bonged the half hour, confirming that the park had closed. Fewer bystanders would be in the line of fire. Something to be thankful for.

An image of Gwen's face flickered through his mind, but he shied away from it. Right now, he had to be a king, not a man. Remembering his wife, in all her softness and fiery temper, would undo every scrap of courage.

Arthur's mouth had gone dry, and he had to swallow twice before he could speak—but when he did, he spoke loud enough to make himself heard by everyone present. After all, he'd been trained to address crowds in a time before microphones. "Greetings, Rukon Shadow Wing. To what do I owe the honor of your visit?"

Rukon let another scrap of flame escape his muzzle. The fire floated like ragged scarves around him, giving the impression of something birthed in a painter's conception of hell. Arthur guessed it was a sign of temper, and a dangerous one. If the arena floor hadn't been dirt, the entire place would be in flames.

"I warned you that I would come," Rukon replied, the rumbling voice grim. "I have already explained what I will do to reclaim fame and glory among the human realms. Are these your reporters?" He snaked his neck toward the news vans, blowing a puff of steam.

"Do you really believe renown will come if you eat me on television?" Arthur said wearily.

"It must be seen and commented upon to be of value. Isn't that how this world works?"

"That is hardly the point."

"That is precisely the point." The dragon snorted more fire.

This wasn't telling Arthur anything new. He gambled then, the ache in his chest an indication of how much he feared. "You've given me words. I will think of them whenever I shovel the stable."

Rukon's head swung back, the yellow eyes glowing hot.

Arthur lowered his sword and shield, but just enough to show his intention to talk. "You could have killed me yesterday, but you did not."

"I spared you so that we would meet tonight, in front of your tale-tellers."

"You are here again, but so far you haven't touched a single blade of grass. Meanwhile, I have received threats from an anonymous fae. These are all part of a pattern, and I don't believe you are a willing participant. Nor was the dragon who fell from the sky. She was chained with magic, a pawn in a murderous plan."

At that, Rukon threw back his head and gave another roar. It was filled with sound and flame, bringing screams from the gathered crowd. From the corner of his eye, Arthur saw uniformed men press forward, but the knights rushed to hold them back.

Eventually the bellow subsided, fading from fury to what Arthur had expected to hear—grief. "Her name is Elosta," Rukon said. "Remember her name well, human, and remember it with reverence. There is no telling what befell her. He will not say."

"Who?" Arthur demanded, wondering if Elosta was Rukon's mate. "What is going on?"

"Treachery," Rukon rumbled. "You are the Pendragon, little king. Figure it out."

But Arthur didn't have a clue. "Tell me more."

But Rukon fanned his wings, spreading them wide until they blotted out the stars. Arthur just had time to lift his shield before he was engulfed in flames.

Gwen had all but ripped the hotel-room door open at Clary's tentative knock.

"Sorry I'm back early, but I had a sense that it was time to come home." The green-eyed witch regarded her closely. "I'm guessing the reunion didn't go so well."

"Ya think?" Gwen snapped, using an expression she'd heard Clary use at least a dozen times that day.

"You're wearing my flannel pajamas."

Gwen looked down at the fuzzy garment, which was covered in prancing pink sheep. "Nothing I bought today felt comforting enough."

Clary finally stepped through the door, closing it behind her. "Do you want to talk about it?"

"No." Gwen said it with finality, but carried on in the next breath. "I thought he was listening. Everything was going so well. He told me about the dragon problem—he actually talked about something important happening in Camelot—and he said he wanted to change. But the moment one of his men called, he left and I had to stay behind. That's not partnership."

"That's pretty patronizing," Clary agreed. "Has he always been like that?"

"He's a king. They're the definition of patronizing." Gwen walked to the bed she'd claimed as her own and sat on the end. "I've never been able to really serve the people of Camelot. Yes, I arranged receptions and banquets and ran the king's household, and that was all necessary, but it wasn't *vital*. And it certainly wasn't anything we could build a relationship over."

"Sounds boring," Clary agreed.

"It was to me. He only let me go to war with him once. Women sometimes did, as laundresses and cooks as well as…other things."

There had been a few wives, but more whores who traveled with the baggage trains. Gwen hadn't considered herself sheltered until she'd seen what went on in the tents at the back of the encampment.

"What happened?" Clary sat down on the opposite bed and kicked off her ankle boots. They fell to the carpet with a thump.

"A fever ran through the camp, and I caught it. I was sick for a long time." There was more to the story, but this wasn't the time for that tale.

"Let me guess. He treated you like a glass ornament after that."

"Exactly. One that can't be chipped or covered in fingerprints. But there's a difference between caring for someone and being careful nothing happens to them."

Clary rose, restlessly pacing the room until she opened

a tiny door beneath the television stand. It rattled as she pulled out two small bottles and tossed one to Gwen. "This kind of a talk needs lubricant."

"I already drank the rest of the champagne." There hadn't been much, but it had taken the edge off her hurt for a few minutes.

Clary tossed a bag onto the bed. "Snack food. The secret is to soak up the drink so you can start over."

"It occurs to me that you're what my nurse called a bad influence."

"I'm the terror of mothers everywhere." Clary fell back onto the bed with her own snacks. "Usually I can't afford the minibar, but we still have the king's credit card."

At that, Gwen pulled open the bag and extracted an orange object she recognized. There had been a bowl of the bright orange worms sitting on the table in Arthur's living room. "What is this?"

"Cheese Wizards."

Gwen stared at it, thinking something that orange was possibly lethal, and then popped it in her mouth. Experience never came without risk. The snack was salty and crunchy, although it didn't quite taste like real food. "I don't understand why they call it a wizard."

"Because they're fabulous," Clary said with a shrug. "A wizard is just an extra-special witch, after all."

"Merlin was born a witch?"

"Yeah," said Clary, "I wonder how he feels living in a world with Cheese Wizards. One day, you're the most magical person ever, and the next they name a snack food after you."

"Someone named these after Merlin?"

"Not really. The normal world has no idea real wizards exist. It's just advertising. Magic is sexy."

"Oh." Gwen really didn't want to mingle images of bright orange worms and reproduction. Not one bit.

"But we're not here to talk about Merlin," Clary prompted.

All the same, Gwen didn't mind taking the spotlight off herself. "Have you met him?"

"No," Clary said, flopping back onto her pillow. "Although he came to my hometown to see the high muckety-mucks of witchdom."

"What about?"

"There's been talk about information sharing between the covens. Boring stuff mostly, though it's meant loosening up on some of the rules we live by. More chances to travel outside our own coven. No more arranged marriages, for which I'm grateful."

Clary rolled to face Gwen, propping up her head on one hand. "I would've gone completely fangirl over the Great One. I mean, I've never traveled without my spell kit since I was a little girl. I would have had him autograph it. But I was out of town for work. Even witches have to eat."

Gwen sat up. "You see, that's what I want."

Clary raised her brows. "To eat?"

"No, to live the way you do." Gwen waved a Cheese Wizard for emphasis. "You have a job, places to go, an independent life. That doesn't make you any less of a witch."

Clary's eyes narrowed. "I agree, though the older generation would argue."

"I can be Guinevere the queen and still exercise my mind," Gwen said, sure of herself now. "You told me that the witches where you come from could help if I wanted to start fresh."

"They can forge identity papers," Clary said, sounding less certain.

"You said they could teach me what I need to know so that I can go to school and eventually earn my own keep."

Clary sat up, setting food and drink aside. Her expression was completely serious. "Yes, but I live on the other side of the country. If you come with me…"

"You live by a completely different ocean," Gwen said quickly. "I looked at a map. If I go with you when you return home, I'll be leaving Arthur and Camelot far behind."

"Are you sure?" Clary frowned. "That's a big step, and even if you turn around and come home again, you've made a statement you can't take back. And you just got here."

Gwen didn't have a good answer. She'd tried to get what she wanted tonight. Rather than argue yet again, she'd shared her feelings with her husband and urged him to share his own. She'd been more than willing to hear him out and find a compromise.

But one text message had hurtled them back to where they'd started. Guinevere, Queen of Camelot, would never be a real partner. Gwen, the woman, was an even-lower priority.

"If nothing else, it will give Arthur and I time to decide what we want." Her words were quiet but firm.

"A cooling-off period?" Clary asked in a cautious voice.

"He will never change his mind about me. To him, I'm still the overeager young girl who came to court and made a lot of mistakes."

"Can't he notice that you've grown up?"

"He's too focused on other things. Perhaps it's not his fault. I've tried making things better, but nothing works."

Clary reached across the space between the beds and squeezed Gwen's hand. "The witches of the Shadowring Coven will have you in school in no time."

Gwen squeezed back, incredibly grateful to her new friend. "I am no warrior queen, nor am I a mighty sorceress like Nimueh or Morgan LaFaye. But I have other talents. Even if Arthur doesn't care about them, I do."

Clary gave a slight cough. "For a mighty king, he's a bit of an idiot, isn't he?"

Chapter 11

"Oh. My. Goddess."

Clary's voice was strident with alarm—loud enough that Gwen emerged from the bathroom, hairbrush in hand. "What's wrong?"

Clary sat cross-legged on her bed, remote control in hand. She'd turned it on for a late-night talk show, which had prompted a whole new flood of questions from Gwen. It appeared the modern world had taken gossip to a professional level, a notion guaranteed to horrify a queen with a crumbling marriage.

Clary pointed at the screen. "They interrupted my show for a news bulletin. This is happening at Medievaland."

Gwen moved so that she could see the screen. "That's Palomedes! I know his armor."

The handsome Saracen knight was acting as a human wall so the reporters couldn't pass. Behind him, Gwen could make out flame. This was about the dragons! Transfixed, she slid onto the bed next to Clary.

Some effort had been made to illuminate the scene, but the field was too large for whatever the news vans had on hand. Only the dragon's glowing eyes and fiery nostrils were clearly visible, the rest a winged hulk with patches of shining scales.

"Look!" Clary pointed again. "The firemen are turning on their hoses."

Bursts of water whooshed through the air, arcing toward a black shape shifting in the shadows. A disgusted bellow drowned out every other sound. Gwen felt her mouth drifting open in astonishment.

The jiggling camera swung around to a female reporter with red lips and hair that didn't move despite an obvious breeze. "There is what appears to be a fire-breathing dragon on the field behind me, along with members of the Knights of New Camelot, an entertainment troupe employed here at Medievaland. Most of the entertainers are engaged in crowd control, along with the police. However, the leader of the troupe, Arthur Pendragon, has confronted the monster."

Gwen gasped as the scene cut to an image of Arthur crouched behind his shield while flame flowed over it. "Arthur!" She jumped off the bed, bounding toward the TV before she realized the futility of it.

The camera focus jerked back to show a draconic head, but a mailed fist immediately closed over the lens. Gwen collapsed back onto the bed, tears standing in her eyes. "Is he hurt?" she demanded. "Tell me if he's hurt!"

Clary put a hand on her arm. "Wait and see what they say."

"As you can see," the reporter continued, "it hasn't been easy to get good coverage of this event."

"But, Megan," said the male voice of the announcer, "isn't this all a publicity stunt?"

There was a second's delay while his question made it to the reporter's earpiece. "Undoubtedly, Kevin, but the authorities at Medievaland are denying all responsibility. No doubt this incident is related to the flaming apparition that dropped from the sky. Animal control officers won't confirm that it was actually a live cow or whether it was dead when pushed from some kind of aircraft or whether it was actually a hologram."

"Is Arthur hurt?" Gwen wailed.

Kevin must have heard her. "Megan, have there been any injuries?"

Gwen realized her nails were digging into her palms.

"None that have been reported," said Megan.

Gwen and Clary exhaled together.

"But with uncontrolled fire in play, all we can do is hope for the best."

Someone on TV shouted and the camera did another stomach-turning swing. Gwen leaned forward, trying to see better, but the screen showed only a muddle of shadows.

"It's hard to see, Kevin, but it appears the so-called dragon is getting ready to fly."

"To fly?" the announcer asked incredulously.

There was a rush and a roar and the camera swung upward, following a trajectory of flame and bat-like wings. "Kevin, these animatronics—or holograms or whatever—are incredible."

"Every theme park in America will want to know how this was done," said Kevin.

Clary made a rude choking noise. "It came from an egg, dude."

The cameras followed the dragon until it was swallowed up by the night.

"Well, that appears to end the spectacle," Megan chirped. "I'll have interviews with the entertainers for the morning show."

"Thank you, Megan."

"Thanks, Kevin. This is Megan Dutton, Nighthawk News."

Clary hit the power button, sending the TV into blackness.

"So that's why Arthur had to leave." Gwen drew her knees up, wrapping her arms around them. "It was for an important reason. But then, it always is."

And their marriage never mattered quite as much.

Clary dialed her phone. "Hey, Gawain, is everyone okay?"

Gwen watched her friend's face darken as the conversation went on. Clary said little before finally heaving a sigh and ending the call. "What did he say?" Gwen asked.

"No broken bones. No major burns. He doesn't know more than that."

Still, it was good news. Gwen realized that she could in fact phone Arthur. He'd put his number in her cell phone. Would her call to him be welcome or would it be considered a bother? Why hadn't he called her to put her mind at ease? Gwen put her forehead on her knees, wishing her heart would stop aching.

Clary turned to face her. "What do you think is going on? With the dragons, I mean."

Gwen considered. "I can't say. I only ever knew one dragon and she was very, very old. She had a cave in the hills near my father's castle. She didn't like humans much and rarely strayed far from her nest, but she'd talk to me sometimes."

"You knew an actual dragon?" Clary sounded impressed.

"I can't say that I actually *knew* her," said Gwen, unfolding herself. "The only ones who are close to the dragons are the goblins in the Crystal Mountains. They live alongside the dragon strongholds beyond the Forest Sauvage."

The Forest Sauvage was a no-man's-land, neither a mortal realm nor part of the Faery Kingdom and beyond the laws of either. Magic dwelled there, as well as the last remnants of demonkind. It was the kind of place young knights went seeking adventure, some never to be seen again.

"You're thinking," Clary said. "I can see it on your face."

"Arthur is asking the same questions we are. He said as much earlier tonight." Gwen slid off the bed to pace. "If he really wanted answers, he'd talk to the goblins."

"And he won't?" Clary asked uncertainly.

"No one talks to the goblins. The court was all politeness to their envoys, of course, but only as far as they had to be."

"You met goblins?" Clary went for more liquor from the tiny fridge.

"Yes. The goblins had mineral resources and came to trade. The Crystal Mountains are filled with gold and all sorts of precious gems, but not common salt, which we had in abundance. I learned all this because I was the one left to entertain the goblin delegation while the knights found urgent business elsewhere."

"Why?"

Gwen waved a hand. "Goblins are repulsive—rude, smelly and unpleasant to look at—but they *are* interesting. They know more about mining gemstones than anyone I know. That's why they live in the Crystal Mountains and consequently know about dragons."

"Which is exactly why Arthur should have you at his side." Clary crumpled up her chip bag and tossed it neatly into the garbage can across the room. "You're the one with the answers."

"No," said Gwen. "I just know who probably has them."

"Then tell Arthur. Tell him to get on it."

"I doubt he'd have much success with the goblins' king. When the ambassador and his retinue came to Camelot, I'm the one who poured their wine and laughed at their jokes. The will to build a relationship counts for much among their kind. I even gave Ambassador Krzak a lock of my hair as a token of regard."

Gwen folded her arms, thinking through what Arthur had told her about Rukon, the female dragon and the fae making threats. One didn't have to be Merlin the Wise to detect the stink of skulduggery and plots. And if she drew that conclusion, Arthur surely had.

But he didn't allow anyone to help bring these enemies to justice. Oh, he'd trust his men to swing a sword on command, but Arthur kept control where it mattered. He'd protect the human realms with his own flesh and bone if necessary—even if that meant facing down Rukon Shadow Wing. That willingness to bear the brunt of sacrifice was the stamp of a good king. But working alone was also Arthur's weakness. It would never occur to him to ask a lowly goblin for aid.

But it had occurred to Guinevere, and only she had a welcome with the goblin king. It was up to her to act.

At that thought, a wave of terror passed through her, strong enough that she had to sit down before her knees gave out. She reached for the tiny bottle of wine and uncapped it, taking a healthy gulp.

"What's wrong?" Clary asked sharply.

"Witches know how to work portals, right?"

"Yes," Clary said suspiciously. "I've been practicing ever since we rediscovered the spell last year."

Gwen's heart leaped at the same moment her stomach sank with a fresh wave of fear. It was a horrible sensation. "I need a portal to the Crystal Mountains."

"Wait." Clary held up her hands. "Why?"

Gwen wanted a lot of things—school, independence, a chance to explore this exciting new world. But she had accepted the role of queen, and that meant putting the mortal realms first. "I can't stand by when there's something I can do, and I'm the only one who actually *can* do it."

"Will Arthur agree?" Clary asked, doubt plain on her face.

"No, but that doesn't matter." Gwen hugged herself, wanting nothing more than to crawl beneath the bedcovers and hide. "I'm not asking for Arthur's permission."

Arthur lay on the bed in Medievaland's infirmary, staring at the cracked ceiling. He could have risen and faced the world five minutes ago, but it was quiet and the ice pack on his head felt good. The lack of sleep last night—not to mention the twin calamities of dragons and Gwen—were catching up with him.

Unfortunately, the peace was short-lived. The door opened and Gawain tiptoed in, forehead creased with worry.

"I'm awake," said Arthur.

"How are you feeling?" Gawain asked, folding his arms.

"Lightly toasted."

"Fortunately, your shield took the brunt of the flame. Your burns aren't serious."

Arthur sat up, swinging his legs over the side of the bed. The room swam, forcing him to brace himself.

"Careful," said Gawain, putting a steadying hand on

his shoulder. "You have a concussion. That was a nasty blow you took."

He could have been incinerated, but once again Rukon had held back. Instead, a flick of the dragon's tail had sent Arthur flying. Again. It was the same trick the dragon had pulled in the forest, and it was getting old. Although Arthur had broken no bones, he'd lost consciousness for a minute or two.

Gawain lifted an eyebrow. "Rukon must have hit you with as much force as a truck."

"The beast did it on purpose. A last insult as it flew away." And the dragon had answered none of his questions—just given him nonsense about his family name.

Gawain handed Arthur a clean T-shirt, and he shrugged it on. It was then he noticed his armor piled in the corner. He vaguely remembered the knights helping him from the field and unbuckling the heavy gear so he could rest. The shield was a charred ruin. "Was that on television?" he asked quietly.

"The flames, yes. Your flying lesson, no." Gawain shrugged. "The news reported that no one was seriously injured."

"Good," Arthur replied.

"There will be a lot of questions. The police, the press and even Medievaland's owners have been trying to contact you. Go out the back way. I'll drive you home. We can think up a cover story in the morning."

Arthur grunted his agreement and pulled on his boots while Gawain picked up a call. As he wasn't listening to the one-sided phone conversation, it took a moment before Arthur realized something was wrong.

The knight had gone beet red. "You what?" Gawain demanded, voice rising.

The faint sounds of a female voice emanated from the

phone. The words were muffled but the tone was clearly excited. Cold dread began creeping into the room.

"Stay where you are. We'll be right over." Gawain stuffed the phone in his pocket. He rubbed his temples, then turned to Arthur with an apologetic look. "It's about Queen Guinevere."

Arthur rose, Gawain's tone instantly flooding him with tension. "What about her?"

"The queen believes she knows a way to gather information about the dragons' recent behavior."

Arthur frowned. "She does?"

Gawain smiled an apology that looked more like a wince. "You should sit down again. You're not going to like what I'm about to tell you."

Arthur complied, but anger was rapidly eroding his confusion. "Tell me!"

Gawain heaved a sigh. "According to Clary, Queen Guinevere has gone on an adventure."

Chapter 12

Clary had made the portal in the hotel closet, saying it was easier for her to draw the necessary arc of light within a defined space. Gwen, who had no magic whatsoever, couldn't comment. The only time she'd gone through a portal was with Merlin just days ago, and stepping through that had been like walking through a door. The mechanics—whatever they were—had been seamless. A wave of his hand, and time and space parted.

Clary's portal, however, had required almost the entire contents of her spell kit, several more snacks and a quantity of curses. It came together quickly, but the effort involved had made the young witch break into a sweat. Eventually, though, there had been a blur of color and light, like the reflection of torches on water, and then a spinning, gasping tumble. Gwen landed face-first on cold, wet grass. For a panicked instant, she couldn't breathe and flopped over onto her back, willing her chest to inflate. A heartbeat passed, then two, and finally she dragged in a long, rasping heave of air as her lungs remembered how to work. The air was sweet and fresh, tangy with mud and growing things. Gwen rejoiced deep in her soul—this smelled like home, not the city with its motors and garbage and thousands of rushing people. Beyond the sound of her panting, there was the rush of water and a distant cacophony of birds.

Only then did she venture to open her eyes to a blue sky untroubled by clouds. She sat up, feeling a twinge where her elbow had hit the ground during her unceremonious landing, and gazed about her. She was on a gentle mountain slope that rolled into a deep valley. She couldn't see the bottom from where she sat, only steep angles blanketed with pines that turned the warm greens of her meadow to a somber blue black. On the upper edges of the valley, a scattering of deciduous trees showed it was autumn here, as well. Slowly, she got to her feet and turned to see behind her. There, the land rose, eventually giving way to enormous boulders. The peak of her mountain was cloaked in mist, but she could tell it was only one of many. All around her were snowcaps shrouded in mist wrought gold by the sun. A cool breeze kissed Gwen's face as she turned, shading her eyes. In the distance she made out twin mountaintops with a distinctive curve to their peaks—an outline she'd seen many times in tapestries and illuminations about the goblin realms. They were called The Fangs—a deadly pass into troll territory. The sight both frightened and reassured her. Despite her inexperience with portals, Clary had indeed sent Gwen to the Crystal Mountains.

But the mountain range was a large wilderness. She'd asked Clary to set her down near the goblin king's palace but there was no such place in sight. She clutched her hand around the bracelet Clary had given her—a simple leather thong strung with painted wooden beads. It was bespelled to open the portal to return home at a spoken command—an innovation the witches had recently invented. Clary had been inordinately proud of her work, but cautioned her that reopening the portal would only work once and there weren't enough supplies in her kit to create another. So, Gwen wasn't giving up and running home unless she was certain there was no other option. She marked the site carefully with a pile of small rocks and began walking.

To her left was a stream flowing down the mountain, light dancing off the churning water. Gwen followed it up the slope, using it as a guide to keep from wandering in circles. She'd dressed in warm clothes, with the sturdy boots she had bought, and taken along a knapsack filled with the food left in the minibar and the small knife she'd brought with her from Camelot. It wasn't truly a weapon—knives were everyday tools, even for a queen—but it could be used for self-defense.

The rise ended in a steep but brief climb. Gwen had grown up scrambling over hills and made it to the new plateau with no trouble. Here, the view was wider and she went to her hands and knees, crawling to the edge of the rocks for the best possible panorama. She was warm from hiking, and her cheeks welcomed the mountain chill. Although she'd found nothing useful yet, excitement bubbled inside her as if she were made of champagne. This was what she had lacked all along—adventure, a purpose and a way to challenge herself.

Her new viewpoint showed more breathtaking views, but also something that made Gwen give a triumphant cry. There was no castle, but there were signs of habitation on the face of the mountain below. Rings of earthworks were held in place by smoothly sculpted rock. They were cut in half by a steep stair that wound out of sight around the face of the steep cliff. Bridges arched over steep crevasses, miracles of engineering and craftsmanship Gwen longed to study up close. All of it led to a doorway in the face of the mountain, a huge arched maw of blackness surrounded by elaborate geometric carvings. When the goblins had said their king lived in the mountains, they meant literally *inside* the mountains. Gwen had found where she needed to go.

She looked a moment longer, plotting the best route to the stairs, and began to back away from the cliff's edge. She had barely moved when a cold, hard point pricked her neck.

"Have you done spying on our home, human?" came a rough, nasal voice.

Goblin, Gwen thought, remaining absolutely still. No other voices had that same rasping quality, as if the speaker was being slowly strangled. The words were obscured further by the speaker's accent—goblins had their own language, though most could speak at least one human tongue. "I was seeking a way to your door, guardsman. I would ask you to escort me the rest of the way."

"Escort you?" he mocked. "I will *escort* you straight to our dungeons."

Gwen's heart skipped in fright, but she kept her voice level. "I request an audience with your king. I am Guinevere, Queen of Camelot and wife of Arthur of Britain. Ambassador Krzak knows me well."

"Krzak died in my great-great-grandsire's time." Now the guardsman sounded incredulous. "What's a queen doing crawling around the mountains alone? Where is Arthur? Where are your men-at-arms?"

Pulse thundering now, Gwen realized she'd made a terrible mistake. Krzak had been young when she'd known him, but too much time had passed for even a goblin to live so long. "Please," she said. "I'm telling the truth."

The blade poking her neck was removed and rough hands pulled her to her feet. She turned to the guard, catching sight of the stone-tipped spear before finding the guardsman's face. If there had been any doubt what he was, one look dispelled it. Goblins came in every shade of the rainbow, and this one was a mossy green that blended into the vegetation. He was perhaps four and a half feet tall but sturdily built, wearing a leather tunic and cap scrunched down over straggly green hair. But what set goblins apart, besides the earthy, mildewed smell of them, was their lumpiness. Like autumn gourds, they were covered in bumps and warts that in any other species would be a sign of a contagious skin disease. To them, it was a natural hallmark of beauty. Gwen had trained herself to see past it long ago, and so she gave no reaction to the guardsman's irregular face.

"I see you are familiar with our kind," he said with a ferocious grin that showed blocky, crooked teeth.

Gwen remained firm. "I am. I entertained the ambassador many times." And she knew better than to ask the goblin's name. Only public figures like Krzak shared their names with outsiders—which meant anyone not born of goblin kind.

"So history says, human, but that doesn't explain how you're here now."

"Magic," she said simply. "And I came for information only the goblins, with their great wisdom, can provide."

The dollop of flattery must have worked, because the guardsman gave a slow nod. "All right. We'll go to the palace and my captain can decide what to do with you."

"Better to let the tall heads roll than risk those bowed in humility," she said, quoting one of the ambassador's favorite lines.

He gave her a sharp look. "My mother used to say that."

"Then she gave good advice," Gwen said, although she knew her tall head was currently at risk.

With the barest flicker of a smile, the guardsman angled his spear until the point prodded her in the chest. He jerked his head toward the stream Gwen had followed to get there. "Walk."

The route to the stairs was arduous, testing Gwen's endurance to its limit as she scrambled over rock piles and up slippery screes of gravel. The goblin, on the other hand, had no such trouble, skipping like a goat over stone and stream and only occasionally using the butt of his spear like a walking stick. A half-dozen times, he had to help Gwen along.

But once they reached the stair, the real climb began. Ever afterward, Gwen tried to forget that upward slog. She arrived at the top gasping, sweaty and with a fire in her legs that promised excruciating muscle cramps.

She collapsed outside the door while the guardsman conferred in his own tongue with a blue goblin wearing a steel chain about his thick neck—presumably an officer of some kind. He glanced at Gwen, but didn't bow, and she knew better than to expect it. Even if he did believe she was the Queen of Camelot, goblins barely recognized any royalty besides their own.

When another guard shoved an earthenware cup of water into her hands, she gulped it without question. Only when she caught her breath did she realize the goblin's captain had disappeared, and the others stood watching her with curious eyes.

"What are we waiting for?" she asked, refusing to admit that anything could go wrong after she'd made it this far.

The goblins didn't answer. They were clearly under orders to wait in silence. Gwen settled with her back to the rock and did her best to ignore the chill of her sweat-dampened clothes.

Minutes later, the blue goblin returned and gestured to his men. They stood at attention, spears straight, while Gwen got to her feet. "Come," he ordered, and led the way inside the mountain. Gwen followed, and the guardsman and his companion brought up the rear. Their small procession had the appearance of an honor guard, but she knew very well she was their captive.

The dark cave mouth gave way to a smoothly hollowed tunnel several times her height. Flaming torches sat in stanchions every dozen yards to light their path, but Gwen barely noticed where they were going. The entire tunnel—walls, ceiling and floor—was lined with glittering mosaics depicting scenes from goblin history. Each tiny tile was a chip of glittering, translucent stone set against a field of gold leaf. The torchlight caught the gold, the reflection making the passage shimmer with light. Her steps slowed as she stared openmouthed, her whole being dazzled by the unexpected beauty.

The captain, however, was impatient and soon spear points prodded her back. She was almost trotting by the time the tunnel emptied into a large chamber set with double doors of carved oak. As Gwen was marched closer, a pair of blue goblins opened the doors wide enough to let them pass through.

Beyond was the throne room, packed with citizens come to beg justice or a favor or leniency from taxes. This was daily business for a court, and Gwen had seen thousands of such gatherings before, though none had smelled quite so bad. She was used to unwashed humans, but a room packed with overheated goblins was enough to make her gag.

The king sat beneath yet more mosaics. The alcove was lit from behind and surrounded the king in a halo of sparkling light. Only when Gwen drew near the throne did she see the goblin king clearly.

He was scarlet and lumpier than any goblin Gwen had ever seen. A crown sat on his hairless brow, a cloak of ermine over a tunic of royal purple. The picture wasn't improved by the fact that he was as wide as he was tall. It was like meeting a royal red toad, especially when he gave an unexpected burp.

Gwen's escort stopped, and then stepped aside, leaving her alone before the throne. "Greetings, Your Majesty," she said, sinking into a deep curtsy. "I am grateful to be granted an interview."

"I am Zorath, King of the Goblins and Emperor of the Crystal Mountains, Spear of the Deep and Blade of the Fangs." The king spoke with almost no accent but plenty of attitude. Every syllable of his title rang with pride.

"And I am Guinevere, Queen of Camelot," she said, bowing before him. "I have come seeking Your Majesty's wisdom, so that I may return to my royal husband and help him save the mortal realms."

Without warning, Zorath burst into a raucous laugh, holding his stomach as if to contain his merriment. The outburst finished in another belch. "Is that so?" he asked wryly, wiping his mouth with his sleeve. "If I were you, I'd be asking for mercy. No outsider has left here alive for the last thousand years."

Chapter 13

"Your Majesty," Gwen said with forced calm, "please explain what you mean."

Their eyes met. Zorath's shrewd gaze was as hard as twin black buttons.

Gwen silently panicked. Krzak had never mentioned anything like this. By all reports, the goblins had always been eager to show off the glories of their mines. Something had changed during the centuries of the stone sleep.

"We have riches. Outsiders have armies. No one visits the goblins for the pleasure of our company." Zorath leaned forward, studying her features with keen interest. "Tell me, pretty human, how did you find our stronghold? Was it the fae who told you of it?"

"The fae? Have they troubled your borders?"

"Ever since the end of the demon wars. Now our lands are closed to any but our own tribes."

That explained much. Gwen rose from her bow, dizzy

with fear and an urgent need for fresh air. "With your in-
dulgence, sire, I will tell you everything."

"A story!" he exclaimed with obvious delight. He
snapped fat fingers. "Bring wine and food."

As servants hurried to obey, he turned back to Gwen.
"Before you start your tale, did you bring me any pres-
ents?"

Gwen was stumped, realizing she should have antici-
pated this. Goblins set great store by tribute, but what could
she offer a king already wealthy beyond measure? "In my
pack," she said, scrambling for ideas. "It is a small gift,
sire, barely worthy of your notice, but it is a great delicacy
among the humans of my new home."

The green guardsman brought her knapsack forward
and watched carefully as she opened the zipper. Gwen
was careful not to reach for the knife, but instead plucked
out one of the cellophane packets. She went down on one
knee, offering up her gift in outstretched hands. "Sire, I
offer you Cheese Wizards."

A murmur ran through the crowd as Zorath delicately
took the bag between fat fingers tipped in long dark claws.
With a frown of concentration, the king wrestled the bag
open. As she expected, he gave a cry of pleasure at the
bright orange color of the treats. He extracted a curl and
chomped it down with relish. The only thing goblins
craved more than color was salt.

"More," he demanded, waving at her knapsack. "Show
me all your tribute."

Gwen emptied the knapsack of food, laying out the
bright packages of snacks at the goblin king's feet. "I hope
the variety pleases Your Majesty."

The king now had a huge golden goblet and was alternating slurps of wine with bites of Cheese Wizards. "It is

acceptable," he said with a full mouth. "Now, rise and tell me your tale."

She did, from Krzak to the stone sleep to the dragons at Medievaland. The story took time, but Zorath's attention did not waver. Neither did that of the audience in the hall.

"You say that you knew our ambassador to Arthur's court in Camelot?" Zorath asked after she had at last finished.

"I did," she agreed. "I knew him well."

"You gave him a lock of your hair?"

"I did."

"We will put your word to the test."

There was a long wait while the king summoned a historian who trotted off to do the king's bidding. Then more time passed until the historian reappeared with a small box on a purple velvet pillow and knelt at Zorath's feet.

"Your Majesty," the historian said in a wheezing voice, "Ambassador Krzak placed the lock in a casket bespelled to preserve it from the ravages of time. That casket has been kept in our treasure stores, for the memory of Queen Guinevere's respect and kindness has been a legend among our people."

"Very well." Zorath lifted the lid of the box. "Step this way, lady."

Gwen obeyed, kneeling at the king's feet. The goblin king lifted a long golden lock tied with sky blue thread and held it beside Gwen's fall of hair. "It is a match. This human woman tells the truth. She is Camelot's Queen."

The assembly of goblins erupted in a cheer, tossing caps into the air and bowing as she turned her head to witness the commotion. Zorath broke into a wide grin and offered an unexpectedly graceful bow. "Queen Guinevere is always welcome in these realms. For her, the borders are always open."

Gwen exhaled a long breath, her heart lifting. "Your hospitality is gratefully received, King Zorath."

A herald called for silence as the king replaced the lock of hair in its casket and motioned its keeper away. Zorath turned to Gwen. "There was something you wanted to ask me, my lady?"

Now Gwen wanted to cheer, as well, to stamp her feet and wave her arms in jubilation. She'd done it—she'd won the goblin king over without threats or swords or magic. She'd done it just by being who she was and never forgetting that a queen owed courtesy to everyone who came beneath her roof. And now she would have something to offer in pursuit of keeping the human realms safe.

"No one knows the dragons of these mountains better than the goblins," she began. "Can you tell us why they are leaving their dens to terrorize the new Camelot? It does not make sense. Dragons do not ever stray far from their hoards."

Zorath opened his mouth to answer, but a commotion came from the back of the room. Dismayed by the interruption, Gwen turned to stare as the great doors to the throne room swung open and a knot of goblins appeared, half marching, half trotting after a prisoner who seemed to be in charge of the procession.

"What is the meaning of this interruption?" Zorath demanded.

The goblins parted to reveal a figure with a large sword. Gwen stared for a moment, disbelief stalling her brain for a beat. "Arthur?"

He was muddy and bruised, and his expression crackled with temper. He fixed Gwen with a look that spoke of relief and fury in equal measure. "You're not hurt?" he demanded.

"No!" she protested. "I'm completely fine. What are you doing here?"

"Kneel before the king!" a blue goblin ordered, prodding Arthur with his spear. Arthur swung around to glare, and the goblin scampered backward.

"Kneel, human," Zorath commanded.

Casting a puzzled glance at the bag of Cheese Wizards, Arthur sheathed his sword and went to one knee. "Greetings, King of Goblins. I am Arthur, King of Camelot and High King of the Britons."

Zorath looked down from his dais with incredulity. "Two outsiders in one day? And one such a mighty warrior of renown."

Arthur glanced up from his bow. "I came in peace to find my wife."

Gwen met his eyes. "Are you trying to rescue me?" she asked.

"Of course. I made Clary send me through her damnable portal as soon as I'd found out where you'd gone."

Gwen huffed in exasperation. It might have been touch and go along the way, but she'd managed to navigate the goblin court on her own. In fact, she'd been about to get the answers she needed before Arthur had interrupted.

Her thoughts must have shown, because Arthur's gaze snapped away. A stubborn angle formed along his jaw. Gwen turned to Zorath. "A thousand pardons for the interruption, Your Majesty. I hope you can find it in your heart to excuse the actions of a protective spouse."

Zorath sank back onto his throne, a hard tone creeping into his words. "Ambassador Krzak wrote of the generous Queen of Camelot. I have no reason to welcome the king."

"Then we shall leave at once," said Gwen, "though I hope you will still give me the answer I seek."

Arthur's brows crooked in question, but he let her speak.

It was Zorath who interrupted with a wave of his hand. "No, those who venture here do not return to tell the tale. In honor of past friendship, we will let you leave, Guinevere of Camelot, but only you. The king stays."

Arthur sprang to his feet, his hand on Excalibur's hilt. He could fight his way out, but that would get them nowhere.

"No!" Gwen cried, pushing past the guards to stand at Arthur's side. Her mind scrambled frantically, reviewing in seconds everything she knew about goblins. "No, I beg you to let us go!"

"Gwen!" Arthur interjected.

He got no further. As theatrically as she could, Gwen fell to her knees and held up her hands in supplication. The crowd, who had fallen silent, responded exactly as she'd hoped. A murmur of sympathy and protest rippled through the room. "Please, great King Zorath," she asked, putting a throb of anguish into the words.

She gambled on what she'd seen so far—the shimmering tunnel, the glowing mosaic over the throne and even the fact they'd kept her token of affection as a relic. Goblins loved theater, especially when it elevated their role in the world. How could they resist an honored queen begging for the return of her spouse? "Word of your generosity would be sung among our people."

A crafty expression came over Zorath's features. His gaze moved from Gwen to Arthur and back again while black-clawed fingers rubbed at his warty chin. "You are persuasive, Queen, and I can hear the approval of my citizens in their cries. But law is law, and what ruler can break it without weakening his position? I cannot grant your wish without exacting a price. Will you pay it?"

Arthur's expression was puzzled. "Clearly my wife had a purpose in coming here. If there is a way I can further

her mission without dishonor to either Your Majesty or the good name of Camelot, I will assist you. And, yes, I would like to go home without the need to battle my way to freedom."

"Spoken like a noble man." Zorath sounded unimpressed. "But a public hall is not the proper place to speak of bargains."

"Do you fear so many witnesses?" Arthur asked coolly.

"I fear your clever wife, King of Camelot. She has them wrapped around her dainty fingers. We will adjourn to my conference rooms."

Zorath rose and stumped his way down from the dais. The guards gestured with their spears for Gwen and Arthur to follow as he led the way to a side passage, ermine cape flapping around his crimson knees. The walk was short, ending in a smaller chamber with many maps pinned to the walls.

"Clear the room," Zorath said to the guards.

The guardsmen looked hesitant, but Zorath shooed them away. The goblin king roamed the room, arms folded, his expression thoughtful. "You are carrying Excalibur, I see."

Arthur's hand went to its hilt. "I am."

"I know your reputation," said Zorath. "You could have killed my men. You let yourself be taken."

"It was the fastest way to find out if you had Guinevere." Arthur's tone was firm, but not challenging. "And I have no wish to start a war with you, King Zorath. There is enough turmoil among the realms."

"We have a common enemy in the fae, it is true." The goblin jabbed at one of the maps. "The fae realms are at our back door. There are those among them who hunger for the treasures in our mines."

"Is that your price? Do you require protection of your lands?"

"Yes, but it has nothing to do with the fae." Zorath slapped a different map. "There is another who plagues us. Here."

Gwen and Arthur drew closer to inspect the map. It appeared to be a network of tunnels with a large red *X* over the entrance to a nest of twisting lines. Arthur frowned. "Something has blocked access to a subsection of your mines?"

Zorath nodded. "Mines, living units, surface access and vaults. Miles of treasure and territory stolen and hundreds of lives lost. We sent our soldiers, but they never came back."

Gwen took a step back, as if the red mark on the map might suddenly come to life. "What is it?"

The crafty look was back in Zorath's eyes. "A troll. Only a charmed weapon like Excalibur will kill it. You'll get your freedom and all the information I can give you about your dragon problem once you bring me the troll's head."

"A troll!" Gwen wasn't even sure what a troll looked like, but she knew their reputation. There was little wonder Zorath needed a warrior of Arthur's caliber to defeat it.

The goblin king nodded. "It has taken our livelihood bit by bit, tunnel by tunnel. There is no family who has not lost a son, a brother or a husband to its ravages. None of my workers will report for their duties. We lose trade, and soon we will begin to fade. It is devouring us in more ways than one. We have been desperate for a solution." Zorath turned to Arthur. "And here you are."

Too worried to stand on ceremony, Gwen grabbed Arthur's sleeve and dragged him to the other side of the room. He followed willingly enough, but his mouth was set in a hard line.

"Can you kill a troll?" she asked under her breath.

Arthur's eyes were dark with temper, but his answer was calm. "They're deadly, but not smart."

She squeezed his arm, feeling the hard muscle beneath his sleeve. "That doesn't answer my question." There was much wrong between them, and she knew the risks every warrior accepted as part of their mission. But she suddenly wanted guarantees, a word, a hint of safety to cling to. She needed to believe this adventure would end well.

"In the stories I've heard, trolls are conquered more often by wit than brute force."

Gwen nodded slowly, remembering that she'd seen dragon flame dousing Arthur's shield only hours ago. She reached up, and cupped his cheek. She wished she could rewind time until they were back in the hotel, drinking champagne and unbuttoning each other's clothes. How did they go from that to goblins and trolls in a single night?

"Have you ever done it before?" she asked quietly. "Killed a troll, I mean."

He shook his head. "I've never seen one. They stay in mountains like these, far from Camelot."

She didn't like that answer. Experience would have been better. She leaned closer. "Why does it have to be a charmed blade that kills it?"

"Ordinary weapons won't pierce their hide."

Her stomach dropped. "Oh, Arthur."

He studied her face, and something in his expression softened. "This is what I do, Gwen. My job is to keep people safe. That includes goblins."

"You're agreeing to this?" She tightened her fingers, holding him fast. She could feel his heat in the cool air of the room. She wanted to press closer, to soak it up and claim it for herself. It wasn't her fault that he was here— he had come of his own accord—but reason couldn't erase the ache in her heart.

Unexpectedly, a faint smile curved his lips. "You paved the way for this exchange of information for my services. Now I'll do my part to close the bargain." He turned to Zorath and gave a sharp nod.

And it was done. Her husband was committed to hunting a deadly, iron-hided troll that had already devastated hundreds. His only advantage would be in a game of wits.

That was her department. She wasn't letting him do this alone. "We're both going," Gwen said suddenly. "Or the deal's off."

Chapter 14

"Under no circumstances!"

The only surprise in Arthur's response was the look in his eyes. She'd expected irritation or pride or resignation that they must retread an argument they'd had so many times. He was the warrior. Even as king, fighting monsters was his stock-in-trade. She was a woman with no such skills.

What she saw was real fear. On some level, she'd assumed he was simply fulfilling a role—the protective male to a hopefully submissive wife. But perhaps the strangeness of the situation had caught him off guard, because the wall he kept between his thoughts and the world was missing and Gwen saw what was in his heart. He truly cared.

An ache settled in her chest as she reached up, cupping his face in her hands. He was hot to the touch, the pulse in his temple throbbing. "Don't leave me behind again," she pleaded.

She wasn't a warrior. She could manage a bow—everyone in Camelot's court knew how to hunt and hawk—but more important, she was another set of eyes. Someone had to watch Arthur's back, even if it was just her.

Gwen could see him weighing his answer and prepared herself to be stubborn. Arthur rarely changed his mind, especially about the things that mattered to him.

"You leave me a poor choice, my lady." His voice was soft, but angry. "If I leave you here, you will curse me. If I take you with me and you come to harm, I will never forgive myself."

As if on a single instinct, they both turned to Zorath, who held up his hands as if to shield himself. "I have three wives and know better than to say a word."

Arthur pulled Gwen's hands from his face. "Promise that if you come, you will obey my every word. Both our lives might depend on it."

He was giving in! Joy and trepidation both stopped her breath—she'd been so focused on changing his mind, she'd barely thought beyond the moment. "I promise," she said, barely managing more than a whisper.

When she kissed him, his eyes were angry, but they were also sad.

In less than an hour, they set off. Gwen watched the stiff line of Arthur's back as he disappeared down the tunnel. Although he'd given her permission to come, he was not happy about it. With grim determination, she hoisted her knapsack and charged after him, breaking into a trot to keep up.

The goblin tunnels were surprisingly comfortable. They were as wide as any castle corridor and high enough for even a tall man to walk without bumping his head. A complex system of crossbeams and bracing kept the tunnels stable and provided an anchor for an ingenious system of pulleys used to move buckets of ore and unpolished stones. Frequent ventilation shafts brought in fresh mountain air, and storage chambers with food, water and other supplies were dotted throughout the tunnel network. The only drawback was the miles of rock over Gwen's head. All that stone weighed on her imagination, making it wonder what it would be like to be buried alive.

And she disliked the darkness. The miners had to carry their own light—either a candle stuck to one of their helmets or a metal lantern. Gwen had opted for the lantern, which squeaked as it swung from its wire handle and cast crazy shadows as it moved. The sounds in the flickering gloom were disturbing—trickles and echoes and mutterings of air in the deep shafts. Since the troll had come, the goblins had deserted the mines, leaving the mountain with only its own voice for company.

Oh, yes, the troll. That had her imagination scrambling, and she desperately needed a distraction. She quickened her pace until she was at Arthur's elbow. "Are you going to refuse to speak to me throughout this entire journey?"

Arthur stopped and turned. He had his sword in one hand and a scowl on his face. "This is not the time for witty conversation, my lady. Too often the hunters turn into the hunted on these quests."

"I saw the map. We're nowhere near the troll's lair."

He made a face. "As Clary would say, color me cautious."

She stilled. "Cautious, or are you still angry?"

"Believe me, if there had been any chance that I might leave you in Zorath's care, I would have." His eyes bored into her. "You left me no choice."

She bridled. "I will pull my weight. You'll be glad of me before the end."

"Slaying a troll is not a Maypole dance. Trust me,

Gwen, the penalty for losing on this hunt is death. You should not be here."

"I'm not playing a game." She poked him in the chest, tired of his judgment. "You should be glad I'm here. I got us this far."

"That's no excuse for behaving in a reckless fashion."

"Reckless? Reckless is confronting a dragon single-handed!" Gwen suddenly felt short of air and struggled to catch her breath. "I was watching the television. I saw what happened. Why didn't you call me? You might have reassured me that you were all right!"

He stalked away, making it three or four steps before he turned again. "By the time I was in a fit state to call, you had left for this realm. I followed as soon as I could."

"In a fit state?"

"I was unconscious," he mumbled.

She buried her face in her hands. "By all the saints, Arthur. The knights might have attacked as a group. Why did you face Rukon alone?"

His expression grew opaque, closing her out. It was worse than his anger. It was like she wasn't even there.

"How can I ask anyone else to risk what I am not willing to give?" he said in a low voice. "Acting as shield and champion for the human realms is my responsibility."

"Others want to help, Arthur," she said softly. "They deserve the chance."

She wanted to reach out, reassure herself with touch, but he turned away and silently resumed his march into the tunnels. The only change was that now he slowed his pace enough for her to walk by his side. It was little enough, but it was something.

Their quiet passage gave her time to think as she stole glances at his rigid profile. If she had to guess, she thought he was cursing himself for imperfections only he could

see. But why? There was so much she didn't know about
her own husband, and what she did know was more legend than man. He never spoke of his childhood, and it was
little wonder. His parents had been murdered when he was
still a baby. It had been Merlin who'd rescued him from
slaughter and smuggled him to Sir Hector, who raised
him as his own son. Every time Gwen heard the story, it
turned her blood to ice.

They kept on walking for what seemed like hours, but
time was deceptive in the lightless silence. One tunnel
looked much like the next. Their only guides were the clay
tablets screwed to the support beams and marked with the
goblins' system of wedges and slashes.

"We're at the twenty-ninth tunnel," Gwen said, running
a finger over the indented clay.

"You can read their tongue?" Arthur asked in surprise.

"Only the numbers, but someday I'll learn more. Ambassador Krzak said their written language is sophisticated, containing many dialects and a long history of epic
verse."

Arthur gave her a sharp look, but this time it wasn't
critical. "You really did spend a lot of time with the goblin delegation in Camelot, didn't you?"

"I liked him. He said what he thought, and that wasn't
easy to find at court."

Arthur gave a wry laugh. "True enough."

"Most of the delegations from other courts were fascinating." There had been humans from other countries, and
once elves from far, far away. Her favorites had been the
fae, but that had been before the demon wars, when they
were still in full possession of their souls. "I made many
friends among them."

Arthur was watching her, a furrow in his brow. "I didn't

know you found them so interesting. Many look on entertaining the castle guests as a chore."

"Sometimes it was dull, but there's usually at least one intriguing thing about any person. I just looked for that."

They kept walking, falling back into silence, but it was a different quiet. They were both deep in thought.

"I'm sorry I trusted the Mercian prince," she said suddenly. It came out before she even knew she was thinking it. *Impulsive as always, Gwen.* "He made me feel important. I didn't know any better."

It had been a disaster. He'd flattered her, danced with her, was always there to hold her horse or play a game of chess. And then he'd drawn her into political discussions—about this treaty or that. She'd divulged too much, and the damage was done.

Arthur nodded. "I bear some responsibility for that. I should have been at home more."

"And I should have known better." Gwen's stomach twinged at the confession. She'd blamed Arthur for leaving her alone, but it was true—she should never have mixed business with flirtation. The truth made her feel small.

"Our instinct is to trust," Arthur said gently. "Knowing when we can't is a bitter lesson."

As they turned down the tunnel, he put a hand on the small of her back as he had in the cocktail lounge. The memory, so out of place, jarred her.

He glanced down, his eyes sad. *Our instinct is to trust.* The one time he'd formed a significant alliance was during the demon wars, and that had ended with the fae swearing vengeance against Camelot and humankind. It was a war they were still fighting.

"I understand why a king doesn't trust, but how can you live with that as a person?" she asked.

"Should I point out that when hunting monsters, it's best to keep your mind on the job?"

"I understand," she said, wincing a little. "But just tell me, was it the incident with the prince that made you question my judgment?"

"It gave me pause, but you misunderstand me."

He stopped, holding up a hand as he edged toward an intersection of tunnels and listened intently before waving her forward. Gwen quickly obeyed, aware that they were nearing the *X* on Zorath's map—the troll's lair. It was time to stop talking, but she couldn't help herself. This was an answer she'd waited years to learn. "How do I misunderstand?"

"All my life, I've been surrounded by assassins. Mordred, Morgan LaFaye and a hundred others. That puts everyone around me in danger. Often it seems better to work alone than expose others to that risk, especially those I love."

Gwen blinked, suddenly understanding much. She wasn't the only one that Arthur shut out. At times he'd distanced himself from Merlin and even his foster father, Sir Hector. On other occasions, it had been his friends—Lancelot or Gawain. She'd assumed Arthur had suspected them all of disloyalty, but perhaps she had it wrong. Maybe it had been a wrongheaded expression of love.

"Family shares your danger, whether you like it or not," she said.

"I know," he replied, his tone grim. "And a king is expected to marry."

He made it sound like a prison sentence, and Gwen recoiled in hurt. "It is that much of a burden, my lord?"

His look was unreadable. "When the enemy knows what's precious, it becomes a weapon in their hands."

"Precious?" she whispered, but he had already moved

on. It suddenly made sense—his distance, his temper and his solitude. Arthur believed he was protecting everyone around him, but he was also protecting himself. Love for him was a perilous risk.

How did I not see this? Gwen cursed herself as she hurried along behind him. She'd known him six years. At first she'd had too little experience to fathom such a complex man, and most of their marriage he'd been away at war. But at some point… She gave up, letting the past slide through her fingers. They'd done a good job of nursing their anger with one another, of making a mess of every attempt to truly connect. The real question was what they would do next.

Arthur interrupted her roiling thoughts with a sharp gesture. Gwen froze, reading the urgency in his stance. Her senses stretched wide, trying to find whatever it was he had detected. For a moment, she was baffled, but she heard it—footfalls, far ahead. They were slow—not just unhurried, but as if the stride itself was long. If that was the troll, it was disturbingly large.

Arthur's glance went to the lantern. Gwen guessed his meaning and slid the lantern's shutter all but closed. In the sliver of light that remained, the blackness around them seemed absolute. The troll's footfalls were silent, but still Arthur didn't move. They waited, Gwen's knees unsteady, for a long time before Arthur advanced again. When they did, he leaned close and spoke in a voice that was nearly a whisper. "When we find its lair, we'll study the beast for weakness. I'll have one chance to strike. Even with a charmed blade, I'll need to hit a vulnerable point."

The prospect of killing the creature became far too real. Gwen's mouth went dry as she all but glued herself to Arthur's side, hurrying into the next corridor. There, the tunnel ended in a dark, cave-like chamber. The map had indicated a series of such rooms, one leading to another. They'd reached their destination. "The map said this is a storeroom," she said softly.

Arthur took her hand in his, his mailed glove rough but welcome against her skin. He pulled her close as they stepped through the arched doorway. Gwen gasped as the faint lantern light swept over the walls.

"By the saints," Arthur breathed. This was no stash of picks and shovels; it was a treasure room worthy of a dragon's hoard. There had been shelves and chests, but the troll had scattered it all. Heaps of gold dishes, coin and jewelry spilled over the floor in drifts, mixing with the gems that gave the Crystal Mountains their name. The lantern picked sparks from the treasure as the light flashed on facets of precious stones. To Gwen, it looked like a scattering of stars in the darkness. She wasn't normally swayed by wealth, but it did leave her a little breathless.

"Is this where I steal the silverware?" Arthur asked, his lips all but touching her ear.

"I feel underdressed."

He bent and picked up a long dagger set with gems. He handed it to her, the gesture almost courtly. "Sometimes the best accessory is a blade."

She took it, not bothering to point out she'd brought her own knife. This one was bigger, and right now she was fine with that. They kept moving, placing their feet as silently as possible on the sea of shifting coins. It was no mystery why Zorath wanted to regain access to this room. The contents were a king's ransom—enough to buy all of Medievaland, perhaps all of Carlyle.

They emerged into a broad empty space, and then into another cave. The scene here was as awful as the treasury had been wondrous. Gwen clamped her mouth shut, swallowing hard. A thick, meaty smell hung in the air and sent a surge of panic through her gut. Every primitive instinct screamed to run, but her legs refused to move. Arthur stepped close, urging her back.

"You don't need to see this," he said, his arm slipping around her shoulders.

But she already had, and she sidestepped his protective gesture. A cool detachment slid over her, freezing the panic into a numbing fog. Her heart beat a little too fast, but she gave no voice to the incessant screaming at the back of her mind.

There were torches burning in the next room, shoved into black iron stanchions along the walls. They gave a clear view of what had become of the missing goblins. What Gwen saw answered the question of what a troll wanted in the goblins' mines. Not gold, but meat. Goblin meat. This was the troll's larder, and it was a messy eater. Most of the torn and bloody limbs strewn over the floor still had clothing attached. Scraps of uniform said some were the soldiers Zorath had sent.

Arthur stood rooted to the spot, his eyes incandescent with rage. But there was something else in his expression—fear. The *thud-thud* of the troll's footfalls was back, and they were loud.

"Run," he said softly. "Run and hide."

Slowly, as if in a dream, he closed both hands around Excalibur's long hilt and took a deep breath. In that moment, he shifted from the man she knew—king and husband—to a warrior she had never met up close. It sent a zing of shock through her bewildered mind.

"Now," he ordered in the voice of command.

Her body obeyed out of reflex, making her back away from the scene of carnage. A protest rose in her—she'd come to help, to use her wits to help Arthur—and yet what could she do against a creature who'd turned the mine into a butchery? There had been more bodies and parts of bodies than she could count. It was hopeless. She was useless. Terror for Arthur choked her, as if her lungs were suddenly gone.

She wasn't sure if panic or despair claimed her first, but she stopped moving. She'd made it as far as the treasure chamber. Here, she was hidden from view but still close enough to see past where Arthur stood and into the larder. It wasn't a good enough hiding place. As soon as she could gather her wits, she would run, but she couldn't remember how.

Then the troll lurched through the door where Arthur stood. Gwen bolted.

Chapter 15

The troll was massive, scraping the high doorway as it lurched forward. Its gait was top-heavy, unbalanced by its barrel chest and massive shoulders. It was wrapped in a kind of kilt made of hides, the long tail of the motley garment flung over one shoulder. What the hides had once been, Gwen didn't want to know.

Her feet moved of their own will, scampering backward until her shoulders hit a towering stack of treasure chests. She spun around with a squeak, flailing out to smack the cold, brass-bound boxes. Her lantern swung, making crazy patterns on the walls. With a curse, she dived behind the chests and sank to the ground, panting and trembling. She'd faced danger before, but a charging bull was nothing compared to this. She wiped her face with her sleeve, mopping away sweat and tears of fright, and then made herself peer around the corner to see Arthur standing firm as the creature charged.

Black lips peeled back from the troll's fangs as it gave a grunting roar and rushed forward with a rolling, side-to-side gait. For all its awkwardness, it was fast, closing in on Arthur in a blur. Arthur swung Excalibur, the blade ringing as it struck the creature's leathery hide. The troll lashed out, its arms seeming far too long for the rest of it. Arthur spun lightly away, sword poised high. The beast grabbed again, sharp claws screeching against the stone walls, but Arthur smacked its knuckles before dancing away. Gwen could see the concentration in every line and angle of his movements. It was a game of cat and mouse, with the mouse the smarter of the two.

Unfortunately, the cat was especially deadly. The shredded bodies in the next room made that clear. All the heat seemed to leave Gwen's body as a fresh wave of fear overtook her. The troll's head thrust forward, its prominent jaw jutting with annoyance as it swung toward Arthur one more time. The dance between monster and warrior could go on and on, ending when the loser made just one mistake.

Arthur launched into a flurry of thrusts and slashes, aiming for eyes and throat, but the troll's long reach made it all but impossible to get inside its guard. The beast hammered its fist, but Arthur dived and rolled, escaping the pulverizing force by an inch. As he rolled to his feet, he swept the sword low in a move that should have crippled the beast.

Excalibur rang against the troll's hide, achieving nothing.

Gwen sprang to her feet, her own fear forgotten in her worry for Arthur. He couldn't keep the fight up forever. Something had to change, and she was the only one with enough breathing space to do it. She jammed the jeweled knife through her belt and left the lantern on the ground. With her hands free, she tore through the treasure room, picking things up and tossing them aside. If she'd had a slingshot, there were plenty of jewels and coins to hurl at the monster. There were dishes and crowns and scepters of fine goblin workmanship, stockpiled and ready to trade at the unearthly markets where the realms met on Midsummer's Day. All those riches were useless to her now.

She kicked a pile of coins in frustration, causing a glittering avalanche. And then she saw what she needed, flung down in panic by some unlucky goblin in flight—a plain ash bow and quiver of arrows. She snatched it up, testing the string. The bow was made for a goblin man and so a good height for her, but the draw was stiffer than she liked. *Too bad*, she thought, slinging the strap of the quiver over one shoulder and climbing onto a chest to get a clear shot. She'd just have to manage.

Gwen was a good shot and the troll made a huge target. All she needed to do was distract it long enough for Arthur to strike. She notched an arrow with trembling fingers and drew the bow, panic giving her the extra strength she needed. The battle was still in progress, a spinning flurry of sword and claw. She aimed, forcing herself to gauge the rhythm of the fight, to anticipate where her target would be. She loosed, snatched another arrow and loosed again.

The first hit the troll between the shoulder blades, the second smacked its forehead when it turned to howl in protest. Arthur didn't miss his chance, driving Excalibur upward at the underside of the troll's chin. The sword tore through flesh, the point sinking deep, but not deep enough. A trickle of black blood coursed down the troll's neck and chest, but it barely seemed to feel the wound.

The troll caught sight of Gwen and charged. Fright stabbed through her and she leaped from her perch, bow in hand. She landed lightly and dodged around a tall golden statue, finding speed she didn't know she had. The troll swung its huge head from side to side, peering among the treasure while she circled the room and dashed behind the beast. In a dozen strides, she was at Arthur's side. With a look of fierce pride she'd never seen before, he grabbed her hand, and they ran.

The only place they could go was through the scene of slaughter. Gwen quailed—though her feet kept flying. Behind them, the troll turned and roared its fury. Gwen kept her eyes fixed forward, refusing to look at the carnage on either side. She didn't see the slick of blood in her path until she skidded, falling to one knee and coming face-to-face with a limbless torso, the rib cage cracked open like a walnut robbed of its meat. She made a gurgling shriek as Arthur hauled her up and dragged her stumbling forward.

Gwen's mind blanked for an instant, surrendering as Arthur led her from the scene of slaughter and into the tunnels beyond. There were torches here, too, but they were farther apart, at times providing only the faintest glow. The troll was behind them, each step a mighty thump, but it was slowing. Fatigue or blood loss was finally taking its toll.

Arthur pulled her down one of the smaller side passages, finding a dark chamber filled with miners' gear. Panting, they squeezed behind a huge wooden cart on wheels.

"Did we lose it?" she asked.

"I don't know."

They sank to their knees, Arthur's arms around her. Gwen buried her face in his shoulder, breathing in the familiar scent of him. Like a frightened animal, she needed his warmth and the comfort of his touch while she steadied her thundering heart.

"Gwen," he whispered. "My brave Gwen."

She couldn't read his tone well enough to tell if it held sorrow or laughter or both. As long as he kept holding her, she wasn't sure she cared. "I couldn't leave you there," she murmured.

His lips pressed against her hair, the sigh of his breath hot as his arms curled more tightly around her. "Thank you."

They were two simple words, but there was an ocean of feeling in them, a bridge between them that she'd longed for. Gwen squeezed her eyes shut, reliving the last minutes. He'd lifted her out of the blood. If he hadn't, she might have died of despair. She dug her fingers into his coat, holding him tight.

"Are you recovered?" Arthur asked softly. "We need to keep moving."

It was then that she heard the troll's footsteps coming down the corridor, each slithering slap of bare sole oddly stealthy. It paused, snuffling the air. Gwen cringed with revulsion as she realized her pant legs were soaked in blood. The stench would surely betray them.

Arthur released her, his hand silently gripping Excalibur's hilt. There was no room behind the cart for Gwen to draw her bow, so she forced herself to stillness, her muscles coiled with fierce tension. The only possible way to survive was to outsmart the beast. Gwen had thought herself so clever as she'd barged her way into this expedition, but her mind was as blank as fresh parchment. The frustration of it burned.

The *slap-slap* of the troll's feet started again and stopped, then resumed. All the while, it sniffed the air like a bloodhound, steadily growing closer. Arthur made a low sound that was nearly a growl, lifting his sword and balancing his weight in readiness to spring. Gwen willed the troll to keep moving past their door, but it lingered outside, the steps dwindling to a shuffle as if choosing a new direction. Gwen shrank down another inch, hope crumbling. The scant light in the room dimmed as the troll's hulking shape blotted everything else from view.

Arthur sprang with a mighty battle cry, but the troll was too quick. A huge, clawed hand scooped Gwen up as if she were no more than a doll. An outraged shriek flew from her lips and she snatched for her bow, but it was lost behind the cart. The troll clutched her to its chest, the thick, hairy arm pinning her despite her desperate squirming. Wheeling in a two-handed strike, Arthur stabbed his sword straight down, driving the point into the troll's bare toe.

This time, the troll felt the sword. With a weirdly high-pitched yelp, it hopped in a circle, one foot in the air. Gwen flailed at the dizzying movement, arms and legs flying. The quiver emptied of arrows and they hit the ground with a clatter, snapping as the troll crushed them in its dance. Arthur stabbed again, aiming for the other foot. The troll howled, tossing Gwen aside to clutch at its feet. She smacked into the stone wall, skull ringing with the impact before she slithered to the ground. Stomach churning, Gwen struggled to her hands and knees. Dizziness made her falter, but Arthur's strong hands were suddenly there, setting her back on her feet. She blinked frantically, clearing her head.

Then her thoughts came into focus. She spun, stumbling a little as she searched for the troll. "Where is it?"

"Gone." Arthur looked down the corridor. Gwen followed his gaze and caught a glimpse of the creature loping away, whimpers fading as it retreated to nurse its hurt. "I doubt it's felt true pain before."

"How did you know to attack its feet?" she asked. "No other blow seemed to damage it."

"Fingers and toes always hurt the most, even when the wound is slight." Arthur gave a faint smile. "I gambled that was true for trolls."

The brief reprieve from danger left her in a strange free fall. She sagged against him, every limb tingling as her panic drained away. Arthur pulled her close, dipping his head to kiss her brow. But that wasn't enough, and he cupped her face, pressing his lips to hers. His skin was salty with sweat and dust. All at once, Gwen hungered for his touch, as if his kiss was the last breath of air before she drowned in endless dark. She returned the embrace, letting that need remind her she was still alive. Arthur's breath caught with a ragged noise. They pulled apart, panting a little.

"Will it be back?" she asked, regret thick in her voice.

Arthur's mouth turned down. "We've shamed it. It will want revenge."

And their luck wouldn't last. "What do we do?"

His gaze darted toward the tunnel where the troll had vanished. "Retreat until we have a better plan and more swords."

"I'm going to strangle Zorath for sending us here alone," she said darkly, scanning the ground for usable arrows. Every one was broken. She tossed the empty quiver aside in frustration. "I understand the goblins are afraid, but these are their mines. He could have mustered some backup."

"I agree." Arthur sighed. "In the meantime, can you run?"

Her whole body ached, but her brief moment as a troll's plaything had been worse. "I can run."

Arthur held out his hand. He'd made the gesture often at dances and during ceremonies, but here it was different. This wasn't protocol. He was offering her his protection when she needed it most. Gwen accepted it, squeezing his fingers, and they set out at a gliding trot.

They retraced their steps to the main corridor, careful to end up in no more dead ends. Gwen hadn't noticed what was in the broad tunnel before, but now she saw carts piled with ore as well as winches and scaffolding. The goblins had been mining a vein near the ceiling, and they had hauled a huge bucket up by ropes. There were still picks and water bottles on the high catwalk, and the bucket brimmed with ore destined for the furnace. Judging from the abandoned worksite, the troll's initial attack had been sudden.

Farther along there was a pool of standing water to her left and what looked like an abandoned pumping station. More personal items were scattered along the path—a pipe, a hat and a pair of boots tied together by their laces. Gwen tried not to think about the fate of their owners. Their retreat led through the cavern littered with bodies.

They had nearly made it when she heard the troll's roar. She started, disoriented. "It's ahead of us!"

Arthur was already pulling her the other way, pelting back the way they had come. Somewhere, there was another parallel route the troll had used to cut them off. Clearly, it was not as witless as they had assumed. And it was fast, so fast. Gwen sped with the desperation of prey, lengthening her stride to keep up with Arthur.

They passed the lake again, bursting into the part of the tunnel lined by scaffolding. Arthur dragged her toward it. "Climb!" he ordered, grabbing her by the hips and heaving her upward.

Gwen grasped the rough wood, scrabbling with her feet to find purchase. The spaces between crossbars were at odd intervals, making her wonder how goblins climbed—and then she was too busy to think. Arthur let go the moment she was secure, leaving her bereft of his comforting touch. A moment later, she heard Excalibur hiss from its scabbard. The urgency of the sound gave her strength and she hauled herself up the wooden structure. When she finally crawled onto the platform, she was far above the stone floor.

The walkway was narrow enough that she knelt, gripping the sides with both hands. She had to twist her neck to see the troll bearing down on Arthur. Her husband stood braced for attack, his chosen ground below Gwen's perch. It was clear he would defend her to the death.

Chapter 16

Gwen screamed as the troll leaped toward Arthur, slashing the air with its claws. The king ducked and rolled, dodging behind one of the carts only to wheel behind the beast and deliver a two-handed blow. Delivered with such force, the strike should have cleaved the troll's legs from beneath him. Excalibur rang with the sound, but the blow had little effect.

Gwen cursed, using a word no lady should even know. She'd seen this battle before—they were right back to where they'd been when the troll first appeared. She knew all Arthur's heroism would avail nothing. She looked around, hoping for another bow and arrow or pot of miraculously boiling oil. What she had was a winch and a bucket of rocks.

That made her sit up, forgetting how delicately she was balanced. She'd seen enough siege engines to understand the principles of the machine. The rope that held the bucket arched over an iron wheel barely a foot from the platform.

The bucket was balanced by a counterweight, making the business of raising and lowering the load of ore more easily controlled. If the rope were cut, the full container would smash to the ground.

Surely that much crushing weight would stop a monster? She glanced down, seeing Arthur aim for the troll's feet one more time, but the creature was wiser now and evaded the flashing blade. Gwen choked on a gasp as one clawed hand streaked out, ripping through Arthur's chain mail shirt. Arthur spun away, links pinging as they hit the ground.

Gwen anxiously forced her mind back to her task. If she cut the rope, the massive stone block that balanced the bucket would drop. That was expected, but parts of the winch were torqued. With no tension to keep the weight in line, it looked poised to crash into the scaffolding's supports. If the platform fell, she fell, possibly into the troll's clutches. Or she might just break her neck.

Another glance at the fight made her decision. She'd just have to take the chance. She drew the jeweled dagger from her belt and inched toward the spot where the rope was easy to reach. It was a matter of waiting for the absolute right time.

For the briefest moment she caught Arthur's eye, and made a frantic gesture.

Arthur saw Gwen waving, but he was fully occupied with the troll, who had picked up a boulder in one hand and heaved it like a toddler learning to throw a ball. Arthur jerked aside, feeling the rush of air as it sailed past. Apparently pleased with this new tactic, the troll bent to pick up another projectile.

It was then Arthur looked up to see Gwen pointing down, and then mimicking a hammer squashing something flat. With a leap of excitement, he understood. A deadly simple plan, but it had a certain elegance. Despite exhaustion, he grinned. He'd all but lost hope, but Gwen—all the saints bless her—had just changed everything.

He ran beneath the bucket, turning and raising Excalibur as if ready to make a final, desperate stand. With a grunt of satisfaction, the troll charged with fangs bared. There was a creak as weight shifted, then a snapping noise. The troll looked up in surprise, but by the time it bellowed in shock, Arthur had leaped away, hitting the ground and rolling as an avalanche of rock crashed down. Wood splintered and dust flew, creating a choking cloud that blotted most of the cavern from sight.

Arthur coughed, scrambling to his feet. "Gwen!" There was no reply. He blinked and sneezed, still blind to anything but dust. "Gwen?"

Rock shifted, and he heard a low growl. The troll was still alive! He groped for Excalibur and prowled into the cloud. It was then he saw her, lying full-length on a beam that tilted at a crazy angle. His heart dropped, and for an instant he forgot everything else. She was dirty and pale, but her eyes were defiant. When a faint smile curled her lips, Arthur forgot to breathe. *She is so brave.*

And she had given him such a gift. He turned to the half-conscious troll, poised Excalibur over its vulnerable throat and swung the mighty sword. The troll's head rolled free.

It was over.

The walk back to the goblin castle was slow and weary, Gwen leaning on Arthur's arm. All the same, there was grim satisfaction to be had as they marched into Zorath's dining hall. All conversation stopped and the crimson-skinned goblin rose to his feet.

"You have returned!" King Zorath exclaimed.

"We have returned victorious." Arthur dropped a miner's sack containing the troll's head before the king. "There is all the evidence you need. Your mines and treasure are safe once more."

The goblin king's expression moved from stunned incredulity to joy. Zorath snatched up a goblet and raised it into the air. "All hail King Arthur and Queen Guinevere, saviors of the goblin tribes!"

There was a general roar and pounding of fists. It went on and on until Arthur raised his hand. "We have fulfilled your quest, and now claim your promise."

"The King and Queen of Camelot are granted freedom to come and go from the Crystal Mountains for as long as they shall live," Zorath declared.

The cheering and pounding resumed for a full minute. It might have gone on longer, but a fresh barrel of ale was borne in by servants, distracting the diners. Zorath sat and beckoned Arthur and Gwen to approach.

"You sense trouble among the dragons," the goblin king said. He kept his voice low, indicating the discussion was not for all to hear.

"Yes," said Gwen, speaking for the first time. "I think they're in trouble."

The observation surprised Arthur. He wouldn't have stated things that way, but she was completely right. "There is a fae involved," he added.

Zorath nodded. "The fae's name is Talvaric. You know well that our borders are closed to outsiders, but he has roamed these parts for centuries and knows how to come and go undetected. He is also a magic user and skilled with portals. It is not easy to bar someone with such skills."

"What is his business here?" asked Arthur.

"Until recently, we believed he simply liked the mountains. Fae walk in wild places."

Arthur shook his head. "That might have been true

once, but fae lost their love of beauty along with their souls. He was here for another purpose."

"I know." The goblin king's expression grew crafty. "As time went on, I began to ask questions. And then I sent eyes and ears to verify what I heard."

Arthur gave a slow nod. Every king had his spies.

Zorath leaned closer. "He came to the Crystal Mountains in search of magical beasts. He takes them prisoner for his own ends. When we tried to put an end to his raids, our trouble with the troll began."

That made a horrible kind of sense. "Is that all you know of this Talvaric?"

The goblin shook his head. "As you well know, the Lady of the Lake has imprisoned Morgan LaFaye. That leaves the Kingdom of Faery without a ruler. Most are not bold enough to risk Morgan's wrath if she should break free, but Talvaric wants to claim the crown."

"How does he hope to achieve this?" Arthur asked incredulously. "He is not one of the high lords of the fae. I've never even heard of him."

"He hopes to win support by proving to the world he can beat the great Arthur of Camelot. You wield Excalibur, the one sword that can kill Morgan LaFaye and cleave through the darkest of fae magics. If he can defeat you, then he will be worthy of their allegiance. Or so he would have them believe."

"How does he hope to achieve this?" Arthur demanded. "And what does that have to do with these mountains?"

"Dragons," Gwen said. "You said Rukon Shadow Wing dwells here."

"His weapon is dragons. Beasts. That's why he takes them." Arthur said it aloud, finding it hard to believe. Dragons couldn't be tamed, and yet the ones who'd come to the mortal realm had behaved strangely. It all fit together.

Gwen made a disgusted noise. "Talvaric needs proof of his victory, so he will use the dragons in the most public way possible, in full view of the human media. Haven't you noticed all the TV cameras?"

Arthur's temper flared. It was bad enough the fae yearned to defeat him, but dragging the hidden world into the full view of mortal eyes was utterly unforgivable. "This Talvaric has a short and undignified future. Where can we find him?"

"We do not know," said Zorath.

"Is there anything else you can tell us?" Arthur asked.

"Unfortunately, no," said Zorath. "Believe that if I knew more I would share it, for you have done us a great service."

"And you have given me the name of the villain who threatens my realm," Arthur replied. "That is also a service of great worth."

The goblin king rose, a wide smile on his ugly red face, and spoke so that all could hear. "King of Camelot, my new friend and ally, you have earned a place at my table, as has the lovely Queen Guinevere. This is an occasion to celebrate, so let us speak no more of dark things tonight."

Arthur bowed, recognizing the honor for its full worth, while Gwen leaned forward and left a kiss on Zorath's cheek. The goblin beamed and called for wine and food, as well as water and towels so they could wash before they ate. Arthur suddenly realized that he was starving. By the way Gwen fell on the many dishes set before them, so was she. And the food was well worth a hearty appetite—tender greens, bowls of delicately seasoned grains, fresh berries and lamb in a rich, spiced sauce. Almost everything came from the mountains, but the spices were hardly local. The goblins had a vast trading network, and Arthur realized the value of an alliance with their kind. Much had been achieved during this adventure.

And without Gwen, he never would have had it. He watched her eat, fascinated by her swift, precise bites and the delicacy of her hands. She wiped her fingers often, for there were few utensils. The goblins used triangles of a nut-flavored flatbread to scoop up their food, sometimes slathering it in a cool, herbed sauce. It was messy but very good, and Gwen gave in to the temptation to lick her fingers like a child. She caught Arthur's gaze, her eyes bright.

"Food tastes good after you've been frightened half to death," she explained.

"I know." He wanted to say more, but his throat ached too much. On any other occasion, he would have been planning, calculating and moving pieces around his mental chessboard to find a path through the future. Now all he could do was relish being next to his wife, grateful they were safe and together. For once, the present was enough.

The feast went long into the night, and Zorath offered them a bed. But Gwen and Arthur both wanted the free air outside the mountain, so they took their leave. The night was clear and cold, thick dew sparkling on the grass. Arthur sucked the freshness into his lungs, clearing them of the peculiar scent of goblins. The air was like iced wine after a mouthful of greasy stew.

Zorath sent a guide to lead them back to the place where Gwen had been captured, and from there she easily found her way to the meadow where the gate had been. Arthur followed in her wake, oddly content to let her take charge of getting them home.

It wasn't hard to locate the gate itself, because there was a queen-size bed sitting in the meadow, along with a collection of coat hangers, bathrobes, extra blankets, the minibar and a nightstand. None of it was neatly arranged, but scattered as if hurled from a catapult, a few of the lighter items stuck in the lower branches of a pine tree.

The bed at least was upright, although the covers were strewn everywhere.

"I think Clary's portal has developed a mind of its own," Gwen said, sitting down on the edge of the bed with a sigh. "I wonder if it's actually safe to use it."

Arthur wandered through the meadow, picking up items as he went. Some things had been there awhile, judging by the heavy layer of dew. Others weren't damp at all. He picked out the driest items and carried them to the bed. He stood for a moment, looking down into Gwen's face. The moon was bright, picking out her features in a wash of silver. He'd always thought her delicate, which was true. Her bones were fine and graceful, and every part of her spoke of an artist's love of harmony. But she was also incredibly strong. Perhaps that wasn't a matter of muscle, but character. He'd seen it expressed in her stubbornness, but now he understood there was more to it than that. She had something the best of his knights had: a willingness to accept their own fear and fight past it.

Arthur sat down beside her, lacing his fingers through hers. "Today I've been roasted by a dragon, captured by goblins and attacked by a troll. I'd rather not face a temperamental portal through time and space. Are you okay if we stay here tonight?"

A laugh bubbled out of Gwen and she tipped her face up to the sky, showing the long line of her throat. "Am I okay? Yes. All I want to do is fall over." And she did, flopping backward with her slender arms spread wide.

Arthur lay down beside her. The stars above were dimmed by the moon's full radiance, but even so they spread into a full canopy of lights. It made him feel tiny, a mote of dust clinging to the high mountains in one of countless realities. It was peaceful.

"There are no people here," said Gwen in a soft voice.

"No cars, nothing electronic, no huge buildings to hem a person in. It feels like home."

Arthur turned to look at her profile, but became distracted by the strip of bare flesh where her neck curved into her shoulder. He kissed her there, nuzzling her warmth. "Camelot is in a different world now."

"I know. And there are so many opportunities for me there."

He heard it then—a note of hesitancy in her voice. She was expressing a desire she thought he wouldn't approve of. It made him wonder how she really saw him. "Is that what you want—opportunity?"

She turned toward him, eyes catching the moonlight. "I think I want to go to school."

It wasn't what he'd envisioned for her, but every instinct told him to change course. Gwen was smart—wasn't it her quick thinking that had felled the troll, just as much as his sword?—and the desire to fulfill that potential was simply part of her intelligence. "If you want school, then you shall have it."

She raised herself on one elbow, the shadow of her form filling his vision. Moonlight turned her fair hair into a halo, as if Gwen were as much angel as woman. "Thank you." And her breath sighed out, as if in profound relief.

Arthur's heart stopped for a delicious beat, hearing the truth of her gratitude. He'd finally touched something essential in her—not the superficial place that could be pleased with jewels or clothes or even one of Gwen's beloved hounds, but something deeper. He'd recognized something about who she was.

He reached up, burying his fingers in the silk of her hair, and kissed her deeply.

Chapter 17

Gwen caught her breath, lost for a moment in the pure sensation of his lips on hers. His breath was hot compared to the cold night around them, and she drank in the kiss as if eager to pull his warmth into her. She cupped her hands around his face, the feel of skin and beard and bone her anchor in the starlit dark.

The kiss ended, but she remained kneeling above him, unwilling to release the intensity between them. A breeze stirred the trees, whispering icy secrets. She kissed him again, the sigh of his breath mingling with the wind.

She shivered, and he pulled her down, wrapping his arms around her. She turned into his chest, feeling the hard, hot solidity of him. All the strangeness of the past few days battered at her, and a sense of spiritual vertigo made her cling yet closer. As if sensing her need for comfort, Arthur sat up and reached for the thick pile of blankets that were still free of dew.

"Wait." Gwen kicked off her boots and shrugged out of her clothes. She'd cleaned up as best she could before entering the feast hall, but she felt a thousand times better without the soiled garments. When she was done, Arthur settled the covers around her as he stripped down to his skin. Gwen watched him while his back was turned, letting her gaze play over the planes and shadows of his form. The moonlight turned his skin to marble whiteness, showing every curve and valley of hard muscle. Gwen knew swordplay had as much to do with speed and balance as it did brute force, and Arthur was perfectly proportioned, every muscle honed by training from childhood. Her pulse skipped as a sweet ache filled her belly.

When he lay down and put his hands on her skin, she gasped at his cold touch. "Sorry," he murmured, kissing her brow. "I'm afraid we'll have to keep close to stay warm."

His voice held teasing regret. Gwen had no words to respond. Desire pushed sore muscles and fatigue aside, but it couldn't restore her wit. Instead, she kissed him again, nibbling at the strong muscles of his throat. He released a pleased groan, rolling her so that she lay on her back. She was warming up now, their cozy nest all the sweeter for the crystalline night around them. This was stolen time, an unexpected gift of intimacy.

Arthur knew how to make use of it. He pulled the covers over their heads to trap the warmth around them, and then set about exploring her form. His hands were rough, but his touch was a caress, arching over her ribs with a firm but gentle pressure. Gwen pushed into it, gasping a little as his lips found her breasts. He had always known exactly how to please her, but tonight—tonight there was a difference in his touch. He was taking his time.

Gwen ran her hands over his shoulders, feeling the tracks of old scars. Her fingers played over them, remembering their shape. It had been a long time since the two of them had twined together this way. The exact months and days were impossible to calculate, with centuries spent in magical sleep. All she knew was that it had been long before the demon wars, before her world had cracked and fallen to bits. Some would say lovemaking might mend any breach, but nothing so broken could ever be put back together. Nor should it, when she'd been so unhappy. And so she'd closed the door to Arthur's bedroom the night she'd come to Carlyle.

But Arthur hadn't left her behind today, so Gwen was willing to relent and build something new. She stroked down the curve of his back, using her nails. He arched into her, finding her mouth and parting her lips with his tongue. She let him in, tasting his unique flavor with a mild shock of recognition. They'd kissed before this, but there was a difference when it was in bed, and all his thoughts were of her.

His lips traveled to her throat, his teeth scraping over the skin as if he might devour her. She drowned in the sensation of it—hard and soft and slick and warm. His hands mounded her breasts, and then his mouth was there, too, closing around one nipple, then the other, leaving her restless and hot.

Her hands found his hardness then, and she teased it with her fingertips. This, too, was familiar but in an entirely different way. They both wore so many masks, and some they kept especially for each other. That was the way of husband and wife, king and queen in a world where only those with nothing could afford to marry for love. She had grown into the role of willing wife, mixing the truth of her desire with the lot she'd been given. And yet tonight, she had a new awareness. He had fought for her life, held her when she'd grown weak with fear and brought her whole out of danger. And he'd let her help him, so she could meet him here as an equal.

The terms of their bargain had changed. He'd earned her honesty, and somewhere tonight she'd earned the right to insist that he accept it.

She guided him home, fitting herself to his embrace with frank need. When he filled her, she cried out, as if the hunger she felt echoed through the vast darkness and into the caverns beyond. It was pleasure to the knife-edge of pain, her ache for him an appetite that only increased with feeding. When he began to move inside her, she was lost to everything but the knowledge of him. It was a claiming of her soul that she had never allowed, but now she wanted it. She wanted Arthur, immediately, tonight.

And he gave himself, hard and furiously. By the end, his gentle, slow caresses hardened to insistent demand. She surrendered, weeping and laughing at once, mad with her own sweet destruction.

Afterward, they tangled together and abandoned to the night.

Gwen dreamed she was back in her father's castle, kneeling on the straw-covered floor of the barn. She was barely sixteen; her dress was covered in dust, her hair in a braid down her back, and she was hammering a wooden frame together. She'd stopped to suck at a splinter in her thumb when she realized someone was watching her.

It was that young man again, the one named Arthur. Everyone said he was the king, but she found that hard to believe. Kings were crusty and ancient and prone to chopping off heads. So far, Arthur had betrayed no signs of any such flaws. All the same, she scrambled to her feet and managed a curtsy, holding her dress in a way she hoped hid her dirty, bare feet.

"What are you doing?" he asked. He looked at the scraps of wood scattered around her feet, his eyebrows furrowing in an intense frown.

"I'm building a trap."

"Really?" he replied. "What for?"

"Foxes. They've been bothering the chickens."

A speckled hen approached, picking at the frame and prancing around it with bobs of her head. Gwen picked her up, tucking her in the crook of an arm before the silly bird could scatter the nails. The hen gave a squawk of protest but settled in happily enough. Gwen could see Arthur trying to assemble the pieces of her trap in his head, but she doubted he could. This was her own design, and not even the gamekeeper believed it would work.

Gwen kept looking at Arthur—he was handsome enough to look at for hours at a time—but couldn't help wondering why he was there, in her barn. She knew plenty of men-at-arms, but he was different. His clothes were never stained with ale or worn through at the elbows and knees. He stood straighter, his shoulders squared as if in constant combat. It clashed oddly with his tendency to stare at her. If she were honest, she found their encounters rather uncomfortable. But she tended to ignore the honest part of herself when confronted with a gorgeous young man who was supposedly a king greater even than her own father.

He looked up from the frame with an amused frown. "A bow and arrow is less work than nailing all this together and then having to cut their throats."

"I don't kill the foxes!" she said in horror. "I take them out to the woods."

He gave a surprised laugh. "You know they'll just come back?"

"No, they don't," Gwen said defiantly. "I give them a

stern talking-to. I tell them to stay away or they'll end up lining my father's cloak."

"And do the foxes listen to you?"

"Yes."

His blue eyes shone with hilarity. "Really?"

"Really," she said with annoyance. "I can tell you don't believe me."

"I am devastated to say it, but I'm afraid I don't."

In her fury, Gwen clutched the hen hard enough that it began to flap. Gwen tossed the bird away, and it settled on one of the low rafters. "I know it's the truth. Not one of the foxes has returned."

"How do you know that?" Arthur asked, a little less certain now.

Gwen shook her skirts back into place, ignoring the dust that billowed from their folds. "Because otherwise the foxes are dead and all I'm left with is heartbreak. I won't accept that."

His slow smile was the first real one she'd seen from him. "I think I understand. You have to try."

The dream ended abruptly when the heavy insulation of the bedcovers was jerked from Gwen's head. Her eyes flew open at Arthur's yell and the rattle of Excalibur's sheath. Cold air slapped her face and she clutched the blankets close—only to see Merlin's astonished face. Excalibur's point was all but tickling his nose, but his eyes were flicking from Arthur to Gwen and back again. She burst out laughing at his mix of embarrassment and amused curiosity—and then realized she was naked. She sank back beneath the blankets, feeling blood rush up her cheeks.

"Did I startle you?" Merlin asked drily.

Arthur lowered his sword, fury fading to annoyance. "The least you might have done was bring coffee."

"Tea," said Gwen, refusing to be cowed. "I like tea better."

Merlin tossed bathrobes marked with the hotel crest onto the bed. "I suggest you get up and follow me back through the portal. I've got it stabilized, but I don't know how long that will last."

He turned his back, and stalked toward a shimmering doorway that rose out of the long grass. Gwen grabbed a robe and pulled it on, her arms disappearing into the oversize terry-towel sleeves. She noticed the sun was high and the air was only slightly cool. They must have slept for a long time.

Arthur offered his hand with a gallant bow. "Your escort awaits, my queen."

Gwen took it, rising on her toes to give him a kiss. She should have felt foolish, standing in bare feet and a robe, her unbrushed hair falling in a tangle, but she felt more herself than she had since childhood. By the light in Arthur's eyes, he was happy, too.

Merlin kept his expression blandly neutral and held out a hand toward the portal. "If Your Majesties would care to step through, I shall return the meadow to its pristine state. I doubt the squirrels have a use for the minibar."

"Hard to say," replied Arthur, retrieving Excalibur. "The bottles are about the right size."

Merlin gave him a withering look. "Not even you can look regal in a hotel bathrobe."

A moment later, they were back in the hotel. Clary jumped up from where she sat on the floor, her expression wild with concern. "Are you all right? You aren't hurt, are you?" She bowed to Arthur, then clasped Gwen's hands and finally gave her a rib-crushing hug.

"I'm fine. We're both fine," Gwen squeaked, realizing her ribs hurt from hitting the wall during their fight with the troll. She probably had bruises.

Clary let go, looking her up and down with a raised brow. "So it seems. I take it the trip was a success."

"Yes." Gwen might have said more, but was distracted by the state of the room. There was a dusty patch on the floor where her bed had been, and the nightstand that had stood beside it was missing. Her gaze went quickly to the pile of shopping bags that held her beautiful new clothes, the black dress tossed carelessly on top. At least the portal had left those alone.

"I met Merlin," Clary whispered in Gwen's ear. "And I'm devastated. He's *horrible*."

There was a flare of light and Merlin emerged from the hotel closet, dusting off his hands. "Next time you want a portal, call a professional." He gave Clary a dark look.

"Hey," the witch protested. "I got the job done."

"And I'm certain the hotel proprietor appreciated the bull moose who traded places with the bed. Somebody needs to review their homework on the principles of portal stabilization."

"I was in a hurry," Clary protested.

Merlin folded his arms. "Get the spell right, unless you want to keep swapping furniture for livestock."

"Nobody died."

"Tell that to the breakfast buffet."

Clary folded her arms and stuck out her chin. "Moose like waffles. Who knew?"

Gwen and Arthur exchanged a look. "Everybody likes waffles," Arthur suggested. "I'll call room service."

Gawain picked that moment to come through the door. His gaze flicked from one face to another, finally settling on Arthur. "I hope you got some rest."

Gwen saw Arthur's expression shift, face settling into hard lines. It was as if an artist had erased and redrawn his features in a single heartbeat, deleting the man who'd slept at her side. She yearned to cry foul, to turn the clock back and bar Gawain from the room. Instead, she took Arthur's hand and squeezed hard.

"What's happened?" he asked, returning the pressure of her fingers.

"Rukon Shadow Wing has been sighted in the woods near where we first encountered him. This time we ride as a company and finish this once and for all."

"No," said Arthur.

Gawain scowled. "Why not? We've tried being nice. We've tried single combat. This is no time to send a basket of home-baked cookies."

"The dragons are under the influence of a fae named Talvaric," said Arthur. "He's the quarry we want."

"And in the meantime?" Gawain demanded. "Sir Hot and Smoky has to be dealt with."

"The dragon is our connection to the fae."

Merlin gave an evil grin. "You're going to use the dragon to draw Talvaric out."

Arthur shrugged. "Or at least provide information on him."

Gawain appeared less than convinced. "One does not simply interrogate a dragon."

"Sure you can," Merlin said helpfully. "You just have to catch it first."

Arthur's expression said everything Gwen was thinking. This wasn't the dragon's fault, and punishing it was unfair—and yet somehow they had to stop it before innocent people were hurt.

"I have an idea," Gwen said before she could stop herself. Last night's dream was fresh in her mind, as if a hidden part of her was already working on the problem. "We could build a trap."

Arthur turned to her, his eyes narrowing. She expected him to tell her to be silent, but he paused a moment before speaking, speculation in his gaze. "Explain."

Chapter 18

Once in a while, it was good to be king.

Arthur, freshly showered, lay on the remaining bed in the hotel room, his hands behind his head and Excalibur propped against the nightstand. Clary had changed to a different room, and Merlin was running interference with the hotel staff. Opening an interdimensional portal in a hotel closet probably wasn't covered by guest-room policy, and even though the portal had now been closed, it would take wizardry to dispel awkward questions. Everyone else was off tracking the dragon in an effort to locate its lair in the woods outside town.

Normally, Arthur would have been in charge of the search party, but not today. They had too little information about their fae enemy, and Talvaric had made a veiled threat against the queen. Arthur's self-appointed job was to watch over Guinevere, who sat at the desk sketching furiously on hotel notepaper. Like him, she was still in a bathrobe, her hair pinned up in a knot that left her neck bare. Arthur was transfixed by the curve of her spine as she bent to her task.

The notion of trapping a dragon seemed ludicrous to Arthur, but he was curious to hear her idea. Their adventure in the Crystal Mountains had reminded him just how much Gwen could surprise him.

She'd been dancing when he'd first seen her. It was hot, even for July, with the sky a merciless sapphire. Arthur was on horseback, Merlin at his side and a company of men behind him. They were near the castle of King Leodegranz when he looked down from the road and spied a hollow of cool grass shaded by elms. There she was, leading a mob of children in a round dance. The children ranged from babies to ten or twelve years, but she was at the threshold of womanhood. Flowers wove a drunken crown around the spill of her gold hair and her skirts were knotted up to display coltish, grass-stained shins. She was hardly elegant, but she drew his eye. How could she not, with so much joy shining from her face?

"Who is that?" he asked Merlin.

"I don't know," the sorcerer replied without much interest. "Some servant's daughter, I expect."

And yet Arthur stared, watching her as his column of men wound up the hill and between the castle gates. That year had been nothing but war, and his soul echoed with the clash of steel. He'd forgotten what innocence looked like, and he'd forgotten about dancing. Now he yearned to bound across the soft green grass to join them, shedding pieces of his armor as he ran.

"She's a pretty thing," Merlin said, amused.

Arthur tore his eyes away, suddenly uncomfortable. "The children look happy, that's all. It's a pleasant change from battle."

A thoughtful look crossed Merlin's face. "Indeed."

Much of that year's war had been with Leodegranz. Eventually the old wolf had surrendered his sword and agreed to a treaty, which was why Arthur and Merlin had come. Arthur's goal was to unite the petty kingdoms of Britain into a single political force, and Leodegranz was the fifth to swear allegiance to Arthur of Camelot as high king. Earlier that month, Arthur had turned twenty-three.

They were received with every courtesy, and a banquet was prepared. To Arthur's surprise, it was no page who filled his wine cup that night, but the dancing girl. She was dressed in a gown of soft gray, the sleeves lined with cloth of silver and her shining hair bound in a fillet of gold. Clearly, she was no servant's child, but a maiden of rank.

"Do you like her?" asked King Leodegranz, eyeing the girl with the same assessment he might show a prize hound. "That's my daughter, Guinevere."

She lowered her eyes as she poured the wine, tawny lashes hiding her thoughts. In the dark and smoky feast hall, the pale dress made her shine like a piece of lost moonlight. "She is very beautiful," Arthur said, fascinated by the graceful curve of her long neck.

Her gaze flicked to his before she moved away, her slim back spear-straight. Furtive though it was, there had been a dare in that look. Guinevere was bold, for all that she was young.

Merlin leaned close. "You know it's no accident that she's here. Leodegranz wants a marriage as part of the treaty. His grandson will be high king, if he has his way."

Arthur watched Guinevere and remembered her joy. If he was her husband, he could protect that bright spirit, or that's what he told himself. In truth, he needed that happiness as a balm to his soul. Happiness and beauty and innocence. Guinevere held the promise of them all the way a new flame holds light.

Arthur lifted his goblet, touching it to Merlin's. "Make it happen."

And Merlin had. Almost two years later, after a long and complicated negotiation, they were wed.

Back on the bed in the present day, Arthur opened his eyes. He'd been drowsing and yawned with the drugged lethargy of daytime sleep. Gwen was sitting on the edge of the bed, the pad of notepaper in one hand.

"I have the door figured out," she said. "The other parts may need magic."

Arthur took the drawing from her and studied it, recognizing a sophisticated and yet simple device of counterweights and pulleys inspired by what they'd seen in the mines. "I wish I'd had this for the drawbridge at Camelot."

"Do you think it will work?" she asked, her fingers twisting the bedcovers.

"Yes," he said. Gwen had a natural talent. She'd already provided a list of materials so the others could get started gathering them, and from the look of it her estimates had been sound. "You're good at this."

Her smile was shaky. "Thank you."

He understood why she was hesitant. There had been some understandable doubt from the knights. None of them knew this side of the queen, but that was only the beginning of their objections. Even if Gwen's unusual plan worked, a caged dragon would be an angry one. There would be consequences. However, Arthur had overruled his men. The trap might give the knights the upper hand for a brief window of time, and maybe that was all they'd need.

Gwen put a hand on his knee. "We must find out how to help your dragon."

With a twist of regret, he remembered her fox trap,

and how she'd lectured the bewildered animals. A dragon wouldn't be so easy to ignore if he came slinking back. "We can try. I can promise that much."

"And if you can't?"

Arthur set the drawing aside and sat up to slip an arm around Gwen's waist. He pulled her close, kissing her hair. It smelled of the sweet hotel shampoo. "Your trap will buy us time. That will save lives."

She nodded, her expression tight, and tapped the notepad. "I won't know how to finish the design until Gawain comes back with a description of its lair."

"You're going to build the trap where it sleeps?"

"If I can. Owen says dragons prefer caves or other rock formations for their home. We can take advantage of the surrounding landscape to provide some of the walls of the cage."

"That makes sense." Arthur was finding it increasingly hard to pay attention. Her lips had taken over his imagination—their shape and softness and his memory of their taste.

She stopped talking and gave him a look of fond exasperation. "I can explain all this later."

"I'm listening," he protested.

"No, you're not." But she smiled, and everything was all right.

He lifted a hand to her cheek, stroking the silken skin with his thumb. "I can't stop feasting my eyes on you."

She caught his hand. "One would think I'd be a commonplace sight by now."

"Never commonplace."

"Then what, my lord?" Her gaze searched his face. Now that the aftermath from their time in the mines was fading, uncertainty had crept back into her expression.

His first instinct was to say she was his wife, his queen,

but he stopped himself. Guinevere belonged to herself. It was one thing to claim a woman, but first he had to respect her. Arthur took her hand and kissed it. "You are exquisite."

She glanced down at the hotel robe, which was made for someone with much longer arms. "I am simply Gwen."

"That is precisely the point."

Her smile managed to be wry and flirtatious at once. She *was* exquisite, the golden goddess poets and painters adored. And yet that was just surface, like the gilt decoration of a jewel chest. The real riches were beneath, where so few cared to look. Where he had failed to look for so long.

Shame speared him and he bowed his head, searching for a plea of forgiveness. She brushed his hair back with a soft hand, prompting him to raise his eyes. "What is it?"

She truly didn't understand the ache of regret inside him. It wasn't just remorse for leaving her behind, or even a wish that their marriage had thrived sooner. He should have been a better man, one unbroken by the path his life had taken. She deserved so much more.

He'd tried to let her go. Now he didn't think he could. He was far too selfish, too possessive to attempt that sacrifice again. The collar of her robe had slipped, leaving one shoulder bare. His lips found it, delighting in the smooth, pale flesh.

Her warm breath tickled his ear. "You're distracting me from my design."

"I'm concentrating on mine," he replied.

"You have a design?" Her tone was arch.

"Of course. A good king always does." He slipped the tie of her robe loose and slid his hand inside the folds of cloth. He palmed her hip, pulling her tight against him. The throbbing low in his body drowned out every other idea. He was only dimly aware of his course of logic—that his men were hunting a deadly beast, that he was guarding Gwen from harm, that he was king and ultimately responsible for them all. Instead, all he wanted was warmth and relief. He wanted to hear his wife laugh and cry out in pleasure. He wanted what any man did—that simple peace that kings rarely enjoyed.

Gwen leaned into him, letting him take her weight. "Then perhaps you ought to show me what you have in mind."

"I am all obedience, my queen."

He pulled her down onto the bed, sinking into the soft covers. She threaded her arms around him, rolling so that she balanced lightly on top of him, her hands on his shoulders and her knees straddling his waist. Eyes dancing with expectation, she gave a feline smile. "What should I choose as my first command?"

Her kiss was deep and filled with a sweet, unconscious lust. Arthur wove his fingers through the long curtain of her hair, glorying in its soft caress. She sat up, shrugging off her robe and letting it fall. The pale afternoon light bathed her skin, showing off flawless, slender limbs and breasts soft as silk.

Arthur suddenly felt far less obedient. He raised himself up until they were nose to nose, their breath mingling. Gwen's neck corded as she arched back, refusing to give ground. "I am queen here," she whispered, voice dark with need.

He shifted, freeing his legs so he could trap her between his knees, but still she met him, skin to delicious skin. She grasped the lapels of his robe and pushed it off his shoulders. He was breathing hard now, almost panting. It was all he could do not to shudder as her nails traced down his chest and belly with sharp, exquisite strokes.

Then she took possession of him in her hands, and he groaned with the hot, throbbing pleasure of it. He suddenly doubted the wisdom of letting Gwen take charge. He might not survive her regal commands. She bent, her lips brushing his tip before she slid her body upward, giving him the full benefit of the soft friction.

"Take me," she whispered. "I'm ready for you."

Arthur was all too happy to oblige. He took her by the waist, lifting her. She settled over him in a tight, wet heat, her wordless cry vibrating through him. They began to move as one, and his mind slid from thought to sensation. All that remained was color and heat and a kaleidoscope of imagery—a slender shoulder, the translucent curl of an ear or the rosebud perfection of a breast. And the mindless, heartless need to possess it all. When it came to Guinevere, he had always been mad with greed.

To keep her had meant putting her in danger. To release her had meant tearing out his heart. And now he was once again the bridegroom drunk on the scent of her skin. He had lost his willpower. Perhaps his mind. He didn't care.

At last they fell apart, sweat slicked and boneless side by side. His limbs were leaden, but his head felt light, as if he'd drunk too deeply of a strong wine. With the last of his strength, Arthur took her hand in his. This was what he wanted, to be man and wife in full enjoyment of each other. She was bold, clever, demanding and his.

"Is Your Majesty satisfied?" he asked, turning to stare into her eyes.

Her pupils were dark, swallowing the blue. Her features were flushed and soft with relaxation. "That was very, um, majestic."

They laughed like drunkards until Arthur's cell phone cut them off with an emphatic buzz. He turned to glare at it, hating the way it turned his stomach hard with the anticipation of trouble. With fae and dragons on the loose, what else could it be?

He snatched it up, fully alert now. "Hello?" He realized too late his greeting was a growl.

"My pardon, Your Majesty." It was Sir Owen's voice, the Welsh accent unmistakable. "We've located the dragon's lair. We thought you would want to know at once."

"Of course." Arthur cleared his throat. "Where is it?"

Gwen stirred as the knight gave directions. By the time Arthur ended the call, she had slipped back into her robe. "The dragon?"

"They found its nest five miles west of town." Arthur tossed the phone aside, too aware his respite from duty was over.

"So what do we do next?" she asked, sitting on the edge of the bed.

The innocent question struck hard. He asked himself again if he should ignore the misgivings of the knights and trust Gwen's design. The chance for success seemed slim, and then there was the question of how to help the creature once it was confined—or even if it wanted help. If it got loose, its vengeance would be deadly.

"Arthur?" Gwen said, prompting him when he didn't answer.

The alternative was to forget the trap and battle the beast until it fled back to its home or died. In all probability, at least one knight would not survive.

And what of Gwen? Did he insist she remain behind, when every path he could see ended in peril? And yet he needed no imagination to foresee how *that* conversation would unfold.

"Arthur?" She put her hand over his.

Ultimately, his word would shape the events to come. This was what he hated most about rulership—the knowledge that a bad decision could end in pain and death. Whatever happened would be his fault.

Some days it sucked to be king.

He squeezed her hand. "We go investigate the lair."

Chapter 19

For the first time ever, Gwen became a partner in one of Arthur's adventures without the need to threaten, cajole, blackmail or sneak her way onto the team. She should have been delighted. Instead, she clutched her notebook to her stomach like an improvised piece of armor as she stood beside him in the elevator, watching the numbers count down to the lobby. She'd been given a chance to prove herself, but by extension she'd also been given the opportunity to fail. It was all part of the same package.

The fact pressed on her like an anvil crushing her skull. It was actually hard to breathe past the knowledge that her failure—a flaw in the design or getting in the way at just the wrong moment—could cost the life of someone she knew. Owen. Percival. *Arthur.*

Shying away from that thought, she put on her most queenly face and hoped that confidence would find its way to her roiling stomach. In the past, she'd guessed at the kind of pressure Arthur was under, day after day, but this was as close as she'd ever come to that much responsibility. How could he stand it? Then again, what choice did he have?

Gawain was waiting for them in the hotel lobby, his usual scowl in place. They'd never liked one another, and his expression said nothing had changed. "Arthur," he said, with a nod that added the implied "Your Majesty."

Then he turned to her. "My lady, did you get the photos I sent?"

Gwen handed him the notepad. "I used them to complete the design."

The knight flipped from page to page, rapidly scanning what she'd drawn. Then he looked up, still scowling, but with something in his eyes she'd never seen before—approval. "This should do the job. It's better than anything I've seen from a master builder."

Gwen kept her face still, but she knew she'd hoard that brief moment as carefully as any dragon. Impressing Gawain wasn't easy. "I'm glad. I know better than to expect empty compliments from you."

The knight gave a wry grin as he led the way to the front doors. Arthur stayed at her side, a hand resting on the small of her back. Gwen looked up at him, and he dropped a quick kiss against her lips before giving a smile of his own.

"What's so amusing?" she asked.

"You two. Your endless arguments."

Some of those had been spectacular. Gawain had a temper equal to hers and was deeply loyal to Arthur. The Scottish knight had gone ahead far enough to be out of earshot, so Gwen ventured a complaint. "He used to shout at my greyhounds."

Arthur made a face. "You spoiled them until they were impossibly ill behaved."

"Well, so was he."

That made Arthur laugh, a rich sound that turned every head in the lobby. Gwen noticed people smiling. No doubt they looked like a couple in love and on holiday, about to head out to enjoy the outdoors. It was a good feeling, and Gwen was so absorbed in it that she barely noticed when Gawain came to a dead stop as the automatic glass doors to the lobby whooshed open.

The hotel driveway curved from the main road to the doors and back again, giving easy access for tour buses and taxis to load passengers and luggage. Camelot's large black Escalade waited among the vehicles, with Clary leaning on the front bumper and typing on her smartphone. Merlin stood a few steps away, for once looking concerned.

And so he might have been, because three news vans crowded the drive, along with their cameramen, reporters and a swelling mob of onlookers. Red-jacketed hotel staff were trying to wave them off, but all they'd managed to do was keep the cameras out of the lobby.

One of the reporters caught sight of Arthur and visibly brightened. She charged forward, but was blocked by a wall named Gawain.

"What do they want?" Gwen asked, letting Arthur drag her back to the safety of the lobby. "Do they still think the dragon was your fault?"

"Right now they believe it was a machine or some other construct the theme park invented to draw more visitors."

That fit with what Gwen had seen on television, though she didn't fully understand how anyone could imagine the dragon was a fake. Many things about the modern world still confused her, and the media was right at the top. "And they think it was a dangerous invention because of the fire? Why not tell them the truth?"

"The shadow world is secret here."

"I know that, but—"

"That secret is the only thing that keeps frightened humans from turning against anyone different."

"Why?" she protested. "In our time—"

"Times have changed," Arthur explained. "Once all the peoples lived side by side, but after the demon wars that's no longer true."

Gwen realized that he was right. Almost everyone she saw was human, and she felt the loss of the others like a missing limb, or a feast reduced to a single, uniform dish. "What happened?"

"There is no time for a history lesson," he said, speaking quickly. "But in short, the witches were nearly wiped from the earth, thousands burned at the stake, and they wouldn't thank us for dragging them back into the public eye. And that doesn't begin to describe what would happen to those like the sprites, dryads or merfolk, who don't even appear human. We keep the shadow world secret for their safety. Even the fae—or most of them—respect that."

Gwen rubbed her forehead, feeling the start of a headache. "And so we have to find a way to put the media off the scent of dragons."

Their conversation had taken no more than a minute, but it had been long enough for the crowd outside the doors to muster their forces. The hotel staff wouldn't hold them off much longer. Gawain returned to Arthur's side. "Should we find a back way out of the hotel?" the knight asked.

Arthur shook his head. "Giving them a chase will only sharpen their hunger for blood."

"Please tell me that's metaphorical," Gwen muttered.

Arthur shook his head. "We will face the lions head-on, and let the good people of this establishment continue their day in peace."

Gwen linked her arm through his as he started forward. She hadn't come this far to be left behind now.

Camera flashes exploded in her face as they stepped outside, and several mics thrust forward. Gwen raised a hand to shield her eyes, and Arthur drew her closer, making it clear Gwen was his to protect.

"Mr. Pendragon, how do you explain the phenomenon everyone is calling the Dragon of Carlyle?" said one reporter.

"Care to comment on the accusations of public endangerment?" asked another.

"This story is beginning to spread to the national media. Was that your intention all along?"

"How do you feel about your increasing celebrity?"

The questions weren't so much asked as hurled. Arthur stopped, drawing himself up as if delivering a speech from the stone balcony of Camelot's tower. An instant hush fell over the crowd, and when he began to speak, he sounded every inch the king.

"I assure you my only desire has been to ensure the safety of the public. This has been in no way a design to increase my own reputation."

Through the forest of cameras, Gwen saw Clary advancing through the crowd. The young witch's eyes were snapping with annoyance.

"Mr. Pendragon has no additional comments," Clary said firmly.

"Who are you?" asked a reporter Gwen recognized as Megan Dutton.

"I'm his social media advisor," Clary announced, sounding rather like Camelot's old court chancellor about to order an execution. "Anything that needs to be said will be said under the Pendragon hashtag. Keep your eyes on Camelot's feed."

She took Gwen's arm while Merlin took the king's. Clearly, the two were working together to get them safely through the crowd.

"And who are you?" The cameras swung toward Merlin.

One corner of the enchanter's mouth turned up. "I'm special effects."

That started a murmur of speculation, and they managed to inch toward the Escalade before the cameras closed in again, halting all progress. Would they never make it out of here? Even with two magic users, the trap wasn't going to build itself, and every hour that passed was another opportunity for the fae to use Rukon Shadow Wing against them.

She glanced at her notepad of sketches, firmly gripped in Gawain's hand, and made a decision. She took a diagonal step that intercepted Megan Dutton. "And I'm Arthur's wife."

Every mic and camera swarmed her way. Gwen gave her best smile. "Didn't you know the celebrated leader of Medievaland's tourncys was married?"

She'd offered the reporters fresh meat, and they obligingly pounced on it. "Why is this the first time we've seen you in public?" Megan asked.

"Of course, my husband is athletic and handsome, not to mention an excellent administrator, but he is also a very private man," Gwen replied.

"For all the danger and excitement of the tourneys, half the attraction is the male eye candy. Did Arthur maintain the illusion of bachelor status to attract female fans?"

Gwen forced a merry laugh. "A truly determined woman would hardly notice my existence."

"Are you sure? I've heard Arthur receives daily offers of marriage from his fan base."

Oh, really? Something with fangs rose up in Gwen's

spirit, but she kept her smile in place. From the corner of her eye, she saw the men slipping into the Escalade while Clary remained firmly at her side.

"So tell us more about your romance," another reporter asked.

Gwen's smile grew genuine as she changed the topic from serious accusations to the romantic chatter village gossips would enjoy. It was something she'd always been good at, and people hadn't changed all that much. They still liked a good love story.

"Have you seen your husband fight?" somebody asked.

"I've seen him fight," Gwen replied. If only they knew about the troll.

"What about children?" asked Megan Dutton.

Gwen opened her mouth, but for a nightmarish instant, nothing came out. It was the one thing she never spoke about, and for reasons no one suspected.

The only time she'd followed Arthur to war, they had begun to settle into their marriage. By then, Arthur had united the kingdom and turned his mind to other things, including Gwen.

War in Camelot wasn't like the images Gwen saw of modern battles. Most people walked to the battlefield, so progress was dependent on the weather. Supplies, including medical support, whores, laundry facilities and family members traveled in the baggage trains that followed the main body of the forces. That summer, the Queen of Camelot had followed with the other spouses.

Gwen had begged to accompany the army because she had a passion to understand Arthur's world. The fight—a border dispute, really—wasn't expected to last long or be particularly bloody. They would march, wave their swords, have a picnic and be home by Midsummer Day. But then halfway to their destination, it had begun to rain, and that lasted until the fields were lakes of standing water. Fever broke out in the ranks.

Arthur forbade her to go near the tents where the sick were tended. Gwen was supposed to do what she did at home—sit with her ladies, read poetry and entertain whatever guests Arthur sent her way. But the friars tending the ailing soldiers needed all the helping hands they could get. Besides, she had learned how to mix herbs and medicines, like any good mistress of a noble household. That included a knowledge of how to preserve her own health—an easy task when she was strong and fit and not yet twenty. She waved goodbye as Arthur and the healthy soldiers went on ahead, and remained behind to do whatever she pleased.

At first, she'd spared a few hours at a time tending the sick, but as the disease spread, she devoted every waking moment to her task. The fever touched all the mortals, both witch and human. Among Gwen's charges were the three sons of the witch-born blacksmith, all of them black-haired, stocky lads. The eldest was just big enough to swing his father's hammer.

The blacksmith stayed away, but their mother came. Every day she thanked Gwen for her care. "They're all I have," she'd say when she rose to leave each night. "Don't let them leave me."

"I won't," promised Gwen each night, for the woman's plea broke her heart.

The youngest boy died first, and then the middle child. Gwen wept with the mother, sharing her grief, but tears could not bring back the dead. The eldest boy died last; his still, cold face a silent accusation when Gwen crept into the tent as dawn broke the sky.

"You swore you would not let them die!" wailed his mother. "Now all my sons have left me."

"I'm sorry," Gwen said, smoothing the woman's hair and patting her back.

"Sorry? Is that all a great lady can say to a poor blacksmith's wife?"

"I can't presume to know how you feel."

"No, you can't," the woman snarled. "Not yet, but you will. There is only one fit punishment for breaking your promise to keep my sons alive. You will never have a child of your own!"

Though all who heard the woman speak cried out in shock and fury, Gwen would not punish her, not even for speaking so to a queen. But the painful emotion behind those words carried weight, especially when they came from a witch. Not long after, Gwen fell ill herself, and in the fever dream the woman spoke to her again.

"As year after year passes by with no babe in your arms, you will come to understand my grief," the woman said. "I'll take from you what you took from me, and you will die unloved and alone."

That night, Gwen nearly perished from the fever burning in her blood, and she almost died twice more before the illness ran its course. The blacksmith's wife went to her grave soon after. That was just as well, for cursing the queen was treason in most men's eyes, even though the woman was crazed with pain.

Gwen floundered, her spirit languishing although her body healed. Her guilt was indescribable, but she sat through Arthur's scolding as he pointed out how he'd forbidden her to nurse the sick, and how that disobedience had nearly cost Gwen her life. He spoke like she was a willful child, which was true, but never mentioned the lives she'd saved at great cost to herself. It was that lecture that had made her decide to keep the tale of the curse to herself. And it sowed the seeds of the unhappiness that drove them apart, because in her moment of grief, he had judged her. That made it impossible to build trust.

She'd never followed him to war again, at first by her own choice, and then by his. She understood that he was afraid for her, but locking her away only gave her more time for regret.

And not once had she conceived a child.

Chapter 20

Hours later, Gwen found Arthur and slumped down on the rough ground next to him.

"Hello." Arthur looked up with a smile. "My thanks for saving me from the slavering fiends."

Silently, she took in the landscape with a frown. The bite of the ocean wind was cool as the late afternoon sun retreated from the sky. Arthur's perch was high above the slash of valley that led down to Rukon's nest. It would be possible to see the dragon coming for miles. It was perfect, except for one detail.

"I don't see the cage," Gwen replied without preamble. She was still rattled from the reporters, and her tone came out sharper than she intended. Her next words were softer. "I mean, did anyone work on it?"

"It's done," Arthur replied. "The men built the gate as soon as we gave them your drawings. It was elegantly simple, after all, and your instructions were clear. Merlin put it in place and reinforced the rest of the nest to form the sides and roof."

Gwen took a second look. The dragon had chosen a deep hollow sheltered by a tangle of trees for its nighttime resting place. She could make out red-barked arbutus trees and the bright splash of rowanberries, but nothing else. She knew the others were supposed to be concealed in pairs around the woods. The scene looked deserted.

"Where is the gate?" She should have seen a frame of wood and steel balanced over the mouth of the cave, ready to drop once the dragon was inside.

Arthur sounded slightly smug. "Merlin's hidden it with magic, erasing even our scent. All we need to do is watch and wait."

It made sense, but it felt as if the trap had become Merlin's accomplishment and not hers. Or maybe that was just the memory of her father claiming her design for the Round Table. It shouldn't have mattered, and the trap might not work, anyhow. That didn't make Gwen any less unhappy. Or defensive.

"What's wrong?" Arthur asked, taking her hand.

Gwen forced herself to be honest. "I'm unsettled."

"Because of the reporters?"

"Yes." They had kept her for over an hour. Afterward, Clary had taken her to a distant tea shop and fed her cups of chamomile and lemon until she was calm again. "The questions they asked were too personal."

Arthur pulled her close until her head rested in the crook of his shoulder. "I'm extremely grateful to you. Your quick thinking made it possible for the rest of us to get away."

"I'm glad it worked." She wasn't sure if she could endure another session like that. She turned her face into his chest, needing to feel his warmth. "They asked things no one has the right to know."

His hand cupped her head, stroking her as he would a cat. "I'm sorry. That's what they do."

"If I'd been any less startled, I think I would have punched Megan Dutton."

"I should have left Gawain there. He could have pinned her arms for you."

She sniffed, trying not to laugh. "Clary was there for that. She wouldn't let me answer some things."

"Good." He kept stroking her hair. It was hypnotic, and she began to relax. "Clary understands the media far better than the rest of us."

"You should talk Medievaland into hiring her. Perhaps we really need a social media advisor."

"Maybe I will. We could use another witch around."

That was true, but not even magic could assuage the ache inside Gwen. The horrible memory of the blacksmith's wife gnawed like an open wound. She'd wanted children, and not just because it was every queen's duty to provide an heir. There were places in her heart waiting for small, young lives. She closed her eyes, forcing back tears.

She'd tried hard to put the memory behind her and move on. Despite her sadness, she'd had to continue living. And so she did, for years, although her marriage had slowly crumbled. Much was due to Arthur's increasing preoccupation with the coming war against the demons, but she had to admit she'd withdrawn as well, crushed by what had happened and too afraid to share her pain.

But since the Crystal Mountains, everything between her and Arthur had improved. It had barely been any time at all, but it was enough to make her hope. Arthur had wanted her, and she'd almost trusted the happiness that brought. She couldn't allow Megan Dutton's curiosity to ruin it all.

"What did they ask you?" Arthur stopped petting her and looked down, clearly worried by her silence.

"How do you take the pressure of looking after a whole kingdom?" she asked, changing the subject. "How do you face it day after day?"

"I was raised to it," he replied, the words flat. "I had a destiny, or so everyone said."

"You were just a baby. An orphan." Demons had murdered his parents. How could anyone consider that a destiny?

"Merlin took me to Hector, who lived far from anything or anyone. I grew up knowing the moment I left home I'd be a hunted man. And yet somehow I was meant to unite Britain and free it from the threat of the demonic overlords. Until I did, everyone I loved was in peril."

Gwen sat back, studying him. Once in a very rare while, he'd spoken about the small things of his childhood—fighting with Kay, his foster brother, and all the usual pranks and spills of boyhood. He'd never spoken of this.

"My father, the great Uther Pendragon, couldn't keep his family safe," Arthur said, reaching over to brush a strand of hair from her eyes. "So how could I do better? It's always been on my mind, especially after what happened to the fae. I thought the demon wars would fulfill whatever the fates had planned, but I only created more enemies. I'm sorry, Gwen. I pulled you into a life I cannot control."

His words made her want to weep, and that made her glad of the gathering darkness. "But beyond a certain point, it's not possible to control what happens. I don't believe in destiny."

"Then explain my life." His eyes were shadowed with

unhappiness. "Explain a sword in a stone that would come to only my hand. Then explain how my reign went so wrong I ended up here. Was one fated, and the other bad luck? Or am I simply doomed?"

He sounded lost, and she folded his hand in hers. "All I know is that you're not responsible for everything that happens. Not to yourself, nor to those around you. We're not puppets."

"I've struggled all my life to figure this out." He shook his head. "I truly believed you were better off if I was far away."

She finally understood the conversation. "I accept your apology for leaving me behind."

He smiled, but it was weary. "I'm glad. I'm not particularly good at saying how sorry I am."

She used his hand to fold herself back into his embrace. When she settled, her back was to his chest, the top of her head beneath his chin. He wrapped his other arm around her and they waited silently as the stars came out, pricking the indigo sky.

When she finally saw the dragon, she nearly mistook it for a shooting star. It skimmed the hilltops, a speeding scrap of red flame. The bulk of its body revealed itself as it drew closer and she saw the fire was the glow of its breath.

She straightened to get a better view. "Look."

Her focus should have been on the monster hurtling through the sky, but Arthur was there, right behind her, and his presence muted everything else. His breath stirred her hair as he sat forward, too. "I see it."

Her gaze followed the dragon as it circled far above, no doubt checking for danger. She could see the long neck and tail snaking through the air, the wings working in a slow, lazy flap. There was no sense of urgency in its flight. She hoped that was a good sign.

It made a last turn and banked, sliding into a long and gradual dive. The rush of air over its wings reminded her of thunder, or wind filling a ship's canvas. Branches snapped as it brushed them and the trees seemed to shudder as it pushed through the canopy. In another moment, it landed with a muffled crunch.

And now came the part where her skills were put to the test. Gwen tensed despite Arthur's reassuring touch, and she moved to stand. Arthur pulled her down. "Wait," he murmured.

Keeping still, she peered down, trying to match sight to the sound of something slithering over rock and brush. Was that the dragon crawling into its cave?

A white flash of magic filled the sky, the afterimage resolving into the gate perched over the mouth of the cave. Gwen heard the telltale click of the gate's release and the bars dropped with a mighty thump. The instant they hit the earth, magic flared up the steel rods, turning them into bars strong enough to hold the great lizard. Merlin had done his work, and done it well but, she thought with pride, it had been her idea that had given his magic form.

Their handiwork was instantly put to the test. Rukon hurled himself against the bars with an outraged roar. Power flared, turning the forest into a phantasm of glowing light and dark, twisting branches. Arthur jumped to his feet, his gaze riveted to the scene.

"The cage is holding." Merlin's voice came out of the dark forest, making Gwen jump with surprise. "Magic works best with a physical shape to support it. Thanks to the queen, we might just survive this."

"My compliments," said Arthur. "To both of you."

Merlin stepped forward, arms folded. His smile was grim. "Who knew that you and I would make a team, my lady?"

Certainly not Gwen. She said nothing, too transfixed by the outraged dragon throwing himself against the bars once more. A hollow pit was forming in her stomach. She had designed the cage for a good reason, but she still hated it. She was sure this wasn't the dragon's fault, and no creature should ever be trapped like this.

Arthur was already descending the path to the lair, Merlin a step behind. Gwen knew she was meant to stay where she was, safely out of sight, but she was responsible for the creature's captivity. It only seemed right to look her prisoner in the eye. She descended a few steps behind Merlin, trusting her feet to find their way despite the darkness.

When they reached the floor of the valley, she could see Arthur's men emerging from the trees. Some had flashlights, but a few carried candle lanterns, as if they still found old-fashioned firelight more comfortable than modern convenience. They barely needed illumination however, for the dragon itself glowed with rage, its nostrils burning like hot coals. Sir Owen stood to one side, his face tight with sorrow. Gwen knew precisely how he felt.

The dragon's head could barely move in the tight space, but it scanned the group with its glittering eyes. "So this is your doing, little king," Rukon said in a quiet voice that was somehow worse than any roar. "I will roast you for this indignity."

"Do your worst." Merlin stood directly before the cage, hands on his hips and an arrogant tilt to his head. "Your fire won't make it past the bars."

Rukon's response was to peel back his lips, showing fangs like swords. "Then one day when you least expect it, wizard, I will eat you for dessert."

Merlin laughed, as if the threat had genuinely amused him. "I hope you have antacids."

Arthur stepped forward to stand beside Merlin, and

executed a respectful bow. "I hope someday you can forgive this practical necessity, Rukon Shadow Wing, but I desire conversation with you and have no wish to fight."

"Because you'd lose."

"Perhaps," he said frankly, "but I don't think the real fight is between you and me."

Rukon's response was an insolent puff of smoke that slid past Merlin's barrier and made them cough.

Arthur cleared the smoke around him with an irritated wave. "King Zorath named Talvaric of the fae as the true enemy of us both."

That got a reaction. Rukon growled, gathering his feet beneath him as if readying for another spring. "The goblin king risks much by revealing that name."

"He had a troll problem like I have a dragon problem. I was able to get rid of the nuisance troubling his mines."

"By slaughter," Rukon said darkly.

"It was a sad necessity." Arthur took a step forward, his hand on Excalibur's hilt. "You're smarter than any troll. There is no need for your death."

"Yet," Merlin muttered under his breath.

"Is Talvaric forcing you to be here?" Arthur asked Rukon. "Is that the treachery you spoke of?"

Gwen had seen Arthur like this before. It was how he dealt justice from his throne—respectful, but firm and always searching for the real issues beneath a problem.

"It's Talvaric's name that the minstrels are supposed to sing, not yours," Arthur said. "Your boasting was a sham. Talvaric wants the other fae to know how powerful he is and how worthy he would be to sit on the throne of Faery. You're just his weapon."

"That is the truth." Rukon bowed his head, both in acknowledgment and defeat. "He took my choices from me."

A ripple went around the gathered men, Owen's outraged voice carrying above the others. Gwen drew closer to Arthur, proud of him for uncovering the facts.

"You are the Pendragon," said the creature, sounding lost.

"What does that name mean to you?" Arthur asked, his voice solemn.

"It is not a name," the dragon said. "It is a responsibility. The first Pendragon was our protector in a time of dire need, and his line was sworn to do the same. But that duty has been forgotten."

"My father died and never had the chance to tell me of it," Arthur said. "You can."

"It is too late. Talvaric knows how to ensnare the beasts of the Forest Sauvage, the Crystal Mountains and the enchanted realms beyond."

"The enchantment over you is not enough to force your every move," said Merlin. "How does Talvaric bend your will?"

The dragon exhaled another angry breath of smoke and steam, causing Merlin to fall back a step. "He came for me first among my kin."

Gwen had been silent, letting the facts unfold, but the pieces were falling into place now. "He came for you first, and you hesitated to kill without cause. So, he went to the other dragon next. The one you call Elosta. But it sounds as if she struggled to escape his snare and fell from the sky."

Rukon bellowed in rage, shaking branches from the trees. Flocks of birds filled the night sky with frantic caws and whistles.

"She is my mate, and Talvaric has our young."

Chapter 21

Talvaric pushed branches aside, ignoring the rake of thorns against his skin. Something was in his trap—the slight spell he'd woven to signal success had drawn him at once to this distant corner of his lands.

The site was ideally situated near a stream where the beasts came to drink. He used the illusion of a struggling bird as bait, but the trap itself was iron. He could have used something magical to actually hold his prey, but that lacked visceral satisfaction. Metal teeth sunk into a creature's flesh left no doubt who was in charge.

He emerged into the small clearing where the trap lay. His first reaction was disappointment when he saw the struggling fox, one of its dainty, black-stockinged legs caught and bloody. Only a fox? He'd hoped for something better. Another dryad, perhaps. They were about as entertaining as potted ferns, but he needed more slaves to clean the cages of his collection.

The fox's desperation was plain—which was some compensation—as it bit and worried at the iron, at the ground, even at its own paw. Left to itself, it would probably chew off a limb. He was tempted to let it, but then saw the splash of green at the tip of its tail. This wasn't an ordinary fox, but a Charmed Beast of the Forest Sauvage.

Talvaric drew near. He saw the fox's ears prick, and then its head turned to reveal wide amber eyes. With a yelp of fright, it started digging with its one good foreleg, as if it could burrow out of sight. Talvaric grabbed it by the scruff.

"Well, aren't you a surprise?" he said, turning the animal so he could get a view of its face. The fox, however, tried to duck away. He gave it a hard shake.

"Please," the fox begged, tucking its tail as low as it could go. "Please."

"Please what?" Talvaric asked, because he could.

"Let me go." The fox started panting with panic. "I need to go, master."

"I don't agree."

Talvaric released the trap with a single word of power. The mechanism clicked open and fell to the dirt. Instantly, the fox's feet began flailing as it wriggled to break free. Talvaric saw with satisfaction that the creature's leg was not actually broken, even though the flesh was torn. A broken bone would have made it less useful.

"Stop struggling!" Talvaric gave the fox another shake. "Be still."

The fox froze. "I want to go home."

"We all want something, vermin."

Talvaric sat on a fallen log and held the beast in his lap. Beside him, the stream bubbled past, autumn leaves spinning in the current. Once, before his soul had been ripped away by Merlin's spells, he would have been transfixed by the natural beauty of the place. Talvaric recalled his wonder, but it was an impression, nothing more. He couldn't recapture the feelings behind those images. The memory was haunting, like listening to a language he no longer understood.

Arthur and his pet enchanter would pay for what had happened to the fae. Talvaric's people remembered what they had been, and that was enough to serve as a springboard to power. He would prove his worth by crushing the enemy. He would rise and Camelot would suffer.

Talvaric let his dreams go and came back to the present to find the fox staring him in the face. The black nose twitched with anxiety. This creature would be disappointingly simple to bend to his will.

"What is your name?" he asked.

"S-senec, if it please you, master," the thing sputtered in its clear tenor. Why was it that the foxes always had such fine voices?

"Tell me about yourself. Do you have a mate?"

"Not yet."

Too bad. It was so easy to control a creature by stealing its mate or its young. That had worked perfectly with the dragons. He had a clutch of eggs that someday would give him the power to conquer entire realms.

"So you're young," Talvaric mused. "That has its advantages. I can train you the way I like."

The fox's response was another, shorter bout of struggling. That was brought to a quick end with a single blow to its hindquarters.

"You're mine now, Senec," Talvaric said. "Whatever I tell you to do, you will do it. You will do it when and how I say. You will *not* attempt to find a loophole in my instructions but carry out my wishes in both spirit and letter. Furthermore, you will not attempt to escape."

"Y-yes, master," the fox replied.

Talvaric knew foxes. Their reputation for craftiness was deserved. He turned Senec so the fox had a good view of the clearing. "There is something you need to know about this place. I cover it with a glamor that cloaks what is truly here from all the senses—sight, smell and touch included. I do that so creatures like you will wander into my trap."

The glamor hiding the clearing fell away, and Senec gave a terrified whine. As Talvaric withdrew his spell, carnage became visible. Pieces of flesh scattered the ground, the bushes and even the lower branches of the trees. White bone protruded from some. Black-and-white fur clung to many. "The last animal I caught in my trap was a Charmed Beast like you. A badger. He didn't want to obey."

"P-please, master," the fox whined.

"I gave this disobedient badger to one of my trolls to play with," he said. "He lasted longer than you might think."

Senec began to shudder, making faint, piteous sounds. It couldn't have been easy to shake that hard when standing on only three paws, but Talvaric still had a firm grip on his scruff. He turned the fox around again.

"Are you going to obey me?"

The fox cringed into a puddle of rusty fur. It seemed to have lost its ability to talk.

"Good." Talvaric curved his mouth into a smile. "I'm glad we understand one another. That will make it so much less inconvenient for us both."

Perhaps this fox wasn't the disappointment he'd originally thought, but a stroke of luck. His plans with the dragons hadn't unfolded the way he had expected—sometimes ambitious leaps fell short. Senec would be so much easier to control. Reliable. Useful.

And if Talvaric's original scheme had unraveled, there had been unexpected developments in his favor. Who could have expected Queen Guinevere's appearance on the scene? Morgan had tried and tried to find Arthur's weakness to no avail. A foolish mistake, in Talvaric's opinion. If any man had a soft side, it would be vulnerable to the human queen's golden beauty.

"In a handful of hours," he said to the fox. "I will have a message for you to deliver. I trust you will be prompt to obey."

Talvaric petted the soft red fur as the animal shivered in mindless terror.

"We have to let him go," Gwen said, shedding her coat.

There hadn't been much more to Rukon's story, as the dragon knew little of Talvaric's actual plans. They'd returned to the hotel room after Arthur and Merlin had deemed it safe to watch the dragon in shifts, with someone skilled in magic there at all times. Merlin, Gawain and Owen were on first watch.

Arthur paced to the window. "I don't think releasing him is wise."

The light from the desk lamp cast odd shadows that made him look tired beyond his years. Or maybe that had just been the day.

Gwen rose to join him, cupping his face between her hands. "But the mystery is over. We know about Talvaric. We know why Rukon's caught up in this, and we know what he's suffered."

"And is still suffering." Arthur stepped out of her grasp and pulled off his jacket, leaving only a long-sleeved T-shirt. He'd pushed up the sleeves, and every motion showed off strong forearms, honed from years of wielding a blade. "If we open the cage, we have no protection and Rukon is still in Talvaric's power."

"But he doesn't want to be. He hasn't hurt anyone yet."

"Yet." Arthur's gaze caught hers. "Talvaric has his

young, and his mate is missing or dead. There will be no more eggs for Rukon. Dragons mate for life."

"So he's going to do whatever Talvaric says, because his children are hostage."

"Exactly."

That made everything worse. "But we can't keep him trapped forever. He'll die."

"I know." Arthur gave a weary sigh and sank onto the couch. "However, I can't let him go until I'm certain he won't kill us all."

It was hard to argue with that, but she did, anyway. "You're the Pendragon. You're supposed to protect their kind." She sat beside him and took his hand in both of hers.

"And I will, by killing Talvaric as quickly as possible."

That was a plan she could get behind. Gwen tilted her head so she could kiss his jaw. His clothes still smelled of wind and pine, and the image of the brilliant, starry night filled her mind. Arthur slipped his arm around her and they stayed that way for a long moment. His shirt was soft beneath her cheek, the steady thump of his heart hypnotic. The night air had left her sleepy and exhilarated at the same time. Every sense was heightened and yet relaxed, as if she were humming with life.

He hadn't pushed the issue of returning to his apartment, and she was grateful. The hotel was a safe space and neutral ground. Whatever they had started to build wasn't ready for the larger expectations of his personal territory. Here, Gwen had a claim, too.

He kissed the top of her head. It was a fond gesture, and it quickly led to more. They tasted one another, tongues tangling. Arthur's breath was hot and urgent as he explored her, claiming her kiss with the thorough determination of a general. His hand found the comb that held her hair, pulling it free so he could run his fingers through the long tresses. Gwen felt the weight of it fall down her back, uncoiling as it went.

Desire flared so easily between them now, as if just waiting for an excuse. She ran her hands down his shirt, glorying in the hard muscle beneath. Then she slid onto his lap, straddling his legs. Her core ached with the anticipation of what would surely happen next, and she settled carefully, winding her arms around his neck and leaning in until he took her weight. He wouldn't stay trapped beneath her unless he wanted to, but it was the surest way to claim his attention.

"How can I help with Talvaric?" she asked.

The question seemed to startle him, chasing the gathering languor from his eyes. "You've done enough."

"Until Talvaric is dead and the dragons are safe, no one has done enough."

Arthur's jaw set. "I don't want to be Rukon, mourning my mate."

That wasn't the right argument. "We don't know exactly what happened to Elosta, but it's clear she was reluctant to be bound by an outside will. She fought until her wings tangled in that net. I admire her defiance."

"Even so," Arthur said, "I think—"

"I don't want to be bound, either," Gwen interrupted.

They locked gazes, and his only grew more stubborn. She slid off his lap, rising to pace the room. Old anger bubbled inside her. Despite everything, it seemed they had to have this argument one more time. She prayed it was the last.

"What's wrong?" he asked with a touch of impatience. It was interesting how he always took that tone when he didn't know what to say.

She spun to look at him. "I've been part of this, at your side, and for once I feel as if we're working together."

He stood, brows drawn together. "I feel the same way."

"Good. Then learn from the experience. You don't have to bear your destiny alone. You have your men and Merlin, and you have me. You especially have me."

She'd never used this snappish tone with him before. He was her husband, but he was also a king. At the moment, she didn't care that she was supposed to be reverent or even polite. After six years of marriage, she'd run out of patience.

"Guinevere," he said, her name an admonishment.

That only made her temper flare hotter. "If you don't want me by your side, doing my part, say so now. I can build a life here for myself that has nothing to do with Camelot."

It was then she saw his anger rise in a slow flush up his cheeks. "Or me."

"That's your choice." She swallowed, taking a breath to rein in her words, to make them true instead of just angry. "I have an idea of the burden you bear, and it staggers me. But if you trust the people who love you, we can share the load. And look at what happens when you do—we caught a dragon and found the truth. Take heart from that. Let me be your asset."

"You are. You provided the trap's design." Arthur's jaw worked, but he made a visible effort at control. "I realize how badly I've underestimated what you can do."

Gwen took a breath, because suddenly she could. They'd turned a corner. There was a glimmer of something better for the two of them. Suddenly even the room felt warmer and more welcoming.

"I want you to go to school and learn everything you can," Arthur said, his voice rough. "You deserve it, and I know it will make you happy. And that makes me happy."

Her eyes stung with tears of hope, but she stood her ground. "No guards dogging my tracks."

"Not unless there's an active threat." He nodded, emphasizing his promise. "And if it matters to you, Camelot needs your skills. You can make a solid contribution to whatever we do."

He was giving her everything she'd asked for when they'd met for cocktails. That night felt as if it had been years ago now—and it was, in terms of experience. Then, she'd been content to build a life alongside Arthur's. But now? Now she wanted to be part of his. "So why is that acceptable, and yet you won't let me help now?"

"Sitting at a desk drawing a design for a cage is sensible. It's not the same as running headlong into danger."

"I don't *want* to run headlong into danger. I'm capable of judgment, and there's a wide patch of ground between real danger and being an involved partner. You saw what I did in the Crystal Mountains."

"You nearly got squashed by a troll."

"Not that part." She flicked a hand. "The part where I talked Zorath into speaking with Camelot in the first place."

"That was useful," Arthur admitted.

Gwen gave an unladylike snort. "Thanks."

"But you never know when to take a step back for your own good." He took a step forward, blue eyes intent, and took hold of her shoulder. "You were sick for months after you went with the army to Wales. It broke my heart."

"And you don't think it broke mine?" The memory slammed her, too painful at the best of times, but worse when she was already stinging from the reporter's questions earlier that day.

And she couldn't face it now, when her defenses were crumbling. She jerked back, away from his touch. "I lost every chance of having a child!"

Arthur fell utterly silent, his face a blank mask. "You what?"

Chapter 22

By the blessed angels! Gwen had blurted out the words without thinking, and she panted now, her pulse thundering in her ears. She put her palms to her face, feeling wetness and the heat of her flushed cheeks. There was no point in trying to bury the truth now. "I was cursed. There was a witch. I nursed her sons, but they died."

Gwen suddenly lost all the strength that had sustained her. She swayed where she stood, feeling stranded far from help.

"You never told me," said Arthur, his face drained with shock. "For years, you never told me."

"I'm sorry." The words were a whisper.

He opened his arms to reach for her, but she backed away. She felt soiled, as if finally dragging the secret into the open had exposed a seeping wound. "I disappointed you. Giving you an heir was the one thing I was supposed to do."

"That's not true," he said. "Honestly, you're enough for me."

But Gwen knew better. "Every king has the right to expect an heir."

"That's what we're told, but my heart is yours, Gwen. I want you most of all."

His kindness only made her feel worse. She'd failed because she'd disobeyed him. If she'd been obedient, none of this sorrow would have come to pass. The words rang in her head, but even now she couldn't bear to give them voice. There were tears standing in Arthur's eyes, and each one pierced her like a blade made of glass. *This was his tragedy, too.* And she hated herself still more.

"I love you," he said, saying the words slowly as if to reassure her. "And I'm sorry. I knew you were sick, but I had no idea you were grieving about this, as well."

But she had been, and he'd ordered complete bed rest. Only calming music, only pleasant visitors. No books, no news, no gossip that might unsettle her mood. He'd meant it with kindness, but it was like being stuffed in a box with no air. *You don't understand me at all.* But she couldn't say that. It would only be selfish to hurt him that much more.

"You didn't trust me," he finally said, sorrow hardening to resentment. "Or you would have told me. We could have asked for Merlin's help, or Nimueh's. They might have broken the curse."

She folded her arms, bracing herself. "How could I tell you? By the time I recovered, I wasn't welcome in the council chamber or your private discussions about affairs of state or anywhere that mattered. I was no longer queen, whatever title you gave me."

"I would not risk your health. You were fragile."

"You were barring the door because I dared to make my own decision when I offered comfort to the sick." She gulped air, refusing to cry. "I was wrong, but it was my risk to take. You had no right to punish me, and you're still doing it every time you leave me behind."

"Is that how you see me?" His eyes were wide with frank surprise. "And you say that *I* don't trust *you*. You never told me anything about how you felt!"

"I disappointed you, and you lectured me! What could I expect?"

Silence simmered between them. They'd backed away from each other until they stood on opposite sides of the puddle of lamplight. The distance was a physical pain to Gwen, a twist of desire's knife. She still wanted Arthur, even though she could barely look at him right then.

And why were they arguing now? They'd just begun to build something fresh—or was that true? Hadn't the same mistakes just been waiting like bandits in their path? Or perhaps she'd had to feel confident enough to tell him what had truly hurt her?

She'd finally been honest, but did it even matter now?

"Well," Gwen said, staring at the floor. "There we are."

"There we are."

She forced herself to raise her chin, but it was hard, her neck almost throbbing in protest. Meeting his cold blue gaze was even worse. "Is there a road forward from here?"

A heartbeat passed. All she could see was destruction, an avalanche begun by a few careless words. She felt hollow, as if all her insides had vanished.

With a sudden, startling motion, Arthur snatched up his coat. "I don't know. I don't know anything anymore."

"Where are you going?" Gwen demanded.

"I don't know that, either."

He stormed out, slamming the door. She froze, listening to his steps stomp down the hallway. When they'd finally faded, she let out a shuddering breath. She felt calm, but it was the calm of devastation. They'd fought before, but this was different. This was falling off a cliff.

Because they'd finally bared their souls. That was supposed to be healing, but it felt like death.

She sank to one of the chairs, staring at the spot where she'd been sitting with Arthur just minutes before. The drastic change wrought by so little time stunned her. And yet? And yet a piece of her felt different. Not relieved, but maybe unburdened. She had no hidden resentments now—they were in the open for all to see.

Sadness overcame her in a sudden wave, and with that came tears—messy, hot, angry sobbing. She gave in to it, letting herself cry in a way she hadn't since her mother's death. There was nothing to hide anymore. She wept for the child she'd never have, wishing she'd been able to hold it and say how much love there was in her heart. She wept for Arthur, who didn't know how to be anything but a king. Finally, she let loose the private griefs, the voices that said no one should be punished for wanting to make their own reasonable choices. There was compromise and sacrifice, and she was more than willing to make them, but as an equal partner. She would not be pushed away like an impertinent kitten, or left behind like someone who doesn't know her proper place.

When the tears stopped at last, loneliness moved in. It was crushing, but when Gwen picked up her phone, she immediately threw it back down. She was heartsick, and there wasn't anything she was ready to share, not even with Clary. She went to the bathroom and washed her face, doing her best to avoid the mirror. She idly considered the freshly stocked minibar, but set the notion aside. These emotions, difficult though they were, held importance. Dulling them would get her nowhere.

But when she left the bathroom, she paused. Something

was wrong. At first she thought her nerves were simply raw, but when her gaze swept the room, she saw her instincts were on point. There was a stranger standing beside the couch, a satisfied smile on his lips. An involuntary cry left her lips when she took in his silver hair, olive skin and the bright, predatory green of his eyes. The man was a fae.

"Queen Guinevere, I presume," he said. "My name is Talvaric."

Gwen stood her ground. She was afraid, but she was also a queen, and this creature had interrupted a very private moment. "What are you doing here?" she demanded.

"Tonight, I am here to see you." Talvaric gave a smile, but it was a movement of lips, no more. "The legend of your beauty was not a lie."

Given her red eyes and tear-blotched face, he had to be insane or lying. "What do you want?" she snapped.

"You shall be of use to me."

Like the smile, his words held no emotion. She'd heard the fae had been stripped of their souls, but she'd never quite understood what that meant. She saw it now in the fae's flat, almost-reptilian expression. There was life there—cold, calculating and hungry—but it was vile. Horror rose until Gwen thought she might be sick. Once the fae had been poets and painters, noble warriors and creators of great beauty. Some had even been her friends. Now they were monsters.

"I'm not yours to use," she said evenly, hiding her nerves with a cutting tone. "I am the Queen of Camelot."

"So you are." Talvaric took a step toward her. "You will be coming with me. It's up to you whether you struggle."

Gwen calculated the distance to her cell phone. It was on the bed, too far away to do her any good. She was nearer the door to the hallway, but fae were fast. Instead, she shot backward into the bathroom and slammed the door shut.

Or tried to. Talvaric's boot wedged itself into the gap just in time. Gwen put her shoulder to the door and heaved. There was a grunt of pain, but the foot didn't budge. Gwen shoved for all she was worth, but fingers appeared in the gap, using the door frame to brace against her weight. Slowly, her feet began to slide across the bathroom tile. She was losing the fight.

This was not the moment to be proud. Gwen screamed every curse word she'd learned from Camelot's soldiers, then ones she'd learned from all the ambassadors to Arthur's court. Desperately, she hoped someone would hear and pound on the hotel-room door to complain. Talvaric was going to use her as a weapon against Arthur, holding her life in the balance as cruelly as he'd used Rukon's family against the dragon.

Or he'd try to. Gwen wasn't having any of it. She would battle to the end.

But then the bathroom door burst open and she flew backward, crashing against the shower door. Her skull pounded, ears ringing as she rebounded, bracing herself against the sink. She'd hit her head already when the troll had tossed her against the wall, and this hurt even more. Her stomach rolled with the pain, but she kept screaming insults.

"Be quiet, human!" Talvaric grabbed a handful of her hair and pushed her down until her cheek squashed against the countertop, muffling her cries. Suddenly, she could barely breathe. His weight bore down on her, an elbow digging into her spine. The hold was impersonal, as if she were no more than a sheep to be sheared. Methodically, he jerked her arms behind her and heavy rope bit into her wrists. Gwen had given every ounce of her strength, but the fight was over in the matter of a minute.

"Arthur will be back at any time," she snarled, wondering if that were true.

"How unfortunate that he'll miss us." Talvaric pulled her upright, his grip back in her hair.

She kicked backward, aiming for his shin, but he shoved her out of the bathroom, letting her stumble before he snatched her back to her feet. Moving was surprisingly awkward with her hands tied behind her.

"Be still," he growled, his lips close enough to her ear that the warning was almost intimate.

"How did you get in here?" she demanded. Her stomach was a cold ball of fear. She was forced to pant around it, her pulse a quick, dizzying beat.

"Someone conveniently built a portal," he observed, opening the closet door with one hand while he gripped her bound hands with the other. "I sense Merlin's hand in it, though he was not the only maker."

"How can you tell?"

"How can you distinguish one painter from another? Every magic user has his own distinctive style. Merlin's is unmistakable."

He said it bitterly, and she remembered it was Merlin's spell that had damaged the fae so completely. She'd even heard they feasted on mortal souls in an attempt to rekindle their dead emotions. The high didn't last, but it turned the fae into desperate addicts.

For a moment, she was at a loss for a retort. It didn't matter—Talvaric kept talking. "I hope the hotel gave you a discount for a room with a breach like this."

"Merlin sealed it."

Talvaric's green eyes glittered. "A portal can be sealed, but it never completely disappears. A competent sorcerer can find a way just as a thief finds an open window. He can also alter its destination."

"You're kidnapping me?"

"Thank you for pointing out the obvious."

When would Arthur come back? Or would he? Their argument hadn't been the kind that would heal quickly. She clenched her jaw, wishing she had one tiny shred of magic that would let Arthur know how badly she needed him now.

As if he could sense her distress, Talvaric was watching her almost eagerly, his pupils large and dark. His nostrils twitched as if scenting her fear. "It will be a brief trip. The portal now leads directly to my front hall."

When she drew breath to scream again, he slammed her head against the door frame of the closet. Her head swam, and time slid away as she desperately gathered her wits again. By the time her eyes focused, it was too late. The portal was open.

The fae's magic burned icy blue, licking like a flame around a hole between realities. Gwen tried one more time to pull away, but there was no hope. When Talvaric spoke a word, the portal flashed so bright Gwen squeezed her eyes shut and twisted her head away. Even then, bright spots danced behind her eyelids.

"Let me go!" she screamed one last time.

Talvaric's reply was a push between her shoulder blades. With a stomach-churning lurch, she fell through an ocean of space and magic.

Chapter 23

Dawn seeped into the sky through cracks between the clouds. To Arthur's eyes, it looked as if the heavens were bleeding. He was taking his turn at watching the dragon, but there was not much to see. The grays and blues of the early morning sparkled with heavy dew, stirred only by a fitful breeze. Rukon was immobile as a large green stone.

Merlin and Owen were also on watch, hidden so well in the trees that Arthur couldn't see their still forms. He alone was restless. He'd chosen a perch on the opposite side of the valley from where he'd sat with Guinevere, not wanting to trigger memories of their temporary truce. The tactic was pointless—thoughts of her permeated everything.

And *complicated* didn't begin to describe his feelings. A chill, heartsick pain seeped through him. In truth, they'd both wanted children, but he'd meant what he'd said about loving her above all things. Discovering that she'd been cursed and kept it secret was an unfamiliar, awkward ache.

They should have been able to face the problem together. She hadn't given them that chance.

He should have suspected something had happened when she'd lingered so long in her sickbed. They'd had a stormy marriage, but after that time, they'd begun to drift apart. There were demands of state—Arthur was busy and often away—but Gwen had turned inward, as well. Now he knew she'd been dealing with a terrible loss.

Arthur picked up a pebble, working the cold, hard shape between his fingers before tossing it down the hillside. Had Gwen really believed he would blame her? In truth, he *was* angry about that. They'd fought, but had he really made her think so poorly of him?

He shied away from answering that. Perhaps he was reluctant to share his burdens, but how could he ask such a young woman to take on such a crushing task? True, she was the same young woman who sweet-talked a goblin king, helped him kill a troll and figured out how to cage a dragon. *Utterly helpless. Obviously.*

Arthur cursed, rubbing his sleep-deprived eyes. He'd done everything wrong. He'd protected her more than she liked—she'd made that perfectly clear these last few days. And she'd been afraid of disappointing him. *Disappointed?* That made him sound like an old, cranky father.

The father he'd never be. A grim sorrow surged through him. In modern parlance, a painful bandage had been ripped off. Beneath it was grief, anger and lack of trust. At least he finally understood the wound. That meant there was a chance to heal, even if it was a slender thing.

The silent dawn magnified the crack and rustle of footsteps coming up the slope toward him. It was Merlin, his hands stuffed in his jacket pockets. His breath steamed faintly, as if he'd borrowed some of Rukon's fire. He crouched beside Arthur.

"You're brooding," said the enchanter. "I can hear it clear across the forest."

"Gwen and I disagreed."

Merlin lifted his eyebrows in question. "Do tell."

Arthur tossed another rock. "Have you begun a career as a marriage counselor?"

"I would sooner teach a pit of demons how to crochet." Merlin turned his gaze toward the dragon's cage. "I suggest you put your differences aside for the moment. This is not the time to be distracted."

"It never is," Arthur replied. "Maybe that's the problem."

Merlin was silent, but gave Arthur a significant look.

"There is no such thing as work-life balance for kings," Arthur snapped. "She wants to solve the problem by involving herself in everything I do."

"Seriously?"

Arthur stopped and rubbed his temples. "I'm exaggerating, and I'm tired. Forgive me."

"When you were a boy, you didn't think it was fair that you had to rule Camelot all by yourself. Now you're complaining that someone wants to help you." Merlin sounded amused. "If anyone should share your burden, it's your wife."

Arthur studied the enchanter. Although he looked about Arthur's age, he was centuries older. He probably did remember whatever it was Arthur said when he was five, but that wasn't the point. "You think I'm shutting her out?"

"I'm merely pointing out an inconsistency."

It sounded more like a character flaw to Arthur. "You told me once good men don't make good kings."

Merlin shrugged. "There will always be sacrifices. Sometimes kingship leaves no room for the heart."

Arthur didn't want to hear more. He rose. "I'm going to check on Rukon."

"I think if he was digging his way out of the cage, we'd know it," Merlin grumbled, but he followed him down the hill.

Owen was sitting on a fallen tree near the dragon's lair, hands on his knees and his expression almost meditative. The only sound emerging from the cave was a slow, rhythmic rumble Arthur guessed was the dragon snoring. A glance inside the lair revealed a haunch and the tip of its tail, but the rest was lost to shadow.

"Report?" Arthur asked Owen.

The Welsh knight was instantly alert and on his feet. "All is quiet, Your Majesty."

There was a snort from the dragon and one baleful yellow eye peered out of the dark for a moment before closing again. Arthur wasn't fooled by the outward show of quietude. He'd already asked Merlin how long he could maintain the spell that kept the cage secure, and all indicators said they needed to make a plan quickly.

Arthur gestured for Owen to relax. The knight sat again, while Merlin lounged against a tree. Arthur paced, forcing his thoughts to the topic of dragons and away from the fight with his wife. It should have been easy. It wasn't, and his head began to pound.

A rustle in the brush broke his concentration. He spun toward the sound, scanning the trees but seeing nothing. His gaze worked downward until he saw a black nose poking from the bushes. It was followed by a long, delicate snout and a pair of upright ears. Arthur stared at the red fox. He had seen hundreds roaming the woods of Camelot, and not one of them had ever approached humans willingly—yet this one was.

There was blood matting its coat. It was also limping,

one black-furred leg obviously lame and his bright brush of a tail so low it dragged through the dirt. A tuft of green fur colored the end of its tail, marking it as a Charmed Beast. Arthur remained still, transfixed as it hobbled up to him and sat, trembling and staring up with intelligent eyes. Slowly, Arthur crouched, cautiously aware this was no ordinary creature.

The fox's nose lowered as Arthur went to one knee. "You are the Pendragon?" the beast asked in a clear voice that was firm despite its piteous shaking.

"I am," Arthur replied.

"He is," Rukon rumbled.

The dragon was awake and watching the fox intently. The fox turned, his ears swiveling toward Rukon before he bowed his head in a gesture of respect.

"I am sorry to see you here, little brother," said the dragon in a voice that was almost gentle.

Out of the corner of his eye, Arthur noticed Merlin and Owen approaching. Merlin appeared fascinated, Owen frowning with concern. Their presence made the animal tremble even more. "What can I do for you?" Arthur asked the fox.

"I bear a message from Talvaric of the fae," said the fox.

The name made Rukon snort fire. The two creatures exchanged a look of mutual commiseration. Arthur's fists clenched, hating their shared pain. "And what does he want?" Arthur said in a strained voice.

The fox cringed then, licking his injured leg. "I did not want any part of this," he said plaintively. "You cannot think I call him master out of my own free will!"

Arthur remembered Gwen lecturing the foxes she caught, warning them away from her father's chickens. She'd loved them. Sadness and anger mixed in a volatile brew until Arthur ground his teeth in frustration.

"I understand. You have nothing to fear from me." *No, these creatures need a protector. They need my sword as much as any human.* He reached out, letting the fox sniff his hand. "What is the message you have been sent to deliver?"

"He wants—demands—that you present yourself at the front gates of your theme park in two hours. He wants re-por-ters." The fox said the word carefully, as if it was unfamiliar.

Arthur cursed, thinking of Gwen's unhappy experience with the press. She had been so upset, so in need of comfort. He cursed again. "To what end?"

The poor creature shook with dread. "You are to surrender yourself to him."

Both Merlin and Owen made sounds of outrage, but Arthur felt a cold hand grip deep inside him. "And if I don't?"

The fox's ears flattened, its chin drooping to the ground. Furry eyebrows bunched in a plaintive expression. "He said by the time you hear this message, he will have Queen Guinevere."

Gwen landed on her knees, unable to catch herself with her hands bound behind her back. On this side of the portal, the floor was marble, and the shock was enough to send spikes of pain through her hips. Talvaric was behind her, his light footfalls scuffing as he spun to seal the portal—and every chance of retreat—closed.

It took him a second, but that was all Gwen needed to scramble to her feet and run. Talvaric shouted something in his own language. It sounded like a curse, but it was just words and she kept sprinting at top speed. At first, she was only aware of where a door was open and whether it led to a dead end. Her experience with the troll had made that hazard painfully clear.

A few turnings later, she realized she'd actually left the fae behind, at least for a few seconds. She ducked behind a curtain, finding a wide window embrasure looking onto a starlit forest. It was too dark outside to see more than trees and grass. No chance of bolting into some public place and screaming for help. Worse, there was no way to open the window and escape.

She had to think, not just react. This was Talvaric's territory, and simply running wouldn't help her. Gwen made herself small, perching in a ball on the window ledge. It was awkward without the use of her hands, but it gave her the chance to calm her pounding heart.

The respite only lasted for moments. She heard him—or someone—moving, and he wasn't alone. Toenails clicked past. An animal. A dog, she guessed—Gwen missed her greyhounds with a physical ache and knew the sound of their feet on the palace floors—but this one was large, given the length of its stride. Then she heard it snuffling.

She was being hunted. She was prey.

Her whole body tingled with fright. She wanted to jump up and run so badly, her toes cramped inside her boots. But running wouldn't help. Run where and do what? Her hands were numb and useless. Even if she found a doorway into the woods outside this house, she couldn't turn the knob. All the same, remaining still and quiet was an act of will.

I'm trapped. She could hear the rasping breath of whatever it was coming closer. It didn't whine or bark like a normal dog on a scent and that made the suspense worse. *Help!* She pleaded silently, wishing Arthur could hear her thoughts. *Help!*

But he wasn't a mind reader, and he was far away in the mortal realm. Worse than that, he probably hated her. She was lost.

A snout poked through the curtains. It was black,

pointed and huge. Gwen cringed back from it, watching a trail of drool dangling from the chops of the enormous animal. It smelled like a battlefield a week after the war. A second later, the curtain jerked aside, revealing Talvaric and a massive red-eyed creature.

"Meet my barguest," said Talvaric.

A barguest. They were creatures of moors and lonely places, and they were the reason no one wandered the roads alone after dark. She'd never expected to see one inside a home—even a fae's home. The incongruity of it broke the spell of terror.

"Is he your pet?" she asked incredulously.

The barguest gave her a withering stare from those fire-red eyes. Gwen held its gaze just long enough to see its defiance fade to something more painful. Monster or not, it was miserable.

"He is your guarantee of good behavior." Talvaric grabbed her arm and dragged her off the windowsill.

She moved awkwardly, her knees stiff from her earlier bad landing. "Where are you taking me?" she demanded.

"To your cage. You will join my other curiosities." He gave her a savage shove, and she stumbled but kept her feet. He snatched her shoulder hard enough a cry escaped her clenched teeth. "If you try to escape again, my barguest will hunt you down and make you his dinner. I never feed him quite enough, you see. That's the best way to deal with picky eaters."

All the same, Gwen did her best to memorize the route through the sprawling residence. It was mostly bare and white, as if decorating it had been too much effort. Not surprising, if the fae had lost their ability to perceive beauty, but it made it hard to find landmarks to anchor the route.

That all changed when they reached his collection. Gwen stopped cold, digging in her heels at the unforget-

table sight. This corridor was all of stone and had a series
of tiny rooms on either side. The walls that looked into
the hallway were plain metal bars, each door fitted with a
heavy padlock. There was straw on the floor of the cells,
but no furniture.

He really meant to put her in a cage. A literal cage.
Gwen's knees went weak as her ability to breathe deserted
her.

Talvaric jerked her forward. "Say hello to your com-
patriots."

She made an involuntary cry when she saw a huge snake
curled in the straw of the first room. It had glistening green
scales and the head of a woman. In the next was a deer-
like creature with a single spiral horn. In the one after
that was a bird with feathers made of flame. There was
no straw in that cell.

Talvaric all but tossed her into the next, and followed
her inside. He held her down with one hand and cut her
bonds with a knife he had strapped to his belt. It was rough,
but impersonal. The second Gwen's hands parted, he retreated and slammed the barred door shut.

Her shoulders sang with pain, but she spun around to
face Talvaric. He stood on the other side of the door, arms
folded, with a speculative look on his face.

"You're mine now," he said. "Just like all the others."

All Gwen's rage screamed in her head, but she was too
appalled to speak a single word.

Chapter 24

As soon as the sun rose, Talvaric strolled into the cells to admire his newest acquisition.

"I brought you something to wear," he said, motioning to the silent servants who shuffled behind him.

They drew close, unlocking the door and opening it wide enough for two of their number to slip into Gwen's cell. Gwen backed away, unsure what to expect. She'd glimpsed green-skinned beings like this in the Forest Sauvage. They were dryads, creatures who shifted at will into trees. How Talvaric had trapped them and made them his slaves was beyond her comprehension, but it had to be with cruelty. Such beings did not belong anywhere but under open skies.

The scent of fresh leaves surrounded them. Their features were strange—humanlike without following the same rules of proportion. Nevertheless, they were beautiful, with long green hair and graceful limbs. One bore a pitcher of water and basin for washing, the other carried garments. Gwen noted their fingers had too many joints, or perhaps it was too many fingers. Nothing seemed completely fixed, but shifted every time she looked.

"I don't want your clothes," she said, although she silently wished for a bath.

His response was terse. "You are a queen. You will dress appropriately."

"Why? Is your collection diminished if I choose to remain as I am?"

He refused to show annoyance. "You will diminish if I choose to withhold your food. The rules here are simple— do as I bid you, or suffer the consequences."

At his sign, the dryads set down their burdens and left the cell, locking the door behind them. "Thank you," Gwen said to the pair, but the green-skinned creatures remained silent, their eyes downcast.

"Don't bother," Talvaric said. "Plants are terrible conversationalists."

Gwen glanced down at the dress he'd given her. It was a long court gown, full-skirted and jeweled and very much like her clothes from Camelot. It reminded her of all the things at stake besides her own life. "Is there a regent on the throne of Faery while Morgan is away?"

To her surprise, he answered the question. "There is a council of nobles. No one person dares to take Morgan's place."

She heard the derision in his tone. He thought them cowards. "What do they think of my capture?"

Silence. That meant he hadn't told them, and possibly didn't intend to. She risked going one step more. "You intend to take the throne for yourself."

"Why not? They are a fractured, leaderless court with no ambition and less courage. Whoever dazzles them enough will hold them like flies in honey. I intend to demonstrate how Arthur and his magic sword are clay dragons, frightening to behold but easily smashed."

This confirmed what Gwen already knew. Still, her stomach plummeted. "I'm bait to bring him here."

"Precisely." His smile was icy.

She wanted to scream that Arthur wouldn't come, that this was all foolishness because he didn't love her, but there was no point. Likewise, begging for Arthur's life would be a waste of time. Nothing would convince the fae to spare their deadliest foe.

And if Talvaric was telling her his plans, he had no intention of ever letting her go, either.

"Are you certain you want a throne?" she asked bitterly. "I've never seen that much power bring anyone joy."

Talvaric's expression didn't change. "I don't feel joy. Not any longer."

"Then why bother?"

He shrugged, the gesture stiff with unease. Perhaps he did feel something, after all—she'd heard some of the fae had recovered pieces of their soul. Did he want revenge? Or hunger for recognition? Or was he simply deranged?

"I shall sweep away the unworthy," he said after a long pause.

She waited for more, but it didn't come. Irritation overcame her fear. "As a plan, it lacks detail."

His smile was feline. "And yet I know what I am worth. I will rise by my own merit. That is more than you can claim."

"I am Queen of Camelot."

"You are a mortal woman, unloved by her husband and cursed to a barren womb. You are worth nothing."

The cold certainty of his words felled Gwen as if they were a physical slap. She dropped to her knees, the shock of violation wrenching a gasp from her throat. "How did you know?" she whispered. *How does he know about the blacksmith's wife and her curse?*

"Please," he purred. "I am a fae enchanter. Your secrets are pebbles on a beach, waiting to be gathered as I please."

The idea of his mind—or any part of Talvaric—leafing through her secrets brought bile burning up her throat. She covered her face with her hands, pushing the image away. But he had stirred something—the aching, scorching disappointment in her own life.

She'd accused Arthur of disregarding her, but was that actually a reflection of her own opinion? Did she blame him for what she felt about herself? The idea sickened her, and yet it felt true—at least in part. She was her own worst enemy.

Talvaric turned away then, the force of his attention shifting like a great weight. It was a relief, and yet she felt obliterated, as if she'd ceased to exist. As if she deserved nothing more.

Talvaric began to walk through the clutch of dryads, returning the way he had come, but then stopped. "I can already feel that this is going to be a momentous day. One worth remembering as a vivid experience." He spun to face Gwen, walking backward. "You've been asleep for many years. How much do you understand about today's fae?"

She had no idea what he meant, so merely shook her head.

He grabbed one of the dryads, holding her face between his hands. The creature, mute until now, shrieked. It was not a human sound, but like the rending of green branches and bark. Gwen flinched, knowing terror when she heard it. Talvaric didn't slow, but brought his face close to the dryad's, almost as if he would kiss her. Horribly, Gwen understood what he meant to do, and a rush of panic prickled over her skin. Arthur had mentioned the fae's hunger for mortal souls, and dryads were long-lived, but as mortal as the trees they called home.

"Stop!" Gwen was on her feet, grabbing the door to the cage and wrenching it. The lock clattered, but would not budge. "Stop it!"

The dryad's eyes, dark brown in her pale green face, had gone wide. She seemed to be screaming, but silently now. She tried to push away, back bowed so far that Talvaric was forced to crouch over her, but there was no escape. Slowly, a mist rose from her lips to his. He was taking her life essence, her spark, and all the emotions that went with truly living.

"Help her!" Gwen reached between the bars, her fingers just brushing the sleeve of the closest dryad. They were all just standing there, faces blank. "She's your sister! Save her!"

At last, Gwen caught hold of the sleeve, winding her fingers in the cloth and pulling for all she was worth. The owner of the sleeve stumbled and turned to look Gwen in the eyes. Then she saw. The other dryads knew exactly what was going on, but he had some hold over them that prevented the slightest interference. That helplessness shamed them beyond anything Gwen could fathom. *Magic. He's holding them helpless with a spell!*

The creature in Talvaric's arms began to shudder as the last of her life was consumed. When the struggle ended, her entire frame went limp. The fae released her, and she toppled like a sapling under the woodsman's ax. Talvaric sucked in a long, noisy breath. As long as the dryad's life essence lasted, he would regain his ability to feel.

"I understand why this is addictive," he said to Gwen, stretching his arms as if waking from a long nap.

Suddenly, there was a leer in his voice that hadn't been

there before. If she'd felt vulnerable before, this was much worse. Something inside her curled into a tiny ball.

"You look terrified," he added, obviously amused.

"I've been told that drinking souls eventually destroys your kind."

Talvaric laughed, the sound harsh and hoarse. Clearly, he didn't get much practice. "Don't think I'm that weak."

"Remorse is an emotion," Gwen said, hating this new Talvaric even more than before. "What will happen when you realize what you've become?"

This time, Talvaric's smile held layers of malice. "Moralists always make one mistake. They assume the fae were universally good to begin with. My old self would applaud what my present self is finally able to achieve."

Gwen's heart dropped. He was right. She'd never considered evil fae. "You were already a nightmare. Merlin's magic simply dulled your enjoyment of it."

"And now I am my own true self, at least for today." Talvaric stirred the dead dryad with his foot, then spared a glance for the other servants. "Clean this up."

"What are you going to do?" Gwen demanded.

"I'm going to have a word with your dear husband." He stepped toward her cage, and she instinctively backed up. "Do put on the dress. If Arthur truly is a heroic fool, he'll give himself up for you. I think you owe it to him to look your best."

With that, Talvaric walked away, leaving the dryads to gather up their fallen friend. As he went, he sang an old and lyrical melody Gwen knew from her first days at Camelot. Sung with such malevolence, the tune made her weep.

Medievaland was in full swing, tourists streaming in and out of the gates. The appearance of dragons—whether or not anyone believed in them—had spurred public interest. During Arthur's brief conversation with management, it was clear they were less concerned about potential bad press than they were sales at the gate. Furthermore, Gwen's interview had turned the conversation to a more manageable direction. On this one front, at least, news was good.

Or it would have been. Despite the fox's message, Arthur hadn't called the media but as he approached the arched entryway to the park, Arthur saw news vans circling the parking lot. Talvaric had been busy.

"I believe there is a movie where two warriors fight at high noon," Owen observed.

The Welsh knight walked at Arthur's side, gaze roving over the crowds. He had a patient stillness that made him excellent security, and Arthur valued his presence. He wasn't so sure about his taste in entertainment.

"I don't know that story," he replied.

"It is a hero tale not so unlike our own."

Arthur would rather have skipped heroism for something involving fewer casualties. Arthur and Owen were dressed in full armor, as were Palomedes and Beaumains, who brought up the rear. Gawain was inside the park, watching for trouble there.

The autumn day had grown sunny and light shone on the polished weapons, drawing the attention of the crowd milling at the gate. Cameras flashed and a few approached for autographs, but the younger knights gently sent the fans on their way. The reporters were less easy to deter.

"Arthur, where's Guinevere? Why do we never see her at Medievaland?"

"Arthur, hashtag Iseedragons is one of the top-trending topics in North America. Care to comment?"

Arthur kept walking, allowing the eternally cheerful Beaumains to deal with the questions. As King of Camelot, he had one purpose, and that was to rid the mortal realms—make that all the realms—of the fae named Talvaric.

"There," Owen said, "by the information kiosk."

A man stood with his back to the knights. He was tall and well built, but slender. A long pale braid escaped a baseball cap to trail down his back. As soon as Arthur saw him, he turned. In spite of the sunglasses, it was clear he was a fae. By the way he moved, Arthur could tell he'd recently consumed someone's life. It was a subtle difference, but he'd learned to spot it—the nervous twitch of the hands, the eagerness in the step. Cold dread weighed in Arthur's gut. Who had died so that this villain could enjoy the pain he caused?

Arthur approached the fae with only Owen to watch his back. For his part, Talvaric strolled to a neutral territory between the kiosk and a photo booth. It was a well-chosen meeting place, public but away from listening ears. Arthur came to a stop a few feet away, leaving distance between them. Neither man bowed.

Talvaric pulled off his glasses, narrowing his eyes against the bright sun. "I see my messenger performed his duty. Where is the vermin?"

Senec was curled up in the back of Owen's truck, sleeping in a nest made of an old sweatshirt. The fox and the knight had bonded at once. "Safe."

"The fox is mine."

"Not anymore."

Talvaric shrugged. "We shall see. For now, there are more important concerns, such as who owns your wife."

Arthur didn't reply, letting the silence speak his contempt.

"I will trade your life for hers," Talvaric said. "Come quietly, and the exchange will be made without fuss or bother to these good people."

Arthur followed the fae's gesture toward the crowd. There were children with balloons, grandparents using walkers, and baby carriages. A sense of nightmare seeped into him, as if Talvaric had literally spread a cloud of horror. Somehow, Arthur had to keep these people safe, but what was the best way to do that? Not by following Talvaric's rules. There was no way Arthur could allow the fae the upper hand.

"Do you truly believe I'm going to give in and hope for the best?" Arthur widened his stance, ready for a fight.

"You don't care what happens to your Gwen?" Talvaric chided. "I took you for the heroic type."

Fury speared Arthur, and his hand flew to Excalibur's hilt. "Do not hasten your death with meaningless chatter."

"I'll take that as a maybe?"

"Touch her and I'll use your guts to lace my boots."

"Then come with me, king of mortals, and I will let her go."

Arthur didn't move. Gwen was foremost in his thoughts, his heart and in the yearning of his body—but he was king and responsible for all the mortal realms. Giving Talvaric control meant condemning everything. He had to—he *would*—save Gwen *and* the girl in the stroller by the ticket booth, her mother *and* her grandfather, who was purchasing a pink balloon with a dancing unicorn. The only way he could save everyone was by destroying the fae here and now.

That was fine. Cutting Talvaric to pieces was going to be a pleasure. "I'll save time and kill you here."

Surprise flickered over Talvaric's face, followed swiftly by derision. "You can't. There are laws here about murder, and I will fight back. You'll never expose the hidden realm to the curiosity of all these mortals. All this press."

Arthur smiled. "I have one advantage you don't."

Talvaric raised a brow. "What?"

"Friends." Arthur held up a hand to signal the figure who stood hidden beside the photo booth.

Talvaric caught the gesture and spun to see who it was. "Merlin!" he snarled.

Merlin gave a finger wave. "The mortals won't see us chopping you to bits. I promise."

"Then see if they'll notice *this*!" Talvaric released a storm of magic.

Chapter 25

The world around him jolted. Arthur fell into a crouch, sword in hand. He didn't need to look at the blade to know it was glowing with a faint iridescent light. Excalibur detected magic and reflected it away from Arthur, saving both sword and man from the effects of any spell. That was why Morgan LaFaye feared it—even her darkest enchantments couldn't keep her safe from its edge.

But Excalibur could only do so much, and the sky was cracking open like a shattered egg, revealing a visible split in the sunny autumn blue. The next moment, Merlin was at his side, chanting a spell under his breath and weaving intricate shapes in the air.

"Not even you can hide this forever, Merlin," Talvaric jeered, and made a tearing motion with his hands.

The crack leaked brilliant flames of light, and then another sky beyond. They were looking through a portal. Was this where Gwen was being held? Heart pounding,

Arthur sprang to his feet, ready to run and leap through. Any chance of finding her was better than none.

As if reading his thoughts, Merlin grabbed his arm. "No! It's not stable."

Arthur understood the enchanter's plea a moment later. Another jolt shook the ground, rumbling like a small earthquake. The babble of the crowd rose in alarm.

"Portals aren't meant to be so large," Merlin muttered.

And neither were they meant to release a Noah's ark of fantastic beasts into the mortal realms. All at once, they spilled out of the air, falling where the bottom lip of the portal sat a dozen feet from the ground. Some were naturally airborne: gargoyles and griffins and birds with fabulous plumage. Others ran on hoofs or paws or claw-tipped feet, bearing the green-tipped tails of the Charmed Beasts. Still others slithered and swam, floating in bubbles of water that bobbed and rolled in the air, seeking a lake or a stream to deposit their cargo. There had to be hundreds of strange beasts, each one a scrap of the hidden world just waiting to be revealed.

So many creatures were impossible to contain, even for Merlin. The enchanter grew red faced from weaving an increasingly complex spell. It forced some of the creatures back through the breach, but just as many streamed past. With a sinking stomach, Arthur saw the television cameras fasten on a griffin wheeling in the sky.

He rounded on Talvaric. "Call them back!"

The fae raised his hands in a mock-helpless gesture. "They're yours to protect, Pendragon. They're all part of the mortal realms, even if they are magical."

Arthur ignored the statement. The attack was meant to overwhelm their defenses, and it was doing a good job. He had to stop the onslaught of creatures, and the fastest way to close the portal was to cut off its supply of power. Excalibur in hand, he rushed Talvaric.

Swords sang as they clashed, the fae's saber snaking through the air to meet Excalibur. Arthur had battled fae before and knew their fighting style, but Talvaric was quick and strong. Arthur's focus narrowed until nothing else mattered but blade and pattern. He had to move faster than with any mortal swordsman, and one misstep would cost blood. At any other time, such an opponent would be a gift, but too much was at stake now. Gwen's life depended on victory.

The saber slashed the air and he ducked, feeling wind kiss his cheek. He parried, Excalibur shedding sparks as blades scraped together. Arthur forced the fae's blade away and circled the tip with his own, following with a thrust that could have skewered an ox. Talvaric stumbled back, falling into a roll that returned him to his feet yards away.

"Well done," the fae said with a panting grin.

His eyes gleamed with excitement, but there was fear, as well. They were evenly matched and Arthur guessed he wasn't used to that. Then Arthur's instincts flared when he saw a flash of deviltry flicker in Talvaric's gaze.

"Look out!" Merlin cried from behind Arthur.

Arthur ducked, and it saved his life. Fangs snapped the air where his head had been moments before. Arthur spun, lifting Excalibur in both hands. He nearly dropped it from sheer surprise.

He'd never seen a manticore outside paintings, but there was no question what the thing before him was. It was the size of a lion, with reddish fur, but a scorpion's barbed tail curled above its back. Black bat wings flared from its shoulders, beating hard to keep it aloft. The noise was like a steady roll of thunder broken only by its blaring, cawing cry. The worst feature was its face, which might have once been human. Whatever had made the manticore—surely it wasn't natural?—had bent and stretched the features into a muzzle crammed with multiple rows of sharklike teeth.

The manticore dived, slashing with claws unsheathed. A spear would have been a better weapon against such an enemy, but Arthur used what he had, leaping into the air to deliver his blow. The tip caught the creature's belly, sending it bolting into the sky. That gave Arthur just enough time to spin back to Talvaric, sure there would be another attack from the fae. Instead, Arthur saw the fae dive into his own portal.

Talvaric had Gwen, and he was getting away. Furious, Arthur bounded forward, hand outstretched to grab him. The two men regarded each other for a fraction of a second, one will testing the other. Arthur expected mockery, or a wild grin, but there was none of that. Talvaric's expression held the cool calculation of a mathematician working out his figures. He was certain everything would end according to his plan.

That he was correct, this time. He grasped both edges of the portal as if they were curtains and drew them together with a flick of his wrists. The portal stitched itself shut in a blaze of light, leaving Arthur behind. Simple grass and pavement took the place of shimmering magic. Arthur spun, dark rage crawling through him.

The manticore swooped, bellowing its trumpeting call. Arthur charged, using the momentum to power his blade. Luck was against him this time, the clack of claws against steel the only contact. He turned the motion into another upward swipe, this time catching the deadly barbed tail. Screaming, the manticore swerved in midair, the damaged appendage spraying blood. The beast rolled in the air, doubling back to make good its revenge.

Arthur readied himself, wishing one more time for a spear's extra reach. But this time the manticore dodged toward Merlin, lashing its injured tail. As the tip swung the enchanter's way, barbs flew as if ejected from a crossbow. One stuck in Merlin's side. He stiffened and fell, shaking as a seizure swept over him. *Poison!*

Fury drowned Arthur in a red haze. This time Excalibur sliced all the way through the creature's tail and the beast screamed in agony. It stooped like an owl, claws extended, but Arthur's armor saved him as the hind legs kicked with razor claws. But where the steel kept his skin whole, it couldn't stop the impact. Arthur skidded to the pavement before the manticore flapped skyward, trumpeting its pain. It banked awkwardly, the missing tail skewing its ability to steer, and disappeared over the midway.

Arthur scrambled to Merlin, placing a hand on the enchanter's chest to feel for breaths. It was there, but faint. With a savage curse, Arthur pulled the barb from his friend's side. The wound wasn't deep, though it released a trickle of blood. "Merlin?"

There was no response. The enchanter's skin was clammy and his eyes were closed. Meanwhile, screams rose from the crowd as a flock of gargoyles tormented a tour group. One man was swinging at the bat-like creatures with his selfie stick. Arthur swore long and hard. The glamor Merlin cast had vanished.

Owen skidded to a stop beside them. "What can I do?" the knight asked. There was a long scratch on his forehead, but otherwise he looked unhurt.

"Call Clary. We need a witch's healing powers."

It was then Arthur saw the manticore circle around again and snatch the girl from the stroller. The pink unicorn balloon floated skyward as the mother screamed.

"And watch Merlin," Arthur ordered as he scrambled to his feet, already sprinting after the beast. He dodged through the crowd, scanning the sky. He glimpsed the manticore weaving past the Ferris wheel and roller coaster, working hard to stay aloft with the child in its claws.

Arthur jumped the turnstile to the rides, chain mail rattling as he landed. He was hot and sweating, but fear for the girl made him put on more speed. The creature was flying lower now, wings angling in a way that predicted a landing. Arthur sprinted toward the Merry Minstrel restaurant, fearing the worst.

The manticore landed in the middle of the restaurant's patio. Terrified patrons streaked past, barely noticing a man holding a huge sword. More were scrambling to crawl over the glass pony wall that separated the eatery from the crowds.

Chairs and tables tipped over. Food was strewn everywhere. In the middle crouched the manticore, the little girl trapped between its front paws. The child was sobbing, long wails punctuated by red-faced hiccups. She had sunshine hair like Gwen's, Arthur thought, hating Talvaric all the more.

Arthur delivered a single swift kick to the pony wall. The Plexiglas panel flew off its brackets with a clatter, bouncing once before it came to rest. When it saw Arthur, the manticore rose to its feet, looming over the child. Arthur couldn't help but glance at the stump of its tail.

"If you choose to return to your home in peace, I will see to it you get there in safety." Arthur made the words clear and loud, hoping manticores spoke English. He repeated himself in French, Greek and Latin, just in case.

There was no flicker of recognition in the creature's eyes. If anything, they looked insane, filled with formless rage. This wouldn't be as easy as helping the talking fox, who had been content with a can of tuna and an old shirt to sleep on. Worse, Arthur could hear the child's mother sobbing somewhere behind him.

This was up to Arthur. Merlin was down, the other knights were chasing their own monsters and Medievaland's security guards were—perhaps fortunately—nowhere in sight. He began advancing with slow, deliberate steps. This would either spook the creature or provoke it, but either way he had to get close enough to grab the girl. Why had the beast taken her? As a hostage? Parental instinct? Dinner? By the drool dripping from the creature's fangs, Arthur assumed the last.

"Let her go," he said softly, not sure he could be heard over the wailing child and the thousand clicks of smartphones taking pictures. He just kept talking, his voice as smooth and quiet as Excalibur was sharp.

The manticore snarled, the nightmarish teeth on full display. While the fangs were appalling, Arthur paid more attention to its stance, watching for any sudden shifts in weight that meant it was about to pounce. Of all its mismatched parts, the lion was at its core. It would be those instincts he had to watch out for. "Just back away," he said. "Then we can all go home."

Miraculously, it did take a step back. But then the manticore rushed him, bowling the girl over as it raced forward. Arthur barely got his sword up in time. Alarm surged through him as the manticore reared up, displaying paws like dinner plates. The thing cuffed him hard, claws scraping on his mail shirt. The links tore, slashing claws flaying the flesh beneath. Arthur staggered, his shoulder suddenly numb. Excalibur dropped to the ground, but before he could dive for it, the manticore lunged, knocking him flat. It landed with rib-cracking weight on his chest, but Arthur slid away, using speed to outmaneuver it. Confused, the manticore looked around for its prey but Arthur grabbed its rounded ears.

Arthur felt an instant of regret, but he twisted its head sharply. Bone crunched and the creature collapsed, neck broken. Arthur sagged, his mind and soul a blank for one heartbeat before the world rushed in.

Then he backed away from the monster and went to

the small girl, who was still crying. Ignoring his wounded shoulder, Arthur gathered her up from where she was stranded amid the broken china and carried her out of the mess. Her warm, soft weight was comforting, but he didn't get to hold her long. The child's mother was there, sobbing words that Arthur couldn't unravel through his exhaustion. She put her arms out for her daughter, relief and gratitude in every line of her body. Arthur surrendered the child.

"I suppose you want me to clean up the mess?" Merlin asked drily.

Arthur spun. "How are you up and walking?"

The enchanter's face was the shade of curdled milk. "I don't recommend manticore venom. It's like the hangover you get after a drinking party with trolls."

Merlin said something under his breath, and the manticore's body imploded into a pile of dust. Half a dozen curious onlookers leaped backward in alarm.

"The glamor fell when you were unconscious," Arthur said.

"My apologies. It's back under control," Merlin replied, his lips white with strain. "All but the most observant will think this was no more than a clever bit of showmanship."

Arthur put a hand on his shoulder to steady him. "Come with me. You need to sit down."

"We don't have time for that."

"I need a better plan," said Arthur.

"You think I can give you one?"

"I need you to open a portal. Gwen needs rescuing and Talvaric needs killing."

Merlin shrugged. "I think your plan is just fine."

Chapter 26

"The good news is that I know where Talvaric took Gwen," Merlin announced. They were in Arthur's SUV, speeding back to the hotel. "I had a look at the portal. He didn't bother to hide the new destination."

"Careless or overconfident." Arthur wasn't sure which was worse. Both said Talvaric wasn't concerned about retaliation. "What's the bad news?"

"Everything else."

That killed conversation for a few minutes. Eventually, Merlin cleared his throat. "Are you sure you want to do this?"

"I thought you said my plan was fine."

"In principle. I'm not liking the logistics. The moment you walk through the portal, you're on Talvaric's turf." Merlin's eyes drifted shut. With a wrench of guilt, Arthur saw the enchanter was still weak.

"There are many reasons I would rather not walk through the portal," Arthur said quietly.

"You prefer to fight on your own ground."

"I do." There was no point in lying. "And I know asking you to open it is a drain of power when you can least afford it."

Merlin chuckled. "It takes more than a manticore to put me out of action."

"You're my oldest friend." Arthur slowed for a red light, loathing modern traffic rules. "I don't take your well-being lightly."

"Appreciated, but I know you," Merlin agreed. "There's a reason you left your men behind to mop up the monsters, including the ones with microphones. You're sneaking off. Owen might be in his own particular zoological heaven with all the beasts at large, but the others would rather be at your side. Logically, they should be."

The light changed and Arthur stepped on the gas. "So?"

"The reason you're going solo is that Gwen is a problem only you can solve. This is really about you and her. Talvaric just happened to step in the middle of it."

"Talvaric is a maniac who wants to slaughter me on television," Arthur grumbled.

"He wants to kill a king," said Merlin. "He made it personal when he took your wife."

Arthur cast a glance at Merlin, whose amber eyes were open now. A familiar irritation crept over Arthur. Talking to Merlin was a mixed experience—half enlightenment, half confusion. "I don't see the difference."

"You're the King of Camelot, but you're also Arthur. And there is the real problem you face, beyond fae and lunatics and monsters. You've always been too much a king, and Gwen too little the queen. She's tried to wear the crown, to find her own way of fulfilling her role, but you haven't truly let her."

Arthur clenched the steering wheel in frustration. Gwen had said pretty much the same thing. "I've tried to protect her."

"Perhaps you should show her how to protect herself." Merlin's eyes drifted shut again. "Don't take away her self-respect."

Arthur's chest tightened. Gwen had been about to walk away and start her own life without him. All at once, the enormity of that unthinkable future hit him. Without her, there would be no adventures to conquer trolls, no clever solutions, no romance under the stars, none of her creative, curious spirit. She was beautiful, yes, but she was brave, stubborn, ingenious and always seeking new and better ways to look at everything, even if it was just a way to keep foxes out of the chicken coop. If she were gone, he'd be bereft.

She was his partner. Arthur's thoughts skipped a beat as he realized the truth. He'd never seen it before. *And I love her. This is what loving someone actually means.* What if she didn't want him now? What if—

Arthur pulled the SUV into the hotel parking lot and killed the motor. Merlin was right—his true challenge was making things right with Gwen. She would either forgive him, or he would have nothing.

Merlin shifted in his seat, easing his wounded side. "You need someone to remind you to be a man as well as a king. You need someone to share your burdens. Without that, it's easy to lose your way. And a lost monarch becomes little more than a tyrant."

Arthur was silent. *This is why Camelot requires a queen.* He sucked in a breath. "We had an arranged marriage. She never actually agreed to wed me."

"Fix it. You need her," Merlin added. "And that's why I'll risk sending you to Talvaric's home."

The knot in Arthur's gut eased. "Thank you, old friend." He'd faced Talvaric as a king, with defiance and principles. The next time they met, Arthur would face him as a man, battling to save the woman he loved.

"Then let's go." Merlin reached for the door handle when his phone rang. When he looked at the caller ID, his expression filled with an irritated disgust. "It's Clary."

The enchanter put the phone on speaker. "Aren't you supposed to be dragon-sitting?"

"I thought you said the magic on Rukon's cave would hold even if you fell asleep." Clary's voice was sharp.

"Of course it will," Merlin retorted, and then a horrified look stole over his features. "Although the fact that I was poisoned and passed out probably changed things."

"Whatever. Rukon isn't in his cage any longer," Clary said in the strained tone of one dealing with a very large lizard, "and he says he wants to go home now."

Arthur instantly saw the possibilities. He hadn't planned on taking backup, but… "Tell him I think we can arrange that."

The jeweled comb in Gwen's hand had long teeth that slid easily into the lock of her cell door. Unfortunately, they were carved from bone and didn't hold up to her attempts to force the pins. Gwen heard the snap of another tooth breaking. With a curse, she pulled the comb back through the bars and examined the damage. The comb was of fae design, rimmed in sapphires and very pretty. Unfortunately, it was now missing three teeth. Despondently, Gwen pushed it into her hair to hide the damage.

Gwen had washed and changed into the clothes Talvaric had provided, and the sapphire comb had come with the gown. She had put off changing for as long as possible, but eventually grime and stale sweat had made her reconsider. Besides that, defying Talvaric without a good reason was foolish.

As if merely thinking about the fae drew him forth, Talvaric's steps rang on the stone floor. Gwen straightened, shaking out her skirts. When he came into view, a pair of dryads followed at a respectful distance, their heads bowed.

"Aren't you a picture?" he said with a sly smile.

The tunic he wore was the same blue as her gown, with the same silver cord around the neck and wrists. The symbolism was plain, even if Clary would have condemned the coordinated outfits as too matchy-matchy. His green gaze swept from her hem to the combs in her hair. Gwen had seen that look before—possession, and it wasn't even for her own sake. Talvaric simply wanted to outrage Arthur.

Her skin crawled with disgust. *This is just another adventure,* she told herself. It was like being in the troll's lair, only worse because she was alone. She wanted Arthur's presence so badly it hurt. She'd been afraid in the mines, but there was a vast difference between then and now. Here, no one had her back.

Talvaric studied her expression with a faint smile. Cruelty lurked beneath the curve of his lips, a blade disguised but by no means sheathed. "Come. I have something to show you."

He took a key from his belt and unlocked the door. There only seemed to be one key, she noticed, but was careful to appear uninterested when he put it away and handed her out of her cage. They set off toward a different part of the house, the silent dryads shadowing their steps.

"I paid your world a visit today," he said conversationally.

"Did your journey have a purpose, my lord?" Gwen asked in her most polite tone.

"Certainly," he said, and added nothing more.

He was baiting her with the vague answer, but she refused to bite.

They passed through a gallery, where pictures might have hung. Instead, there were a lot of swords and she guessed he used it as a practice room for fencing. At the other end, a short flight of steps led to an octagonal chamber surrounded with windows. While most surfaces in the manor were painted white, the floor was a colorful pattern of blue and orange. The design was a starburst in a circle of hammered bronze and in the center was a plinth holding a crystal globe. Gwen knew at once it was a room for working magic. She had no powers of her own, but the energy in the air prickled her arms.

Talvaric stepped up to the globe and made a swiping gesture with one hand. The crystal fogged for an instant, and then the mist parted to reveal an outdoor scene of utter mayhem. A crowd of ordinary people milled about, ducking and screaming and trying to snap pictures with their phones. Above them, gargoyles flicked to and fro, diving with the speed and agility of swallows. Gwen's shoulders tensed. The creatures were harmless, until they weren't. In a pack, they could be savage.

"My world doesn't have live gargoyles," she said, doing her best to smother her horror. "What did you do?"

"I gave Camelot something to chew on. It wasn't my first intention, but Arthur refused to take me seriously."

Gwen looked up with a frown. "I find that hard to believe." Arthur despised the fae, but he would never discount them.

"Perhaps I'm saying this the wrong way. Let me try again." Talvaric tapped his chin with one finger, mimicking someone deep in thought. "He refused to give himself up to save your life, so I sent my beasts to show how serious I truly am. Does that make more sense?"

The fae's smirk deepened. *He refused to give himself up to save your life.* That was what Talvaric wanted her to hear. She wasn't loved. No one would come to rescue her.

Sick despair froze her veins. Arthur was king. Of course, he couldn't drop everything to mount a rescue. Wife or not, she was just one woman. One woman who would never give him the heir he needed. A woman who couldn't find it in her heart to trust him. The question wasn't whether Arthur would come, but why he would bother.

"You could have asked," she said lightly, even though her knees shook. "I could have told you he can't be manipulated for my sake."

Talvaric's eyes narrowed, a flush of anger creeping up his cheeks. "Then what good are you?"

None. "You should have sent spies to check your facts. If you want to be King of Faery, you should know that every good king has spies."

"I have this." Talvaric pointed to the crystal ball. "What I saw between you looked like love to me."

And love was a weapon he could use.

Gwen swallowed, thinking of the past days with Arthur, and trying not to think of Talvaric watching them through his crystal ball. What she'd shared with Arthur might have been love and maybe even a brief partnership, but she would never admit it to this monster. "You have no soul. What would you know of true affection?"

Talvaric's eyes met hers, and there was murder in them. Gwen's blood turned to ice, but she set her jaw. Pride refused to let her look away.

Then the windows behind them shattered. Shards of

glass fountained in a thousand tiny, stinging pieces, catching in clothes and hair and biting exposed skin. Gwen ducked, shielding her face as her ears rang with a deafening roar. A sudden rush of wind brought the scent of forest and smoke. Dragon smoke.

A furtive glance told her Talvaric had forgotten her. His pale face was slack, eyes transfixed on whatever was behind her. Gwen spun around to see Rukon's giant green form outside the window. The dragon was flapping in place, toothy jaws bared in a snarl.

Gwen bolted. After enjoying the freedom of light modern clothes, the gown felt unbearably heavy, tangling her feet as she moved. All the same, she flew through the gallery with the swords, bursting past a clutch of dryads. They watched her with curiosity, but didn't move to stop her.

"Run!" Gwen called out. "The dragon has come for Talvaric."

She had a small window of time to get out of the manor house and find the portal Rukon had used. Hopefully, it would take her home.

She turned, and turned again, frustrated because every room and corridor was the same featureless white. Before long Gwen suspected she was going in circles.

One more burst of speed took her into a long, long hallway that sloped downward. It was wide and high ceilinged, more of a tunnel than any household corridor. Her first instinct was to retreat. This wasn't the way outside, and she'd had bad luck with underground lairs. Still, she stopped, poised on tiptoe and holding her breath. There was a sound coming from the darkness that reminded her of…peeping chicks?

Given what she'd seen in Talvaric's manor, there was no telling what was down there. Gwen wished she'd grabbed a sword when she'd raced through the weapons room, but all she'd been thinking about was freedom. Which was what she should have been thinking about now, except it wasn't just her own safety that mattered. She had to consider all the creatures in Talvaric's zoo. Some of them were dangerous, but none of them deserved to be his captive—and whatever was down here sounded as if it was very, very young.

She ran forward on light feet, glad the passageway was smooth and straight. There was a soft, rosy light coming from the other end, throwing just enough illumination to find her way. A slight crook at the end of the tunnel angled into a large natural cave. Gwen stopped, grabbing the stone wall for support. Her lips parted in surprise.

Elosta, the blue dragon, lay curled around a clutch of eggs, and they were hatching.

Chapter 27

The fight was on, and Arthur was betting that a willing dragon was far deadlier than a dragon forced to obey.

Whatever magical leash the fae used on Rukon had been weakened by exposure to Merlin's spells. As for the rest of the fae's hold—it was a two-edged sword. Talvaric had Rukon's mate. That was a powerful control, but it was also a reason to fight.

Merlin had opened a new portal—one big enough for a dragon—that sent them just outside Talvaric's manor, on the lush green of the lawn. Rukon had gone through first, but only by seconds, and was aiming for the north end of the house. As Arthur followed, the portal snapped shut, magic tingling like the air before a storm. Arthur took off at a run, aiming for the other end of the sprawling structure. If Talvaric had any wits, he'd run in the opposite direction from the dragon's attack—and straight onto Arthur's blade.

Arthur circled the perimeter of the place, looking for a way in with no success. Frustration mounted quickly. The house didn't simply lack a formal entry—there wasn't even a tradesman's door. With a stable and gardens and large property to maintain, there should have been many ways for the servants to come and go. Unfortunately, they were invisible.

Arthur drew Excalibur and stood with his back to the manor. In the sword's bright blade, the reflection of the house was clear and, as always, the charmed sword cut through magic. Arthur saw the entry and its guard—a creature that resembled something between an insect and a uniformed footman. As he turned and stormed toward the entry, the glamor broken, the creature scuttled away.

The door wasn't locked, and Arthur was inside just in time to hear Rukon's outraged roar. A surge of panic sharpened his focus. If he was going to find Gwen, he would have to work quickly.

Gwen stood openmouthed. The eggs were so large she could have barely held one in both her arms, and the shells were iridescent shades of blues, purples and greens. The colors reminded her of the riches of the goblins' treasure hoard, but this was even more wonderful. The rosy light was coming from the eggs themselves. The gentle heat of the cavern was boosted every so often when Elosta breathed licks of flame into the air.

The tiny dragonets nearly made her laugh out loud. They were as big as full-grown cats, if cats had bat wings and necks as long as their tails—but they were clearly newborns. Four or five were tumbling around the clutch, clumsy but determined, with their translucent wings spread wide for balance. If all the eggs were viable, there would be a dozen young, each matching the color of its shell.

Arthur's story of Elosta plummeting from the sky jarred Gwen's memory. She had nearly perished, and these eggs would have gone cold and dead. A glance at the dragon showed her wings were charred, the fine membranes that webbed them in tatters.

"Human?" Elosta said, the single word filled with warning. Gwen had never heard a female dragon speak. The voice was feminine, but as resonant as Rukon's.

"Pardon me," said Gwen, giving a curtsy because she was the intruder in this mother's very private domain. "I am Guinevere, Queen of Camelot."

"Why are you here?" the dragon asked, clearly suspicious.

There was no time to waste, so Gwen explained as quickly as she could. "I'm glad to see you well," she finished.

"I was spared from death so that my eggs might live. The fae is careful of his investment." Her tone was dark with anger.

"Perhaps he did this one thing right. Your children are beautiful."

The dragon made a soft crooning noise that didn't fit with her size or the sharpness of her teeth. Or maybe it did, Gwen thought as Elosta righted a floundering youngster with her long snout.

"Thank you, human, your words are courteous," said the dragon. "Someday your children will be beautiful, as well."

The statement made Gwen flinch. "I'm afraid not."

"No? I see the shadows of younglings around you. Dragons are rarely mistaken in these things."

"I was cursed by a witch." Gwen drew breath with effort. "Even Talvaric said I will mother no heirs."

The fae's name drew a plume of angry smoke from

the dragon's snout. "He has no gift of prophecy, but he thrives on the ability to see another's fears. Do not take his word on this."

A tiny blue dragon peeped agreement—or perhaps it just peeped. Gwen wasn't sure when they began to understand spoken language.

"How did you find my den, Queen of Camelot?"

"I am seeking the way out of this place. Rukon is attacking the house and I got away."

"Rukon is here?" Elosta rose to her feet in excitement, though she was still careful where she placed her talons.

It was then Gwen saw the slender gold chain that bound the dragon's hind foot to the cavern wall. It had to be magic, because nothing that flimsy would have worked otherwise. The dragon saw her looking. "Yes, he has me bound, and one day he will bind my heart by stealing my children."

"No," said Gwen. "Not if Rukon has any say in the matter. He's coming for you."

"And where is the King of Camelot?" asked Elosta. "Surely he is coming for his queen?"

Gwen straightened her shoulders. "A king is wherever his people need him the most." But she wasn't certain of her husband.

Arthur was looking for Gwen, but he found Talvaric first. He'd just entered a long room hung with weapons when the fae slid to a stop at the other end of the space, panting. Arthur drew up short, surprised. The fae's singed appearance spoke of a narrow escape. Tiny shards of glass glittered on his hair and clothes as he moved.

A roar shook the manor, shaking plaster loose from the walls. Talvaric's panicked gaze swept from Arthur to the windows. A dark shadow flicked over the lawn, marking the circling dragon's passage.

"You've annoyed a lot of people," Arthur observed. "Especially the wrong ones."

Talvaric's response was to dart to the wall and snatch a blade from a rack of swords. He moved with a limp—had that cut come from the dragon, or perhaps the glass?— but Arthur knew better than to count that too heavily in a fight. Fae could fight past pain like no others.

"What have you done with my wife?" Arthur asked, swishing Excalibur to loosen his injured shoulder.

"So you came for her, after all. How endearing." Talvaric grinned, his panic suspended long enough to enjoy the gibe.

"Gwen was always coming home."

"Not when you refuse to obey my rules."

Arthur made a disgusted noise. "Grow up. Answer the question. Where is she?"

Talvaric's lip curled. "Beat it out of me."

With pleasure. Arthur grinned as Talvaric launched toward him. Their skirmish at Medievaland had been intense, but this fight was the one that mattered.

They were staggeringly different swordsmen, with distinct styles and weapons. Arthur was quick for a man in armor, but Talvaric's attack was like water—swift, changeable, seeking the tiniest gaps in Arthur's guard. Arthur's blows hammered in return. A two-handed great sword like Excalibur was made for strength, not speed.

Arthur brought Excalibur down in a mighty, two-handed slash. Talvaric dodged and rolled, laughing as he did it. The fae was a natural acrobat, and knew it. The fae lunged, turning the motion into a cutting blow with a twist of his wrist. It caught the underside of Arthur's arm, finding a slight gap between mail and plate. Arthur roared in pain, but used the sound as a distraction. With a backslash, he left a wide slice along Talvaric's ribs. The fae screamed.

Talvaric's blue tunic was instantly soaked in red, but he moved as fast as ever, shrinking back from Arthur with a string of Faery invective. Arthur swung again, but Excalibur whistled through empty air. Talvaric bolted for safety. With an angry roar, Arthur charged after him.

He was not as fast, and in armor he was nowhere as quiet. He kept the fae in sight for several turnings through the anonymous white house, catching a glimpse of the blue tunic or the swing of Talvaric's long white braid. Eventually, though, Arthur was left panting and lost. Humans could never match a fae in a footrace. However, they weren't helpless.

Arthur's gaze fell on the trail of scarlet drops on the stark white floor. Talvaric had drunk a mortal soul, and was experiencing emotions after a long time without. Apparently, he'd forgotten how panic could make one careless. Arthur began to run again, but this time he knew exactly where to go. He hoped, desperately, that the fae would lead him to Gwen.

The blood drops led past cages filled with creatures that left him sad and disturbed. A barguest, black furred and red eyed, peered from the back of its cage, shuddering in fright. He passed dryads standing helpless, as if their wills had been ripped away. They should have been dancing in the woods, far beyond the sight of anyone but the moon. But then he heard Rukon's frustrated roar, and the crash of the dragon smashing its way into the manor. There would be justice.

When the path descended down a long, broad tunnel leading under the earth, Arthur heard the roar of another dragon. The sound rang off the walls, the echoes magnifying it until it became a physical force. After that he slowed, sword raised to strike. He could smell smoke and blood and the leathery scent of a dragon's lair. The last time he'd ventured into one, he'd been reminded that humans were a nice-sized snack.

He swung around the corner, ready for anything. A glance took in the female dragon, her young and Talvaric holding a sword to Gwen's throat. Gwen's eyes were wide, the blue almost shocking in her pale face.

Arthur did not stop to think. He moved with a speed Talvaric did not, could not expect. The sword went flying from the fae's hand, taken by the heavy great sword with the delicacy of a rapier. It shouldn't have been possible, but Arthur was first among the mortal swordsmen for a reason. He understood the value of surprise.

He could have killed the fae then, but he reached for Gwen instead. Talvaric thrust her into Arthur's arms and ran, crossing just out of the reach of Elosta's snapping jaws. Arthur caught Gwen's weight against him for a delicious moment, savored the scent of her skin and hair. It was only for a single heartbeat, but it was long enough for the fae to snatch up his blade.

Arthur spun with a snarl, pushing Gwen to safety behind him. Talvaric's eyes flew wide at the sound, delivered with the savagery of a man at his limit. When the fae had taken Gwen, he'd pushed Arthur beyond any expectation of mercy. One more time, the fae fled.

But Rukon was at the other end of the tunnel, and he was coming to protect his mate. Talvaric stopped, arms flying wide in an effort to stop his forward motion. Eyes red with fury glared from the darkness. The fae raised his blade and turned to face Arthur, ready to make one final defense.

A series of images flashed through Arthur's mind: Rukon, Elosta, the barguest, the dryads, Senec wounded and trembling. Gwen, with the blade to her throat. Feeling its even, perfect balance, Arthur swung Excalibur, showing what a great sword was made for. Talvaric's head flew wide.

Silence rang as loud as any roar. Fountaining blood, the fae's body fell. Arthur took a step back, and then another as Rukon's flames turned the remains to ash, scouring the world clean of Talvaric's presence. But Arthur was not quite done. He spun on his heel, once more hefting the long blade that was so much a part of him. With a shout of victory, he slashed it downward, severing the chain that bound the blue dragon. Light flared as Excalibur's power severed the spell, burning the links apart. Elosta roared in triumph, bounding free to twine her long, sinuous neck with Rukon's.

Slowly, Arthur let the weight of Excalibur drag down his arm until the point dug into the stone floor. Gradually, his pounding heart slowed, the furious thunder abating until he could breathe at a normal pace. He leaned into his sword hilt, exhaustion finally making its claws felt.

Gentle hands touched his arm and he lifted his head. Gwen was there, her eyes shining with tears. "You came for me." Her voice was soft, almost wondering. "You saved my life."

"Of course I did." He tried to make it sound matter-of-fact, but his voice shook.

She cupped her hands around his face, leaning close so their foreheads touched and breath mingled. "Thank you," she whispered.

Arthur said nothing. He could not, with Gwen's tears burning against his skin. Common words would have been sacrilege.

Chapter 28

The dragon's fire had destroyed the key to the cages, and it took time to find the spare. It was dark when the creatures were finally freed. Not one made any move to harm their fellows, and each bowed before the King and Queen of Camelot, for he bore the name and duty of the Pendragon, protector of magical beasts. After they paid homage, they ran one by one into the darkness, vanishing back to wherever they belonged. Only the barguest stayed an extra moment to lick Gwen's hand before he fled.

"He knows I like dogs," Gwen said, but Arthur looked dubious.

The only part of the manor that remained occupied was Elosta's underground cavern. She could not fly until her wings healed, and she had to remain until the eggs were fully hatched. But that was safe beneath the ground, and it was time for the dryads to have their say. Gwen watched from a safe distance as they placed their long fingers against the walls and seemed to grow into the stonework, long tendrils crumbling the structure just as roots crack pavement. But rather than taking years, the process took minutes. In no time, Talvaric's manor—and prison—was reduced to rubble. The dryads cleared the tunnel mouth for the dragons to come and go, and then they, too, vanished into the woods.

After that, Arthur and Gwen used the portal to return home. Clary, who had been waiting, drove them to Arthur's apartment. The destination was Gwen's choice. "I can't go back to the hotel," she said. "I know Talvaric's gone, but I'd still be jumping at shadows."

Still, the apartment held memories, too. Their reunion. The first awkward night when she'd shut Arthur out of his bedroom. Walking out to face the knights who'd left her behind while they'd traveled to the future.

Gwen stood in the living room, still in the blue gown Talvaric had made her wear. It was dark outside, the city lights beautiful but as alien to Gwen as the place she'd just left. Someday this world would look like home, she supposed. Just not yet.

Arthur came out of his office. "I phoned Merlin to let him know we're safely home. He'll tell the others."

"Good," she replied.

"The knights rounded up most of the creatures," Arthur added. "Merlin and Clary have been sending them back through the portal. Some probably got away, but no one's sure."

"No innocents were hurt?"

"Not seriously, or not that we know of. We were lucky." He looked tired, his hair rumpled and his feet bare. His armor was piled in the corner, waiting to be cleaned.

They stared at one another for a long moment, neither wanting to say more. The crisis was past, the villain vanquished and even the barguest was safe. She should have been content.

And yet nothing had changed. Not really. The last time they'd been together, they'd parted in anger. "I'm sorry," she said, her voice cracking on the words. "I don't know if I can change who I am."

If the shift in topic startled him, he didn't show it. "Would you be surprised if I said I don't want you to?" His smile was wistful. "You keep me humble."

She wasn't certain how to take that, and stiffened. "I'm not your possession. I can't be put on display or locked up whenever you like."

His gaze lowered, a flush spreading over his cheekbones. "No."

She could see he was sorry, but her hurt went too deep for a single word to cure it. He'd left her too many times. "I can't be the queen you want."

"And who is she?"

"Someone else."

He choked a laugh. "I don't want someone else. I want the difficult woman who fought beside me in Zorath's mine."

Her breath caught, not sure she could trust the intensity in his eyes. "You never wanted her before."

"I never let myself know her until now." He reached forward, running his fingers down the length of her arm. The featherlight touch made her shiver. "I want that woman, every day and every night."

"Are you sure?"

"Only the best of my knights have your wits and nerve. You and I make good partners."

In other words, she'd proven something in the Crystal Mountains. She suspected they'd both changed perspectives over the last few days. "Do I deserve such praise after keeping secrets from you?"

His expression grew grave. "What you're really asking is whether you can finally trust me."

"And whether you'll ever trust me back," she said in a small voice. It was true. Everything he said was true. "In some ways, I've been selfish. I'm one person, and I never understood how many lives you touch. I wanted too much from you."

"No." He shook his head. "If anyone deserved my best, it was you. I'm the one at fault, and I would give much to atone for that."

"I don't want to be right at your expense. That was never what I wanted."

He didn't answer. Instead, he went to the corner, where his armor lay in a jumble, and picked up Excalibur. When he turned back to her, he held the blade balanced across his palms.

"There are moments of faith. Moments when the only choice is to leap into the future. Should I pull the sword from the stone and rule Camelot, or walk away and live a peaceful life? Those decisions make us what we are, and nothing should ever take them away."

Gwen stood very still, barely breathing, and wondered where he was going with this.

"You were never given a choice about your future. When it came time to wed, others selected a husband for you. That wasn't just."

He fell to one knee, offering Excalibur in outstretched hands. Reflexively, she took the sword, balancing the weight with care.

"My lady, this blade is everything I am—my weapon, my power, the symbol of my rank and right to rule. I surrender it to you as a king to his queen, and as a man to his woman. Return Excalibur to me when I prove myself the husband you deserve."

He reached up, cupping her hands where she held the sword, helping her bear the weight of it. "Will you marry me, Gwen?"

He was giving her a choice, the freedom to go or stay. She'd never had this decision, never known what she might have chosen if her father hadn't sent her to Camelot to be the queen. And here, in this modern age, the options were beyond counting. If she struck out on her own, she could be anything.

Yet this wasn't a flight from the familiar into the unknown. It was from one unknown to another. Camelot was utterly changed, even if the dangers facing it were just as deadly as before. The knights lived in secret, using their wits as much as their blades. The trappings of monarchy meant nothing here. If she stayed, she would have to work hard to help this new Camelot thrive.

Gwen was numb, her body tingling with shock. Arthur was giving her the power to direct her future. This was her moment to pull her own sword from the stone, and leap.

She met his blue eyes. There was uncertainty in them, but there was also hope—and love. He was the same man that he had always been, but in this strange time and place they had finally seen the truth in each other.

It was like coming home, but to the home and the husband she'd always wanted.

"Yes," Gwen said, and pressed Excalibur into his hands.

His eyes grew darker as he lowered the sword to the floor. It rattled slightly as he released it, the sound loud in the sudden, profound silence. It was as if the air had suddenly grown thick.

Arthur rose and stepped over the sword to take her in his arms. "Gwen," he whispered. "My wife and queen."

His hands slid from her waist up her ribs, caressing her. She felt suddenly fragile, as if made of eggshell or the finest glass. And yet, here she was, spanning centuries to be in his arms again. Queen Guinevere wasn't so easy to leave behind as all that. The thought made her laugh even as her throat ached with tears. It wasn't unhappiness, just the relief of a long journey successfully completed.

"What are you thinking?" he asked. "You have the oddest expression."

"I belong with you." When it really mattered, he'd crossed worlds to come for her, to be her hero.

"Yes." His smile was confident. "I never doubted it."

"My character is flawed," she said. "I'm independent and willful."

"I know. I've always made the error of trying to control you. I think I'll count on you instead."

He stopped her mouth with his before she could say more. When she closed her eyes, she saw him opening cage after cage of beasts, great and small, horrifying and beautiful. He had saved them all, and he had held her hand as they watched them run free. Finally, in that moment, she'd understood why he was king, but also who he was as a man.

The kiss lasted a very long time, and her hands found the hem of his T-shirt, warming themselves against the heat of his bare skin. The sensation brought tension to her belly, as if the fire in him had passed through her palms and into her core. Impatience prompted her to finger the buckle at his waist. His stomach tightened at her touch, hard and vulnerable at once. She stroked the ridged muscle with her fingertips, pleased by his intake of breath.

His lips ran down her throat, tasting her. She let her head fall back, nuzzling the softness of his hair as it fell against her cheek. And then his mouth was on her collarbone and his thumbs stroking over the swell of her breasts. She leaned into it, the sweet ache inside her turning liquid. When his caress roved over her nipples, she shivered. Moaning softly, she arched her back for more.

"Are you going to shut the door on me tonight?" he teased.

"Perhaps not." She nipped the lobe of his ear. "Prove to me you're worthy of entrance to my bower."

"Shall I come as a supplicant to Your Majesty?"

"Supplicants are as common as sheep in the field. I think something with more resolve."

In a swift motion, he caught her up in his arms. Gwen's stomach swooped as her feet left the floor and she instinctively clung to his shoulders as he carried her into his bedroom. The bedside lamp was on. She hadn't seen the room since she'd slept in it, and a bit of the confusion from that first night returned—but only for an instant. As soon as her toes touched the carpet, she was in his arms once more—and when Arthur kissed, it was impossible to think about anything but him.

He pulled off his shirt, revealing the angry, scored flesh where the manticore had clawed him. She traced the skin around the hurt, then over the swell of his chest, where older scars seamed his skin. He had a warrior's physique, muscled from the long use of weapons. Her mouth went dry, as it always did when he offered his body for her pleasure. Even after years together, each time seemed new.

"He gave you this dress?" Arthur asked, his voice so low she barely heard the words.

"Yes."

He gripped the wide neck of the gown and tore it in a single, angry wrench. When he released the fabric, the garment fell away, leaving Gwen in her chemise. She instantly felt cleaner. Nothing of Talvaric's had a place here. "Thank you," she said.

The rest of their clothes vanished soon after. Gwen fell on the bed, reaching up for Arthur to join her. He stretched out beside her, the length of him a hot line against her side. For a moment, she was lost in the sensation of touch—smooth and rough, firm and yielding, the crispness of hair and softness of lips. He arched over her, settling her back into the pillow. The musk of his skin was a familiar mix of leather, steel and man. She buried her face in his shoulder, wanting more.

His palms found her breasts, kneading and caressing until her core burned with new heat. Gwen bowed her back, stretching her arms above her head and inviting him to do more. She felt flushed and heavy, her nipples aching from his attention. He nuzzled her, licking and sucking and loving her until she grew restless, needing to feel him in other places.

His hand stroked her belly, working its way down and down until he found the wetness between her legs. She startled under his touch, sparks of sensation firing through her. But he didn't hurry to slake that need, nibbling his way over her skin instead, every touch of tongue and teeth building the tension inside her. She kissed and squirmed and rubbed him back, the taste of him like a drug. She was lost in him, hypnotized and addicted.

When he at last turned his full attention to her aching core, Gwen was slick with sweat. His mouth teased her, parting flesh that tingled with every gust of his breath. As his fingers slid inside, her body tried to grip them, but they weren't nearly enough to satisfy. She was slick and swollen and greedy. His thumb stroked her into spasms of pleasure as tears of release escaped her lids, trickling down her temples and into her hair.

"Please," she begged, just once because she was a queen, and because his mouth covered hers before more words were possible.

He slid inside, the fullness of it coaxing a groan from her throat. She gripped him, digging her fingers into the hard planes of his back. He loomed over her, but she wrapped herself around him, binding herself with desire. She was already drunk on it, loose and eager with the heat of their bodies. When he began to move, they surged as one.

Gwen's mind slipped then, blank of everything but the need to move with him, to release the gnawing wildness spiraling up inside her. Her breasts brushed against the roughness of his chest, the sensation a pleasure and a goad at once. She bit his shoulder. There was no explanation for it beyond savage glee.

Cursing at the pain, Arthur held her hips, angling her body. He had given, and now he took possession. With driving thrusts, his rhythm quickened and broke as he plundered her. The mad thing inside Gwen sprang free. She cried out, speared on the sharp pleasure of her surrender. He plunged once, twice more before he stiffened and shuddered.

Afterward, they curled together like a single being, their limbs tangled. Gwen's face buried in the crook of Arthur's shoulder, the world beyond the bed a strange and distant thing. She listened to Arthur's slow, deep breathing as sleep claimed him. The darkness wrapped them like a soft, black cloak.

For once, Gwen's thoughts were still. She had drawn her sword and leaped, and she had landed in the arms of the man who was meant to catch her. With a smile tugging at her lips, the Queen of Camelot drifted into peaceful slumber.

Chapter 29

Arthur woke to a kiss. It was an excellent kiss, bringing him to full wakefulness in seconds. Some dim and distant part of him was aware of aches and bruises from yesterday's battles, but all of him that mattered was focused elsewhere. Guinevere was naked and wrapping her clever fingers around his shaft.

The morning light bathed her, making her skin glow as if white fire burned inside. Pale blue veins showed in the most tender places—her temples, her throat, her breasts. He kissed them all, keenly aware of the life flowing so close to his lips. Gwen was a never-ending wealth of sensory experience. Soft skin tempted him and the rich scent of her tantalized him. Fair hair sheeted like a gold river around her, teasing as it swung to obscure the most interesting views.

He was hard in her hands, every part of him straining to claim her again. But this time, she was in command, her hot tongue refining his desires. "What are you planning, woman?" he asked, his voice dropping into the region of a growl.

She drew herself up, straddling his waist. "You know I have an interest in how things work," she said lightly, lowering herself so that she slid neatly over him.

He swore, the tight heat of her so perfect that his pulse stuttered with pleasure. But then she rolled her hips. He reached up and she caught his hands, placing them over her breasts. Telling him what she wanted. As a knight sworn to serve his lady, Arthur had to obey. He caressed her as she caressed him, exploring and testing every angle and motion. Arthur held himself in careful control, letting her discover her pleasure, but he had to clench his teeth.

When she began pushing and rocking, he thought he might die. She sat high and proud like the Amazons of legend. Every undulating motion rippled her belly and swayed her breasts, the nipples winking from the curtain of her hair. Years in the saddle had made Gwen fit and strong, and the glove of her body around him squeezed with every move.

She came with a soft, gasping cry and then sank, draping herself across his chest in a pool of silken hair. He loved her languor and the elasticity of her pleasured body, but mostly he loved the fact she'd taken what she wanted. He rolled her over so that she spread out beneath him, boneless and sated.

"Did you solve your engineering problem?" he murmured in her ear.

She gasped a laugh, surging to life beneath him. "What do you think?"

"A theory has to be tested more than once."

She wriggled away, playing now. Her eyes sparked with laughter. The sight of it shook him deep and hard, for it had been so long since he'd seen that look. When she slid off the bed, he followed, drawn by an invisible thread that refused to allow distance between them.

He caught her, trapping her between his body and the cool white of the bedroom wall. She kissed him standing on her toes and holding his face in her hands. It was frank, her lust unfettered. He was tinder in its path.

Arthur hitched her up, hooking her legs around his hips and bracing her back against the wall. Her nails dug into his shoulders as he pushed into her. Her head flung back, throat bare to him. He pushed and pushed, stirring her as he might a banked fire. A flush of heat crept up her pale skin, staining it pink. Only then did he let go, releasing himself and filling her as she melted against him, hot, sensual and shivering with pleasure.

"Gwen," he whispered.

"I don't think I can stand." She let loose a throaty giggle as she drooped against him. Her eyes were closed, the sweep of her lashes like wing tips against her cheeks.

Arthur's chest ached with the miracle of her. He had stepped between worlds for her, but it seemed such a paltry thing compared to her courage. He had lost everything—his kingdom, his castles and his armies. No one in this time recognized him as their king. All he had left was his war against the fae.

But Gwen had stayed. When it had counted most, she had chosen him.

He kissed her softly, reverently, loving her with all his being. "What can I do to please you?"

She twined her arms around his neck. "I'm still new to this world. Show me what you like."

"I'd love a hot shower."

Their eyes met, and he could see her working out the possibilities. Watching her think was arousing all on its own.

"Together?" she asked.

"Of course."

Her grin was wicked.

"I think," said Merlin, fussing with the sleeves of his brand-new enchanter's robes, "the happiest person in all the realms is Medievaland's accountant."

"The park is certainly busy," Gwen agreed, eyeing Merlin's costume. The park had hired him as part of the troupe of entertainers, and wearing the outfit was part of the job. The robes were covered with moons and stars and had come with a tall staff and a pointed hat that he refused to wear.

It was nearly two months since Talvaric's defeat. The knights and ladies of Camelot were waiting inside the service building next to the tourney grounds. Outside, a noisy throng of guests filled the large white pavilion where that day's event would be held. Banquets at Medievaland had always been sellout events, but now there was a waiting list for tickets. The recent media attention, for good or ill, had brought the theme park to national attention.

"What about the lawsuits?" she asked nervously.

Merlin shrugged. "No one was actually hurt beyond a good scare, and there's no physical evidence that any of Talvaric's beasts were anything but fancy puppets. The park settled with the family of the child the manticore abducted, and they're paying a fine for some sort of violation of the peace, but they'll make the money up a hundred times over with increased sales."

Merlin turned to Clary, who was wearing a medieval costume but still typing on her smartphone. "What do the mysterious gods of the interwebs say?"

"We're still trending on the top five things to know about King Arthur. There are always a few trolls, but—"

"Trolls?" Gawain spun around from where he was chatting with his brother.

Beaumains put a hand on his sword. "Where?"

Clary rolled her eyes. "Not that kind."

The conversation was interrupted by Arthur's arrival. He was wearing a tunic and cloak of deep claret trimmed with gold. Excalibur hung at his side. When he saw Gwen, his step quickened and a smile dawned in his eyes. She held out her hands and he took them, kissing her lightly.

"You look breathtaking," he said, his gaze drinking her in as if they had been apart for weeks, not hours.

"Thank you." She'd had a dress made for the banquet, though she'd added some of her own touches. The fabric was a shimmering confection of palest yellow—definitely not a product of her own time, but authenticity was hardly required. If she could have the best of both worlds, she would.

He looped her hand over his arm, still smiling. They'd both done a lot of that in the past few weeks. "Any last words of advice for a debut performer?" she asked. This was the first time she'd appear in a Medievaland show.

"Just remember they all want to fall in love with you, and who can blame them?"

With that, he gave a signal, and trumpets sounded the arrival of the king and queen. They stepped into the night and walked beneath garlands of glittering lights. Arm in arm, they were the head of a procession, followed by Merlin and Clary and then the other knights falling in behind. Fans cheered and cameras flashed. For a moment, Gwen was startled, but then she realized she already knew what to do. She'd been a queen before, and this was just the same. She smiled and waved, and caught the glances of as many people as she could, giving them a moment of personal connection.

They sat at the high table, while the guests were seated around trestle tables that formed an open square inside the tent. Senec the fox sat in Sir Owen's lap, pointed snout sniffing the air as platters were brought by liveried servants. The pair had been inseparable since the knight had bound the animal's wounds. With some coaxing, Senec had been convinced not to speak in public, but he'd refused to be left out of the fun—or the food. Gwen watched the fox snag a chicken wing and disappear under the table. The sight gave her a feeling of contentment—Camelot might no longer be a sprawling kingdom, but those who needed its protection still found welcome.

A servant offered her a basket of rolls and she took one. Even after many meals in the modern age, she marveled at the light texture of the bread. "So," she said to Arthur, "what is it that Merlin will do here?"

"Special effects," Arthur said with a twinkle. "At first he said pandering to the entertainment industry was beneath him, but even an enchanter has to eat. Compared to his other clients, we're schoolchildren."

Gwen frowned. "Who are these other clients?"

"Those members of the hidden world with no other place to go."

In other words, outcasts and criminals. She shivered slightly, and Arthur picked up her hand, kissing it. "We've had our difficulties with Merlin. Do you mind that he is once again in our circle?"

"No." She was a little surprised to find she meant it. "He's proud and difficult, but he cares for you. I am grateful for that devotion."

Arthur's smile was lopsided. "He's also made a deal with Rukon to do the occasional flyby. Medievaland's reputation for dragons is secured."

Their conversation ended as the entertainment began.

Singers, jugglers, storytellers and magicians each took their turn. Palomedes and Beaumains picked a mock fight over one of the pretty young guests and staged a bit of swordplay. The public cheered and wept and swooned exactly as they should, their problems forgotten for the night. It reminded Gwen of the times when traveling minstrels visited her father's castle, and everyone gathered in the great hall to hear love songs and tales of mighty heroes. People hadn't changed much.

Her opinion was confirmed later, when she made the rounds of the guests. All members of Arthur's court, including the king and queen, spent a few minutes at each table to make the diners welcome. Gwen enjoyed the experience, answering endless questions about what it was like to live in a castle. Young girls asked a great many questions about the knights. It was delightful.

When she returned to her seat, Arthur was doing an interview outside the tent, but Clary was there. "How do you like celebrity?" Clary asked. "I see you and Arthur made the front page of the entertainment magazine."

"It's interesting," Gwen said. "But I can't wait to get into school. I'm not giving up on that plan."

"You shouldn't," said the witch. "Every time the fae strike, there's a new twist. We need a lot of different skills to combat them. You have a great deal to offer."

"Having something to work toward makes me feel rooted." That was important, coming from such a different world. But even more vital was that for the first time in her life, Gwen was shaping her own future with the support of the man she loved.

Clary watched her with a curious expression. "Did you say once that you were cursed?"

Gwen went still, her pleasant mood wavering. That wasn't something she cared to discuss in a public place. "Yes."

"May I ask what kind of curse?"

"It was of a very personal nature." Though she was almost certain Clary had guessed what it was.

"Uh-huh." Clary shrugged. "For what it's worth, witches can see most curses. I don't see one."

What was it Elosta had said? *I see the shadows of younglings around you. Dragons are rarely mistaken in these things.* "That is good news," Gwen said carefully, reaching for a glass of wine.

Clary put a hand over hers. "I wouldn't touch that."

"Why not?"

"Even if you were cursed back in the day, most such spells don't last more than a hundred years. It would have dissipated centuries ago."

She rose, kissed Gwen's cheek and wandered off to beg Merlin one more time to teach her the proper way to open a portal. Gwen sat very still, the untasted glass of wine just outside her reach. She withdrew her hand, folding her fingers in her lap. The sound of the banquet seemed to meld into a solid roar as she considered what Clary had said, and what she hadn't.

A piece of knowledge, one of the million random facts Merlin's spell had put in her head, said alcohol and babies didn't mix. Gwen shot another look at the witch, wondering exactly what that intense gaze of hers had meant. Clary looked up and winked.

It was impossible to block the parade of thoughts that rushed through her mind. How many weeks had she been here? How many times had she been in Arthur's bed and on Arthur's couch and in the shower and… They had been well and truly reunited. Still, it was very early.

But witches were witches, and they saw what was hidden. She'd missed her monthly courses, but after being turned to stone for centuries, wouldn't her body take time to adjust? And wouldn't it be normal if unfamiliar food sometimes made her queasy?

Feeling more than a little shaky, Gwen rose and left the banquet, glad of the fresh autumn air outside the tent. She saw Arthur at once, bidding the reporter farewell. For an instant she saw her husband as a silhouette, the lights strung in the trees rendering him in black and white. But then he turned and saw her, and in an instant his arm was around her waist.

"How did it go?" she asked.

"Well enough." He smiled, but it was rueful. "I think the young lad wanted to know how to sign on as one of the knights."

"Perhaps training new knights is not the worst idea," she mused, but her mind was elsewhere. "I need to speak to you alone."

His brow creased, but he led her away to a stand of trees that gave them shelter and privacy. He held her close, his fingers linked behind her back. She wanted nothing more than to lean into his warmth, but held herself back so that she could look into his face.

"What is it?" he asked.

"We've talked a bit about the future," she said, "and all the things that must be done. Protecting this world from the fae, finding more of the knights and waking them from the stone sleep and running these shows at Medievaland so that we can pay for food and shelter."

"And you have your schooling," he reminded her. "Don't forget that."

"I won't," Gwen said. "I want all of it. I'm happier than I've ever been."

"As am I." He kissed her forehead. "Leading you into the banquet tonight, as my wife and queen and partner, was one of my most joyous moments. Everything was right."

"I have one more responsibility to add to that future list," she said softly.

She took his hand and pressed it to her stomach. "It is very soon. I am going on the word of a witch."

She wasn't sure what his reaction would be. All kings required an heir, but Arthur was a man. Since their last real fight, she'd learned to expect honesty from him. That was healthy, but sometimes uncomfortable.

A child was a new vulnerability and, as she said, another responsibility. Arthur didn't need more.

But she needn't have worried for one instant. Arthur picked her up, spinning her around with a joyous whoop that made the park workers stop and stare.

"Hush!" Gwen put a hand over Arthur's mouth.

His eyes went wide, as if he would explode with the news. She laughed, contradicting the tears that suddenly blurred her vision. She wanted to laugh and cry and dissolve all at once. The happiness seemed too much, but she would fight like a tigress to keep it all.

This was her kingdom, and she would make her home and raise her babies in it. She would study and build marvels and take part in the fight to keep it safe. And she would do it in the arms of this man, this king and her husband.

Some days, it was good to be queen.

* * * * *

HARLEQUIN®

Save $1.00

on the purchase of **ANY**

Harlequin® series book.

Redeemable at participating Walmart
outlets in the U.S. and Canada only.

Save $1.00

on the purchase of any Harlequin® series book.

Coupon valid until December 31, 2017.
Redeemable at participating Walmart outlets in the U.S. and Canada only.
Limit one coupon per customer.

52615229

5 65373 00076 2 (8100)0 12316

Looking for inspiration in tales
of hope, faith and heartfelt romance?

Check out **Love Inspired**®,
Love Inspired® **Suspense** and
Love Inspired® **Historical** books!

New books available every month!

CONNECT WITH US AT:

www.LoveInspired.com

Harlequin.com/Community

 Facebook.com/LoveInspiredBooks

Twitter.com/LoveInspiredBooks

www.ReaderService.com

Love Inspired®

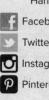

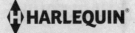

LOVE
Harlequin
romance?

Join our Harlequin community to share your thoughts and connect with other romance readers!

Be the first to find out about promotions, news, and exclusive content!

Sign up for the Harlequin e-newsletter and download a free book from any series at

www.TryHarlequin.com

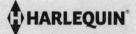